C0-AKZ-312

The Return

The Return

Mark Mustian

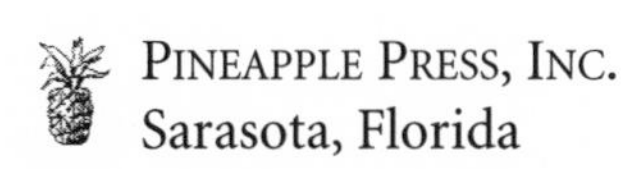
Pineapple Press, Inc.
Sarasota, Florida

Inquiries should be addressed to:

Pineapple Press, Inc.
P.O. Box 3899
Sarasota, Florida 34230
www.pineapplepress.com.

Library of Congress Cataloging in Publication Data

Mustian, Mark T., 1959–
The return / Mark T. Mustian.—1st ed.
p. cm.
ISBN 1-56164-190-1
I. Title.

PS3563.U843 M37 2000
813'.54—dc21

99-045716

First Edition
10 9 8 7 6 5 4 3 2 1

Design by Shé Sicks
Printed and bound by The Maple Press, York, Pennsylvania

To G. L. S.

Many thanks go into the making of a first novel. Thanks to my earliest readers: Will Butler, Bryan Desloge, Ann and Emory Hingst, Elise Judelle, Terry Lewis, and Leo Sandon; thanks to my Paulista friends Jeri Scott and Luiz Salles for their advice and consultation; thanks to novelist Jim Grippando for some good early advice; thanks to Lesley Kellas Payne and Jeff Burdick for making this book better; a special thanks to Sue Ecenia for great feedback and a marvelous piece of artwork; thanks to my secretary Maree Koch for help above the call of duty; thanks to my friend and legal assistant Terrie Ream, for liberal doses of assistance, suggestion, and humor; thanks to the fine folks at Pineapple Press; and thanks most of all to my wife, Greta, and my children, Bern, Eva, and Jackie, for their love and patience.

The Return

1

For many shall come in my name, saying, I am Christ;
and shall deceive many.

Matthew 24:5

The Very Reverend Joaquim Sebastião Silva cradled the rusty weapon in his hands. His mind played over the options again, dropping on each like a hammer. He could, when exposed, as she had promised he would be, admit the truth, brave the storm of negative publicity, and launch a desperate and probably futile battle to save his once-promising career. He could yield to her wishes, suffer much of the same negative publicity, repudiate the only life he had ever known or wanted, but be with her. Or he could end the nightmare, even through sin. She would understand, and she could explain when the child was old enough. There would be talk, stories, shame, but he wouldn't have to endure it. He would be somewhere else, anywhere else, free of the hurtful shell of human existence.

How had he allowed it to happen? Why had she entered his life? How could it be part of God's plan, this travesty, this suffering, this . . . this child? Was it a test? He grasped at the possibility. Must he endure this to better serve Him?

He put down the shotgun and checked again to make sure the room's door was securely latched. Behind him, he knew, a single crucifix adorned the São Paulo rectory's plain white wall. He kept his back to it, edging away from the door. Maybe such posturing would shield the impending action.

Trembling, he scoured the depths of his cupboard in search of whiskey vaguely remembered from many years before. Ah! One very small victory. He poured a glass and drank, the liquid burning his throat and eliciting a shudder from his insides. He poured some more.

She had entered his life out of the blue some six months ago, in the drabness of a government meeting on the plight of the homeless. He had found her undeniably attractive, phenomenally so, but he had known other attractive women. In fact, the chastity part of his vows had never tormented him as it had many of his brethren, even during his youth. He enjoyed serving God, happily enduring hectic days and a consuming workload. Perhaps that was why he had risen rapidly through the Church hierarchy to the bishopric, a culmination that had been the happiest moment of his late mother's life. He was respected, even revered. There had been whispers a line might exist to the papacy. What an honor for his continent, not to mention his country. But not now. He shuddered again, feverishly. Thank God his mother was dead.

They had seen each other again on the street one day, in the *Praça da Sé,* and on the spur of the moment he had invited her for coffee. He remembered chatting amiably about the poor and the children, conversations he had every day with scores of different people, and being attracted to her in an innocent way. Against his better judgment, he had accepted a position on her steering committee advocating social causes. Thereafter he had seen her more often, and her allure had grown. Recognizing his feelings, he had tried to distance himself, discontinuing the committee meetings, immersing himself in prayer. Still, he had found himself thinking about her constantly, even dreaming about her. Masturbating guiltily one night, he had asked for strength and forgiveness even as his mind remained on her. The next day she had suddenly appeared in his office, pulled the door tight behind her and as if in a dream had disrobed and mounted him, her mouth tightly on his. The image remained burned into his brain, as if he could see himself from above: clumsy and foolish and guilty and ravenous. She had left quickly and quietly. He wondered later if either of them had uttered a word.

He had seen her often afterwards, even as he fought not to. Cutting back his workload and spending more time in meditation and prayer had not helped; it was as if he lived only for her. He was an addict, he had realized then, no better than the junkies who prowled the streets at night outside the cathedral. Frustrated with himself and with God, he had decided he must leave the city temporarily to escape her. Praying constantly, for fifteen hours some days, he had emerged after two weeks feeling refreshed and determined.

A message awaited him on his return: she must see him immediately on a matter of utmost importance. Opening her apartment door with a smile, she had handed him a home-pregnancy test. He vaguely remembered finding his way to a chair, his world crashing around him. He must leave the Church, she had insisted; she didn't care about marriage, but she would not allow the child to grow up in this type of situation. If he refused, she would not hesitate to expose him. They had blood tests for such things.

The whiskey against his throat made his eyes swim. Did he love her? He wasn't sure what exactly he felt for her—love or lust or something altogether different. There was a magnetism between them he had never known before. But love? He shook his head, tried to clear his eyes. He loved children, but never in his wildest dreams had he envisioned one of his own. Abortion was, of course, out of the question; he would not have considered it under any circumstance. Still, he found himself thinking the unthinkable: if something happened to her, no one would know. He could keep his life.

He slammed the glass on the counter. What was he thinking? His sacred vow violated and exposed. No, the gun offered the best solution. He staggered back to where it lay, and slowly inserted a moldy shell into the chamber. Would the thing even shoot? He would have to pull the trigger with a toe to get the barrel in his mouth.

His thoughts ran to the unborn child, and for a minute he envisioned it, with his dark hair and her emerald eyes and smooth skin. He wavered, tilting his head back and emitting an audible sob. "My Lord! I am so weak!"

He put the barrel into his mouth and pushed off his shoes. The old gun's rusty smell caught in his nose. Metal ground against his teeth.

For a minute he thought he had done it, that he could taste the salty tang of blood in the back of his throat; instead, he realized the tears trickling down his face had reached his mouth. With a miserable moan he flung the gun across the room, grimacing as it clanked loudly against the wall. He was too weak even to take his own life, a monument to weakness, a pillar to failure. He tried to tell himself he was forgiven, but it did no good. Laying his head on the table in front of him, he wept tears that tasted of whiskey.

The same dream again. Michael Mason kicked the blanket off his legs and sat up in bed.

In the dream he walked in a dream-familiar courtyard he had never seen in waking life, toward an old green building with green shutters. Women in white, nurselike uniforms strolled in the courtyard, ignoring him. The scene was peaceful and pastoral, like a country home. At the building he opened the door but was unable to see inside.

The dream always ended there. It was as if a power kept him on the stoop, even as the door stood open. Even after awakening, lying in a frustrating half-sleep, he could not force himself to visualize the interior. He felt its coolness, somehow smelled the coolness, yet he could not envision moving his feet. The effect was frightening; he almost always awoke kicking the bed covers, convinced his legs had become paralyzed.

He shook himself and sat up on the side of the bed, his T-shirt clinging to his chest. The dream itself was not lengthy, yet invariably he awoke exhausted, soaked in perspiration. He couldn't tie the dream to any particular factor in his life, nor could he explain its sporadic reoccurrences weeks or months apart. He'd had the doctor check him out, so it wasn't physical. What was it?

He stood under the shower and revisited the dream, the vision dimming the longer he remained awake. Why couldn't he step through the doorway? Maybe he needed to see a psychiatrist or psychic or something; this thing had been going on for over two years now. He had never told anyone about it; it just seemed too personal, too stupid, too hard to explain. What was he going to say—I've been dreaming again and again of a green building with green shutters that for some reason I can't enter?

Disgusted, he turned off the water, shaking his head as he stepped out of the shower. Maybe it was metaphysical. He was, after all, the religious affairs correspondent for the *New York Herald*: burning bushes, weeping madonnas, sightings of the Virgin—the search through the fraudulent and the doubtful had become his specialty, a byproduct of his own desire to confirm, to know, to atone. He would be leaving New York soon for Brazil, to investigate yet another self-proclaimed "messiah," a woman calling herself *Zhézush da Bahia.* Jesus of Bahia, in Portugese. Jesu, Jeza, Jayzus—it was always the same. The healing of the crippled, the raising of the dead. He sighed and toweled himself off, the dream dislodged from consciousness.

Strolling through the crowd at São Paulo's Guarulhos International Airport, Mason surveyed the sweating throng of people waiting for other passengers. A cardboard sign reading "MASON" in block letters caught his eye, and he pushed through streams of people and luggage to reach the dark-skinned young woman holding it.

Freckles and reddish hair greeted him. Straight white teeth that flashed against deep brown skin made an otherwise unremarkable face attractive. "Are you Mr. Mason?" she asked in accented English.

He grinned and nodded. The *Herald* bureau chief in Rio had suggested that he get in touch with a freelance writer who had done work for the *Herald.* He'd been told that her given name was Maria Lambosa de Lima but that everyone knew her as Perola, "pearl" in Portuguese.

She extended her hand and shook his with a strong grip. "I'm Perola. Welcome to São Paulo." Another smile lit her face. He noted the wedding band on her finger.

"Thanks." Perspiration beaded on his forehead, and he wiped his face with the back of a hand. He was nearing forty, his once-thick dark hair beginning to thin, his slender body starting to sag. "Where to?"

"We will go to your hotel. We have some time before the service tonight."

A large group of schoolchildren swept by, laughing and talking in high-pitched voices. It seemed that all of São Paulo was at the airport. "Where and when is this thing?" he asked.

"It is being held at the football stadium. They are expecting a large crowd. I think it starts at . . . seven or seven-thirty. I must check."

Outside the airport, he could hear her more clearly. Her accent sounded almost British, her words clipped and precise. He considered mentioning his rusty knowledge of Portuguese, learned during a temporary station near Lisbon as a child, but decided against it. There would be time to embarrass himself later.

He followed her to a battered Fiat parked at the curb, climbed into the passenger seat and threw his bags in the back. Waves of heat radiated from the vinyl seat through his pants and across his back and shoulders. Perola rolled down her window and edged into traffic, hands and feet working stick shift and clutch.

"So, you are the expert on religious matters such as this, yes?" she asked brightly.

"I guess you could say that. I've spent years examining religious phenomena: miraculous healings, mysterious sightings. Jesus on the side of a building. Jesus on the face of a tortilla."

"And other purported messiahs?"

Mason shifted in his seat. "By my count, this is the twenty-seventh such claim I've investigated. Black, white, men, women, children—you name it. Some fairly famous ones along the way, the so-called St. Louis Messiah, for one."

"And what have you found?"

He smiled. "Mostly fraud."

"Why do you do it?"

"Do what?"

"What you do. Do you enjoy it? What keeps you going?"

He pursed his lips. These were questions he had asked himself a thousand times. "The satisfaction of exposing falsehoods. The rare cases where I stumble onto something truly remarkable, something I characterize as . . . a glimpse of God. The one percent, if you will." And the unspoken craving to replace uncertainty with faith, to rediscover God.

"Do you sometimes find glimpses of the other side, of a one percent of undeniable evil?"

"Yes. Sometimes."

Ten years of working and searching, in so many cities and so many countries one started to blend into another. He gazed out the window at familiar urban clutter, unable to distinguish it from the gray, garbage-laden landscapes of Cairo or Mexico City or even Manhattan. Gray concrete gave way to smoggy gray sky. Grimy waterways ran along roadways, between broken-down buildings. City buses coughed by, so jammed with people it looked as if the air had been sucked out of them. Infrastructure failing to keep pace with the crush of humanity. Humanity searching for God.

"How many people live in São Paulo?" he asked as exhaust from a diesel truck blew in through the car's open windows.

"In the greater area, close to twenty million." She shifted gears and sped around the blue cloud of smoke.

"Wow. That has to be one of the largest in the world." He squinted out the window at the rows of skyscrapers making up São Paulo's inner city. "Mexico City, Tokyo—yeah, that's right up there."

"And it is still growing in great leaps. São Paulo is the king of sprawl; it goes on forever and ever. The roads and the water and sewer, they are never enough." She shifted again and muttered under her breath as a foolhardy bicyclist cut in front of the Fiat. "The city originally grew because of coffee. When the coffee began to make big money, everybody came to São Paulo. First the people from southern Europe to grow the coffee. Then the Japanese, the Syrians, the Lebanese. Big factories were built to produce automobiles, electronic goods, rubber, machinery. Now São Paulo is the economic heart of South America." Her voice rose with what he took to be civic pride. "Many people in the U.S., when they think of Brazil, they think of Rio—you know, the beaches, Carnival, all that—but São Paulo is the engine."

She smiled again, the white teeth gleaming against the smooth dark skin. He felt his facial muscles retreat in return, caught in a familiar sexual hunger that crept through his body like a virus, the frailty that had so impacted his life: the blessing and curse of helpless fascination with the opposite sex.

They stopped at a stoplight. A disheveled boy of about twelve leaned in the car window, waving a brown package in one hand as he rattled off something in incomprehensible Portuguese. Before Mason could do or say anything, Perola yelled something and gunned the car through the intersection, the light still red.

"*Meninos de rua,*" she said stonily as Mason fell back in his seat. "He was offering to sell you drugs, but probably he meant to rob you. They work in gangs. One will distract you while the others steal from you. You have heard of the death squads, no? The police militia who have murdered youths such as these? It is a terrible situation, leading to desperation. You must avoid these children. Remember this."

2

Suppose ye that I am come to give peace on earth? I tell you, Nay: but rather division:

Luke 12:51

The cold bottle of Brahma beer felt good in his hands. Across the rounded booth in the São Paulo Hilton's large bar, Perola's white-collared shirt lay open, exposing an expanse of brown skin. He tried to direct his thoughts elsewhere.

The Hilton stood in the midst of glitzy, concrete downtown São Paulo, straddled between luxurious apartments and modern high-rises. The contrast with the poor, overcrowded areas they had passed through earlier could not have been greater. Torrents of people dressed in conservative business attire flowed by outside the bar's darkened window. Doormen and porters directed traffic and goods. It was obvious that, whatever the massive city's other problems, major money flowed in São Paulo.

Mason signaled for another beer, then turned back to Perola. "So tell me about this Jesus, or Zhézush, or whatever you call her."

"Until a few months ago, no one had ever heard of her. She was a kind of faith healer—there are many in Brazil—preaching on street corners to whoever would listen, first in Salvador, a large city on the coast with many poor people. She moved at some point to Rio and only recently to São Paulo. When I first heard of her, I thought she practiced *candomblé* or *umbanda,* one of the African-based—how do you say? voodoo?—cultlike religions to which many Brazilians belong. Most people in Brazil are

Catholic—though less so in São Paulo—but many, particularly blacks, also believe in other mystical religions. We call this *macumba.* So when I first heard of her, I know that she is black, I figure she is a mystic for one of these groups.

"I saw a small article in the Rio paper about some miracles she supposedly performed there. A month or so later, I got a call from a friend of mine in Rio who tells me of these huge crowds following her. The police and the city, they are ready to get rid of her because she is messing it up for the tourists. So she comes to São Paulo, and she is even bigger here! Thousands and thousands want to see her. There are stories on the TV and in the papers. They say she was an orphan, on the streets since an early age."

The beer arrived, along with Perola's soft drink. Mason fished in a pocket for money.

"Has any of this been verified?"

Perola looked slightly pained. "I have tried, but it is very difficult. As for her childhood, as you will see, there are thousands, maybe hundreds of thousands, of street children in Brazil's major cities. They exist day to day by scavenging and stealing. The births of many of these children are never registered. If she was one of these, as she claims to be . . ."

"What about schools?"

"I have an associate in Rio who is checking with area schools. It is a time-consuming and tedious task. It is possible, even likely, she never attended school."

She handed Mason a folder containing copies of several Portuguese-language newspaper articles. "I will translate for you," she said brightly.

Mason scanned the articles quickly. Several he had been given before leaving New York, tabloid-ish pieces with oversized headlines and outlandish claims he could decipher well enough: "Jesus walks across a reflecting pond!" "Jesus cures baby born with two heads!" All within the messianic template, he decided, with the possible exception of reference in several of the articles to ex-Bishop Joaquim Sebastião Silva's resignation and his appearance with "Jesus."

"We can look at these later. Has there been much TV coverage?"

"Only in the last two days," she replied. "Once the bishop became involved and the services reached the size where they had to be held in the stadium, the TV people became interested."

Mason began to jot some notes on a pad. "What about this bishop?"

"That is an interesting story. Bishop Silva was the head of a prominent diocese, a well-respected man in his late forties. He was somewhat famous internationally—even before all of this—because of the young age at which he was made a bishop, one of the youngest bishops in the history of the modern church. Several months ago, he abruptly resigned his position for no stated reason. This received much attention in the Brazilian press, for, as you know, it is uncommon for a priest to do this, and almost unheard of for a bishop. There was speculation about a woman, or a serious illness, but I heard nothing more. Then he started showing up with Zhézush at her services, but he will say nothing to the press. As you can imagine, this dramatically increased her notoriety and credibility."

She took another swallow of her *Guaraná*. "I have been told parish priests have been warning their congregations not to attend these services. But you must understand, Brazilians often pay little attention to what the clerics say. Black Brazilians have a kind of love-hate relationship with the formal Church. Since the days of slavery, the Church has been one of the firmest pillars of the status quo. Of some twelve thousand Catholic priests in Brazil, maybe two hundred or so are black.

"When every metaphor, religious and otherwise, signals white as good and black as bad, that Zhézush is black is a significant thing. 'I am the way, the truth, and the *light*.' No? Anyway, race in Brazil is very . . . complicated. Probably ten times as many African slaves were imported into Brazil as into the United States. Particularly in São Paulo—where there are fewer blacks percentage-wise than in some of the other Brazilian cities—blacks have had a difficult time. In Rio there have always been more opportunities for *mulattos* and *pretos*."

"Who?"

Perola dipped her head. "Although all *Paulistas* may seem dark to you, there is very much a . . . what do you call it? stratification, I think. Yes, stratification. I am what is known in Brazil as a *mulatto*, a "brown," if you will. Those of strict African descent are called *pretos*. There is a big difference between the two socially and economically, but essentially we are both treated as black. Being labeled black is not a generally desirable thing in Brazil; blacks are still banned from white social clubs and dancing societies and otherwise discriminated against. To improve your lot in São Paulo is often called *branqueamento,* which means to whiten. Want ads in local newspapers often seek *boa aparência,* which translates to good appearance but means white."

A cough, then another flash of white teeth. "So you would think Zhézush would be an African phenomenon, confined to black culture and limited to black followers, but this has not been so in São Paulo. The audiences at her services have been a mixture of whites and *mulattos* as well as *pretos.* What has perhaps influenced this is that Bishop Silva is white."

Mason drummed his fingers on the table. "Is every person touched by this woman supposedly cured, or is it selective?"

"I do not know. I think that it is a large percentage—but not everyone."

"Are the cures immediate?"

"Apparently so. In the service I saw, a number of people threw away crutches or rose from wheelchairs."

Perola twisted the wedding band on her finger, then continued. "Zhézush's other primary lieutenant is a woman named Elisabeth. She is fairly well-known in her own right, having been active in local organizations supporting progressive and union causes. There is a political coalition of those who seek to change things, to spread Brazil's wealth into the poor areas and get the children off the streets. There have been protests, peaceful and not so peaceful. Elisabeth's husband, a man named Jorge Mendes, was a leader of these protests. He was killed in a large demonstration about a year ago when a rubber bullet fired by state military police hit him in the head."

She looked up at Mason, steepling her fingers, resting her elbows on the table between them. "My husband Henrique and I have known Elisabeth casually for several years. I have tried to reach her to discuss Zhézush, without success. I will continue to try. I believe I can eventually arrange this."

"Has Zhézush been interviewed by the media?"

"Not to my knowledge. Her access is tightly controlled by her advisors: Elisabeth, the Bishop, a man named Ricardo Cunha."

Mason finished his beer in a gulp. "Undoubtedly worried she'll say something to embarrass them or give away the fact she's not who she says she is. Who is Ricardo Cunha?. . . And what about her mother?"

"Ricardo Cunha is a former state governor who has somehow become connected with this group. He is like their . . . how do you say? political man? He helps work things out with the government, helps set up the services, arrange for the stadium, things like that. He, too, is well known within the São Paulo area and controversial. But he gives additional credibility, because he is a white man and a former politician. I do not understand your other question. Her mother?"

"Is there any claim that her mother is divine, that there was a virgin birth, anything like that?"

"I have not heard of such."

A truck rumbled by outside, tinkling glasses throughout the bar. "Any evidence of the stigmata?"

"You mean the scars on the wrists and side?"

"Or bleeding, yes."

Perola shifted her gaze around the bar. "I have not heard of anything like this."

"What reason does she give for being here?"

"I do not understand what you mean."

"Well, if she is Christ returned, does she claim that Judgment Day is near?"

"I do not know what she has said about that."

An awkward silence ensued. Mason sought the safety of scanning the bar crowd.

"Do you believe in God, Mr. Mason?" Perola asked softly.

"Michael, please." He swallowed uncomfortably. "I'm searching for certainty," he said slowly, settling back into his chair. "That's why I do this—I need to find the one thing that solidifies it for me, the clear evidence of God. For some reason I need proof." Proof that would absolve his guilt in leaving the Church. Proof that would restore meaning. He had to *know.* "What about you?"

"Yes, I think so." She smiled the face-lightening smile again.

São Paulo police Major Henrique Lambosa nudged his Ford police cruiser into the traffic flow in a light, misting rain. A muscular man with an easy manner and a shark's smile, Henrique guided the car with a single finger as he inquired about Mason's trip. A whistling sound when he spoke marred otherwise perfect English.

"Is there any chance of this being canceled?" Mason asked from the back seat in the best Portuguese he could muster, shouting to make himself heard over the increasing rain.

They turned in surprise. "I did not know that you speak Portuguese," Perola exclaimed. "This is wonderful. I thought we would have to translate for you. How did you learn? Have you spent time in Brazil?"

"I lived in Portugal for several years as a child." Mason struggled with the words. "I haven't spoken the language in over twenty years." The time in Portugal had been a good period of his life, a time of happiness and friends, a simple trust in God.

"This is very good," affirmed Henrique. "It will certainly assist you here. As far as the service is concerned, these people would stand in a hurricane for this woman. The service will be held."

The rain eased as the traffic crawled forward then picked up speed. The downtown area, with its high-rise buildings and conglomeration of neon, gave way to a sea of seemingly identical gray office and apartment buildings. Perola acted as travel guide, pointing out various churches and points of interest, alternating between English and Portuguese. To Mason's surprise he had more trouble with certain accented English words than with the Portuguese.

They exited the expressway and executed several turns, suddenly bringing into focus a huge concrete football stadium. From a distance it resembled a giant spacecraft, flags flying across its rounded crown and concrete ramps extending from its sides. According to Perola, the stadium could accommodate up to a hundred thousand people. It appeared that at least several thousand were congregated outside. Traffic ground to a halt, but Henrique edged the police cruiser around a barricade and was waved into a pedestrian channel. Several quick bursts of the siren parted a path for the car.

Nearer to the stadium, orderly single-file lines snaked into the entrances of the massive arena. A number of young people in black, hooded jackets, who appeared to be mostly women, assisted in organizing the lines. The crowd seemed generally subdued and cooperative. Either the event was extremely well organized or its religious aspect had instilled an unusual calm in the participants.

Off to one side of the stadium crouched a number of low-slung armored personnel carriers, a small army of uniformed military personnel arrayed in front of them. Most of the soldiers carried black submachine guns across their chests or slung across their backs. Moving in and around them, the crowd seemed oblivious to their existence.

Henrique pointed to the men. "This is new," he said. "This is the third service at the stadium, and the first time the military has been here. I do not know if they are expecting trouble or just want to show strength."

"Do you have to have a ticket to get into this thing?" Mason looked at his watch. Darkness was about half an hour away.

"No," Perola replied. "It is first come, first serve, although we are assured a place because of Henrique's status as a police officer. These people queued up in the morning to get the good spots." Henrique nodded in agreement.

Mason's mouth dropped open. "They stand here in this heat all day?"

She nodded. "It truly is unbelievable. . . ." She paused, smiling. "Perhaps that is not the best word. The stadium was about one-quarter full the time I came before. I think there are at least twice as many people here tonight."

"Do you believe she's who she says she is?"

Perola did not answer immediately. Seconds passed, and Henrique glanced at her, also awaiting her response.

"I do not know," she said finally. "If she is not, she is in her own right a remarkable woman."

The car stopped in front of a large orange barricade, and they climbed out into the muggy evening. Henrique led them straight toward a uniformed guard at a side stadium gate, breaking through several queues along the way. The guard gave a brief semi-salute, then stepped aside to usher them inside. Beyond the gate, the open-air interior was filled with the sound of shuffling feet and muffled conversation. Thousands of people trudged in different directions, shepherded along by the cajoling instructions of the ubiquitous black-jacketed women. Pushing through several more queues to a concrete overhang smelling of beer, sweat, and urine, Mason and the others merged with the tightly compressed crowd and moved rapidly down concrete ramps into a larger area where concession stands did a brisk business selling soft drinks, coffee, and some kind of tea. Hugging an outer wall of the stadium, they pushed through the concession area past several more of the black-jacketed women and edged down onto the field itself.

The dark, cramped depths underneath the stadium's substructure gave way to the bright lights and tangible anticipation of the half-full arena. Thousands sat cross-legged in orderly rows on the grass as if arranged by a kindergarten teacher for a songfest. At one end of the field a makeshift stage had been erected; beyond the stage, hundreds of metal wheelchairs glinted in the light. Concrete stadium bleachers surrounded the field, their pedestrian traffic arteries clogged, much of the seating occupied. Overhead, clouds hung low and dark, the stadium lights illuminating their underbellies.

Henrique led them to a spot just to the right of the stage, where they stood for a while gazing around at the crowd. The misting rain had ceased, but heavy humidity remained in the air, almost like a fog that left moisture on everything it touched. Mason and Perola decided to sit on the damp grass. Henrique remained standing, arms folded, his gaze sweeping methodically around the stadium. His uniform stood out in the crowd, highlighting the absence of any identifiable security personnel other than the women in the black jackets. The military presence they had seen earlier appeared to have remained outside the stadium.

"How do they maintain order with no security guards?" Mason asked Henrique.

"They have representatives among the crowd," he replied, pointing to a stout, black-clad woman jostling by. "People just seem to cooperate. The organizers' understanding with the police department is that we don't mess with them as long as things stay under control."

"I don't see any TV cameras."

"For some reason, the organizers, or perhaps Zhézush herself, do not like video cameras at these functions. They say it is a religious service and that the video disrupts the service. The TV people complain, and I think they have gone to court about it, but so far with no results."

People continued to stream through the gates into the arena. Mason looked skyward, then back again. From above it must look like an ant colony, the workers coming home to the queen. Two-legged ants of all ages and racial hues, from *pretos* to blonde Caucasians and all shades in between. The black-jacketed assistants for the most part would fall into the *mulatto* category, he decided, while trying to estimate the percentages of each group in attendance. He soon gave up; in the fading daylight and the bright glare of the stadium lights, the colors had begun to blur.

The submissive crowd stirred, emitting a low rumble like distant thunder. The immense stadium pulsated as the field filled and the concrete bleachers darkened with people. Mason rose to his feet with the rest of the crowd as exhilaration built in the damp air to an almost palpable force.

The stadium lights darkened, eliciting a massive, pent-up roar. Spotlights beamed onto the stage. Any pretense of calm evaporated, swelling into a rock concert–like rush of anticipation. A woman appeared suddenly in the spotlight at the back of the stage, the lights following her as she glided to a podium at the front where a single microphone awaited her. He saw her clearly from his position only thirty feet away: long, luxurious dark hair pulled back from copper-colored skin, dark features offset by a medium-length white dress. She stood silently at the microphone as the crowd's buzz became a rhythmic clapping. The rhythm quickened, and the clapping grew into enthusiastic, staccato thunderclaps. The woman raised her arms, and the crowd quieted.

"Love," said the woman softly in Portuguese.

"Love," the crowd gushed in response.

"Peace," said the woman.

"Peace," rumbled the reply.

"Justice."

"Justice!"

"These are the words of Zhézush da Bahia. These are the words of our savior."

Mason glanced at Perola. Was this beautiful woman not Zhézush?

A drumbeat from somewhere near the stage propelled electricity into the crowd. "The *bateria*," Perola whispered. "The rhythm section at the core of the *samba*."

On its feet now, the crowd swayed to the rhythm, chanting in unison with the woman on the stage, words unknown to Mason but obviously familiar to the others in attendance. The crowd writhed as if a singular living thing, the beat loud and pressing, the chant channeled into pressurized downbeats. The drums abruptly ceased, but the chant continued unabated, folding in upon itself until it transformed into the familiar cadences of the Lord's Prayer. The effect sent shudders up Mason's back, the now-recognizable words cascading into a thunderous crescendo. The woman on stage bowed in prayer at the recitation's end, prompting heads to lower around the stadium in waves.

After a time, she lifted her head and spoke again. "Tonight we have a special happening. This is our last service in this stadium for . . ." He could not make out the last words.

"Nooooo," wailed the crowd, the sound echoing off the top of the stadium.

"Zhézush will return," said the woman calmly, as if speaking to small children. She bowed again, then repeated the "love, peace, justice" call and response. Each response became more urgent and animated until it bordered again on hysteria, then receded.

The stage lights dimmed as she stepped away from the podium and glided in the darkness to the corner of the stage nearest Mason. Even in the dim light he saw her more clearly than before. She stood with her back to him, her figure evident beneath the white dress, without hint of any undergarment. He could see her manicured fingernails, smell her perfume, almost touch her dark silky hair. He felt his mouth go dry.

The stage darkened to opaqueness, obscuring his vision of the white dress. The restless crowd groaned in the blackness. A low, wordless wailing broke out, emanating from the front of the stage, amplifying, and wrapping around the stadium. The drums began again, accelerating into the heightened tempo of a heartbeat. Roaring in delirium, the crowd joined in, the enormous noise of the full stadium rising and falling like waves pounding a darkened beach. Mason felt movement in the darkness, the swaying and dancing of an awakening beast.

"This is one of the features of *candomblé*," whispered Perola. "A dance until the dancer becomes possessed. Then the deities descend."

The stage remained dark, and the wailing slowed to an identifiable chant: "*Mestre, Salvador, O Senhor.*" Master, Savior, Lord, over and over and over. Finally the drumbeat stopped. The chanting grew louder, until the words cut like a cracking whip across the stadium and sound waves reverberated off the concrete. A light pierced the stage's blackness, as if generated by the chanting crowd, revealing a squat figure with short dark hair clad in a dark smock draped to the ground like a robe. The crowd stilled momentarily, then in a tidal rush surged closer to the stage.

3

The eyes of your understanding being enlightened;
that ye may know what is the hope of his calling,
and what the riches of the glory of his
inheritance in the saints,

Ephesians 1:18

Mason peered closely at the figure on stage—a black woman with very dark skin, a flat nose, and protruding girth. She looked pregnant or grossly overweight. Small white flowers anchored coarse, braided hair. A momentary hysteria gripped him; this looked like a black sumo wrestler, not the self-professed daughter of God. He turned to Perola and Henrique to find someone to share in the joke, but their gazes remained fixed on the stage. The woman stood silently until the chanting quieted into stillness.

"My people," she said, her voice pleasing, deep, resonant.

The crowd responded as if at a lover's touch: "Zhézush! Zhézush!"

"God is love. I am love. I am yours." She paused, then continued in a voice that filled the stadium. "Let us give thanks to God for all that we have."

"Amen!" the crowd thundered in response, then just as quickly quieted to a mesmerized silence. Birds cried and flags flapped at the stadium's crest, but no coughing, rustling, or shifting interfered in the quiet below. It was as if everyone in the stadium had stopped breathing. Although he recognized the mass hypnotism, a tinge of fear crept up Mason's back, fear of total dominance, or something more. He coughed lightly, against the spell.

"I have been, I am, and I will always be," the voice continued softly. "I died on a cross, yet I stand before you today." She spoke slowly and distinctly; he had no difficulty understanding the Portuguese. The crowd remained silent. In the distance, the sound of traffic floated on the night breeze.

She conducted a mass of sorts, assisted by the woman in the white dress and a tall, dark-haired white man wrapped in a dark robe. Mason found himself disengaged, attuned to the rise and fall of renewed calling and chanting as if visiting from another planet. What appeared to be an offering prayer commenced, followed by a dispersion of columns of the black-jacketed figures, collection plates in hand. They worked the crowd quickly and efficiently, directing brimming, heavy plates with military precision.

"In the previous service, with only half this many people, they supposedly raised over one half million U.S. dollars."

Perola's thoughts obviously ran in the same direction as his. "Are these people in the black coats paid anything?" he whispered, jerking his thumb toward one of the figures.

"I don't think so."

A loud prayer of thanks for the offering followed. There would be no celebration of the Eucharist, he assumed, given the size of the crowd and impossible logistics. As if in answer, more columns of black-clad women brought small quantities of bread and wine to Zhézush at an altar set up behind the lectern. Instead of blessing the bread and wine, she slowly passed them in front of her face, seeming to blow on them, like candles on a birthday cake.

She bowed her head, and the toneless wailing began again. Armies of black-clad young women sprang into action, moving in lockstep to distribute loaves of coarse bread through the crowd. Each participant pinched off a morsel, adults also breaking off pieces for young children, then passed it on. Person after person placed the bread into his or her mouth and made the sign of the cross, sending ripples down the rows. When a loaf reached Mason, he hesitated a moment, then tore off a piece and bit into it, passing the loaf on to a man standing on his other side. The bread was chewy, with an odd but pleasant taste. Somehow it made him feel part of the crowd again, a participant rather than a spectator.

Another black-clad wave followed behind the bread providers, toting large plastic jugs containing a red liquid. Each member of the crowd drank, then passed it on. By the time a jug reached Mason, it was a quarter full. With some distaste he tilted the community bottle to his lips, his eyes on Perola as the red liquid hit his tongue. To his surprise it tasted sweet and wonderful, and he rolled the liquid around in his mouth, savoring the flavor.

Perola bent her head toward him. "Supposedly, this is one of the miracles," she whispered. "She provides bread and wine for the multitudes, as in the Bible."

Mason shook his head. A marvel of engineering and administration, perhaps; a miracle, no. Nonetheless, it was undeniably a moving experience. Participation in Communion had always affected him deeply; even the thin juice of a thousand dingy worship services seemed a reaffirmation that he believed in something, a justification for his search, a renewal of his determination.

"I speak to you tonight of the world," the voice began again, "and of its people, for there is no difference. For as a mother revolves around her child, so we are connected through a power greater than you or I." The words were flat, yet reassuring, and the crowd reverted to ethereal silence. A plane roared somewhere far overhead; the occasional clack of rosary beads broke the solitude.

"Do you believe in me?" Affirmative cries erupted, only to be silenced by the wave of her hand. "It is not necessary that you believe in me, but only that you believe in yourself and those beside you." The words softened against the packed stadium. "For I believe in you, and God believes in you. One could ask no more.

"Let me tell you a story. There was a woman named Ana. Ana was walking to the market one day when she saw a bundle of clothes lying in the road. She started to walk past them but decided to move them out of the way so that others did not step on them. As she picked up the rags, she saw that they held a newborn baby boy. She guessed that his mother did not want him and had left him there for someone to find. Ana did not need or want any more children. She had four of her own already. But

Ana picked up the baby and took him home and raised him as if he were her own child. Ana took compassion on this child. She sacrificed of herself for this helpless baby. She saw something was wrong, and she gave of herself to right it. Leaving the baby to die on the road would have been injustice. It would have been cruel. Ana exercised love.

"For you see, to give is to love, and to love is to give. *We* must change our world. We must seek justice and love. We must make our enemies see the light through love. We must make our every act an act of love.

"Look about you. Look on the road outside this arena. Do you see our children? Do you see their hunger, their hopelessness? Do you see injustice? Would you stop to help these children as Ana did? Do you love these children?" She paused to catch her breath, sweat pouring off her broad face. A vigorous shake of her head sent moisture flying like rain off a dog.

"Will your government help these children?" The voice hardened somewhat. A few cries of "No!" rang from the far reaches of the stadium.

"When will your government help these children?" Transformed into a roar, her voice rocked the stadium on its own.

Instantly the crowd was on its feet. Faces contorted, voices moved to full volume. Mason's pulse quickened.

Zhézush's raised arms brought magical calm. Those in the crowd returned to their seats. "*You* must stop injustice. *You* must save your children. *You* must save your world. If your government will not do it, . . ." she paused dramatically, "you must do it for them.

"People ask me," she continued, "what must I do to reach heaven? What must I do to achieve everlasting life? I tell them that to solve injustice on earth is to reach heaven. To make another life better is to find true happiness. To truly love is to glimpse everlasting life. If you follow my teachings, you will understand.

"Do you see injustice?" she asked again, softly.

"Yes! Yes!"

"Do you want to change your world?"

"Yes!" The crowd was on its feet again, hands outstretched, fists clenched.

"How do you change things?"

"Love, peace, justice! Love, peace, justice! Love, peace justice! Love!

Peace! Justice!" The ground trembled with the stomping of thousands of feet.

Zhézush bowed her head again, quieting the tumult. Turning to her left, she opened her arms to those in the wheelchairs. By craning his neck, Mason counted over one hundred of the metal chairs huddled together in a roped-off area. The occupants appeared to be mostly children, flanked by adults who stood or sat on folding chairs. Other children sat on the ground nearby, crutches strewn in front of them. Still more lay in wheeled cots and gurneys in front of the wheelchairs, their faces hidden until a spotlight illuminated the area. Those who could lift their heads eyed Zhézush with rapture.

The crowd shifted to focus its attention on the wheelchairs, the motion of one hundred thousand turning heads rippling like a fluttering flag. Soft singing, a jumble of words incomprehensible to Mason, accompanied a hushed drumbeat that ushered Zhézush down from the stage and among the wheelchairs. Straining to see over the stage and around the podium, Mason caught only the top of Zhézush's head as she bobbed up and down, moving methodically left and right. As she moved into his view he saw grasping hands as she stopped at each chair or person. The singing grew louder, and the crowd oohed, aahed, and cheered as several children in wheelchairs stood and cried out after being touched.

Mason turned to Perola. "Can we get around there? We need to get a better view of this."

She looked at Henrique, who shook his head. "After the service they will go out the exit near us," he whispered. "We can try and approach them then. Otherwise, we will be crushed in the crowd. They maintain tight internal security in the wheelchair area."

Mason grimaced. It figured that the service's only security surrounded the supposed miracles. Wheelchair healings were easy enough to fake or influence by the hypnotic power of suggestion; he had seen plenty before. The children would be preselected, permitting some afflictions, excluding others. Those with chromosomal defects such as Down's syndrome would be turned away. Chafing to be closer to the healings, Mason glanced at his watch. Nearly an hour now.

A light rain began, yet no one appeared to consider leaving. Zhézush worked the back row of the wheelchairs, those farthest from the stage. Oohs, aahs, and cheers continued to greet the newly healed as the singing and drumbeat continued unabated. Finally Zhézush straightened, turned, and made her way back to the podium through a sea of grasping hands. The noise of the crowd subsided as she wearily regained the stage.

The lights dimmed. Zhézush stood spotlighted at the microphone. "*Amor . . . Paz . . . Justiça! Amor . . . Paz . . . Justiça!* Love . . . Peace . . . Justice!" The throb of the mantra pounded the stadium. Mason watched as the stout, sweating woman on stage raised her arms above her head like a prize fighter, her mouth drawn and firm. The noise of the crowd intensified to pandemonium level as the stadium darkened. When the stage lights burst on a few minutes later, the stage was empty.

The attractive woman in the white dress Mason surmised must be Elisabeth appeared and stepped to the microphone. "I have an announcement to make." The roar quieted. "This will be our last service in São Paulo for several months." The crowd gasped, its breath sucked away. "Zhézush is planning to visit the United States. She will hold services there to spread the good word of her return and her message for all people. She will travel in the United States for several months and then return to her home, Brazil."

The full lights of the stadium beamed on. The service's end. Elisabeth turned from the microphone, strode to the back of the stage and down some steps. A number of the black-clad young women and seven or eight large men surrounded Zhézush behind the stage. Mason felt numb. He turned to Perola and Henrique, not wanting to convey his sense of . . . what? Wonder? Perola looked drained. Henrique wiped moisture from his eyes. At Henrique's signal, Perola and Mason followed him toward a gate further behind the stage.

"Zhézush! Zhézush!" chanted the crowd, outstretched limbs forming a canopy through which Zhézush's entourage ducked. Black-jackets hurtled through the tunnel of hands, followed by Zhézush's bulk and the Bishop's dark form. Thousands of dark, tentacle-like arms plucked at them. A few of the hands reached Zhézush's dress, now darkened with perspiration, but she seemed oblivious, trudging behind a bodyguard, her head bowed. Elisabeth, her head held regally high, brought up the convoy's rear, followed by flanking bodyguards.

"Elisabeth!" Perola shouted as the group passed in a wall of pressing torsos. Elisabeth swiveled at the sound of her name, momentarily halting the traffic flow. She faced Perola.

"Yes," she said, a quizzical look on her face. She eyed Perola through a break in the human shield.

"May we speak with you?" Bodyguards and black-jacketed women shifted into position between them, blocking their view of one another until Elisabeth ordered them out of the way. The crowd on either side converged, as if drawn to suddenly wounded prey. Guards and women assistants surveyed the scene, their eyes darting back and forth.

Mason gazed at Elisabeth from several feet away. Undeniably African in heritage, her flawless eyes and face offset perfectly formed full lips and magnificent high cheekbones. Green eyes seemed to shine with a light of their own. But her skin proved the most alluring, so dark and soft and magnetic that he found himself longing to touch her arm, her face, any part of her body. He stood mesmerized, realizing he should be inspecting Zhézush and the other members of the group but unable to tear his gaze away.

A security guard shifted his position, blocking Mason's line of sight to Elisabeth, allowing him to focus on the other members of the party: the heavy eyebrows and dark, brooding eyes of the Bishop, looking back to see what was happening; the large form of Zhézush, still staring at the ground; an attractive sad-eyed white man with a mustache and a mane of white hair brushed back from his face, clad in a business suit; the bland black-jacketed young women and hulking bodyguards, collapsing defensively around Elisabeth and Zhézush. Perola entered his field of vision as his focus returned inexorably to Elisabeth, and he found himself comparing the two: the young, freckled wife with the attractive smile who had so beguiled him only a short time before now appeared dowdy compared to Elisabeth's presence.

"Perhaps later." Elisabeth was responding to Perola's request, recognition now showing on her face. "We are leaving soon for the United States."

As the entourage resumed its passage, Henrique led Perola and Mason out through the same gate. It took almost twenty minutes of maneuvering to reach the car and its heavenly blast of air conditioning. Mason felt the moisture on his face evaporate as they inched away from the stadium.

Perola turned to him from the front seat. "Well, what did you think?" she asked, her teeth shining even in the darkness of the car's interior. "Could you understand everything? I would have tried to interpret for you, but it is difficult in such a situation."

"I understood most of it," Mason said. "As you say, it was remarkable. It certainly has to rank as one of the top exhibitions of audience control I have ever witnessed." He paused, drinking in the cool air. "What's with all the women in the black outfits? There must have been hundreds of them."

"They are called *ajudantes,* helpers or assistants. I have heard others refer to them as *filhas,* which in *candomblé,* and I believe also in *umbanda,* are assistants to the primary mystic. The word means daughters of saints. Many of these women are from Bahia and have been with Zhézush since they were themselves small girls. Others, I have been told, were recruited. They help with the services and logistics."

"What's the significance of the black jackets?"

"I do not know. Perhaps nothing."

Mason stared out the window at São Paulo's nighttime galaxy of lights. There must be billions of them, he thought absently. "Her message was so elementary, so . . . so secular. Usually they are putting forth a 'New Covenant' or a 'New Light' or fire and brimstone or warning of Armageddon. If you want my bottom-line evaluation at this early stage, I think Zhézush is probably a great manipulator and hypnotist, but ultimately an elaborate fabrication." He sat back in the seat and folded his arms. He had not been entirely forthright about his own reaction. He had seen fervor before. Still, there had been something more than the excitement of a dynamic performance. He just wasn't sure what.

"Maybe you are right," said Perola, facing forward now. "She is very unusual." She turned to face him again, the outline of her head framed against the background lights of São Paulo. "How do you want to go about the story?"

"I'm going to talk to New York in the morning. My suggestion is that someone from the national desk in the States pick up the coverage there and we continue to work on getting more information down here. I think you know the areas where we need to concentrate. As you are probably aware, the *Herald* way is to let others cover the day-to-day grind of these stories while we concentrate on producing the well-researched, definitive story. The advantage here is that the international press seems to be oblivious to this story, at least for the time being. If she is able to draw anywhere near this size crowd in the U.S., they'll be all over it. Follow up with Elisabeth and continue to work on obtaining historical information on Zhézush. I'll try the Church angle, see what I can find out about the Bishop and the government's view on things. Let's plan on talking tomorrow afternoon. We ought to be able to find out by then exactly when she is leaving for the U.S."

He stopped at the bar before going to his room. Perola's face flashed through his mind. The curve of her chest. Mechanically, he jotted notes on a pad. A wave of guilt washed over him, guilt only an ex-cleric could understand. He could never completely assuage it, even with the exposure of falsehoods, even with the secret reporting of his findings to a certain monsignor in the Vatican. The Vatican would want him to follow this, he knew, as would Aaron Rhodes, his editor in New York. It wouldn't matter that he had just arrived in South America or that there was a ton of work still to do here. Circus coverage loomed before him, from tent to tent across the U.S.

4

Many shall be purified, and made white, and tried; but the wicked shall do wickedly: and none of the wicked shall understand; but the wise shall understand.
Daniel 12:10

Perola weaved her way through traffic in the concrete maze of downtown São Paulo. Street vendors hawked their wares between horn-blowing autos and frantic pedestrians, all squeezed into too-small avenues. Uniformed traffic officers waved traffic in different directions with no apparent success. Wealthy shoppers juggled packages and purses. Just like any other day in any given year in smog-central, she thought, except for one small difference: the sobering presence of the military, from the pair of soldiers standing in a doorway with automatic rifles slung over their shoulders to the camouflage-painted jeeps pulled up on the sidewalk, their occupants solemnly drawing on cigarettes in the morning sun.

Military visibility on the streets had increased considerably over the past several weeks, in actuality over the past year or so, commensurate with the increase in the protests. Until a bus bombing in the downtown area several weeks before, São Paulo had not suffered the terrorist activities experienced by Rio de Janeiro. But then, overnight, the armored personnel carriers and grim-faced soldiers had appeared, their weapons gleaming against the drab cityscape. For several days the press had lambasted the increased military activity, but the government held firm. After a week or so the troops slumped in boredom and the populace went on about its business, adjusted to the presence of artillery and military personnel as another fact of life.

Perola slowed her car to enter a hastily erected military checkpoint at an entrance to the vast *favela* known as Bras. She was looking for Moraes, the *candomblé* medium said to know Zhézush better than anyone else. Supposedly he frequented an area of Bras near an old church in the *favela*'s center.

Originally settled by Italian immigrants, Bras had deteriorated into a breeding ground of crime, discontent, and despair for the thousands of impoverished immigrants who continued to pour into São Paulo from other parts of Brazil, convinced jobs and a better way of life could be found in the city. Bras had so degenerated that over the last several years police patrols entered only in protective packs, usually only in reprisal for heinous activities perpetrated elsewhere by a Bras resident or gang. Even the distributors of municipal milk coupons reportedly worked in teams.

The last time Perola had ventured into Bras had been several years earlier during a bitter feud between two rival bankers for the illegal but widespread "animal" numbers game, when police in tanklike urban assault vehicles had cleared a path behind which a few timid journalists trailed. Perola had found the rival groups scraggly and pitiful, the other *favelados* resentful and uncooperative. A writer for one of the major São Paulo dailies had recently finished a series of award-winning articles on that episode as part of an examination of the dismal life facing Bras' residents. It was a topic Perola had long considered looking into herself. After all, over fifty percent of São Paulo's population lived in slums on a par with Bras.

Perola's journalistic career had begun at *Noticias de São Paulo*, a large Brazilian daily. It had taken only a few days to encounter the subtle discrimination meted out to those characterized as black: a higher standard was applied, mistakes were magnified, and good performances warranted only additional mounds of work. She determined to do something, anything else, resigned to the helpless feeling of many of her black compatriots. *Não adianta* was the catchphrase in Bras and across São Paulo: it won't get you anywhere.

A stone-faced *mulatto* officer glanced briefly through her car.

"Where are you going? Do you know this is a dangerous area?"

"I am going to visit a friend. I know where I am going. I know the risks."

With a grunt the guard waved her on. The old Fiat belched and lurched as she eased past the gate and into a jumble of peeling and boarded turn-of-the-century buildings seemingly jammed on top of one another, many with burned-out superstructures like blackened eyes. Interspersed were dirt streets and shanties and cardboard shacks, low-slung concrete-block hovels and other hodgepodge dwellings created from metal sheeting and other makeshift materials. A fetid, trash-filled stream ran alongside the road, serving as a boundary of sorts for the score of black children cavorting in an adjacent cleared area. The children reminded her of birds, the way they swooped and changed directions without warning, moving in a pack, chasing an invisible ball. Here and there commercial establishments poked through the rubble: a tiny restaurant advertising "the best food in Brazil," beer shacks fronted by grimy tables, a windowless building adorned on its side with the word "food."

The main road eventually deteriorated from asphalt to dirt. Smoke from cooking or trash fires mixed with the city's omnipresent smog to form a deep haze matching the road's color. The acrid smell of raw sewage assaulted Perola's nostrils.

The Fiat chugged slowly along, past a failed attempt at a modern affordable housing complex, its windows black and gaping like the spaces for missing teeth, past an improvised soccer field where a dozen or so boys chased a battered ball. Carcasses of burned-out cars and dead animals littered the roadway. An obviously intoxicated man weaved his way alongside the road, head down, jaws working vigorously. A lone dog, its haunches gaunt, hobbled in front of her car and offered a mournful glance. A group of women standing in front of a low building eyed her suspiciously. Other cars passed heading in the opposite direction, throwing off a dust cloud that deepened the haze to near-darkness.

Rounding a curve, she screeched the car to a halt in front of a dozen or so scruffy-looking children blocking the roadway. They ranged in age from perhaps six to twelve. Despite blasts of her horn, they showed no intent to move. Panic began to grip her as she realized no one else was visible on the street. A glance at the rear-view mirror showed several kids approaching from the rear of the car, cutting off her avenue of retreat. One of the youths advanced on her door, a crooked grin across his face, a baseball bat in his hand.

"I am looking for Moraes!" she shouted through her cracked window as she prepared to shift the car into reverse.

The boy with the bat wrenched open the car door. The Fiat groaned as another boy leapt onto the hood. Perola stepped on the accelerator, careening the car in a backward arc and flipping the assailant on the hood off to one side. The other boy maintained his grip on the driver's door, his feet in the air. The car slammed into something and stopped.

Reaching in, the boy grabbed Perola by the hair. She frantically tried to shift into first gear. Bolts of blinding pain flashed through her head. Dimly, she heard rocks strike the car and a Plexiglas window shatter. The salty taste of her own blood streamed into her mouth. The car lurched forward, the sneering youth still clinging with one hand to the driver's door, the other hand knotted in her hair.

"Let me go!" she screamed, trying to push him away. He spat at her, let go of the door, then yanked her hair to pull himself in. The car hit a bump, spilling the youth backward out of the car with a big clump of her hair still in his grasp.

She groaned with pain. Blood poured down her face, burning and blinding her as she sped back the way she had come—back through the dirty, now-crowded streets, past the "best food in Brazil," past the military checkpoint and the jeering, I-told-you-so look of the stone-faced guard.

Her hands shook as she dialed Henrique's number on the mobile phone. Abruptly, she put the phone down. She would handle this herself, at least for now. She wiped the drying blood away from her face.

Heat shimmered off Miami's aluminum foil–like buildings, radiating outward in a muted glare. Mason surveyed the haze with a lack of enthusiasm. Miami was not much different from São Paulo, just thirty years farther down the road. Or maybe thirty years hence Miami would be São Paulo, concrete as far as the eye could see, gray to grayer to grayest, the greenery of the Everglades bulldozed over or dried up by the constant infringement of humanity.

Flipping the rental car's air to max, he edged into the traffic, enjoying the feel of driving again. Mason had succeeded only in obtaining an agreement for a one-week-only engagement. The *Herald* bureau chief in Miami was on vacation.

He nosed the car toward downtown, past portly taxi drivers in faded guayaberas. Zhézush's entourage would be arriving later in the afternoon and staying at the downtown Conquistador Hotel. The group's "publicist" had not known their itinerary beyond Miami nor how long they would stay nor even who exactly was included in the group. She had, however, told Perola that the first service in the U.S. would be held the evening following Zhézush's arrival in Miami. Perola's efforts to reach Elisabeth had been unsuccessful.

Mason swung the car onto the Conquistidor's parking ramp. So far, none of the major U.S. network news programs or the cable news networks had carried anything on Zhézush. A two-inch article had appeared the day before on the AP wire, describing the size of the crowd in São Paulo, the purported healings, the ex-bishop, the planned trip to the U.S. According to the New York desk, the article had run inconspicuously in several of the major U.S. dailies. If no further stories ran and Zhézush produced significant numbers in the U.S., the *Herald* might pull off a scoop *and* the definitive story, if there was any story. Such concerns were to him secondary, however. Was he closer to real knowledge, or farther away?

Settling into a red leather seat in the hotel's Lobby Lounge, Mason had taken the first long swallow from a Red Stripe when a man at a table a few feet away caught his eye. A familiar, thick plume of white hair fell back stylishly from the man's face, just touching the collar of his white dress shirt. He wore gold cufflinks and no tie. For some reason, he looked like a man waiting on a mistress. Mason sat for a few minutes trying to place him. Someone from another paper or TV, a celebrity? Nah. Then . . . click. This guy had been part of Zhézush's entourage at the rally in São Paulo—the guy with the business suit and big eyes following behind the guards as they exited the stadium. Mason scanned the lobby. Had Zhézush already arrived? He glanced at his watch, wondering if he had miscommunicated with Perola on their arrival time.

Fortified by another hard pull on his beer, he stepped toward the white-haired man. The man looked up blankly as Mason approached. Large brown eyes sagged in a brown face above well-developed jowls, as if a strong magnet had dragged the entire face downward. For a moment, Mason considered he might be mistaken.

"Good evening, my name is Michael Mason." Mason produced what he hoped was a friendly grin. "You look very familiar. Did I see you in São Paulo recently?"

"Perhaps," said the man in slightly accented English, the big eyes widening in surprise. "That is my home." He sipped from a cocktail glass, a cigarette dangling from his other hand.

"Are you part of the group traveling with Zhézush da Bahia?"

The man hesitated, then nodded. "I am with her, yes." He smiled, his eyes wrinkling sadly, drawing farther downward. "My name is Cunha." He pronounced it *coon-ha.* With an easy gesture he motioned to a chair. "Sit down, please."

Mason's senses sharpened as he seated himself. This was the "political man" Perola had mentioned, the former governor.

Cunha lit another cigarette. "Why do you ask, Mr. Mason?" His accent sounded European.

"I'm a reporter for the *New York Herald.* I'm covering Zhézush and her story."

"Ah," said Cunha with a wry smile. "That explains why you were in São Paulo." A gold wrist chain clinked against the cocktail glass. "I suppose I should be on my guard speaking with you. I might end up in the newspaper, no?"

"I don't know about that." Keep him talking, Mason told himself. Friendly, easy. More drinks. "How long will you be in the U.S.?"

"I am still working on that. Hopefully two or three weeks. We will be in Miami a week or so."

"Her first , uh . . . service is tomorrow night?" He was never quite sure how to refer to these events. Revivals? Masses? Congregations? Rallies?

"Yes, at the Miami Arena. You will be there?"

"Yes. I attended the one in São Paulo a few days ago."

Cunha pulled hard on the cigarette. "Yes," he said, almost to himself. "The word is spreading."

He paused for a moment. Mason emptied his beer.

"What did you think of the service in São Paulo?"

"Very impressive. The size of the crowd, their behavior, the control she had over them. I could not see the miracles very well. I would like to know more about them: whether all who touch her are cured, what type of illnesses have been cured, that sort of thing."

Cunha smiled again, ordered another scotch and returned his attention to Mason. "Everyone is interested in the miracles. If not for the miracles, would you or I be sitting here? Would the Brazilian government—or your government for that matter—allow these services to be held? If not for the miracles, would anyone believe Zhézush is the daughter of God? Would anyone go to these events?"

He sipped his scotch then swirled the liquid in the glass. "It is fascinating to me that when people search for God they look for evidence of the supernatural. We must have proof of God's power, proof evidenced by something that is beyond the capability of man." He pulled the glass to his mouth again and stared into the distance.

"Do you not believe these are miracles?" asked Mason.

"Oh, they are quite definitely miracles, my friend, at least in the context we define them. Although not everyone is cured, feel free to follow closely those who claim to be. Medical tribunals will be established to substantiate the cures. You will see truly remarkable things."

"But if she is the daughter of God, why isn't everyone cured?"

"I guess you will have to ask her." The sad eyes sparkled with amusement.

"How long have you known her?"

"You have many questions." Cunha seemed suddenly tired. "When is your story printed?"

"I don't know. Soon, I hope."

"I do not want to be quoted."

"Fair enough. You won't be."

Cunha lit yet another cigarette, smoke enveloping his head. The clown face fell farther. "I have known Zhézush for a number of years. I was formerly the governor of the state of São Paulo in Brazil. I have much experience, my friend, in dealing with the press!" He laughed, tilting his head back to expose large teeth. "Anyway, as governor I was a proponent for the underclass in São Paulo. If you have been to São Paulo, you know there are many poor people. I accomplished much, but I developed powerful enemies.

"I first met Zhézush when I was in office, in the course of the civil rights struggles. I had heard of this woman who preached on the street corners and was said to heal people. There are many such people in Brazil. But when I met her, I know that there is something different about her. You have met her?"

Mason shook his head. "No. I want to."

"When you meet her, you will understand. I became intrigued with her. Entranced, you might say. I did not see her for several years, as she was back in Salvador, then in Rio, only occasionally in São Paulo. But I kept up with her through Elisabeth. I had occasion to meet her again within the past year, after she returned to São Paulo. I was asked to join her group and pursue the good things she is doing. I accepted immediately."

"What about the bishop who has left the church to join her?"

"What about him? I predict that there will be many clergy who will be won over. If you think about it, religious people are the most inclined to receive her message. It seems only natural for clerics to hear her call. Just as Jesus originally won over many Jewish priests, so will the Christian clergy flock to her."

"Is she really who she claims to be?"

Cunha seemed put off. A frown creased the loose skin of his face. "Are you really who you claim to be? Am I really who I claim to be? Judge for yourself."

Silence followed. Mason wasn't going to let the old pol off so easy. "Why is she here?"

"In Miami?"

"Yes, and in a larger sense. If she is who she says she is, why has she returned?"

"You have heard her message?"

Mason nodded.

"Then you should know. Understanding. Peace." He stood and offered his hand. "My companion has arrived. Good luck with your story."

A tall, well-dressed woman approached their table. She looked briefly at Mason. Cunha did not introduce them.

"Thank you very much." Mason stood. "Perhaps we could talk some more tomorrow."

"Perhaps," Cunha said without looking back, grasping the tall woman's arm as he propelled her toward the lobby entrance.

Mason watched them leave the bar. Cunha certainly had not seemed a religious fanatic, or, for that matter, a disciple or crusader for Zhézush. He seemed more a stage manager or promoter. Mason peered around the empty lobby, pulled a notebook from his jacket pocket, and scribbled some notes. At least one of Zhézush's lieutenants should recognize him now.

Glancing up from his notes, he caught a glimpse of Elisabeth strolling through the Conquistador's electric front doors. Dark glasses perched atop a brightly-covered scarf that wrapped her hair, but it was the revealing slit up the side of her tight black business suit that commanded attention. Across the lobby heads turned. Several large, dark-skinned men pushed forward a mass of baggage. Behind them trudged the Bishop, dark and scowling, followed by a waddling Zhézush, then more dark-skinned security men. Seconds later, thirty or so high school- to college-aged women followed, dressed in baggy dark clothing, their hair uniformly short and severe. The previously empty lobby was now noisy and crowded.

Several media-types filtered in. Mason noted with satisfaction no sign of video cameras. He recognized a tall, thin, balding man who worked for the *Global Press*; another man with sagging shirttail and several days' growth of beard looked vaguely familiar. They showed a keen interest in Zhézush, but three of the dark-skinned men formed a protective wall around her. Behind the human curtain, Zhézush beamed radiantly, unresponsive to the questions the tall reporter posed in English.

Did she understand English? Mason hadn't previously considered it, but the thought struck him it was unlikely that a child of the Brazilian streets spoke anything but Portuguese. The language barrier would make for an interesting and much less effective interaction with her audience in the U.S. Squinting his eyes, he tried to imagine someone translating for her at her service.

While most of the group congregated near the front desk, Zhézush escaped from her three protectors and lumbered over to a sofa across the lobby from Mason. She moved slowly, almost painfully, clad in what looked to be the same dark smock she had worn in São Paulo, the frayed bottom of which dragged the floor as she walked. Seating herself, she cradled her face in her hands. Two of the bodyguards quickly recovered, moving to positions on either side of her.

Should he try to speak to her? The fate of his erstwhile colleagues cautioned against it, yet he ambled over in what he hoped was a nonthreatening manner.

"For many shall come in my name, saying I am the Christ," he said in halting Portuguese.

Caught unawares, the guards tensed and began to stand. Zhézush forced them back to their seats by silently grabbing their arms. She did not look up. The guards stared at Mason, but did not speak.

A strong odor, the odor of human perspiration, emanated from the group in front of him. Still bowed, Zhézush's broad face shimmered with oil or sweat, the liquid beading up on acne scars crisscrossing her forehead. The smock had hiked up some as she sat, revealing heavy ankles above dirty-looking feet in worn sandals. On the top of each foot a bloody weal glistened, as if from a new scab or injury.

A shot of adrenaline hit the pit of Mason's stomach. The stigmata? As he raised his head, giant brown eyes bore into his. He felt himself wanting to run, to break the gaze, to apologize, to say something, to do something, anything. Instead, the eyes held him paralyzed.

"So they shall," she murmured in unaccented English, the words warm and comforting.

"Come!" Elisabeth interrupted, motioning to the two men seated on either side of Zhézush. She turned her back to Mason, spreading a waft of perfume over the perspiration odor. From somewhere a voice announced the group's destination as the fifteenth floor.

Mason's gaze returned to Zhézush's feet, but by now she had hoisted herself to a standing position and the smock again reached the ground. He examined her wrists, searching for evidence of other wounds, but they, too, were almost completely covered by the smock. As he stared after her, trying to think of something to say in parting, a guard stepped directly in front of him, blocking his view and prohibiting him from following. Out of the corner of one eye, he saw the tall, thin reporter similarly held at bay by another guard.

The guard in front of Mason said nothing. After thirty seconds or so, he turned and followed the last of the *ajudantes* to the elevators. Zhézush appeared to have already boarded the elevator, but Mason saw Elisabeth's scarf among the heads of the young women outside it. Elisabeth turned and gazed directly at him for a long moment before turning back and disappearing into the elevator.

Mason slumped into a lobby sofa, suddenly fatigued. The tall, thin reporter sauntered over. Mason closed his eyes, his head beginning to pound.

"Mike Mason! There must be something to this if you're here."

"Not necessarily." His name was Reynolds, Mason remembered. They had met in India, in the early days of Mason's journalistic career when his focus had been less on a search for truth than on a new beginning for himself. Afghanistan, Kosovo, Sri Lanka—he had sought solace in movement. Gradually, his journalistic interests had merged with the growing need for spiritual affirmation, until his life had become in essence a single-minded quest.

"Whaddaya think of her?" Reynolds jerked his thumb in the direction of the elevators.

"I'm not sure," Mason said. "I was in Miami and told to check it out." He was remembering he didn't much like this guy. "I'd better run, but good to see you again. Maybe we can have a drink in the next day or so."

"Sounds good to me. See ya."

Mason walked toward the elevators, his mind on Zhézush and their encounter. He had seen manifestations such as those on her feet before, including several obvious self-mutilations. Why should he be surprised Zhézush and her friends had also gone to such effort? Still, memories of other, less explicable exhibitions of spontaneous bleedings washed over him: a woman in California, a man in Seville. He remembered one woman in particular, an elderly nun in a Belgian convent whose wounds opened and closed of their own accord as her mouth worked in silent prayer, Mason and others watching in fascination, gripped by the truth that the inexplicable did occur—a glimpse of the supernatural that had whetted rather than satisfied his hunger for truth. He rolled his shoulders, in an attempt to ward off the chills creeping up his back.

The elevator dislodged him into a vacant fifteenth floor hallway. Feeling vaguely like a burglar, he listened for signs of Zhézush or her group. Maybe they had gone out for dinner. A brief survey of the lobby and restaurant produced nothing. Moving those Young Assistants, as he had begun to think of the *ajudante* group, would be the equivalent of a Wichita trail drive; if they were out and about they would be hard to miss.

He sat in the bar for a few hours, watching a ballgame and doodling in his notebook. Was this one any different from those before? His mind played over the surreal São Paulo service, the encounter with Zhézush, the stigmata, the eyes, the voice. All within the pattern. He sighed, his gaze drifting from the game to the red-headed barmaid and back. By midnight he was in bed. Alone. Mechanically, his hands traced the sign of the cross before sleep overtook him.

5

So he carried me away in the spirit into the wilderness: and I saw a woman sit upon a scarlet coloured beast, full of names of blasphemy, having seven heads and ten horns.

Revelation 17:3

He was dreaming the dream again. It was even more vivid than usual: the green building, big as a mountain in front of him; his legs moving, almost running, toward the door; the sensation that he was making slow progress, past the green hedges, past a little white picnic table. The women in white, ignoring him as usual, moving soundlessly about their business. The doorknob, cold and hard in his hand; the door itself, big, brown, and worn. The coolness of the air inside, sweeping against him as it escaped around the edges of the door. Then he was awake, disappointment sour in his mouth, his legs moving in a bicycle motion trying to carry the dream to conclusion. Mason lay back, closing his eyes again, wanting to continue. Light peeked through the hotel room's partially closed curtains. The dream was gone.

Angrily rousing himself, he sat on the edge of the bed for some time. Was the dream some kind of sign? It wasn't that it was painful, or particularly frightening, or anything like that. It was just so . . . frustrating. Struggling into the shower, he tried to clear his head.

It was early, and he decided to cruise the fifteenth floor again before going downstairs to breakfast. Gray-uniformed housekeepers were already at work cleaning rooms as he exited the elevator, forcing a detour around a cleaning cart on his way to the end of an empty hallway. The floor was even quieter than the previous night. No sound of TVs or blow driers or even running water, only the faint chiming of an elevator bell from another floor.

He had just turned to walk back to the elevators when a woman's scream shattered the calm. Turning awkwardly, he sprinted toward the sound. A series of thumping noises in a room several doors down seemed to confirm its location. Seconds later, an elderly housekeeper backed into the hallway, moaning excitedly in unintelligible Spanish and pointing to the doorway. Another housekeeper materialized out of an adjacent room, peered into the doorway and let out a sharp screech. By the time Mason reached the door, one of the maids had scrambled down the hall toward the elevator, sniffling and crying. The other remained rooted by the door, stammering hysterically, pointing inside.

Doors squeaked open in the hall behind him. Mason pushed past the woman to open the door more fully. Inside, Ricardo Cunha's face peered up at him. The ex-governor's arms were wrapped around a chair, as if he had been trying to raise himself. His face and hands were blue, as blue as if they had been painted, his sad clown's face stretched by bulging eyes, a white line of spittle at the corner of his open mouth. He had the look of someone trying desperately to say something, or perhaps just to breathe. In either case, he looked quite dead. Mason touched a bluish arm to make sure. The body fell to one side, the swollen blue face leering suddenly in his direction as the body toppled.

Stepping back quickly, he edged toward the door. He had seen plenty of corpses before—in India and Sri Lanka—but he had never seen skin turn this hue. He took another look at the body. Usually, corpses reminded him of wax museum replicas, their life sucked away by some malicious vampire. There was something different about this. Maybe he had just never seen someone who had died in this fashion. Headlines danced in his mind. Had Cunha been poisoned?

The room behind the body appeared undisturbed; only the chair the dead man had recently grasped seemed out of place, so close to the hall the door could almost not be opened. He wondered if the chair had been placed against the door, perhaps in an effort to keep someone out, and the maid had dislodged it when she entered the room.

A light-colored hardback book lying partly under the fallen body caught Mason's attention. Focusing, he realized it was a Bible, probably one of the millions worldwide placed in hotel rooms by the Gideons. A passage had been marked with a red pen. As Mason took a step forward to identify it, a short, heavyset man with a portable phone in one hand entered the room. A brass nameplate on his breast identified him as "Collins."

Collins looked at Mason, then at the body, then back at Mason. "What are you doing?"

"I saw the open door and the body and wanted to see if he needed help."

A crowd formed behind Collins, peering over his shoulder into the room, whispering excitedly.

Collins pulled the door partially to, leaned over the body, and felt for a pulse. "He's dead." He stood and faced Mason. "Did you touch him?"

"Just as you did. It knocked him over. He was holding onto that chair before."

"Please give me your name. You are a guest of the hotel?"

Mason nodded and gave his name, his gaze on the Bible. The noise outside the room reached a crescendo.

"Don't touch anything." Collins stepped out to disperse the onlookers. Mason knelt by the body, squinting to read the highlighted passage. Revelation 17:4-5. Half-listening to Collins outside the door, he read quickly:

"And the woman was arrayed in purple and scarlet colour, and decked with gold and precious stones and pearls, having a golden cup in her hand full of abominations and filthiness of her fornication: And upon her forehead *was* a name written MYSTERY, BABYLON THE GREAT, THE MOTHER OF HARLOTS AND ABOMINATIONS OF THE EARTH."

Mason swallowed noisily, a queasiness churning at his stomach. He knew this passage well; the launching pad for the Antichrist. He stood. The room felt cold.

Collins returned, Elisabeth behind him. "Oh, my God," she exclaimed in Portuguese, her gaze moving rapidly from the body to Mason to Collins. She stared open-mouthed at the prone figure for several seconds, turned, covered her face with her hands, and pushed back into the hallway.

Mason and Collins followed, the security officer closing the door firmly behind him. Outside, Zhézush's security guards filled the hall. The Bishop and Zhézush stood off to one side. A handful of Young Assistants peeked from doors farther down the hall.

Elisabeth relayed the discovery in a strained, hushed tone. The Bishop's face paled further as he took in the news, his dark eyebrows splotches of black against his sallow skin. Unsmiling for once, Zhézush stood with arms folded across her ample waist, big tears on her plump cheeks. Mason tried to edge through the crowd to her. As he approached, the Bishop took Elisabeth's arm and led her down the hall away from the others.

Mason took the opportunity. "Will you bring him back, like Lazarus?"

Zhézush's face was wet with tears. "No. I think Cunha was supposed to die. It is God's plan."

"But don't you have the power to bring him back?"

Several of the bodyguards noticed Mason and rushed to block the conversation.

"It is God's plan," she repeated, almost to herself.

Someone tapped Mason's shoulder from behind. Collins. "I need to ask some more questions. You wanna come with me?"

The security guard motioned toward the room's door. Mason followed. Out of the corner of one eye he saw several of the bodyguards leading Zhézush down the hall away from the scene.

Collins punched some numbers on his cellular phone. "Casey? Collins, at the Conquistador. Yeah, I got a cold one here. I dunno. Heart attack or somethin'. Yeah, right. You know the service elevator. Room fifteen-twelve. I'll be here."

He motioned Mason away from the body toward a sliding glass door. "Don't touch anything. Now, did you know this guy?"

"I met him last night for the first time."

"I see. Where did you meet?"

"In the bar downstairs."

"Did you return to the room with him last night?" He moved over to examine the body again.

"No," Mason shifted from one foot to another. "I had a drink with him about seven. I recognized him from seeing him before in South America. He was an advance man of sorts for this Brazilian traveling evangelist, Zhézush da Bahia, who is staying in the hotel. I am a reporter for the *New York Herald,* covering the story. He left after our with a woman he'd apparently been waiting for and I did not see him again last night. This morning, I was walking down the hall and I heard one of the maids scream. I looked in, and there he was."

"Is your room on this floor?"

"No. I came down to see if I could find anybody to talk to about the story."

Collins pulled out his phone. "Your name again?" He punched in some numbers. "Room number?"

"Sixteen fifty-eight."

Mason pulled his room key from his pocket. Collins verified the registration with the front desk, called the housekeeping department, and asked that the maids who had discovered the body return to the room. One had apparently already left the hotel. He put the phone back into a holster and returned his attention to Mason. "Why don't you hang out for a little while. The cops are gonna be here in a few minutes, and they may wanna talk to you."

"Where will the body be taken?" Mason asked.

"To the county morgue. Why?"

"I've never seen anyone turn blue like that. Think they'll do an autopsy?"

Collins scratched his head. "It's up to the coroner. They don't do a lot of autopsies anymore—too expensive. When they do, it usually takes awhile. We do have a new coroner who likes to move things along, though. Maybe they'll just do drug screenings. They've got that big facility near Jackson Memorial for that sorta thing." He stepped over and looked critically at the corpse. "He does look kinda funky. Call the coroner's office if you wanna find out. It's in the phone book."

Collins poked around the room some, checking the bathroom and the windows. Mason returned his attention to the body and the Bible wedged partially underneath it.

"What's that underneath there?" Collins squatted next to the body.

"I think it's a Bible."

"Hmmph."

A light knock sounded on the door. Collins directed two cowering women in gray housekeeping uniforms deeper into the room, out of sight of the corpse, and began to quiz them. Another knock interrupted him and he reopened the door to admit two uniformed men pushing a gurney, followed by a police officer. With some effort the two men loaded the corpse onto the gurney and wrapped it in a sheet so only the outlines of head and feet were visible. The maids whimpered and spoke softly to one another; one appeared to be reciting the rosary. With a good measure of grunting, swearing, and banging of walls and doorframe, the men edged the gurney out of the room. Collins followed the others outside.

Mason itched for a pen and pad. Was it just a heart attack? Poison? Maybe the ex-governor had killed himself. The room showed no obvious signs of foul play or burglary or anything like that. No suicide note or telltale bottle of pills. Just the Gideon Bible opened to an apocalyptic passage. It seemed strange. He had shared a drink with the guy only the night before. Barely twelve hours later, Cunha was cold and blue.

Collins and the young police officer reentered the room. The policeman asked a few perfunctory questions, recorded names and addresses, and left. Collins asked the maids a few additional questions, inquired how long Mason would be staying at the hotel, then gave permission for everyone to leave.

Back in his room, Mason picked up the phone. He reached Perola on the second ring.

"Cunha is dead."

"What?!"

"He either committed suicide or was poisoned or died the most bizarre natural death I've ever seen." He described the blue body, its positioning, and the Bible.

Perola uttered a stream of incomprehensible Portuguese.

"Whoah, wait a minute. Slow down."

"I cannot believe this. What was the reaction of Zhézush, Elisabeth, the rest of the group?"

"Kind of strange. I spoke to Zhézush right after it happened and asked her why she didn't prevent this or raise him from the dead. She said he was supposed to die, that it was God's will."

"Holy mother of God."

"It certainly adds a twist to the story. Anyway, I'd like to be ready to go with the final tomorrow. Anything new on your end?"

"I am attempting to contact a mystic who supposedly knows Zhézush well. I will let you know."

They signed off, and Mason pulled out his notebook computer. He began with a description of the service, the healings, and Zhézush herself, followed by a discussion of her claim to be the messiah. He had just input a segment on the Bishop's defection when the phone rang.

"Hello," he growled, resenting the interruption.

"Mr. Mason." The voice was accented, husky, familiar.

"Yes?"

"I am Elisabeth Obrando, disciple of Zhézush da Bahia. I believe we have met before."

Mason stiffened. He thrust the computer aside. "Yes. How are you?"

"Fine, thank you. I would like to speak to you in private."

"Of course. When and where?"

"I am in room 1527."

"I'll be right down."

He hung up the phone, torn between excitement and skepticism. Why did she want to see him? The image of her face flashed in his mind. He brushed his teeth, gave his thinning hair a push into place. Grabbing a notepad, he raced to the fifteenth floor.

Slowly, tantalizingly, the door to 1527 eased open. She was even more attractive than he remembered, her long hair pulled fashionably back and black earrings framing her face. She wore tight dark pants and a white sleeveless shirt with no bra. Mason's knees shook.

Smiling, she invited him to sit down. "Do you take coffee?"

She had more of an accent than Perola. Somehow, it made her seem more cosmopolitan, more foreign and alluring. She seated herself in a chair across from him and pulled her chair close to his.

"No. Thanks." His mouth was as dry as cactus. "I'm sorry about Cunha."

She seemed not to hear him. "I want to talk to you about Zhézush," she said forcefully, her gaze locking on his, "and about our time in this country. I know you are anxious to speak to her, to ask her questions, to interview her, to do the things reporters do. She is willing to undergo this, but only under certain conditions."

"Okay." He felt like he had been drugged, his sluggish mind conscious of little but her.

She shifted in her seat, uncrossing and crossing her legs. "We do not want chaos and shouting. We want an orderly, respectful discussion."

"That's fine," he heard himself say. "I will treat her with the utmost respect."

Elisabeth smiled again. "No offense, Mr. Mason . . . Michael, is it?" Her gaze bore into him, leaving him feeling suddenly naked. "We do not want to speak only to you. We want a limited interview with a limited number of the press. We want you to help arrange this."

Mason nodded, straining to think clearly. She wanted him to set up a press conference? Hell, he would be willing to be interviewed himself if it would make her happy. His mind lurched into gear. Wariness cut through the fog.

"Newspapers and TV?"

"Yes."

He leaned closer to her, the smell of her perfume permeating the air between them. Their faces were only a few feet apart. A light-headedness swept over him.

"Why are you asking me to do this?"

She grabbed him by the shoulders and kissed him full on the mouth, her tongue slowly grazing the outside of his lips. He fell backward in surprise, overwhelmed with the sensation of her. The chocolate skin pressed against his, warm and insistent. Then, without warning, she stood, her hands on her hips.

"Because I want to," she said in a low voice. "Because the world must be reformed. Because power must be altered."

He regained his feet, weaving like a punch-drunk fighter. Extending long arms, she pushed him back. He grinned weakly, a man overboard with the lifeboat moving away.

"Okay," he managed to gasp, his mind returning with effort to the matter of Zhézush. "When do you want to have this conference?"

"Tonight, after the service."

"Where?"

"Here."

"At the hotel?"

She nodded, impatience now showing in the perfect features.

"Anybody in particular you want me to have there?"

She shook her head, sending black hair flying like a horse's mane. "I want there to be no more than ten people. I want them to act respectfully."

"I can't control other people."

"Then we will end the interview."

"I'll set it up for tonight. How long will the service last?"

"You've seen one before." She turned her back to him, arms hugged tightly against her sides. He stepped over to her, intending to place his hand on her shoulder, but she shied away like a startled colt. He stood awkwardly for a long moment, his hand still frozen in the air, turned, and left the room.

His head spun. He walked down the hallway, past several staring security guards. This woman had him hooked like a big fat grouper. How did she know so much about him? Of course she was using him. Now that Cunha was dead she needed a front man, an advance man. What the hell did she think he was? Still, he would do it, if for nothing more than the opportunity to worm his way closer, to distinguish fiction from fact, to edge nearer to the truth.

6

And there appeared a great wonder in heaven; a
woman clothed with the sun, and the moon under
her feet, and upon her head a crown of twelve stars:
Revelation 12:1

The *bateria* drums sliced through Joaquim Sebastião Silva's skin into his soul: the throbbing of the *atabaques*, the rasping of the *cuíca*, the jingle of the *agogô*, the rapping of the *batuque*. The beat merged with the wordless wailing of the crowd, a smallish one this time, swelling until it took control of the arena. Rising and falling, it reached a crescendo, then fell back again, as if the sound waves were manipulated by a far greater force.

His mind floated, disengaged from his body, reflecting on it all but then on none of it, rather back on himself. That he was here at all was a testament to what: lust? deceit? fate? nothing? She floated by, gossamer in black, and his heart moved to bound free of his chest. The service, the savior, the adoration, the voice, all existed in a universe parallel to his own.

Only the children seemed real: afflicted, deformed legs poking beneath blankets and bedding, some hideously twisted, others desperately thin. One young man balanced upright on his hands because he had no legs at all. Heads bobbed from side to side. Occasionally, a child cried out, an adult moved to assist.

One by one they sought to claim victory over their ills. One by one they grasped the great figure before them. He glanced from the large form to the lithe ones, then back again, fingering the clerical collar he continued to wear. Cunha dead. Would he be next? The thought failed to bring even fear.

Mason slipped under a restraining bar down into the wheelchair area on the Miami Arena's floor. The spent crowd had begun to disassemble. The service had been a microcosm of São Paulo's, only this time in flawless English, with a much smaller but no less ecstatic and mesmerized crowd and the same emotional healings. Searching in vain for a young boy with no legs he had seen from the bleachers, he dodged people and metal chairs as the floor became mass confusion. A black youngster who had been in a wheelchair in front of him hobbled by, yelling excited gibberish as his weeping mother stood beside him muttering "Praise Jesus! Praise Jesus!" over and over.

"About your son," Mason said to the black woman with the young boy. "What was wrong with him?"

Her words tumbled together so fast he could barely understand her. "Oh, praise Jesus! He got crippled in a car wreck when he was six years old. He ain't walked since. Ain't it a miracle? Them doctors, they told us he wasn't gonna ever walk again."

Mason pulled a pad from his coat pocket and began to scribble. "What's your name? I'm a reporter and I'm doing a story on, um, Jesus."

She gave it to him, along with an address and phone number.

"Would you mind if I talked to your son's doctor?"

"Heck, no. I wanna see him myself. He ain't gonna believe it. Lord, I don't believe it. Just look at him moving around!"

The boy grinned broadly, hopping to and fro with only modest difficulty.

Mason thanked her and promised to call, anxious to speak with others before they departed. Hundreds of people and wheelchairs clogged what appeared to be the arena floor's only open exit. Pressed against other "healees," as he mentally referred to them, he struck up a conversation with an obese woman standing next to a double-wide wheelchair that had evidently housed her bulk.

"How long were you in the chair?"

"Thirteen years," she replied, her jaw working in rapid motion on a wad of chewing gum. "My life has been useless. I had to have a special seat just to go to the bathroom. Now, look at me! I feel like I could dance!"

Mason suppressed a smile. "What's your name?"

"Gladys Hinson. You know what else she told me? She told me I could lose this weight. I weigh five hundred and thirty-five pounds," she said, spreading her hands across her girth. "Only weighed one thirty-five in high school. She told me I could go back to what I was then. Ain't it wonderful?" And with a lunge that caught him off guard she hugged him, her sweaty arms barely reaching around his neck. He pulled away, holding his notepad between them like a shield.

"Would you be willing to let me speak with your doctor? I mean, after he or she examines you? We're trying to verify some of these cures."

"Sure, honey! What's *your* number?"

The gridlock at the gate cleared, allowing the crowd to pour into the moist evening air. TV lighting flared as a crew interviewed several children in wheelchairs and their parents. Catching sight of a dark-skinned girl he had noticed on the arena floor, Mason dodged another wave of wheelchairs and weaved his way across the parking lot, arriving out of breath as a large man adjusted a hydraulic lift poised to hoist the girl into the back of a van. The girl's head flopped back and forth spasmodically.

"What do you want?" the man asked in Spanish, his arms flexing in front of him as if to push the intruder away.

"I am a reporter," Mason explained, sucking in gasps of the humid air.

The man did not return Mason's smile. "I have nothing to say," he said abruptly, returning his attention to the lift.

"Was your child not healed?" Mason asked in elementary Spanish, hoping the words made sense.

The hydraulic lift hoisted the little girl and her chair skyward with a clang and a jerk. She offered Mason a gap-toothed smile, her head held still for a brief moment, and flashed her fingers in a "V" sign as the chair rotated into the van. Disengaging the apparatus, the man closed the van's back door and turned to face Mason again, his mouth taut and hard. He said something Mason couldn't understand, then took a step forward, his large brown eyes widening. Mason moved backward.

"We believe," the man said softly in accented English, his face close to Mason's. "Maybe not today, maybe not tomorrow, but she will return." He held Mason's gaze for several seconds, turned and retreated to the driver's door of the van, fired up the engine and pulled away.

Mason jotted down the tag number as he stood rooted in the parking lot, his eyes following the van as it vanished from sight. Had he understood the man correctly? Did "she will return" refer to the little girl or Jesus/Zhézush? Clearly, the little girl had not been healed. It angered him that someone gave such people false hopes of miracle cures. This so-called service might be entertainment for some, even spiritual enrichment for others, but for these folks it had to represent the bitterness of crushed dreams. He ground his teeth in disgust as he made his way back toward the arena.

Had anybody really been healed? He doubted it. Gladys Hinson's cure was nothing more than psychological suggestion, and the same could probably be said for the black boy who had been in the car accident. As in São Paulo, the remarkable thing about the service was the control exerted over the crowd. Still, another fabrication. Another fraud.

Elisabeth stood on the steps of the arena as Mason walked back across the parking lot to retrieve his car. "Do we have a news conference?" she called out to him. A breeze whipped her hair and she pulled it back from her face. She looked as if she could be posing for a fashion shoot. His spirits lifted.

"Yes. Back at the hotel at eleven." It dawned on him she must have been watching as he spoke with the man and little girl.

"Where?"

"In one of the meeting rooms downstairs at the hotel. Take the escalator and look for the lights and cameras. It will be in one of the big rooms behind the escalators."

She nodded and stepped quickly down the arena steps and into a waiting car. The car roared past as Mason continued across the rapidly clearing parking lot. For some reason the press conference seemed ridiculous now. A waste of time. No, more than just a waste of time: a charade. How had he allowed himself to be roped into doing this? Truth seemed to dissipate in the night air.

On his way out of the parking lot he spotted a police cruiser and pulled his car over to speak to the officer inside. "So, what'd you think?"

The cop, a heavyset black man with a small mustache and big sideburns, shifted in his seat and squinted up at Mason. "That was some *shit* in there, wasn't it?"

Mason nodded. "Yeah, I guess so. You ever see anything like it?"

The cop grinned, a toothpick appearing between his lips. "Man, people are crazy about religion. I seen a thousand people tromping on everybody's lawns up in Miami Lakes, all to see this woman says she can see the Virgin Mary in the sun. They all stare at the sun and say they can see it too. But this, tonight, I don't know. Those people were wild in there. Like she brainwashed 'em or something."

"I know what you mean."

The large room housed maybe a dozen people, including at least three wielding hand-held TV cameras, all congregated near a set of chairs on one end of the room in front of a small rostrum. A number of microphones clung like vines to the rostrum. Mason felt relief that enough press had actually shown to make it look good. Several South American papers were represented. An attractive blond TV reporter in a tight red business suit with a "TVKY" emblem was obvious evidence of the giant Brazilian television network.

Several minutes passed, then more. By 11:15 the group had grown restless. Flustered and thirsty, Mason had just risen to look for a house phone when Elisabeth entered the room. All conversation ground to a halt.

She had changed from the black outfit she had worn at the service to a sleek business suit, slit up one side to reveal an expanse of brown leg. Her hair had been pulled back into a bun and blush added high on her cheeks. She looked tough, radiant, and beautiful. Striding purposefully to the podium, she grasped the lectern with both hands and addressed the gathering in a clear voice.

"It is my pleasure to introduce to you Zhézush da Bahia, the messiah, the savior, the daughter of God," she said quietly in English, her accent making the words stilted, almost brittle. Drawing her arm majestically, she directed all eyes toward the door.

Her hair still in braids, clad in the same sweat-stained dark smock, Zhézush entered the room. The rank odor of perspiration followed, so noticeable that Mason sought and found confirmation in others' wrinkled noses and furrowed brows. The torn sandals flopped loudly as she laboriously made her way to the podium. Mason had the uncomfortable feeling that the group was expected to applaud or stand or something. Instead, awkward silence accompanied her entrance. Stone-faced, Elisabeth sat in a chair behind the podium, crossing her legs demurely. The Bishop, who had followed Zhézush into the room, took a seat next to Elisabeth. He was taller than Mason remembered, and still wore a clerical collar. His long black robe brushed the ground as he walked.

TV lights clicked on, and sweat shone on the sides of Zhézush's face. The podium hid her wrists and feet, obscuring any sign of the stigmata. She stood silently for a long moment, during which the bizarre notion filtered through Mason's mind that she might begin cracking jokes. Instead, the room erupted with a dozen questions, prompting Elisabeth to stand and raise her hand for silence.

"You may ask your questions now," she said coolly, and several reporters simultaneously started to speak again. She whispered something to Zhézush, who pointed to Mason for the first question.

"Is it true you that you are Jesus Christ, returned to earth, the son . . . er, um, daughter of God?" The room erupted in snickers and guffaws. Grimacing, he avoided looking at Elisabeth; he had not intended to be flippant. Zhézush seemed unfazed.

"Yes." Her thick lips widened into a smile. "But so are all of you sons and daughters of God. You died on the cross as I did." Mason marveled again at her perfect English. He waited for her to say something else, but instead she turned to another questioner.

A dark-skinned woman from one of the TV stations posed the next question. "It has been said that you are also God himself. Is this true?" Her tone was cynical, hostile.

"No." Zhézush looked for another question.

"If you are not God, but the daughter of God," the woman continued, "are you human? Do you have a navel?"

"I am as human as you are," replied Zhézush quietly. "I have a navel, a liver, a vagina, a mind, a heart. I eat, urinate, defecate, and do all of the other things that you do. If I am cut, I bleed. If my heart stops beating, my body will die." She pointed to a large man with a mass of unruly hair in the back of the room.

"Was your mother a virgin?" the man asked, kicking up a new round of snickering.

Zhézush smiled again. "I do not think so."

"Is your mother still alive?"

"I do not know. I never knew my biological mother."

A large-haired woman in front picked up the attack. "How do you know you are Jesus Christ?" she asked. "Have you always been? Was there some change that came over you? Did you realize your powers when you were baptized?"

"I have always known that I was different, but not until several years ago did I realize that I had become a vessel of God. I was baptized as an infant, but I took the opportunity to be rebaptized several years ago in Rio de Janeiro. From that point, I knew."

"Was there anything in particular that happened?" The man with the flapping shirttail stood.

"Yes." An awkward silence ensued.

"Why are you here?" Mason asked. "What is your purpose?"

"If you have been to my service, you know the answer to this question. I teach love, peace, and justice. If we love our children and our neighbors, we must change our world. We must stop overpopulation. We must overcome violence and ethnicity. We must share our wealth." The calming voice had begun to cast its hypnotic spell. The words themselves offered nothing but simple platitudes. "Ethnicity" sounded like something from a sociology professor. Yet the delivery made it seem eloquent and meaningful.

He pressed ahead. "So if this is really the return, where is the apocalypse? Is Armageddon near? Is this the beginning of the millennium, the thousand-year reign? Is something about to happen?"

"I believe you will find the Bible states clearly it is not for you to know the timing or season of my return. As was the case with the creation of the world, seven days is not seven revolutions of the earth, nor is a thousand years a thousand revolutions around the sun. As for Armageddon, have you been to the slums of São Paulo, or perhaps the bowels of Africa? Would you not characterize these areas as at war? Would you not agree that if these conditions continue, the world cannot survive?"

"I don't understand," Mason responded. "You're saying Armageddon is at hand and being fought in the slums of the world?"

Zhézush nodded affirmatively, her broad arms folded.

"What about the Rapture, Judgment Day, the Beast, the building of the Temple in Jerusalem, all the other things referenced in the Bible in connection with the return of Christ?" The press conference had evolved into a two-person debate.

"Remember that the Bible is filled with imagery, that many of the things you mention are prophesies. Obviously, the world will end as we know it when the sun no longer shines and darkness descends. This may not happen for many thousands of years, or it could happen tomorrow. My point in being here, my message, is to provide a means of reconnection in an isolated world. That connection is love."

"But you haven't answered my question," Mason continued. "Will there be a Judgment Day? Was John correct in the Revelation? Will there come an Antichrist, or is he already here?"

"There will be a Judgment Day. There already is a Judgment Day, although not in our lifespan or in the way we might envision it. God has a plan for each of us. But in His wisdom, He leaves room for each person to forge his or her own way. Perhaps there will be an Antichrist, perhaps not. Many will claim I am the Antichrist. You must judge for yourselves."

A broad-shouldered man standing next to Mason interrupted the debate. "Zhézush," he said in a thick Spanish accent, "your services are marked by a significant number of healings of the ill and afflicted. If you are who you say, why must these people suffer in the first place? Would a loving God impose this upon his people?"

"The power to heal is God's, not mine," Zhézush responded calmly. "Why one person is healed and another is not, or why one person is afflicted and another is not, I do not know. All I ask when I place my hands on someone is that God's will be done. God made this world in a certain way, with choices, risks, happiness, sadness, sickness, health, loveliness, ugliness. This challenge and conflict is the beauty of existence. We cannot control life, but we may direct it in a way that its burden upon our brothers and sisters is eased. Such is my humble request."

"Let me make sure I understand something you said earlier," Mason said. "Do we agree nothing in the Bible indicates this kind of prophetlike return you ascribe to yourself, maybe to come again, maybe to come many times? Everything in the Bible indicates one triumphant, cataclysmic return in the end time. It seems to me you must be saying the Bible is wrong."

"Not at all. Two thousand years ago, did the Jews expect their promised messiah to be a carpenter's son, whose message was 'love your enemy' and 'turn the other cheek'? My appearance on this earth signaled a new covenant from God, it produced a 'new testament' that became the guiding light of the faith. I present to you today a further modification of the original covenant. This is not to say the prophecies in the Bible are incorrect regarding the final days, any more than the prophecies in the Old Testament regarding the messiah were incorrect."

"And what about First Timothy two-twelve?"

Zhézush's face flattened into a grin. "If your point is to produce a statement that the Bible is inerrant, let me assure you it is not."

"Any comment on the death of your associate, Ricardo Cunha?" This from the broad-shouldered man. "How did he die? Couldn't you have saved him?"

Elisabeth slid in front of Zhézush at the podium, cutting off a response or further questions. "It is necessary that we end this conference," she said, to groans from those assembled.

"Will there be another one?" someone asked.

"Perhaps," she replied. "You will be told." She smiled, the white teeth gleaming majestically in the light.

"What is your schedule from here?" asked another.

"There will be another service in Miami tomorrow night, and we will provide further announcements at that point." She paused, her gaze sweeping the room. "Thank you for coming. Good night."

7

For dogs have compassed me: the assembly
of the wicked have inclosed me: they
pierced my hands and my feet.
Psalm 22:16

Mason rolled over in bed. No dream, and no concrete answers. Still, he felt exhausted, as if he had struggled internally all night. The questions and responses at the press conference had been the usual, although with less emphasis on the "wrath of God" and the "end time" than most. Zhézush's hypnotic powers of persuasion were extraordinary, but not supernatural. He stretched, rose from the bed, and stepped over to the desk.

Both the *Miami Tribune* and the *Gazette* had run small articles on Zhézush and the service, each relatively skeptical in tone and relegated to an inside page. The *Tribune* gave more play to Cunha's death, calling it "suspicious" and stating that the coroner's office had not yet made a decision regarding the cause of death. A youthful picture of the late ex-governor, his hair slicked back, sad eyes smiling, accompanied the article. So far, so good; the *Herald* would probably have the benefit of doing the breakout definitive story if it so chose.

Mason called room service for coffee and toast, then checked with police headquarters to confirm the newspaper reports regarding the status of the inquiry into Cunha's death. He called Perola, but reached only her answering machine. After breakfast he dressed and went down to the lobby again, stepped outside to check the weather, and decided to go for a swim to clear his head. A quick change later, he was back at the outdoor pool.

A figure caught his eye as he entered the pool area. Elisabeth pulled herself out of the water, droplets cascading off her dark hair and skin. She wore a white one-piece bathing suit that clung tightly to her body, the moisture rendering the suit essentially transparent. Full breasts and large dark nipples were as plainly visible as if she had worn nothing. Mason felt his breath catch in his throat as she picked up a towel and stepped toward him.

"Hello," she said warmly. "You should know the tabloids and TV news shows are bombarding us. I have already had thirteen calls this morning: *Inside Copy,* American Public Radio, everything. We are accepting no interviews. Thank you for setting up the conference."

"I hope everything turned out okay." He cleared his throat uncomfortably.

"It was adequate. Will you be attending the service tonight?"

"Yes," he replied, forcing his eyes away from her to scan the pool area. He saw no one else he recognized as part of Zhézush's group.

"I am alone," she said quietly, as if reading his thoughts. She stood very close to him, so close he began to backpedal when she shook her head and sprayed his face with water. She dabbed the towel on the side of his face that had been sprayed.

"Tell me," she said, stepping away a foot or so, "what do you think of Zhézush?"

He was thrown off balance by the question, so excited by the prospect of physical contact he could barely think. Somehow she seemed to know his point of vulnerability. He backpedaled again, marshaling his defenses. "Zhézush?"

"Yes, Zhézush," she responded with the barest hint of a smile. "Is that not why you are here?"

He struggled to regain his composure. "I think she's a fake," he said forcefully, jutting his jaw forward.

She surprised him by laughing aloud, her head tilting back, the damp hair flapping against her back. "And why do you say that?" she asked, seeming to suggest no one could be foolish enough to entertain such a thought. "Do you meet people every day with the power to heal?"

"No," he said, folding his arms across his chest, "but I'm not sure Zhézush really has such power either. She doesn't heal the difficult cases, the cures that would be truly miraculous: the guy with no legs, the child who is terminally ill, the youngster with Down's syndrome. If she really wanted to prove herself, why not go to the children's hospital and heal those who are really sick, not a select few in wheelchairs?"

He paused to catch his breath, unconsciously pulling back in case she tried to slap him. Instead, she leaned forward and kissed him again, a long, slow, wonderful kiss that brought murmurs from others in the pool area.

"I like that idea," she said, disengaging, her voice low. He felt himself becoming aroused, in the middle of the pool area, clad only in a bathing suit. She stepped away, laughing at his apparent discomfort. "Set it up for tomorrow."

Mason eased himself into a lounge chair. "Okay," he muttered, placing a towel over his midsection.

"Let us know the time and place."

"Okay."

She stepped over to another lounge chair, collected her belongings, and sauntered back to the door of the hotel without a backwards glance. Most gazes in the pool area followed her, then refocused on Mason after she had gone. He busied himself with the magazine he had brought, the blood still pounding in his veins.

The Reverend Arnold Lee Lovrun scratched his flaking scalp as he read the article in the *Miami Tribune*. He muttered angrily to himself, as was his way, tilting his head back, teeth clenched. Some Negress claiming to be Christ returned and purporting to heal people. What blasphemy! What was the world coming to? How could anyone with half a brain believe this? People were ignorant. It was his job and that of all Christians to educate the masses before it was too late. He read through the article again, scowling. Surely this was an indication the end was near. A woman, and black nonetheless! This certainly was the work of the Devil.

He rose unsteadily to his feet and shuffled over the rippling, cracked linoleum. His church, the Old Springs Baptist Church, sat only a few hundred yards away, just outside La Belle, Florida. La Belle was citrus and cattle country, with a rural population and a conservative outlook. With its concrete blocks painted white and a weathered cross tacked to the front, the church sat just off Highway 80, about a mile outside of town. Reverend Lovrun had been pastor for going on fifteen years and knew his flock well—mostly poor farmers and menial workers in the nearby groves. No blacks, and that was the way it should be. He considered himself an unprejudiced man, having made a decision years ago to stop using the word "nigger" on account of his status as a man of the cloth. Blacks should get the same chances everyone else did, no more, no less. He did not, however, want to socialize or otherwise have anything else to do with them.

He stumbled past the framed picture of himself and the Reverend Joe Farriday, the leader of the National Conference of Christians, taken some seven or eight years ago. Now there's someone who would take this seriously! Reverend Lovrun always listened to Reverend Farriday's weekly sermon on the radio and watched his syndicated TV show when he could make arrangements with someone who had a satellite dish. Reverend Farriday had predicted just such a thing: false prophets would multiply, taking the Lord's name in vain. Reverend Lovrun wished he could talk to the great man, just for a couple of minutes, to tell him what a hero he was to Christians everywhere and to warn him of this infidel. Maybe he should try to call. Still, he was just another country preacher in podunk Florida. He probably couldn't get past Reverend Farriday's secretary, even though he had met the Reverend personally three times before. He sighed, and spat into a nearby trash can.

Reverend Lovrun brought the *Tribune* story with him to the church, still stewing over the sacrilege of the whole thing. He could drive the two hours down to Miami and challenge the heretic, but Reverend Lovrun hated Miami. The city represented everything wrong with the modern world. Instead, he would engage in one of his favorite pastimes and write a letter to the editor of the *Tribune*, warning the heathen of Miami to beware false idols as the Good Book instructed. Shoot, he would even see if his friend Luther down at the store would fax the thing in for him. He paused and prayed briefly for guidance and for triumph over evil.

The phone in Mason's room rang as he opened the door.

Rhodes' bulldozer voice was on the other end. "Got anything new?"

Mason informed him of Zhézush's apparent willingness to visit the hospital.

"You know, given your reputation, these people could be setting you up. You're the perfect foil: 'Well-known authority on religious phenomena verifies Christ's return.' What more could they ask for?"

"Don't think I haven't thought of that. I'm taking it very carefully."

"Who else is going to be there at the hospital?"

"Press-wise? Nobody, if I can help it. I'm not even sure how to go about doing it."

"The hospital is tomorrow and the service tonight?" Rhodes cleared his throat with a loud harrumph. "Call me after each. I think we want to run this soon. What's your impression of the whole thing?"

"I think it's the usual fraud, but intricate and well thought-out. They've spent a lot of time with this, and they're slick."

"I agree with nothing of the sort. They're rank amateurs, and it only points to the incredible gullibility and stupidity of the public that they pay the slightest attention to this shit."

"Then why are we covering it?"

"Because I want to expose it for what it is. Garbage. Call me after the hospital. I'll bet you dinner you won't see anything approaching a miracle."

Mason replaced the receiver then stretched out on the bed to contemplate how he might orchestrate the hospital visit. He couldn't really demand that hospital administrators make their pediatric patients available to a faith healer. What he really needed was a hospital contact in a town where he knew no one, and the local *Herald* bureau chief was still on vacation. Fumbling in the drawer of the nightstand next to the bed, he pulled out the voluminous Miami telephone directory, overturning a Gideon Bible in the process. Health care providers consumed a number of the directory's yellow pages. Figuring he had nothing to lose, he began cold-calling.

Officials at Miami Memorial Hospital and Sisters of Charity Health Center were less than helpful. But the woman who answered at the Dade Memorial Hospital pediatric department was surprisingly enthusiastic. "Oh, yes, I have heard of her," she exclaimed when Mason described Zhézush and the visit's intent. "I saw her on TV this morning. That would be so wonderful." She introduced herself as Rosanna Self, a pediatric floor nurse, and suggested Mason obtain the approval of the hospital's assistant administrator for public relations, then stopped herself. "No, they'll never agree to that. Still, I think the idea is wonderful," she said excitedly. "I'm a devout Christian myself—Pentecostal—and I deeply believe in Christ's power to heal. I don't know if this Zhézush is who she says she is or not, but we see unbelievable heartache and suffering here every day. I don't see how it could hurt. Show up here at three tomorrow afternoon, and I'll get you in to see several patients. No more than three in your group though, okay?"

Thanking her profusely, Mason replaced the receiver. He put off calling any of the other hospitals.

Work on the story consumed the remainder of the afternoon. He updated his earlier version to include the Miami service and the press conference. He struggled with the article's lead—a depiction of the moaning, riveted crowd in São Paulo—and changed it to a detailed description of Zhézush herself, perspiration pouring off her face, wounds visible on her feet and wrists. Reaching an impasse, he stood and stretched.

The Bible he had overturned earlier caught his eye, and he stooped to pick it up, rubbing his hand across its shiny top. This version with the gold cover looked identical to the one he had seen in Cunha's room. He opened the front cover to see if anything had been marked inside.

The inside cover was blank except for a single penciled quotation: Isaiah 53:5. He found the passage and read aloud to himself: "But he *was* wounded for our transgressions, he *was* bruised for our inequities: the chastisement of our peace *was* upon him; and with his stripes we are healed." Prophecy of Christ's suffering. Even after all the training and all these years, he still found the Bible more confusing than illuminating.

He flipped back to Revelation 17, the language highlighted in Cunha's Bible, that of the purple-clad woman with the writing on her forehead, and continued reading. "And here *is* the mind which hath wisdom. The seven heads are seven mountains, on which the woman sitteth." He skipped down: "These shall make war with the Lamb, and the Lamb shall overcome them: for he is the Lord of lords and King of kings: and they that are with him *are* called, and chosen, and faithful." Then, Verse 18: "And the woman which thou sawest is that great city, which reigneth over the kings of the earth."

Closing the Bible, he watched a great storm cloud advance across the Miami skyline. The cloud moved rapidly, then split into smaller clouds. An opaque screen of water followed. Weird stuff, Revelation, cloudy as a liquid wall. The thought struck him that Rio de Janeiro was built on seven hills.

Fifteen minutes later, the thought was still with him as he drove through the rain to the next appearance of Zhézush da Bahia.

8

> And the fifth angel sounded, and I saw a star fall
> from heaven unto the earth: and to him was
> given the key of the bottomless pit.
>
> Revelation 9:1

This time, Perola did not venture into the *favela* alone. Henrique accompanied her in his squad car, along with a giant police recruit named Ricardo. She had gone home and cleaned herself, appalled at the clump of hair missing from the side of her head but determined to proceed with her mission. Nursing a slight headache, she had wrapped a scarf around her head and convinced Henrique to take time off to accompany her back into Bras.

The streets past the military checkpoint bubbled with afternoon traffic: autos of all shapes, sizes, and ages; bicycles; motor scooters; pedestrians; even a long-faced mule. They drove past the area of Perola's confrontation, empty now save for a few men sharing a bottle on a street corner and a large woman toting a load of laundry. The Y at the center of the *favela* was only a mile or so away, but the cruiser moved slowly down the crowded street. As if on cue, the *favela*'s entire populace appeared to have taken to the streets, clogging automobile traffic, further stirring the dust.

They found the Y an extension of the people and trash of the roadway, somewhat on the order of a populated open-air landfill. Lazy-looking men sat on abandoned cars and appliances. A group of children stalked a soccer ball on the dirt street. Several middle-aged women sat in front of a beer shack sipping afternoon brews, their backs turned to the chaos and squalor only a few feet behind them.

Perola shook her head and wiped her face. This was the dark underbelly of the Brazilian economic miracle—for every middle-class subdivision there were two of these ugly urban ghettos. They pockmarked Brazil's cities, absorbing peasants fleeing rural poverty like giant cancers.

Off to one side of the Y stood a tall black man in a battered black hat, frock coat, and trousers, speaking loudly to three people cowering in front of him. He held what appeared to be a Bible in one hand and a small bottle in the other, the two objects sailing around like weapons as he gesticulated wildly to make a point. Some of his words were caught on the wind, blowing to where Perola could make out phrases: a "Holy Zhézush" here, a "dark and abominable evil" there. Dark stringy hair flowed from under the hat, shreds of a dark beard clouded his face. Even at some distance Perola could see his eyes darting excitedly to and fro.

She knew a little about *candomblé,* which originally referred to communities in Salvador in which groups of freed slaves established temples of worship. The gatherings developed into cults of sorts guided by religious leaders known as fathers or mothers of saints, *pais de santos* and *mães de santos.* The *mães de santos,* which seemed to outnumber the men, were generally known as "aunts." *Filhos* and *filhas,* sons and daughters of saints, served as mediums to reach the cult's deities, usually identified with the Catholic saints. The relationship with the Catholic icons helped to anglicize the cults, making it possible for blacks to profess fealty to both religions.

"Make your decision before it is too late," the man in the black hat bellowed in a voice much louder than it needed to be to reach men standing only a few feet away. Spittle spewed from his mouth. "Exu is upon us." Perola recognized the term for the *candomblé* icon identified with the Devil.

The man's body shook feverishly, and his eyes rolled back in his head. Others milling around the area stopped to watch. His body jerked, as if jolted by electricity, lifting him a surprising foot or so off the ground and back. The three gathered around him gave way as he continued to twitch and flail his arms, his eyes tightly closed. A lather of white foam appeared at his mouth.

"Christ! Christ! Christ!" the man shouted, coming out of the trance. "Hurry! There is not much time!" Veins stood out in his neck like giant knotted ropes. Turning slowly around, he shrank at the sight of Henrique's uniform. He muttered something under his breath, then edged away as they neared him.

"You are Moraes," said Henrique.

"And if I am?" The man looked as if he might break into a run.

"Do not be afraid. I am not here to arrest you. My wife would like to ask you some questions." He nodded in Perola's direction.

"I am a reporter," she said to Moraes, who still seemed ill at ease. Pockets of people congregated around the group.

"Go away," shouted Henrique, turning to those behind him. "There is nothing here for you to see. Leave us alone." Ricardo started toward them menacingly, and they scattered like chickens.

"I am doing a story on Zhézush da Bahia," Perola said quietly. "I understand that you have known her a long time. I am seeking information about her."

Moraes pulled at his straggly beard, his eyes so vacant she thought for a moment he might be blind. His lips curled up into a smile. "My Zhézush," he said softly, tenderly. "My Zhézush. Yes, I have known her for quite some time. I nurtured her. I baptized her. I was her lover. I preach her gospel every day. The question is, do you know her?"

"I am trying to. You were her lover?"

"I have known Zhézush for many years, since she was practically a child! I knew her in Rio, before she came to São Paulo. We first met in Dona Marta, in the *favela*." Moraes had a sing-song speech pattern, as if he were used to speaking in rhyme.

"She was like many others," he continued, "stealing, doing drugs, selling her body. But there is something different about this woman. She came to me one night in Rio, the first time we met. She brought me food. I do not know how she came by it. She told me of a vision. She had been chosen. She was to teach and preach. I knew she was special. I knew that God had sent her to me. I knew she had special gifts." His eyes lit as the last word hissed from his mouth.

"So Zhézush was at one time a prostitute?" Perola asked, jotting on a notepad, sweat forming on her forehead.

"Yes, yes," clucked Moraes, "just like many of the girls around here." He waved his arm melodically.

"And you baptized her?"

"Yes, under a drainpipe in Dona Marta. That was seven or eight years ago. It was then I realized she was truly a gift from God. When I pulled her out from under the water, I said to her, 'I realize now who you are. I am at your service, my master.' "

"What gave you this realization?"

"I do not know exactly. It was one of those things God permits you to see clearly for a few moments. I knew."

"You knew she was Christ, returned to earth?"

Moraes nodded, his eyes filling with tears. He pulled a filthy rag from a pocket and dabbed at his face, then wiped at what appeared to be lesions under his hat.

Perola pursed her lips. "Do you also know a woman named Elisabeth Obrando?"

Moraes furrowed his brow. Across the Y a group of black and brown children gathered near a rusty drainpipe, taking turns dousing themselves. "Yes, I have known Elisabeth. Even longer than Zhézush. Elisabeth is also a child of the *favelas,* although different from Zhézush and most of the others. Elisabeth was smart and beautiful. She did not have to be a prostitute; she organized the others. She and Zhézush were always close. When Zhézush first evidenced her gifts, Elisabeth was doubting, skeptical. But they stayed together and became colleagues, moved to São Paulo together."

"You mention gifts Zhézush evidenced. What were they? When did they begin?"

"One of the first I remember was probably six months after her baptism at Dona Marta. A young pregnant girl had given birth to triplets. Here in the *favelas,* the hospitals are bad. There is no health care. There is nothing. Many babies do not live, and a teenage girl who has triplets, little tiny things, she does not expect any of them to survive. But Zhézush came to this girl, and she held these little things, no bigger than the palm of my hand. And they thrived. This was a sign. The people recognized it. There were others. Once, in a ghetto in Rio, the only source of water went bad. Everyone who drank it became sick. The whole slum was in danger. Zhézush put her hands over the water, and it was safe to drink. The sickness went away, like a rain cloud. This too was a sign. Just like the wedding, just like the feeding of the multitudes. Christ has *returned!*"

Perola stepped back nervously. "Just one more question. What about Zhézush's mother? Is she alive? Do you know where she is?"

Moraes shrugged. "I do not know," he said, pulling himself up to his full height. He looked each of them in the eye, as if about to propose a toast, then strode across the road, weaving his way in and around people and trash, his words echoing after him as they watched his retreating form: "Repent! Your savior has returned! Repent!"

Mason's expectation proved correct: television and newspaper coverage of Zhézush's first Miami service produced a much larger crowd for the second. It also produced some protesters. Twenty or so marchers paced back and forth in front of the Miami Arena's entrance, chanting and singing, protected by a half-dozen uniformed policemen. As he grew closer their signs became legible:

"Ignore the False Prophecy!"

"You Blaspheme Our Lord!"

"Christ Jesus Warned There Would Come False Prophets!"

Inside the arena, the wheelchair group had grown in number. At least two hundred chairs occupied almost one-third of the space on the arena floor, their occupants a mixture of children and adults. Some suffered obvious signs of congenital defects, while others exhibited no apparent malady. Caretakers hovered as before, this time in folding chairs thoughtfully provided and placed to one side so that those in the wheelchairs could see the stage. Adjacent to the wheelchair area a woman lay bound on a gurney, the light refracting off the whites of her eyes as she stared upward at the ceiling.

Mason was struck by the need on the faces in the crowd, the hunger for . . . for something. Was it the same as his own? It seemed depressing, somehow, a shared wretched attempt to give empty lives meaning. If Zhézush was a fraud, it made it that much more heinous; not only was false hope given to the physically ill and disabled, false promise was given to the emotionally afflicted as well. Was the world this desperate, this . . . wanting?

The crowd sang as before, swaying like wheat in a field. Elisabeth made her entrance, dressed in the shimmering gown of a starlet. Mason's pulse leaped. The tune died out in a flush of anticipation.

"Love!"

"Love!"

"Peace!"

"Peace!"

"Justice!"

"Justice!"

The now-familiar call and response. The crowd grew louder with each recitation, like a dog straining at a leash. Elisabeth broke into the Lord's Prayer, and the sound of twenty thousand voices droning in unison sent shivers up Mason's back.

". . . for thine is the kingdom, and the power, and the glory *forever*." The words hung like a cloud over the arena, forced finally to earth by a crushing "Amen."

The drumbeat started from behind the darkened stage, spreading around the arena and drawing the crowd into its force. The wailing and chanting began, the words tumbling over and over until they became the rapid thrust of a locomotive: "Master, Savior, Lord. Master, Savior, *Lord.* Master, Savior, LORD."

Floodlights beamed on to reveal Zhézush alone in the middle of the stage, her head bowed. No microphone was visible. Her dark smock crinkled together like a flower ready to burst forth. She raised her head slowly, almost painfully, and lifted her arms as her voice filled the arena.

"My people," she rumbled. Again, chills swept up Mason's back. She must have some sort of cordless mike, but the sound was nonetheless overwhelming, captivating, and all-encompassing, totally different from the ringing metallic reverberation of Elisabeth's voice only moments before. Was it possible that through some miracle this voice carried on its own? The crowd quieted in awe, heads bowing, the unworldly hush of the previous services descending.

"I am yours," gushed the voice, eliciting a moan from the crowd like a lover's prod. "I have returned."

Mason felt goose bumps on his arms and back. Even though he had witnessed two previous services, even though he had seen quite a bit of Zhézush these last several days, this voice, this power, amazed him. The red lights of television cameras blinked from below, and he wondered how much of the effect carried over the airwaves. He closed his eyes and tried to envision other mesmerizing speakers: Roosevelt, Martin Luther King . . . Hitler. Even as sweat trickled down the side of his face, he shuddered.

From the back of the darkened stage, Joaquim Sebastião Silva felt rather than heard the crowd before him, directed as he was to the voices inside his skull. Every now and then a pinprick of extraneous noise entered, only to be isolated and shut out immediately.

"I am, I have been, and I will always be." Only that voice seemed capable of entering from the outside, and he marveled at it. The thought crept across the back of his mind, unformed at first, then rejected, but insistent. Was it possible? He focused in again on the children, on those desperately hoping and waiting, bound up in the grasp of that voice. He fingered the collar at his neck. The wounded mind would seek to rationalize anything, he decided, part of its attempt at delusional self-healing. Even a mind like his, battered with sin and bitterness. He dismissed his fantasies and rose, prepared to assist in the preparation of the sacraments.

Zhézush walked among the wheelchairs. Two of the afflicted closest to Mason commanded his attention: a hefty black teenage boy, whose head lolled continually from side to side; and a thin white girl, who looked to be suffering from advanced muscular dystrophy, her limbs contorted into odd, unusable shapes.

Before Zhézush could reach the two chairs, a thin woman behind the girl cried out and clutched the dark figure, her entire body shaking violently as she whispered into Zhézush's ear. Zhézush held the woman for some time, then turned her attention to the smiling little girl. Big black hands massaged the bent limbs, slowly working down the girl's body to reach misshapen feet and ankles uncovered from beneath a blanket. With a rush Zhézush took the girl up in her arms, lifted her into a bear hug, then held her with one arm as she ran her hand down the girl's spine. The crowd convulsed in applause and cheers as the little girl gamely waved one of her hands while Zhézush continued to hold her aloft. Zhézush set her softly in her chair then knelt in front of her, head bowed in prayer. Moments later, she lifted her head and instructed the little girl to stand. The girl inched forward to the front of the chair and gingerly placed one foot on the ground, then the other, then straightened herself until she finally stood upright. The girl's legs and feet, visible again beneath a yellow dress, had become perfectly straight and normal.

Mason sat rigidly in his seat. There had to be some deception or illusion. The distance that separated the crowd from the action allowed plenty of maneuvering room. Still, he was impressed. He had clearly seen the girl's grotesquely disfigured legs. The fakery was extremely professional—the little girl must be double-jointed, must have been willing to hold her limbs in impossibly awkward positions for some period of time. She stood now, her hands clasped like a boxing champion, a beaming smile stretching ear to ear. The woman who had previously stood behind her had collapsed behind the wheelchair, one of several fainting victims rendered aid by security guards and Young Assistants.

The crowd floated in complete pandemonium, the arena a cacophony of sound, neighbor hugging neighbor, black kissing white. Zhézush continued her work, moving to the black boy closest to the arena floor's edge. She wrapped her large hands around the child's neck, quelling his head's incessant side-to-side flopping. She stood in front of him for several minutes, still holding his head, her head bowed over his. Eventually she disengaged and stepped back away from him as if to admire a painting. The boy's head remained still for a few moments then slowly cocked back to emit a high-pitched, eerie laughter that pierced the crowd's roar and echoed off the walls.

More healings followed. The woman on the gurney rose to straddle it like a horse. The crowd approached delirium, receded, then approached again.

Mason retreated to the Conquistador. He reached Perola, and they traded information on the service and Moraes.

"The newspapers and TV here are blanketed with stories of Zhézush," she said. "Pictures of her are everywhere—on the TV, in the magazines, everywhere. It is almost that she is even more in the public eye by leaving the country. Everywhere I go, I hear people talking about her. I think much of it has to do with the TV coverage of her service in Miami. They play it around the clock."

"I think we need to run our story," Mason responded, kicking off his shoes. "The national news networks are going to be all over this soon. The tabloids are already in high gear."

After signing off, he dialed Rhodes at home and relayed the situation. There was a pause on the other end of the line.

"Send me something by morning. I wanna think about it. On the one hand, I hate to give this fraud any publicity, even bad publicity. On the other, everybody else damn sure will, soon. We've been here before, haven't we? Get it to me. Let's sell some papers. We may go tomorrow. I wanna see what happens with those fucking hospital visits. Are you the only media attending? Jesus Christ, what shit."

It took Mason almost four hours to finish the story and get it on the modem to New York. He was pleased with the final product—a lead describing the services and the healing, a description of what he understood to be Zhézush's message, references to the Bishop and to Cunha's death. He considered sending a message on to the Vatican, his private thoughts on the situation, but didn't. He would wait until after the hospital. Hungry and restless, he took the elevator to the ground floor with the thought of stretching his legs and finding an all-night food place.

The lobby appeared empty as he entered, the restaurants and bar closed for the night. Mason checked his watch: 4:15 A.M. He had just turned to retreat to his room when a figure near a giant potted palm caught his eye. The Bishop's dark gaze connected with his.

Mason moved over to him. "I'm Mike Mason with the *Herald*." He extended a hand.

The Bishop nodded. "I know."

"What are you doing up at this hour?"

A thin smile crossed thin lips. "I have difficulty sleeping. And you?"

Mason shrugged. "Actually, I've been working." He glanced at the darkness outside the hotel's double doors then back at the Bishop. "Mind if I join you?"

"Okay. I was considering a walk."

"Me, too."

The Bishop led the way out into the darkness. They walked silently past towering office buildings gleaming lifelessly in streetlights, stopping at intervals to glance along side streets barren except for an occasional parked car. Here and there a homeless person lay propped against a building or asleep on a bench. As they reached the heart of the downtown area, doors clanged and engines revved as early morning trucks unloaded produce and newspapers. The Bishop walked quickly, purposefully, his back straight underneath his dark garments. He looked out of place, thought Mason; this enigmatic man should be strolling the corridors of some abbey, not patrolling the dark streets of downtown Miami.

"Tell me about yourself," Mason asked, trying to appear friendly and nonthreatening. "What led you to go into the priesthood?"

To his surprise the Bishop pulled a small case from his robes and extracted a cigarette. He lit it and inhaled hard, the ember glowing red.

"I was raised in a religious family," he said evenly, offering Mason a cigarette. He turned back and continued down the empty street. "From the time I was a small boy, I had a special relationship with God. When I was fourteen, I told my parents I wanted to join a religious order. At first they protested, but they relented. I went to a special school for religious training in Brazil. We worked primarily with deaf people. One of the priests took an interest in me, and I was permitted to travel to Rome for a special study program. I elected to continue my religious education and was ordained as a priest several years later, after I had returned to Brazil. It was all that I ever wanted to do. I had a wonderful parish near Rio de Janeiro. I loved my work.

"As time went on, I had the honor of being selected a bishop, the high point of my life. Then I met Zhézush, and everything changed. I had devoted my life to the church, and suddenly I was being pulled in a different direction, in the grip of a powerful current. My thoughts, my dreams, every waking moment was caught up with this woman." His voice caught momentarily, and he paused. "For a while I thought Satan was tempting me, as he tempts all believers at one time or another. But soon I became convinced Zhézush was in fact who she claimed to be, the messiah, the chosen one. Once I became convinced of that, my devotions merged, and there was no other course of action I could take."

"Our backgrounds are similar in some respects," Mason said. Even more similar than he was willing to admit. He fought the urge to confide, to reveal that he too had once had a special relationship with God. "I worked with the deaf as a youth, at a hospital on a military base in Portugal. That's where I learned to speak what little Portuguese I know."

"But you speak it very well."

Mason stopped on a deserted corner to tie his shoe. The air was wet from the morning dew, and a cool breeze crept in from the bay several blocks away. "Bishops don't just leave the Church every day. When did you first meet Zhézush?"

"I met her through Elisabeth. For some time I had been involved with the political struggle in Brazil. I was among the last of the liberation theologians, you might say. I believed—still believe—Christ has a special message for the destitute, the homeless, those with nothing, and there are many of these in Brazil. My views were somewhat controversial. Elisabeth had been involved with these groups for many years, and I got to know her and her husband quite well. She told me of this friend with special powers, but I never thought much of it. In Brazil there is much mysticism, many strange religions and beliefs, many who claim to have special powers. But Elisabeth said, come, you must see this, it is truly extraordinary. You must talk to this person. So I went to this little meeting in the middle of the ghetto, and I met this woman. She was so warm, so . . . different that I was mesmerized. Then I saw her perform extraordinary feats of healing. I experienced her teachings of love and compassion. I heard her voice and I knew she must be the one. Once I knew that, I knew I had to leave the Church. Yes, it was difficult, but so are many things in life." His face tightened into something between a smile and a grimace. "I have no regrets."

"So, was there something specific that made you realize Zhézush was the one?"

The Bishop paused. "Do you believe in God, Mr. Mason?"

He swallowed. Everyone seemed to be asking him that question. "I think so."

"Given your occupation, does it enhance your belief when you encounter circumstances that can only be attributed to the supernatural?"

"Yes."

The Bishop spread his hands before him. "If everything about Zhézush is good, and then you witness the otherwise inexplicable . . ."

"What about Cunha?"

"What about him?"

"Was he meant to die?"

The Bishop looked sideways at him. Silence ensued. "I am not sure what you mean," he said finally.

They had circled back so that the front of the Conquistador was in sight. "It is probably time I depart," the Bishop said quietly, cutting off Mason's response. "Perhaps we can speak another time. Take care, my friend."

The morning papers were being delivered as they entered the lobby, and Mason grabbed copies. Propped against pillows in his room, he flipped drowsily through the pages, noting the more prominent coverage of Zhézush's latest service. Gone was the skeptical tone of the previous day, replaced by one of curiosity. The descriptions of the service were more detailed, the fervor of the crowd better captured. The healings were given prominent play. One article described the healing of the woman in the gurney as the "modern-day equivalent of the resurrection of Lazarus."

Fumbling with the light switch, Mason noticed in the folded paper a small headline, "Beware False Prophets." Intrigued, he picked up the paper again and scanned the article, a letter to the editor on the editorial page.

> All Christians should be forewarned. Beware false prophets such as the woman who claims to be Jesus

> Christ returned to earth, for the Bible has prophesied such. The Book of Revelation says that before Christ returns in triumph and in judgment, the Antichrist will rule the world for seven years. John's vision includes a beast with many heads and horns, ridden by a woman. Beware, all Christians, this woman deceives you! She is Satan in disguise. Who but Satan would be so diabolically clever as to return to earth in the guise of our Christ Jesus? The prophesies of the Book of Revelation are being fulfilled. Repent and trust in the Lord God Jesus Christ before it is too late. Do not be misled!

Below the letter appeared the name "Arnold Lee Lovrun, La Belle, Florida."

Eyes burning, Mason put down the paper. Another part of the pattern. Dissent. Paranoia. He fell into a restless sleep, in which he dreamed of a multicolored, horned beast with several heads, each of which seemed to be laughing at him.

9

Then touched he their eyes, saying, According to your faith be it unto you. And their eyes were opened; and Jesus straitly charged them, saying, See *that* no man know *it*.

Matthew 9:29-30

Perola waited patiently in the vestibule outside the offices of the Most Reverend Jorge deLonious, Archbishop of São Paulo. Copies of the morning's newspapers lay on a coffee table, their pages filled with articles describing Zhézush's visit to the United States and lengthy interviews with several of the healed. According to the lead article, regular television programming had been interrupted late the previous evening to bring footage of the service to Brazil. News of Zhézush's visit crowded out other news stories, including a precipitous drop in the value of the Brazilian *real,* which threatened to further destabilize the country's economy. Again, in what was becoming a daily occurrence, crowds protesting the government's policies had thronged to the centers of Rio de Janeiro and São Paulo, only to be dispersed by police lines, water cannons, and rubber bullets.

A small door opened and an elderly nun motioned for Perola to follow her into a dark hallway. Perola's stomach churned. Who was she to be asking questions of one of the most powerful men in Brazil, maybe even in South America? They emerged from the hallway into a modest office almost devoid of furniture, but blanketed in piles of paper. A wizened little man in a purple cassock peered from behind several mounds of it. He looked to be in his sixties, with thinning hair and horn-rimmed glasses.

"How are you?" he asked pleasantly once they were seated. "What can I do for you?"

"I am fine, thank you. My name is Maria; my friends call me Perola. As I told your secretary, I am a reporter. I would like to talk to you about Joaquim Sebastião Silva and Zhézush da Bahia."

A frown crossed the archbishop's face, and he leaned back in his chair. "Yes, I see," he said almost absentmindedly. "What would you like to know?"

"How long have you known Joaquim?"

"Oh, twenty-five years or so. He is younger than I. I first met him in Rome, actually. He was a very impressive young man, and he became sort of my protégé, if you will."

"Were you surprised when he did what he did?"

"Surprised? It was one of the great shocks of my life. Most people do not understand the dedication it takes to become a priest. It is much more than just a vocation one might decide to change at some point in life. It is a way of life. To break from the church . . . is like disowning your family. It is as if your child has told you he no longer believes you are his father and desires never to see you again."

The pain in the man's face was evident, and Perola hesitated before continuing. "Why did he do this? Did he talk with you about it?"

The archbishop paused for a long time, staring at the ceiling, his hands folded under his chin. "He told me he was convinced this woman was the messiah, returned to earth. I asked him, 'What makes you think that? How can you know that?' His response was that he just knew. I told him he must wait for the Church to make a decision, that this was not something he could unilaterally decide, any more than I could decide a miracle had occurred. I suggested he receive psychiatric counseling. He would not listen. He told me that once I met her, once I saw the things she was doing, I would do the same thing. But I have not."

"Then you have met her?"

The old man nodded, his hands covering his mouth, his eyes down.

"You do not believe that she is the messiah?"

"I do not know for certain," he said slowly. "Nothing has touched my heart to tell me she is. I hear she does great things, but I am unsure. For me, the Church must decide who and what she is. That is the nature of my belief."

The nun knocked on the door, stepped into the room, and handed some papers to the archbishop. He stood, signaling the end of the interview. "Whatever she is, she is very powerful to have convinced Joaquim to do this. Joaquim was, and is, a very good man, a very strong man, a very smart man. He would not easily be led astray. If I were to meet the messiah in the flesh, I believe I would be overcome with rapture and joy. Somehow I did not see joy in Joaquim's eyes when he told me of this. I saw pain. That troubles me. Good day, young lady."

The Reverend Joe Farriday, President of the National Conference of Christians, stared at the fax of the *Miami Tribune* articles and unconsciously smoothed his lacquered hair. The fax had arrived unannounced, displaying articles describing a black woman claiming to be the messiah and a letter to the editor denouncing her from a Reverend Arnold Lee Lovrun in La Belle, Florida. Reverend Farriday picked up a ringing phone as he continued to read. "Yeah?"

"There's a call on line four for you, sir," his secretary informed him. "It's a woman who wouldn't give her name, some kind of foreign accent. Says it's about some woman in Miami whose name begins with a Z. I tried to get rid of her, but she insisted you would take the call."

"Put her on." He listened intently without speaking as the call came through, snapping his legs off his desk, hunching over the receiver. After several moments he smiled. "I know what to do," he said softly, and replaced the receiver.

Tawanna Morrison's son's doctor was a slight, light-skinned African American named Lawrence Raley. He studied a chart as Mason looked on and twelve-year-old Leron moved around them. Leron's legs still looked as thin as reeds, and his movements were slow and labored, but he appeared to be moving with greater ease than when Mason had last seen him following the first service.

"Ain't it a miracle, doc?" breathed Tawanna, her arms clasped against herself. "I wouldn't have believed it if I hadn't seen it with my own eyes."

Dr. Raley frowned, still reading the chart, finally peering up over wire-frame glasses. "This is truly unusual," he agreed. "The boy suffered a severe spinal injury in the automobile accident some . . . what was it? . . . six years ago? One of his vertebrae was essentially crushed at that time. He was fortunate to continue to have the use of his arms. He went through years of physical therapy, but was never able to use his legs. To say I am shocked he is able to move around like he is today would be an understatement. I have heard of this type of recovery before, but it is extremely rare." He paused and looked at Leron again as the boy grinned widely.

"I would like to have some X-rays taken of his spine, to see if there have been any visible changes, and I would also like to have him examined by some of the doctors at the teaching hospital here in Miami," Dr. Raley continued in measured tones. "Whether this was physiological, psychological, divine intervention, or some combination thereof, it deserves more study."

The image of the hyperactive boy occupied Mason's mind as he drove to the hospital to meet Zhézush and the others. Why this kid and not the little dark-skinned girl he had also seen that first night? Had Tawanna Morrison and her son evidenced some special worthiness? Was the mind simply strong enough to effect physiological changes in the body? For that matter, was anything truly a miracle? His mind clicked back to the image of the little girl's withered legs. Would people have believed in the original Jesus if he had not performed miracles? Were Zhézush's healings performed only to buttress her claim to be the messiah?

Proof—it flew in the face of faith. Without faith, did Christianity exist? Depressed by his line of thinking, he edged through parked cars toward the hospital's main entrance under a sign proclaiming the facility "The Healing Place."

Perola put down the newspaper, poured herself another coffee, and stared out at the mid-morning rain. The television news droned in her living room's background, running over and over again the footage from

Zhézush's Miami service of the night before, interspersed with discussions of the falling *real* and the ever-increasing street protests. It was almost as if Zhézush was a national treasure, she thought, sort of like a championship football team, something for Brazilians to take pride in and hold out to the world as proof of Brazil's status as an important nation. It also helped take the focus off the country's mounting problems.

Henrique had worked another double shift the previous night, stumbling home about 1:30 A.M. and leaving again by 5:00. The protests were taking their toll on the São Paulo authorities, and there was talk additional army units would be called out soon in a show of strength against any civil unrest. She and Henrique had barely seen each other this week, with the exception of their trip into the *favela* the previous day.

Gingerly fingering the scab on her scalp, she leaned back on the couch and closed her eyes, trying to follow her thoughts as they shifted among Henrique, the street protests, Moraes, the archbishop, Zhézush. A familiar voice on the TV awakened her, someone she knew but could not place. Her eyes fluttered into focus in time to see Moraes gesticulating wildly as he addressed a crowd from a street corner platform. The image flashed back to a news reporter shouting to make himself heard, standing on the opposite corner of what she now recognized as the *Praça da Sé,* the downtown plaza fronted by South America's largest cathedral. As she watched, someone handed Moraes a bullhorn. His voice became a metallic staccato, rasping over the crowd noise, imploring the group to action. The camera panned to a line of policemen approaching from the other side of the plaza, riot shields, clubs, and guns in hand. Old women leaving the cathedral skittered out of their path. A policeman edged in front of the television camera, deliberately blocking the view just as the camera swung back to focus on the shouting, rock-throwing crowd. A few seconds later the transmission ended abruptly, leaving the screen in blank silence until the news announcer returned with a statement that the report would be "updated as soon as possible."

Perola scrambled into her shoes and rushed out of the apartment, slipping into the subway terminal just in time to catch an inbound train. The spotlessly clean train carried her in quiet efficiency toward downtown. Would she be too late to see anything? How had Moraes commanded the attention of such a crowd? There had looked to be at least several hundred in the plaza.

A sea of mayhem and discord greeted her at the *Praça da Sé.* People scurried in a crazy-quilt of different directions, trampling over one another as if fleeing an invading army. Thick, noxious, black smoke blanketed the entire plaza, attacking all senses at once as it squeezed lungs and rendered sight almost impossible. The smoke smelled of things not meant to be burned, like charred plastic or flesh, and she bent low to avoid it. It seemed palpable, a force unto itself, and she found herself waving her arms frantically against it as she tried to find her way through the plaza. She had expected a virtual lockdown of the area by the police and the military; instead, it appeared the forces she had seen on television had retreated to regroup and press the offensive.

A body hurtled through the blackness and knocked her to the ground, the crunch of bone on bone a split-second antecedent to the inevitable explosion of pain. A heavy-jowled black woman struggled to her feet, clutching her head with one hand, blood on her fingers. Bloodshot eyes gaped wide with fear, glancing back hurriedly for pursuers before returning her gaze to the still-prostrate Perola. Even through Perola's haze of pain, the woman appeared comical and sad, grubby unmatched knee socks falling about her ankles, a torn, dirty dress exposing a broken bra strap. Prominent whiskers dotted her chin. She stared stupidly at Perola for a moment, then charged ahead, forcing Perola to roll aside to avoid another collision.

"Save yourself!" the woman bellowed. "They are right behind me!"

The smoke thinned somewhat, and Perola could see the approaching line of a riot squad, menacing in the gloom, like an onrushing medieval army. Heaving herself to her feet, she fell into step behind the bullish woman. Her head throbbed.

"What happened?" asked Perola as she caught up with the woman, who made for an alleyway off the plaza.

The woman glanced fearfully over her shoulder. Blood dripping into her eyes forced her to stop and dab furiously at her face with a dirty sleeve. A hundred yards or so behind them the riot squad moved slowly in lockstep, their heels clicking on the pavement.

"They attacked us. What do you think?" she responded brusquely in the rough dialect of the Mato Grosso area. "We were protesting and we were attacked!"

Perola nodded. "I saw something of it on TV. What happened to Moraes?"

"Moraes!?" the woman half-wailed, as if remembering a child left behind. "I think they killed him! I saw these men grab him off the platform and beat him with their fists and with the microphone. His head was full of blood when the smoke bombs went off and the panic started. Oh, Moraes!"

"Do you know Moraes well?" Perola felt faint. Her head knocked with pain.

"Why are you asking all these questions?" the woman asked, peering back at the riot squad, which had stopped and appeared to be turning around. "Who are you?"

Perola leaned back against a doorway, suddenly tired, her feet slipping beneath her. She was dimly aware the sun had broken through the smoke and haze, making things bright and blurry. The woman peered over her, the whiskers shining in the sunlight, a single broken tooth visible beneath cracked lips. A vile plume of foul breath singed Perola's mind before unconsciousness overtook her.

Dade Memorial Hospital resembled most other hospitals Mason had ever seen; big, white and antiseptic, its wide halls permeated with a faint smell of body fluids. Elisabeth and Zhézush were already seated in a small waiting area off the main lobby, conversing in low tones. They rose without greeting him, and he followed them to the elevator. They rode in silence to the fifth floor, his gaze alternating between Elisabeth and the scars readily visible on Zhézush's wrists. Elisabeth avoided eye contact, yet he stared at her anyway. The thought of touching her arm made his hand tremble.

Disembarking from the elevator, they proceeded to a nurse's station at a crossway of two corridors. Blue-garbed nurses moved quietly around the station, studying charts and talking quietly on the phone. Bright pictures of balloons and animals identified the area as a pediatric ward.

A gray-haired portly woman approached them and identified herself as Rosanna Self. "I have been expecting you," she said, bowing slightly. She looked at the dirty, rumpled Zhézush in awe. "Wait just a moment, please."

They seated themselves in some plastic chairs adjacent to the nurse's station. The moment turned into fifteen minutes. Zhézush closed her eyes, her face frozen in concentration. Elisabeth paced slowly, deflecting Mason's attempt at conversation. Mason watched a pair of older women communicate in sign. Something about surgery. Complications. He glanced through a dog-eared, yellow-covered book of children's Bible stories: Jonah and the whale, Daniel in the lion's den, the Tower of Babel, Joseph's coat of many colors, the crossing of the Red Sea. Times when God actually spoke to people directly, not obliquely through symbols and such.

"Follow me, please." Rosanna had returned. She led them down a side hallway, through a set of double doors, and stopped before a wide hospital door. "This is Lina," she whispered. "Advanced kidney disease." She knocked briefly before entering the room.

Inside were two beds, the first empty, the second occupied by a frail, dark-haired girl of about seven with tubes connected to her arms and nose. An older woman, apparently a grandparent, sat in a chair by the side of the bed. A male nurse adjusted something on one of the nearby machines.

The older woman stood as they entered the room, grasping Elisabeth's hand gratefully in the apparent belief she was Zhézush. She stepped aside when Elisabeth informed her of her mistake, allowing Zhézush to approach the bed. Mason looked on from near a curtain used to separate the other half of the room. Rosanna Self waited, arms folded, near the room's entrance. The other nurse straightened and moved toward Rosanna. The little girl ignored him, her gaze fixed on Zhézush, wisps of dark stringy hair matted to the side of her head.

Zhézush eased her bulk down on the edge of the bed, and they sat silently looking at one another for some time. Finally, Zhézush began singing softly, a tune Mason did not recognize, words he did not understand. The words seemed of a foreign language, not Portuguese or Spanish or anything else recognizable. After a few minutes, the little girl joined in, her high-pitched voice mixing with Zhézush's resonant deeper one. The male nurse shuffled his feet restlessly then stepped quickly toward the bed as Zhézush reached forward to grasp the girl's head in her hands.

"What are you doing?" he squealed. "Get your hands off the patient!"

Pulling on Zhézush's large shoulder, he motioned for Rosanna to help him. Zhézush turned slowly, her face still a picture of tranquility, and firmly removed the man's hand from her shoulder.

"Let go of me!" The nurse, whose nameplate identified him as Reilly, turned toward the door. "Rosanna, call for help!"

"Please," said Zhézush serenely, the soothing voice calming the situation like a mother's voice to a crying infant. "Look." She gestured to the little girl, who had removed the tube from her nose and was in the process of disengaging the lines connected to her wrists. The others stared in shocked silence. Reilly sputtered but could get nothing out.

Lina sat up, brushed the hair back from her face and pulled her legs over the end of the bed. The grandmother's legs buckled. Reilly caught the woman with one arm before she hit the floor, then pulled her over to a chair. Lina was out of the bed now, moving to aid the grandmother.

"It's okay, mama," said the girl, holding the older woman's face in her hands. "I feel better. This doctor has healed me."

The woman, revived, hugged the girl to her chest, her body shaking with sobs.

Reilly rushed to the nurse's call button. "Send security immediately!" he ordered the metallic voice on the other end. He gasped for air as if he had been punched in the solar plexus. "Rosanna, what are you *doing?*"

"My God," Rosanna Self's voice cut through the clatter, quieting the others. "Lina!" she said softly as she went to the little girl, held aloft in Zhézush's massive arms. "I . . . I don't believe it! You . . . you must reinsert the tubes . . ."

"I feel all better! My stomach doesn't hurt anymore. See?" She pulled up her dress to expose her belly.

"I . . . I must call Doctor Smith," Reilly stammered. "This is . . . ah . . . we didn't think . . ."

Mason felt a blast of exhilaration. Something had happened. Even these charlatans could not have staged this event. He had set this up, had selected the hospital, arranged for the patients. He had informed Elisabeth only that morning of the hospital they would visit. It would have been almost impossible for this to have been arranged in those intervening hours.

Zhézush turned to Rosanna. "I apologize for the disturbance," she said calmly. "May we visit the next patient?"

She led them to another room two doors down the hall, a larger, private room occupied by a tow-headed boy of about five and several adults. One of the adults, a sandy-haired man who looked to be the boy's father, shook hands gravely with Reilly and introduced himself to Zhézush. The man's wife, a slender, attractive woman, and an older woman whom Mason took to be the child's grandmother stood in the back of the room.

The boy resembled a skeleton, his cheeks sunken, eyes deep-set in his skull. The smell of death lingered in the room, and images floated back to Mason of children he had seen dying in the Indian subcontinent, in his earliest days as a correspondent. Two other nurses poked their heads into the room, evidently alerted by the commotion, and the group swelled to ten. The room quickly grew warm and uncomfortable. They stood in silence, the only sounds those of the boy's labored breathing and the ethereal hum of fluorescent lights and medical machinery.

Mason stood elbow to elbow with Elisabeth and Rosanna as Zhézush approached the child. She reached over and pulled the tubing out of the boy's arm, eliciting gasps from several present, quickly shushed by the boy's father. Gently, Zhézush picked the child up in her arms and carried him around to the other side of the bed, where a nightshade was pulled against a window. She released the shade, flooding the room with late-afternoon sun. The boy's eyes fluttered open as the sun's rays hit his face. He squinted against the light, then closed his eyes again.

"Do you see what God has given you, my child?" Zhézush asked as she rocked the boy in her arms like an infant. She began to speak again in the unfamiliar tongue. It was like a language understood as an infant but incomprehensible as an adult, Mason thought, something out of the subconscious. She sang again, rocking the child to and fro, but this time the child did not waken and return the song. After some time she laid him gently on the bed again, turned and faced his parents.

"He will be fine," she said comfortingly. "When he wakes, he will be well again. It will take some time for him to regain his strength, but he will suffer no more." The father looked dubiously at the child, who lay motionless as before.

"Thank you," he said graciously. "I don't know what you have done, but thank you for trying." The mother and grandmother nodded listlessly, and the entourage began to back out of the room. Several uniformed security men and a short young man in a business suit waited outside the door. Nurse Reilly hovered in the background.

"Please leave the hospital immediately, or I will be forced to call the police," the short man said. Mason supposed him to be an administrator.

"As you wish," said Zhézush, and they began to retrace their steps to the nurses' station, past the double doors, and toward the elevator.

Behind them double doors burst open, and the rail-thin, blond-haired boy, cheeks now flushed with excitement, thrust himself forward and made a beeline for Zhézush. The father followed a few seconds later, equally flushed, trailed by the mother and grandmother.

"I don't believe it," the father shouted, tears streaming down his face. Heads turned among the nurses and visitors in the vestibule. "It's a miracle! We . . . we had no hope! Oh, praise God." He broke down in great racking sobs as his son rested in Zhézush's arms. The mother and grandmother held one another, muttering incoherently and crying.

Mason felt a shiver creep down his spine. He looked around at the assembled group. Big alligator tears rolled down the sides of Rosanna's face; Reilly blew his nose and wiped his face with a handkerchief. Only Elisabeth seemed detached, standing off to one side and moving impatiently to and fro. The sight sobered him. He reminded himself he hadn't seen a limb regenerate or anything purely paranormal, only children who looked very sick suddenly appear better. Unusual, but not necessarily unworldly.

"This woman has healing powers," the sandy-haired man was saying. "My little boy is in the advanced stages of leukemia. He hadn't spoken in days. This woman spoke to him, and now look! He is better than he has been in weeks! I . . . I can't explain it. Maybe it's only temporary, or psychological. But from our standpoint, it is hope and additional time."

"Okay, okay. Let's go, all right?" the administrator broke in, flustered but adamant. "Take the patient back to his room, okay?"

Rosanna took the elevator down with them. "Thank you so much," she cried, grasping Zhézush's arm and not releasing it. "I . . . I just can't say anything more." She burst into tears. The others in the elevator looked on quizzically.

"Would you mind if I got the names of the children's doctors and followed up with you?" Mason asked.

Moments later he was back in his car, rushing back to the hotel. He reached Rhodes' voice mail and left a message to dial the mobile number. Minutes later Rhodes' snarl filled his ear.

"Well, what is it?"

Mason relayed the saga of the two patients. "Something definitely happened here," he said in conclusion. "It'll probably be several days, at least twenty-four hours, before lab reports and X-rays are back and anything conclusive can be ascertained. That's assuming the physicians will speak to me. Anyway, it would be better if we could hold the story another day."

"Nah, we gotta go. The World News Network is already on with a little segment about last night's service. Not much, but we need to go. Layer this onto what you got and get it here."

Mason hung up. His mind played over the hospital events again. He had seen so many purportedly healed over the years he was usually numb to the experience; in fact, he often found himself contemplating the irony of supposed revelations of God by means of making whole something permitted to become diseased in the first place. His usual skepticism, however, had begun to melt. Children somehow opened an avenue to his soul. Medically proven yet or not, the faces of the families of the desperate children at the hospital told a wondrous story. He pounded the car's roof with his fist in a brief blast of euphoria. These could not have been setups, he was virtually certain. Somehow, Zhézush had effected a real change in the medical condition of seriously ill children, a change he had seen with his own eyes. He glanced skyward, offering something approaching a prayer. The Return? Perhaps he had been granted a glimpse.

10

Believe me that I *am* in the Father, and the Father in me: or else believe me for the very works' sake.

John 14:11

Perola awoke slowly, shifting in and out of consciousness until at last her eyes opened and she became fully awake. She lay on a pallet in a dark, damp room smelling of mildew and urine. Light shone through cracks in a boarded window. Her head hurt, not a bad hurt, but enough to make her feel slightly nauseous.

A door to the side of the room opened to admit a woman, a familiar-looking woman with prominent facial hair. Suddenly it came back: the plaza, the police line, the crunching impact. The woman wrung a wet cloth in her hands, evidently intent on placing it on Perola's forehead. The room's stench seemed to intensify. With a grunt Perola attempted to rise to a sitting position, only to find the room spin in a greenish whirr. Reclining again, she permitted the woman to place the cloth on her head.

"Who are you?" she finally asked the woman, her eyes still covered by the cloth.

The harsh sound of a throat being cleared echoed in the room, and a wisp of strong body odor floated by. The compress shifted. "I am called Velda," the woman replied huskily. She spoke almost with a lisp, and her words of the previous day—or was it the same day?—came back.

"Moraes," said Perola suddenly, attempting to raise her head again only to fall back once more in dizziness. "What has happened to him?"

She removed the compress from her head.

Velda shook her head sadly. "We do not know for certain. The last I saw him, he was bleeding badly about the face from the beating by the troopers. He may be dead. The authorities will give us no information regarding him." She dabbed the cloth against the sides of Perola's face.

"What happened to me?" Perola asked. "Where am I?"

"You passed out after we ran from the troopers. Jacko and I brought you back here."

"Who is Jacko?" Perola forced herself to sit upright. This time, the vertigo melted away.

"You will meet him. He is my friend." There was something in the woman's tone that seemed strange, as if she presumed Perola her prisoner.

"Well, I must be going. Thank you for your assistance." Perola slid off the pallet and moved unsteadily toward a makeshift door.

"Who are you, dear?" asked Velda. "Are you one of us?"

Perola stopped, her hand on a peeling green doorknob. "I . . . I am not sure what you mean."

"You knew of Moraes. Are you a believer? Or perhaps from the police?"

Perola swallowed hard. Velda's face was in the shadows now. Fear crept through Perola. "I am not a policewoman," she stammered against another onrush of nausea. "I am a reporter. I know of Moraes because I am doing a story on Zhézush da Bahia. I had interviewed Moraes several days ago about his relationship with Zhézush. When I saw him on television and the start of what looked like a riot, I came down to the plaza." She paused, peering at Velda through the gloom. "What do you mean when you say 'believer'?"

Velda stepped forward so her face was more visible. Her mouth opened into a homely smile, exposing the single chipped tooth in front. "Why, dear, if you are doing a story on our beloved, you should know what we believe. We are Zhézushians; we believe in the teachings of Zhézush. We are her followers."

"Miracles or Mirages?" The front-page headline made Mason cringe, but the majority of his story had been left intact. He stretched in the morning south Florida sun.

He had filed to New York by ten o'clock the previous evening then spent the next several hours on the phone with Rhodes and the other editors, fighting their attempts to recraft it. The resulting story ran almost a full column on the front page and comprised the majority of an interior page. It included a lengthy description of the hospital healings and more information on Cunha and the Bishop, as well as information Perola had obtained from Moraes regarding Zhézush's past.

Mason had received no calls from the physicians he had left messages with at the hospital. He would attempt to follow up today, but he knew the full onslaught of the alerted media would make things difficult. A check with hotel security chief Collins about the inquiry into Cunha's death had revealed that an autopsy was to be conducted. Collins had agreed to follow up with his contact on the results.

Mason sipped black coffee and read his story carefully. He was relatively pleased with the final result. His eyes lingered on Zhézush's picture on the inside page, obtained from a freelance photographer. Her outstretched arms struck a crucifixion-like pose.

A glimpse of Zhézush on the TV across the room made him put down the paper. It was near the end of the half-hour segment, a time when "soft news" and human interest stories were often given brief coverage. A dark-haired woman reporter stood in front of a mass of people milling around what appeared to be a hotel lobby, shouting to make herself heard. Pointing to those behind her, the woman described them as people wanting to be healed by a woman named "Zhézush." The camera focused on several in wheelchairs before the coverage jumped to a shot of Zhézush, her large arms raised heavenward at a service, then to a brief interview with none other than nurse Reilly. Signing off with a shrug, the reporter directed the cameras again on the straining, surging crowd. Rosary beads and statues of the Madonna peeked from hands among the compressed bodies.

With a start Mason realized the people he had just seen on TV must be downstairs at the hotel. Striding to the window, he pulled back the curtains to gape at the scene below. Scores of police cars ringed a crowd blocking the driveway. Metal wheelchairs sparkled in the morning sun.

A rap at the door pulled him away from the window. Slipping on his pants, he unlatched the chain and cracked open the door. Elisabeth pushed past him into the room, followed by Zhézush and the Bishop. Mason self-consciously ran his hand through his hair.

"Mother of God!" Elisabeth exclaimed darkly in Portuguese. "These people are relentless. They are all over our floor, banging on the doors." She switched to English. "The hotel, they can do nothing. It is if they have been invaded."

She turned to Mason, seeming to notice him for the first time. "May we stay with you for a while? Zhézush needs to rest." She gestured toward Zhézush, who appeared to have already fallen asleep in an arm-chair.

"Of course. I see the authorities have been called to help control the situation." He jerked his thumb in the direction of the window. Elisabeth glided over to take a look.

"I do not know what we are to do," Elisabeth said, almost mournfully, seating herself gracefully in a chair next to Zhézush. "What do you think, Joaquim?" she asked the Bishop, switching back to Portuguese. "They all want to be healed, I suppose." She gestured to the window as if referring to household pests.

The Bishop shrugged his shoulders and glared out at the growing crowd. "You or I could go now and try to convince these people to return for the service tomorrow night."

"Do you mind going?" She smiled sweetly. "I understand Mr. Mason has written his article, and I should like to read it."

The Bishop nodded stiffly and left the room. Elisabeth turned to Mason, swinging her legs so that her skirt opened to reveal black stockings. "May I?" she asked impishly, reaching across him to pick up the copy of the *Herald*. She sat back in the chair and read the article, laboriously crossing and uncrossing her legs, her face melting into a mask of concentration. Soft snoring from Zhézush's chair rippled like waves through the room. Mason felt uncomfortable, like an artist showing a portrait to his subject for the first time. The image of Elisabeth, aloof at the hospital healings, flashed across his mind. He stood and stretched, looked out the window again. The crowd seemed to be dispersing; apparently the Bishop's entreaty had been effective.

"Where will the next service be held?" he asked.

Elisabeth continued reading. She put down the paper moments later, eyes blazing. "A prostitute? Moraes' lover?" She glanced up furiously at Mason. "Where did this come from?" The sharpness of her voice woke Zhézush, who rubbed her eyes sleepily. "Who told you this?" Elisabeth demanded.

"Moraes spoke to my colleague in São Paulo."

Zhézush's eyes swung shut. Elisabeth snorted derisively. Eventually, she put down the paper. "Well," she said coldly, her eyes shifting away from him. "I suppose it is probably the best we could expect." She returned her gaze to him, as if suddenly remembering he was the article's author. "Of course, I am sure it is much more accurate than what we will find in the other papers. Have we been on TV this morning?"

"Yeah, you and the thousands besieging the hotel. I'd say most of the United States knows of Zhézush by now, probably a good portion of the world, as well."

Elisabeth smiled, evidently relishing the thought. "Yes, you may be right. The next service is tomorrow night. We have changed locations; this service will be held at the Orange Bowl stadium. The police are requiring us to sell tickets."

Mason whistled in surprise. Someone had moved mighty fast to arrange a service at the Orange Bowl. In fact, Cunha must have made arrangements for the Orange Bowl weeks before, in anticipation of this scenario. The thought heightened his unease, and he considered again the possibility he was being used as a pawn to obtain publicity for the cause. Why had Elisabeth and her group been so willing to talk to him, even showing up in his room? The Orange Bowl would produce national publicity, probably live television coverage. He could envision people flying in from all over the country, ill people anxious to be saved.

Realizing Elisabeth was looking at him, he shifted his position on the bed to face her. She stood, glanced at Zhézush still snoring in her chair, then moved to him, her hands against his shoulders. The room seemed to move, as if it revolved around her axis. She unwrapped her skirt, exposing her brown body, the fragrance of hair and body and the closeness of her overwhelming his senses. His breathing quickened in quivering response. If a meteor had hit the Conquistador, he would not have noticed. It was as if the world ceased to exist but for her.

"Do not think too much, my friend," she whispered in his ear, her hands pushing him back on the bed, the brown body now on top of his. He felt himself falling in a wonderful, exhilarating spiral. The snores from across the room, now deeper and longer, muffled the sound of the unzipping of his zipper.

The Reverend Arnold Lee Lovrun stared at the overnight delivery package lying on the table. Overnight delivery packages did not come often to La Belle, and Reverend Lovrun had never received one before. This was truly a day to remember. His letter to the editor of the *Miami Tribune* had appeared the previous day, with more stories about the blasphemous woman claiming to be Christ returned. His blood boiled again just thinking about it. Maybe someone would read his letter and see the light. It was so clear—right out of the Bible! Still, people were so *dumb.*

Then there was this package. He eyed it suspiciously for a few minutes, wondering vaguely if someone had sent a bomb. Curiosity eventually won out, and he ripped open the cardboard. Inside he found a plain white envelope addressed in block capitals to the Reverend Arnold Lee Lovrun, with a return address for the National Conference of Christians. Again, he stared suspiciously at the envelope, turning it over and over in shaking hands before finally slashing it open with a finger. The envelope contained a single sheet of plain white paper on which a message had been printed in the same block capitals. "God needs your help against the Devil!" the heading announced, followed by a smaller paragraph. Reverend Lovrun read slowly, forming the words with his lips as he went, his face contorting with excitement as he reached the end of the paragraph and the signature of the Reverend Joe Farriday. A handwritten letter from Joe Farriday! He dropped the paper onto the rickety card table, blood pumping through his veins, oblivious to the language at the bottom of the letter dictating that it be immediately destroyed. He yelled for his wife.

"I'm going to Miami tomorrow, honey! The Good Lord is gonna take care of a few things!" His wife nodded and waved her hand mechanically, absorbed in the soap opera blaring from the television set in the adjoining room.

Perola eyed the motley group assembled around several upturned cardboard boxes. A deafening rain pounded hard on the metal roof of the lean-to. She had unintentionally stayed overnight at Velda's, collapsing into a deep, dreamless sleep and waking in surprise to find morning light streaming through cracks in the boarded window. She had not spoken with Henrique, and she knew he must be worried she had not returned the previous evening, but there had been no easy way to contact him. Velda had brought her this morning to a shack a few dwellings over to meet the other "Zhézushians."

The damp dirt floor seemed to seep its way into her shoes, and she shivered involuntarily, even though it must have been over twenty-five degrees Celsius outside. Ten people sat around the makeshift table: seven women, including Perola and Velda, and three men. All were black, although maybe one or two could be counted *mulatto*s; Perola couldn't be sure in the gloom. Behind them on the floor sat a child of about seven or eight, his face ballooned in the moonlike countenance of Down's syndrome. A large, bearded man with unruly hair seemed to be the leader, and in a gravelly voice he began a prayer which the others joined in. The sounds of the human voices mixed eerily with the noise of the rain. Candles provided the only light in the room, their flames flickering to and fro as if caught by unseen spirits.

The shack's door, really an expanse of corrugated metal somehow held together by metal wire, opened, and a blast of rain accompanied a figure into their midst. Droplets rolled off matted hair, splattering against several of those seated on the floor or in nearby rickety chairs. Thin hands pulled back the graying hair to reveal the pointed, pockmarked face of a middle-aged black woman. Her gaze jumped around the room, focused on Perola, then shifted away.

"Who is this?" the newcomer asked the bearded man, without making any reference to whom she was referring.

"She is a reporter who was covering the riot at the square yesterday. She was injured, and Velda brought her home. She is doing research on our Lord." The bearded man bowed his head in deference to the gray-haired woman.

The woman walked over and thrust her face close. Perola pushed away instinctively, then held her ground, returning the gaze steadfastly for what seemed a long time. The thin woman finally broke it off and stood, turning her back.

"Moraes is dead," she said tonelessly. A moan swept through the room, finding no words, brittle in its anguish. "I spoke to someone who saw him die. He was tortured, as you might expect. They chopped his toes off, one by one, until he bled to death." She spat angrily onto the earthen floor, turning to face the group again. "I am sorry that our Lord was not here to help him in his final hours. Let us pray for his soul and those of his killers."

The bearded man led a recitation of the Lord's Prayer, his deep voice rumbling like cannon fire. The words echoed off the tin ceiling, bouncing around and over one another. Perola imagined being transported back in time to a prehistoric cave tribe, huddled against the elements, offering entreaties to unknown gods. The end of the prayer cast the room into silence interrupted only by the rainfall's incessant drumbeat.

"Should not we contact Zhézush in the United States?" asked an elderly woman, hands clasping a shawl around her shoulders. "Surely she would want to say a mass for Moraes."

"Perhaps she could raise Moraes from the dead!" chimed in another, a fat woman with long dark hair pulled back straight from her head and braided. She issued a command to the Down's child, who left the room.

"What was being done with the body?" asked the bearded man, whom the others called Vicente.

The thin woman shook her head, wet hair still dripping on the floor. "I do not know."

"But, Aide, what do we do now?" asked Velda, her voice bordering on hysteria. "Do we continue the protest?"

"Of course!" the thin woman responded vigorously. "That is what our

Lord has commanded us to do. We will be more vigilant than ever!"

She walked over to Perola and seated herself cross-legged in front of her. The others inched forward to form a semicircle. "You have been brought here as a friend," Aide said quietly. "We are happy to provide another means to spread the word of Zhézush. But do not betray us. Even were you to try to do so, you could most likely not find us again. Be concerned for your safety. If you are found to be a friend of ours, you are in danger." She rose to her feet in the fluid motion of a dancer. "Just ask Moraes."

"Th . . . thank you," Perola stammered, teeth chattering. "I will not betray you. What more can you tell me about Zhézush? When is she returning to Brazil? What are her plans? What are your plans?"

Aide poured some water from a filthy-looking container into an equally dirty mug. "I can tell you only what she has told me. I do not know when she will return to Brazil. I do not know her plans. But I know the plans she has for us." She gestured to the others. "I know the plans she has for her people." She stopped, as if she intended to keep the information to herself. "Perhaps we can talk again."

Velda accompanied Perola back to the *Praça da Sé.* The scene of the previous day's turmoil now bustled with ordinary morning activity. Vendors hawked sweet rolls and coffee, commuters scurried by, mothers strolled with their babies. Perola had almost convinced herself she had dreamed the entire episode, until she noticed municipal workers scrubbing dark stains on the concrete at one end of the plaza. Dark stains of blood.

Mason slammed down the receiver on the hotel room phone. No one at Dade Memorial Hospital would return his calls. Even Rosanna Self was "unavailable." Calls to the rooms of the "healed" patients were blocked. He gritted his teeth. He would have to return to the hospital and attempt to ferret out information amidst what was by now undoubtedly a media horde.

His thoughts drifted to Elisabeth. Their coupling earlier replayed across his mind like a broken tape, his body tingling in remembrance. Zhézush, snoring not five feet away. A familiar montage of guilt, then remorse, then excitement washed though him. His weakness. He rubbed his face with his hands, determined to concentrate on the story, to avoid becoming a part of it himself.

The phone rang loudly, startling him. He picked it up immediately, the image of Elisabeth on his mind. Instead, Zhézush's familiar melodic voice came over the wire.

"Michael." The voice rose and fell like water in a stream. "The Catholic bishop from Miami and the president of St. Andrew University are coming to see me this afternoon. I would like you to be there. Will you come?"

He was speechless. Zhézush had rarely spoken to him directly, much less called him on the phone. For a moment he thought someone might be playing a trick; he imagined Reynolds laughing as he held his hands over the mouthpiece. Still, no one could fake that voice.

"Hello? Are you there?"

"Of course I will come. What time should I be there?"

"If you could come now, that would be wonderful."

"I'll be right there." Mason hung up, torn between opportunity and continuing unease about his role. Still, the Church had to address the issue of Zhézush; she was becoming too big to be ignored. Parishioners would be asking their priests about her, and they would need a response, even if a temporary one. Would Elisabeth be there? His heart fluttered. His mouth went dry.

Adrenaline still coursed through his veins as the metal door to room 1515 opened moments later. He smiled in Elisabeth's direction, a big, moronic grin, instantly regretted. She did not return the smile nor seem surprised to see him. His face grew hot. Seated across the room, the Bishop likewise seemed to expect Mason. He directed Mason to a chair across from Zhézush's broad form.

The Bishop offered Mason a soft drink, which he accepted. The usual perspiration smell permeated the room.

"We received a call this morning that the Catholic bishop and the president of St. Andrew University wanted to meet," explained the Bishop, his white clerical collar rigid against his chin. "We thought it might be useful for you to hear what they have to say."

The thought distressed Mason. Useful to *whom* for him to hear this conversation? To their propaganda efforts? He started to say something, then changed his mind. The drink tasted vile in his throat.

"I know the bishop, the Most Reverend Jorge Cruz, quite well," continued the Bishop. "He is a fair man, very intelligent. I do not know the other gentleman."

"What do they want to talk about, specifically?"

"We do not know for sure," Elisabeth said from across the room. She looked at Zhézush, avoiding Mason's gaze. "We have heard rumors of a fact-finding commission to investigate the healings as miracles." She shrugged her shoulders dismissively.

"Any comments on what's been going on in Brazil?" Mason asked.

There was no immediate response. It was as if such a question were off limits. "What do you mean?" asked the Bishop finally.

"I'm sure that you've heard there have been additional demonstrations against the government. I have been told that Moraes was killed in one of the protests." Neither the Bishop, Elisabeth, nor Zhézush showed any reaction to the statement. A Young Assistant brought a bucket of ice into the room, then left quietly by a side door.

"We have heard this," the Bishop said quietly. "It saddens us deeply."

"We are worried," Elisabeth agreed. "Perhaps we shall return more quickly than planned." Her eyes met Mason's, and he glanced away.

"Is this group, the Zhézushians, actively involved in the struggle against the government?" Mason continued to probe. They had, after all, invited a journalist to this meeting. "Was Moraes their leader?"

Elisabeth started to protest, but Zhézush cut her off. "The Zhézushians were never intended to be a lamp kept under cover," she said evenly. "Yes, Moraes was involved, but ultimately I am their leader. Moraes helped keep the . . . how do you say it? . . . lines of communication open." Her thick lips creased into a smile. "I am much saddened by his death, but he and I both knew he would die at the hands of evil, as will I."

"What are you saying, that you expect to be killed by the Brazilian government?" Even though he'd half-expected such a response, shivers raced down Mason's back.

"Unfortunately, the Brazilian government is not the only force of evil in this world, my friend." Zhézush's lips parted to expose giant, white teeth. "But yes, I will die soon. That is what has been revealed to me. That is why it is vitally important my message be as broadly disseminated as possible."

The room erupted in a volcano of protest. Elisabeth exhorted Zhézush to explain the premonition. Veins stood out in the Bishop's forehead as he said something in Portuguese Mason did not understand.

Mason sat back in his chair. All messiahs had a death wish. Some acted on it by means of suicide; at least two had faked their own deaths to enhance claims of resurrection. A too-familiar pattern.

A rapping on the outside door silenced the room. Seconds later a Young Assistant appeared, escorting two men: a short, dark man wearing a business suit and a much older man clad in a bishop's red cassock, his blue-veined hand wrapped tightly around a cane for support. The clamor in the room ceased as ex-Bishop Silva approached the visitors and kneeled. Bishop Cruz's bejeweled finger remained at his side.

"My friend, Jorge, it has been a long time," ex-Bishop Silva murmured in English, rising. The old man nodded, gold flashing in his mouth.

"Let me introduce you to Father Alfredo Castiogne, the president of St. Andrew University," said the older man in a guttural voice. The short man bowed, and the Bishop completed introductions around the room.

Bishop Cruz peered over his glasses at Mason. "I was not aware the press would be present," he said quietly in accented English.

"Forgive me, your grace, but I asked him to come." Zhézush's voice filled the room, an orchestra unto itself. "I want the world to hear my message."

"I do not intend to be quoted." Bishop Cruz looked sharply at Mason, who nodded in agreement. "Very well. We asked for this meeting because we too have heard much about you. I, like many of my brethren, was shocked to hear that Joaquim," he gestured toward the ex-bishop, "left his life's work to follow this path. This says much about you, for I had the utmost respect for Joaquim."

The word *had* hung heavy in the air, and the ex-bishop looked away. "Your claim to be the messiah we take with the utmost seriousness. The Church has seen many over the years who have made this claim, including some who appear to have performed miracles." Another significant pause. Beady eyes peered over the top of half-glasses, like those of a bird searching for food. "You are familiar with the Scriptures, no doubt? For instance, Matthew, chapter twenty-four, verse four?"

" 'Take heed that no man may deceive you,' " Zhézush rumbled responsively. " 'For many shall come in my name, saying, I am Christ; and shall deceive many.' "

"Yes," said Bishop Cruz softly. "Another of the verses with which you are undoubtedly familiar is Matthew twenty-four, twenty-four: 'For there shall arise false Christs, and false prophets, and shall show great signs and wonders; insomuch that if it were possible, they shall deceive the very elect.' So you see, madam, the Church is not unaware, or particularly surprised, for that matter, at someone claiming to be Christ returned, even someone who allegedly produces miracles. We have seen this before and will undoubtedly see it again. This has been foretold, and we have been waiting."

He twisted the cane between the gnarled hands. "We have seen on TV that you have performed supposed miracles at the hospital. My brother Father Castiogne has attended one of your services. We see the media in a frenzy, if you will, about you, and our priests are overwhelmed with questions and curiosity from both believers and nonbelievers. As you can well appreciate, the Church moves cautiously and slowly in matters of this nature. We know there will be false prophets, because the Scriptures have told us so." He paused, and silence enveloped the room. Mason swallowed hard. If only Bishop Cruz knew what three of his brethren in Rome did.

"I have received a message from the Vatican," Bishop Cruz continued finally, softly, his voice a padding of slippered feet. His gaze flitted to ex-Bishop Silva and back to Zhézush again. "It has been asked that I convey it to you. Since you are not an ordained priest, I have also been instructed to inform you you are forbidden to conduct a mass or bless the sacraments."

Zhézush climbed to her feet with effort, saying nothing, and waddled to the window. She gazed into the bright sunshine for a long moment of tense silence. "You are familiar with Matthew twenty-four, verse forty-four as well, I presume," came the voice. She turned to face Bishop Cruz. A faint nod evidenced his assent. " 'The son of Man will come at the hour you least expect it,' " she recited. She shifted her bulk from one foot to another. "It would seem to follow that this return would also be in the form and in the place that we least expect it. A woman, a *black* woman, in South America, is the child of God returned? Where is the reconstructed temple, you say? Why are we in Miami and not Jerusalem? Where is the darkened sun, the darkened moon, the stars falling from the sky? The Bible says all these things shall come to pass before Christ shall return." She paused, her breath coming in great gasps. Sweat droplets had begun to inch their way down her broad cheeks.

"My time is very short on this earth," Zhézush continued solemnly, arms folded across her width. "What I do is done for a reason. The healings, the miracles, they are necessary now as they were two thousand years ago. The publicity, the frenzy, as you call it, is required for the dissemination of my message because there is such little time."

"And what is your message, exactly?" interrupted Father Castiogne.

"The same as it has always been. Do you remember my teaching that the greatest commandment is to love God with all your heart, soul, and mind? That the second greatest commandment is to love your neighbor as yourself? These two principles are intertwined. God is all around us—in the trees, the forests, the animals, the people. If we do not love these things, how can we say we love God, or our neighbor? If we do not care for the tiny fish in the bottom of the ocean, so eventually will we destroy it. If we do not care for the plant in the corner of this room, it will die as surely as if we ripped its leaves and mutilated its trunk. If we do not care for the crying baby abandoned on the street corner, the homeless man who has no food, they will certainly perish. My message is the most simple of all messages, for it is one of love." Her voice had grown softer, but remained intense. The tendons in her massive neck jumped and knotted, while a row of scars on her forehead gleamed purple against the dark flesh.

"Read Matthew twenty-five, gentlemen," she whispered. "Read it again and again. Inasmuch as you have clothed, and fed, and given drink to the least of my brethren, so you have given these things to me. If you have not,"—massive shoulders shrugged, lighter-colored palms outstretched—"you have done nothing." The two visitors sat in cowed silence as she approached them.

She crouched on her haunches to look them directly in the eye. "There are forces of evil, Your Excellency, which are real. Some are present in your

Church. In the days to come, you shall see many great and terrible things. Remember my words as you see these things; you, the most holy of the righteous." She stood, her pendulous breasts swinging under the dark smock as she turned away again. "In Jerusalem, so many years ago, my authority was also questioned. I need no outside authority for what I do. I think you understand this." She raised her arm to her head, exposing the sleeve of her smock, now darkened with blood. A large, crimson drop splattered onto the carpet. The other gazes in the room riveted on the drop. Either Father Castiogne or Bishop Cruz, Mason couldn't be sure which, emitted a choking sound.

Bishop Cruz rose to his feet, his knuckles showing white against the cane, his face ruby red. "*You* are the evil one," he said, spittle flying from his mouth. He pointed an accusing index finger at Zhézush. "Maybe you have the healing power, *but you are not Christ!* My savior will return on wings of glory, the clouds trembling at His feet, not as a fat *woman* who drips blood from fake wounds, who surrounds herself with these . . . people." A thin stream of saliva edged out the side of his mouth. He wiped it with a red sleeve. "The Bible speaks of *Jerusalem,* not of Brazil, not of Miami. Are you saying you know better than the Scriptures?" His words collapsed into a high-pitched, choking cough. With the flap of an arm he waved off assistance from Father Castiogne.

Zhézush's body shook in laughter, jolting and jiggling and bumping against itself. Her skin looked almost violet in the light, Mason thought, in contrast to the red blood on her wrists. The description of the woman "arrayed in purple and scarlet" from the passage in Cunha's Bible jumped back at him, and his mind recoiled.

Bishop Cruz's gaze locked with Zhézush's for a long moment. With a quiver he silently crossed himself, then pivoted on his cane and moved toward the door. Zhézush reached out and clamped a large paw on his shoulder. Cruz leapt almost a foot in the air, fear in his eyes, a mouse caught in a hawk's grip. "Do not be afraid," Zhézush whispered softly to him. "Open your ears and your mind."

With a brusque flip of his shoulder Cruz broke away. "May God have mercy on your souls," he spat over his shoulder as he scuttled from the room, Father Castiogne on his heels.

11

Be sober, be vigilant; because your adversary the devil,
as a roaring lion, walketh about, seeking
whom he may devour:

I Peter 5:8

Mason lay in his bed in the Conquistador, propped up against every pillow he could find, the remains of a room service breakfast scattered around him. He was sick of the Conquistador, sick of this room, sick of Miami, and sick of the hoopla now surrounding Zhézush and her group.

The *Herald* editors had decided the night before to postpone a follow-up story for at least another day, even though Mason had put together what he considered to be an adequate piece describing the medical reports and reactions of the various religious organizations. The follow-up would run in the next day's edition, after the Orange Bowl service.

As he had expected, television coverage had riveted the attention of the nation. Footage from the previous service captured the stigmata in detail, and seeping blood played over and over on the tube, like one of those displays in department stores designed to look like a continually dripping faucet. Tabloids screamed the story of Zhézush from every newsstand, headlines ranging from "Mysterious Black Woman Heals Millions" to "Fat Jesus Returns, Hypnotizes Stadiums" to "Is The End Near? Jesus Returns." Media and the curious swarmed the Conquistador like flies, and the hotel resembled more than ever an armed camp, police lines surrounding it on all sides. A bellman told Mason the hotel management had asked

Zhézush's group to leave because of the disruption, with no apparent success.

Although he had been unable to communicate with Zhézush, Elisabeth, or their group since the previous afternoon, he had uncovered one bit of interesting news from Collins. The security chief had conspiratorially pulled him into his office and drawn the door carefully shut behind them.

"They did the autopsy, and the results are out," Collins said dramatically. "The official finding is that he died of cardiac arrest; however, the coroner is a pretty good friend of mine and I called him up to see what he had to say. He said it was the damndest thing he had ever seen, that he had put down cardiac arrest because he couldn't find a single thing physically wrong. Now that in itself is not completely unusual, but Doc Stephens said that in light of the situation he ran all the toxicology tests, you know, for poison and everything? Nothing. He's sending some tissue samples off to a lab out of state to review—probably be a few weeks before that gets back. He said he cut open the guy's heart and lungs and—get this—he says you would have thought he was examining a thirteen-year-old! He said the guy was perfect! No fat in the arteries, lungs clean as a whistle; he said even kids have more shit in 'em than that. Weird, huh? I thought you might like to know, but don't go quoting me or him, you understand? He just told me this 'cause we go back such a long way."

"What about the color of the body?" Mason asked.

"I asked him about that. He didn't know what the hell I was talkin' about. Said the exterior of the body looked normal as well. Shit, I don't know. Damn sure looked strange to me."

The plumes of cigarette smoke surrounding Cunha and the clink of ice against cocktail glass filtered through Mason's memory. Cunha hadn't looked the monastic type. Collins was right; it was weird.

A knock on his door jolted Mason back to the present. He pulled back the door to find the large form of Zhézush, perspiring as usual and dabbing a handkerchief to her forehead. Peering around her, he was surprised to discover she was alone.

"Come in," he said. She flashed a smile and shouldered her way into the room. The stigmata appeared to be in remission, the scars barely visible on her broad wrists. The body odor, however, was in full force.

"I must speak to you," she said quietly, looking down at the floor then into his eyes with a directness that made him look away. "I will not live much longer." Her gaze continued to bore into his. "I know who you are."

His blood froze. She must mean his connection to Rome. How could she know? Only three other people alive knew, unless somehow there was a leak at the Vatican.

"This much has been revealed to me: you will perform a great part in the drama." The familiar soothing voice surrounded him in a vise grip, and he sat down heavily in a desk chair.

"You have been witness to the truth about me; you know my message is true. I have come to you because danger surrounds me, my mission, and my country. It is a long conflict. This is but one battle.

"You must make sure that my message is received," Zhézush continued, the intensity of her speech knocking him back in his chair like a palpable force. "And you must make sure that it is not distorted. There will be others who claim the things I have done for themselves, claim to be the chosen one, claim I was no more than a prophet. You must watch and guard against this. I will rise again, and all the world will know it. I will return again, to bring God's love. In the meantime, do not be deceived."

Mason cleared his throat. "What do you mean I am to play a great part? What am I supposed to do?"

"You will know the truth when you encounter it. When you do, open it to the world."

A knock came at the door, an impatient six raps, followed by another, then another. Zhézush held her finger to her lips. They sat, scarcely breathing, as the raps continued. Mason heard Elisabeth's voice outside, hard and angry, then eerie silence. He wondered if she might be still out there, waiting them out, and a haunting feeling of being pursued swept through him. Creeping to the door, he glanced out the peephole to a warped view of an empty hallway. Seconds later the phone rang. After six rings it quieted.

Zhézush stood to leave. "You will know what to do when the time comes," she whispered.

"When is . . . ?"

But she had already left the room.

The Reverend Arnold Lee Lovrun punched the pedal on the old Buick, down the two-lane blacktop through the brown expanse of the Everglades. He hated the Orange Bowl. The place was decrepit and located in one of the worst parts of Miami, with parking hawked by Hispanic-looking youngsters at ten dollars a spot. After witnessing a near–race riot on his previous visit, he had vowed never to return. God's will was strong to bring him back to such a place.

He had called the number he noticed in an advertisement for the service, explained he was in a bad way from arthritis as a result of a Vietnam War injury, said he was a believer and wanted to be healed. The efficient young voice on the other end had explained he would have to arrive at the stadium four hours early and go to a special gate for admission to the field. She could not promise him admission due to the huge demand, so the earlier he arrived the better.

He shook his head violently, catching a glimpse of himself in the rearview mirror. The idiots! The ignorant idiots! Didn't they know? Hadn't some preacher gotten it into their heads that this entire thing was a sure sign of the Devil? If people were this damn stupid, they deserved to be left behind on Judgment Day. He reclined in the driver's seat and envisioned a great ball of fire engulfing the stadium, roasting the occupants as they sat before their false idol. Better yet, the fireball whirled from the stadium and consumed the entire city of Miami, casting a great black pall upon the sky. He opened his eyes again, feeling better.

He turned the radio up loud and, when he was safely away from La Belle and the prying eyes of congregation members, stopped at a convenience store and bought a tall-boy for the ride. The cold beer filled his throat, warmness enveloped his head, and he rolled the window down to let more hot wind hit his face. He felt young again. Wasn't it amazing how God worked? Like that overnight letter from the Reverend Joe Farriday, then a phone call—an actual phone call!—from the great man himself. He had told Reverend Farriday of his plans and had received a blessing over the phone. Could there be more clear evidence of God's hand? He offered a prayer for guidance, then punched harder on the accelerator.

Perola awoke refreshed, her head clear for what seemed like the first time in days. She stretched, torn between the thought of her morning cup of coffee and the pleasure of remaining in bed. Coffee finally won out, and wrapping a robe around herself she shuffled into the kitchen, opened the curtains to let in bright sunlight. Henrique had made his usual five-hour visit during the night, plopping into bed for a few hours and arising to leave before she awakened. She considered calling him now that she was fully awake, then remembered he had asked her not to discuss the Zhézush matter on the telephone.

This was not the first time in their marriage he had made such a request. The government routinely monitored phone lines, particularly within the police department. Given the sensitive nature of his position, internal affairs types maintained a constant concern he would leak some vital information to his wife that would be reported in the press. Perola and Henrique had worked diligently during their four-year marriage to ensure confidential information was not compromised. As far as she could tell, their efforts had been successful, and Henrique had obtained a series of promotions and managed to avoid any controversy resulting from her stories. They had arranged a code for matters not to be discussed: if Henrique mentioned his mother, long since dead, she knew to drop the subject immediately. Any reference to Perola's father signaled crisis.

Fumbling in the cupboard for the coffee, she detected movement out of the corner of her eye. She turned to chastise her cat, Iguaçu, and instead confronted the pockmarked face of a thin, gray-haired woman. Screaming involuntarily, Perola clutched her robe about her and grabbed for the phone.

The woman spoke, and a flash of recognition hit. Perola replaced the phone in the cradle. Aide, the intense woman from the Zhézushians who had informed the others of Moraes' death, had begun chanting the Lord's Prayer. Perola stood silently, the hair on her arms on end, the feeling of being violated like a sour taste on her tongue. Aide seemed to look through her.

". . . and lead us not unto temptation, but deliver us from evil . . ."

Perola wanted to stifle her, to throw open a window, to run from the house, to do anything to escape those vacant eyes. Yet she stood rooted, paralyzed not by fear but by something else.

". . . for thine is the kingdom and the power and the glory . . ."

She found herself mouthing the words along with this weird woman, unable to break eye contact, the hand holding her robe dropping limply to her side. She could focus only on the gray eyes.

The recitation ended and they remained transfixed in each other's stare for an indeterminate period in which Perola felt she had somehow been lifted above her body, as if her soul had been separated from her flesh. She could see her robe, now fallen open to reveal her bare chest, see her unbrushed hair, the puffiness around her eyes. Aide seemed a skeleton, frail as a scepter, gray hair perched atop her skull like a cap.

"Come," said Aide, and Perola was once again inside her own body, her hand closing the robe about her. The vacant eyes still penetrated.

"What do you want from me?"

"We need your help."

"Why? How did you get in here?" She felt her blood pound again, and the eyes seemed less ominous. This was her home, her refuge.

"I walked in the front door. Now that Moraes is dead, the dissemination of our message is even more important. Tragic things await our city and our country. We must make sure the true message of our savior gets through. We must count on you for that."

"But how? What am I supposed to do, go underground or something? Shave my head so that no one will recognize me? I have a husband and responsibilities and commitments. As a journalist, I must be impartial. I cannot act as a messenger."

A long, thin arm unfurled from beneath Aide's wrap and a hand snaked out to grasp Perola's. The touch was as cold as a mountain stream. Aide's face broke into a smile, the cracked thin lips spread purple by the pressure. "We will not hurt you, I promise. Your integrity will not be compromised. We only want you to see what we see, day after day. How can you know Zhézush unless you have walked in her shoes? That is all that we ask." The cold hand disappeared. The vacant eyes bored in again.

"Okay," Perola heard herself say.

12

Jesus answered them, Many good works have I shewed you from my Father; for which of those works do ye stone me? The Jews answered him, saying, For a good work we stone thee not; but for blasphemy; andbe- cause that thou, being a man, makest thyself God.

John 10:32-33

Mason turned the Gideon Bible over in his hands. Zhézush had said he would know what to do when the time came. Like what? He felt unnerved, caught between waves of skepticism and blasts of anticipation. He picked up the phone and reached Rhodes in New York.

"What's happening down there? Christ, this is all over the networks." Rhodes was on a speaker phone with Michael Hammond, one of the national desk editors.

"Yeah, I know. It's like covering the White House. Although I did have a visit from Zhézush this morning."

"What? Alone?" Rhodes' tone moved up a notch.

"Yeah."

"What did she want?"

"She wanted to talk. She thinks she's going to die soon."

"Why?" asked Hammond.

"It's not atypical for messianic types. She hinted around at the same thing a couple of days ago. She said she wanted me to help get her message out, that I was to perform a big part in the upcoming drama."

"This babe's headed off her rocker." Rhodes again. "Does she say she's gonna rise from the dead?"

"She intimated that. Anyway, the next service is tonight, and this place is crawling with media. We're falling all over each other. I'm not sure how much more I can do."

"Are you kidding? You've got direct access," countered Hammond. "Who else has that?"

They agreed to talk again the following morning, and Mason hung up the phone. Was it fear that made him want to run, to distance himself from the whole thing? Fear of another disappointment? Desire to know welled within him like a sickness. He glanced at his watch, his head beginning to pound, his throat dry. Maybe it wasn't too early for a drink.

The Reverend Arnold Lee Lovrun crumpled the tall-boy can and tossed it in the back seat of the Buick. He had arrived at the Orange Bowl early enough to find a parking spot relatively near the stadium that he didn't have to shell out ten bucks to some kid for. He pulled over to a corner of the small parking lot next to an abandoned service station, the side of his car against the building. With an effort he heaved himself out of the car, lightheaded from the beer, and after a brief struggle unzipped his fly and relieved himself between the car and the building. A scrawny kid watched him from a building across the lot, but Reverend Lovrun paid no heed.

He rezipped his pants. Rain clouds were forming to the west of the stadium, and the sky was darkening. The Reverend Lovrun's spirits sank like an anchor. Rain could spell the cancellation of the service and defeat his purpose. "God damn you, Devil!" He raised his fist at the sky. "You will not defeat the forces of Christ, not if it takes a million years!"

As if in response, the wind shifted, the raindrops ceased, and the smile returned to Reverend Lovrun's face. With the turn of a key and the creak of old metal he wrenched the wheelchair out of the Buick's trunk. A search of the trunk yielded an ancient, rusty can of spray lubricant, and Reverend Lovrun proceeded to lubricate the wheelchair. The sky darkened as he worked. With a series of clicks the stadium lights crackled on, their beams extending as if from a big orange spaceship.

Reverend Lovrun pulled a worn, dingy blond wig from the car and adjusted it on his head, then placed a filthy baseball cap over it. Grabbing a blanket and an extra T-shirt from the back seat of the Buick, he dropped heavily into the wheelchair, positioning his Smith & Wesson underneath the blanket. The wheels moved surprisingly easily, considering the age of the thing, and with a swing of his arms he began to propel himself toward the stadium.

Wind whipped dust around him. The sky had blackened to the point that it seemed like the dead of night. For a moment the Reverend Arnold Lee Lovrun imagined he was the only person left on the planet, that everyone else had been sucked into a giant spaceship, leaving him behind to battle the forces of evil. He fingered the gun underneath the blanket, edged it down into his boot. Damn this weather. Maybe it would blow through by the time the service started.

He rolled himself through a growing crowd to the will-call gate, presenting his driver's license for identification to the squat girl in the black jacket seated behind the window. He had told the girl on the phone he suffered from degenerative arthritis, which rendered him unable to walk. Hell, the way he felt right now, it wasn't even a lie. Another of the black-jacketed women pinned a large card to his shirt, with the words "Lovrun" and "arthritis" in bold letters.

A host of the walkie-talkie women escorted a wheelchair brigade of seekers down several large ramps and onto the field. The chairs clanked together as they funneled into the gateways. The women didn't say much, and what they did say was mostly in a language Reverend Lovrun couldn't understand. Their black jackets against the orange girders of the stadium looked like Halloween. Witches, that's what they were, thought Reverend Lovrun, and he traced a cross with his fingers. Fear gripped him for the first time. What could be a surer sign of the Devil?

People with all different sorts of afflictions passed by, led by a woman with no teeth and one leg who pulled her wheelchair along at breakneck speed, the thrust of her arms outpacing a walkie-talkie woman running along behind. A child with a head swollen up like a balloon rolled by on one side; a gurney holding an emaciated man swung along on the other. Up ahead, an enormously fat woman had fallen off her chair, and four of the walkie-talkie women struggled to right her. Damn if it weren't like the freak show at the fair. The thought crossed his mind that all sorts of infectious and hideous diseases were probably carried by these vermin, and he pulled his arms in from the wheelchair to avoid any possible contact.

He screeched in protest as one of the walkie-talkie types grabbed the back of his wheelchair to propel him along. She pushed him toward yet another of these women—God, were there any men in this place?—who examined his card and positioned him along a row of other wheelchairs about thirty yards from the stage. A clearing of several feet separated his row from another row of wheelchairs immediately in front, and he could see gurneys lining several other rows closer to the stage. Although his watch showed only a little past three in the afternoon, the sky was the color of charred wood. The sweet smell of rain hung in the air. Off in the distance, the horizon glimmered with lightning, followed seconds later by a muted roll of thunder. Some of those around him donned ponchos or pulled out plastic sheets to put over their heads.

Reverend Lovrun glanced around him. He was getting a little hungry. The woman who had provided information to get onto the field sure hadn't told him to bring a sack lunch. The thought of a hot dog set his mouth watering. He could see a couple of the weird women passing out bread or something and little plastic things of water in the row in front of him. God, was he gonna have to eat from the hands of these heathens? Thankfully he had seen a few Christians—a few folks with some sense!—marching in a circle outside the stadium in protest of this blasphemy. He had hailed them as he wheeled by, but they had blankly stared at him and begged him not to go inside. At least some people in this city had not gone stark raving crazy.

He focused on the chair next to his. A pale, thin woman with sunken eyes smiled at him. Behind her stood a large man with a bristly mustache who eyed Reverend Lovrun and nodded his head in acknowledgment. On the other side rested twin strollers with Negro children of two or three years of age, their heads lolling about on rubbery necks. The strollers were manned by a slender girl of maybe seventeen and an older, hard-looking Negro woman who stared at him impassively.

The thin woman in the chair next to his started to speak, but Reverend Lovrun turned his head away. Reaching beneath the blanket in his chair, he retrieved a battered portable radio and earphones he had brought along to keep the Devil's voice from working any kind of hypnotism on him. He slapped them on his head and turned the knob to a country station, leaning his head back to look at the swirling indigo sky. He offered a quick prayer the batteries would hold out.

Mason glanced with concern at the dark sky as he exited the hotel parking lot, weaving his car through the police barricades and crowds of onlookers. He had neither poncho nor umbrella, and the idea of getting soaked held little appeal. Pushing the scan button on the radio, he searched for an announcement the service had been canceled but found nothing. Reluctantly, he pointed his car in the direction of the Orange Bowl.

A broad raindrop or two plopped against the car's windshield, but the deluge held off. As he entered the traffic stream near the stadium, enterprising youngsters descended with armloads of orange ponchos they hawked at inflated prices. He rolled down his window and bought one, a flimsy piece of plastic that looked like it would deconstruct completely in a good rain.

The bad weather did not appear to have deterred many. Several hours before the service's scheduled start, the parking situation was already chaotic. A large number of those who couldn't get tickets had shown up anyway in the hopes of seeing Zhézush. Sitting at a frustrating standstill, Mason glanced at his watch; at this rate, he might be better off to park and walk.

He fought his way to a parking space on a side street several blocks from the stadium. Huge black thunderclouds, barely discernible against the darkened sky, galloped west to east. He tried the poncho on for size, discovering to his chagrin it reached barely below his waist. Grumbling, he slipped into the crowd of humanity moving toward the service.

Near the stadium, the cause for some of the delay became more apparent. Corralled into a squared-off area adjacent to the stadium ringed by dozens of police officers, the ranks of the protesters had swollen to several hundred. Marching in an ill-defined circle, they held placards above the throng carrying familiar refrains: "There Is Only One True Christ!"; "Do

Not Be Fooled!"; and "Christians, Unite Against the Antichrist!" The protesters included a greater number of clerics than before, or at least a greater number clad in religious clothing; the habits of a small cadre of nuns flapped in the breeze. The police officers, arms linked, struggled to hold the surging crowds from one another. Chants and organized prayers from the protesters produced jeers and catcalls from the crowd. Incoming sirens added to the commotion, signaling an influx of police cars into the area. The newly arriving officers formed a vehicular barricade between the groups.

As he neared the gates, the Young Assistants' system seemed to work more smoothly. Despite impassioned pleading, those without tickets were channeled away via a human tunnel of police officers and Young Assistants. Ticketless himself, he gained entrance only by insisting Elisabeth and the Bishop demanded his presence, and even then a Young Assistant stood with him just inside the stadium gates until the Bishop could be found to verify his standing. Inside the stadium, police officers stopped every third or fourth person for pat-down searches and examinations of purses and other items carried through the gates. The stadium fencing, the harsh stadium lights, the wind and the early darkness gave the scene an eerie feeling. The Bishop's deep voice pulled Mason out of his thoughts. "Yes, he's okay," he intoned solemnly to the Young Assistant, who nodded graciously and melted back into the army at the gates.

"Thank you." Mason grinned weakly, his stomach sour and hot.

To his surprise, the Bishop's dour face broke into a smile. "It is no problem. Will you come with me? You may witness the service with us from behind the stage."

Mason jumped at this unexpected opportunity. Some of the stomachache melted away.

"The crowd is unbelievable," Mason said, struggling to keep up with the Bishop's long strides. "I'm worried someone might get trampled outside, between those without tickets and the protesters. It's a zoo out there."

The Bishop nodded gravely. "We too are concerned about that. If we had known it would be like this, we would probably not have proceeded with the service. On the other hand, with God's help and Zhézush's hand, everything will be okay." He led Mason rapidly around the end of the stadium, past another barricade of Young Assistants and into an area underneath one end zone's seating. They reached what looked to be a communications center of sorts, which Mason assumed had a direct link with the light and sound technicians in the press box area above the stadium.

"Are there any male *ajudantes*?" he asked the Bishop.

"No." The Bishop's face wrinkled again. "By their nature, they are women. There are men involved, of course, like myself, but the *ajudantes* are only women. Zhézush prefers it that way. She said to me once this is a counterbalance to the fact that all of Christ's disciples were men. I do not know if the *ajudantes* necessarily equate to the disciples—for one thing, there are so many of them—but this is what she said."

"Where do they come from?"

"Mostly the areas Zhézush, Elisabeth, all of us came from. Many were street children helped by Zhézush and her ministry."

They entered a door beneath the stadium and climbed some stairs to a small indoor reception area complete with bar and sandwiches. More Young Assistants bustled about, black jackets bobbing. Their mouths set in firm lines, they spoke in tight whispers and smiled infrequently.

Beyond a door, in a smaller room adjacent to the bar area, they found Zhézush and Elisabeth, the latter resplendent in a shiny silver dress, her hair pulled back from her head to highlight her prominent cheekbones. The usual dark tent-dress hung, sweat-stained, over Zhézush.

Elisabeth stood as they entered, surprised but not displeased to see him, Mason thought. She greeted him, kissing him lightly on both cheeks, the smell of her hair and perfume and the touch of her hand on his arm sending a pulse through his groin. The hint of disdain from earlier had dissipated as if it never existed, and he basked in a warm glow of reconciliation. Zhézush smiled absently in greeting before retreating into concentration, her eyes tightly closed, legs drawn up underneath her arms.

"You may sit with me, just off the stage," the Bishop said from across the room. "As you know, you probably do not want to be directly in front of the stage. People there are so excited. You will have an excellent view."

"Thank you," Mason responded, sinking back into the depths of the couch as Elisabeth's leg rubbed against his. He struggled to stay focused. "I hope we don't get wet. It's miserable-looking out there."

A shadow crossed Elisabeth's face. "So it is," she said solemnly, then brightened again. "But . . . how do you say it? The show must go on, right?" She laughed. "These people have come from very far and waited very long. They must not be disappointed."

A Young Assistant interrupted, asking politely in Portuguese to speak privately with Elisabeth. Elisabeth rose from the couch and listened intently. Mason stared at her backside, transfixed, his mouth as dry as parchment. God, she was unbelievable. Every time he saw her, she looked more fabulous. When he was around her he found it almost impossible to think of anything else.

Elisabeth gave what sounded like orders, then dismissed the girl and rejoined Mason on the couch.

"They are worried, because of the weather and because of the lines at the gates, that many attending the service will not be seated by the starting time." She looked inquiringly at the Bishop, then at Mason.

A bell sounded somewhere above the room, precipitating a renewed burst of activity. Zhézush rose from the couch, rubbing her eyes, and followed a Young Assistant down the steps toward the field. Elisabeth trailed regally behind them, flanked by more Young Assistants. The Bishop motioned to Mason, and they descended next into the glare of the stadium lights and the excitement of the crowd. The blackness of the sky had given way to a sort of gray twilight, and a brisk wind whipped through the stadium. Hundreds of gurneys and wheelchairs, metal frames sparkling in the light, stretched like a used car lot across the entire field in front of the stage. Mason took a seat along with the others to the right of the stage, out of sight of all but a sliver of the crowd, and waited for the service to begin.

The Reverend Arnold Lee Lovrun's bladder ached so badly that he seriously considered going in his jeans. His scalp itched under the wig, and continual scratching had caused the thing to sit up on his head like a hat. The weird woman with the big eyes to his left kept staring in his direction, which was beginning to annoy him. He glanced at his watch for probably the hundredth time in the last hour, shaking it again to make sure the thing still worked. Another half hour until the scheduled start of the service. Shit.

Gritting his teeth and squirming, he tried to make himself more comfortable. He was beginning to feel for the poor souls who had to sit in these contraptions day in and day out; the things sure weren't built for comfort. His earphones firmly on, he had ignored wave after wave of walkie-talkie women offering to wheel him to the bathroom or give him something to eat or drink. He didn't trust those bitches, their hair cut so short they looked like men. For all he knew, they'd take him underneath the stands and then demand money to take him back. Besides, he wasn't going to risk giving up this spot he had arrived so early to claim.

At least it hadn't rained, though black clouds still swirled and the smell of rain clogged the air. Every now and then rolls of thunder boomed far away. The crowd in the stands milled around, looking at one another, purchasing snacks and drinks from vendors working the aisles. Down on the field, however, everybody pretty much sat and waited. At one point during the wait, the crowd quieted, necks craning toward the southern stands underneath which Reverend Lovrun had entered the stadium. He released an earphone long enough to hear whisperings that Zhézush had revealed herself to the crowd under those stands. He let the earphone slap back against his skull, and sweet country music filled his head. His fingers sought the dial—maybe there was a gospel station within range.

He had at least made some good use of the time by carefully contemplating his escape route. He would move along the aisle of chairs to his right, then down the field away from the stage to the other end zone, away from the conflux of guards near the stage. He figured it would take fifteen, thirty seconds at most, with nothing to block his way but incapacitated people in wheelchairs and maybe a walkie-talkie bitch or two. He'd ditch the blond wig, switch into a different T-shirt, and blend into the crowd, another of the ignorant and disappointed heading home. The thought made his pulse quicken.

"Let's get this show on the road!" he yelled loudly. Those around him turned and stared.

13

And the sun was darkened, and the veil of the temple
was rent in the midst.

Luke 23:45

The wind gusts whipped Zhézush's robes against her body as she prepared to mount the stage. Mason sat above her on a platform, far to one edge of the podium, with little view of the audience due to a large audio speaker almost directly in front of him. A twin speaker was visible on the opposite side of the stage. He had never noticed the speakers in any previous service, and the thought struck him that perhaps the magical voice had benefitted from some mechanical help. The Bishop sat next to him in another metal folding chair, his back taut, his long, thin hands resting in his lap.

The speakers rumbled as Elisabeth delivered the service's opening. Below him, Zhézush waited at the foot of the stage steps, head bowed, arms wrapped in front of her as if holding her massive body together. As the stage darkened, the drumbeat began. The amplification from the speakers gave the sound a louder, harder edge, so dominating it seemed a giant heartbeat, rendering his own unnecessary. Flashlights blinked below the stage, and as the usual toneless wail ensued, Zhézush rose the steps to the platform. She reached the top step, slowed, and squinted in the half-light toward Mason and the Bishop.

"You will know the truth," she whispered fervently up at them. "You will know what to do when the time comes!"

The voice was overpowering, even at a whisper, and with a start Mason recognized the same words she had spoken to him earlier in the day. The Bishop stiffened beside him. Elisabeth passed by on her return from the podium, her eyes glistening in the darkness, her face quizzical, as if she had heard the voice but not understood. She locked gazes with the Bishop for a long second, then took a seat to Mason's left, with a better view of the audience. Several Young Assistants scurried in the blackness to remove the podium. Zhézush took the stage.

The spotlight shone, illuminating the squat figure to the euphoric crowd. Those able to stand rose to their feet, roaring with the noise of a thousand jet engines, the atmosphere immediately bordering on hysteria. Zhézush stood with head bowed, dark robes flapping around her, as the crowd's excitement flowed in waves: easing, then swelling again. At length she lifted her head, extending her arms to the sky.

"Master, Savior, LORD! Master, Savior, LORD! MASTER, SAVIOR, LORD!" Mason's scalp tingled from the sheer physical impact of it. What prompted this? This . . . this answer to desperation. It frightened him the way it had before, in São Paulo, and in the other instances of messianic mania he had witnessed in St. Louis, Jerusalem, Rome. For a moment he imagined himself on stage with the Fuerher, experiencing the same sense of mass mania, of being pulled along by the crowd. He shivered and rubbed his arms.

"My people!" The supernatural voice worked its magic again, quieting the screaming crowd to a whisper and then to the familiar ethereal stillness. Mason could hear the stadium creak in the wind. The speaker next to him did not rumble.

"I am yours!" The crowd roared in response, then just as quickly silenced itself. Again, the unworldly quiet, the creaking of the metal beams.

"I have been, I am, and I will always be." She sounded weary, yet the voice reverberated a thousand times around the stadium.

"I died on a cross." A tumultuous response of amens and hallelujahs, giving way to silence. "Yet," a long pause, "I stand before you today.

"Let us think about life and love. Why are you and I here today? Why is there life? Why is there Christianity and Islam and Judaism and

Buddhism? Why are there countries and races and languages and peoples? Why is there hatred and war? Why is there not love?"

A car horn blared somewhere far in the distance, filling the silent spaces between her words.

"I have said before I am here as a conciliator," she continued, "to present a modern message for a modern world. Just as my appearance two thousand years ago brought forth a new covenant from God, so my appearance today renews that promise. Not all things may be understood, as not all is familiar. That is why I return to earth in a human form. Such fits within understanding." She spread her hands before her.

"We are all given choices in life. We may think that all is happenstance—the beauty of a face or the strength of a mind—but in reality how we live our lives shows the path we have chosen. God permits us to choose a life of goodness and selflessness or to go another way." She paused again, as thunder rumbled in the distance.

"We believe in grace, that Christ died for man's sins on the cross, that he who believes in Christ is automatically forgiven and assured everlasting life. God's concept is broad and inclusive. The key to the everlasting is love, love for oneself, love for one another, love for God. If our time on this earth is not engaged in love, what worth can be ascribed to it? The importance in believing in me is to believe in my message. Remember this above all else." A dark sleeve mopped sweat from her forehead.

"Some will say I am what the Bible predicts—a false prophet—one of the many who will claim to be Christ returned, even producing so-called miracles to support that claim."

The crowd erupted in protest, and Zhézush paused again. "Yes, according to some, I am but one of many pretenders, a sure sign the end times are upon us." Surging in response, the crowd growled before calming. "It is said the Bible specifies believers will be raptured up to meet Christ in the clouds before the second coming. Truly, then, I could not be who I claim to be.

"Listen to me, people." The voice took on a deeper tone, grasping the stadium in a great fist. "I am here because God sent me. I will leave this earth soon. I will return again, maybe several times, and you will not know the hour or the day. Remember the parable of the fig tree? The fig tree blooms not once but every season. Look for me again, maybe once, maybe several times. For I love you, and God loves you." She spread her arms wide, crucifixion-like again, as if trying to hold the entire stadium up in them.

She repeated the entire message in Spanish, to the delight of a large portion of the crowd. The Bishop rose to his feet and, leaving Mason and Elisabeth in the little alcove to the side of the stage, directed several Young Assistants waiting at the bottom of the platform in preparation for the mass. The Lord's Prayer echoed throughout the stadium, mixing English, Spanish, and Portuguese in a howling, drumbeat-assisted cadence. Young Assistants emerged like ants from underneath the stage. The drumbeat pressed on, so ubiquitous now it seemed to emanate from different parts of the stadium, as if the stadium itself pulsed with life. There was something primal about it, something as basic and fundamental as the deathly silence that followed its cessation at the blessing of the sacraments.

The crowd picked up in song again as the bread and wine passed from row to row, a wordless tune that rose and fell as if at the direction of a master conductor. Completing their mission, the Young Assistants began to make their way back to the stage platform, worker ants returning to the queen. Zhézush remained on stage, head bowed, palms outward. Only as the music swelled to a new crescendo did she seem to return to life, raising her head slowly and turning to give Elisabeth a nod. Several Young Assistants sprang to their feet behind the stage, then followed Zhézush as she slowly descended the steps on the stage's opposite side, down onto the field.

The Reverend Arnold Lee Lovrun's pulse quickened at the sight of the dark figure descending the stage steps. A bolt of electricity seemed to hit the field, arms raised skyward from the confines of gurneys and wheelchairs in anticipation. The thin woman to his side practically glowed with excitement, her pale face lit now by a flush of hope. Even the bristly-mustached man behind her seemed animated, pushing the hair out of his eyes repeatedly as his mouth moved in song. The Negro women on Reverend Lovrun's other side also remained transfixed, their faces contorted, the hand claps of the older one puncturing the protection of his headphones. The two young children in strollers nodded their heads.

The dark heathen stood perhaps five rows and twenty-five yards in front of him, moving slowly from one group to another, pausing to bow her large head toward someone in a wheelchair or to reach down to arms grasping from a gurney. Several of the women in the black jackets surrounded her, and Reverend Lovrun's face tightened in concern as he contemplated the difficulty in getting off a clear shot. He would definitely have to wait until she was almost on top of him, then scoot out in the confusion. He noticed with satisfaction that the security guards stayed close to the stage, leaving the big one unprotected on the field. Thinking she might have a bulletproof vest on underneath all those robes, he debated going for a head shot, then decided against it; she would be too close by the time he got his chance. He would have to fell her like a big grizzly, with a shot to the gut. He leaned forward and eased the pistol out of his boot, taking care that it remain covered under the blanket.

". . . from victory unto victory, his armies he will lead, 'till every foe is vanquished and Christ is Lord indeed. . . ." The music sounded in his ears.

His heart pounded loudly, so loudly it drowned out the gospel twang and eclipsed the crowd cheering those rising from wheelchairs and gurneys in front of him. Slowly, over and over, he repeated the Lord's Prayer, stopping at each iteration to ask assistance in ridding the world of this evil. Closing his eyes tightly, he held his face in his hands, the world pounding in one big drumbeat of heart, crowd, handclap, drumbeat. Boom, boom, boom, boom.

With an effort he opened his eyes and looked around. The blasphemy and her entourage had reached his row, only a few people to his left. Carefully, he positioned the pistol in his lap under the blanket, one hand gripping the side of the chair, the other the gun. Trying not to move his head, he examined the escape route to his right, noting with relief that the aisle seemed clear, aware that every other eye remained focused on the dark form approaching him.

He shifted his eyes back left to watch as the group approached the thin woman adjacent to him. The big black face was bathed in sweat, a dark line of scars on her forehead shining through the sheen of perspiration. Reverend Lovrun stared at the scars, shuddering involuntarily, and for a moment he considered he might be wrong, that perhaps this woman really did have some connection with the Almighty. With a violent shake he disabused himself of the notion. This was another of the Devil's tricks, designed to fool even the most devout. Still, he could not tear his eyes from those scars, seemingly seared into the flesh. As she reached to lift the thin woman to her feet, glowing wounds shone in each mammoth wrist.

He watched closely, scarcely breathing as she hugged the woman to her sweaty face, black-clad women bouncing on either side of her like beach balls. The bristly-mustached man behind the girl's wheelchair gazed upward with rapture, tears running down his face into the thatch of mustache. Ever so slowly, the dark figure lowered the young woman to the ground, big arms cradling frail legs. The girl stood unsteadily. She turned around to face the man behind the chair and took a few tentative steps, holding on to the dark robes for support. The figure whispered something to her, the broad lips parting in a smile, and the young woman's motions grew more rapid until she covered the remaining space to the man.

"Daddy!" she squealed, the sound cutting through the earphones' protection. The bristly-mustached man and his daughter were sobbing together now, the girl turning in her father's arms to thank the smiling figure in front of them, who was now turned to face the Reverend Arnold Lee Lovrun.

His pulse jumped at the sight of the large shape looming over him. He found he could not look the figure in the face, instead focused on the giant hands and the wounds in the great wrists. Gently, the hands removed the headphones. The noise of the chanting, singing crowd rushed around him. The hands were soft and warm and comforting, and he wanted to hold them and look at them and rub his fingers across the wounds. Instead, the hands took his face in them and held it tight, turning his head so he had no choice but to look into the black being's eyes.

Reverend Lovrun felt paralyzed and faint. His eyes focused on the big brown pupils in front of him. He was falling, out of control, unable to stop himself. The hands on either side of his head were his mother's, warm and loving, healing. The gun lay forgotten in his lap, and as she placed her face near his, the whole of his being one with hers, he could not imagine wanting anything other than to look into those great brown eyes.

She removed a hand and whispered something in his ear, in a language he did not recognize but somehow understood. She seemed to seek out all of his longings, all of his hurt, from the time he was a small boy through the remainder of his life. He felt himself open to her, wordlessly, drawn by an irresistible force. Then a voice from behind the figure broke the spell.

The figure disengaged in surprise, turning to reveal behind her the most beautiful woman Reverend Lovrun had ever seen. She wore a shimmering gown of silver, her large, full breasts silhouetted underneath, her hair and face perfect in every way. She spoke to the black one in a language he did not understand, then to Reverend Lovrun, her gaze puncturing him as though her eyes were daggers. With a flash he remembered the headphones, the hypnotism, the gun, the blasphemy; he remembered it all. The big black mass turned before him again. He had to get the gun up before those eyes . . .

The Smith & Wesson spat fire at the dark figure, piercing the clamor of the crowd. The girl to his left screamed, and for a split second silence enveloped the stadium. The force of the blast pushed the figure full upright, so much so he feared it might fall on top of him, but instead it tottered for a few seconds until the massive knees buckled and it sank to the earth. Blood spouted from the creature's forehead, opening an additional cavity between the great brown eyes. He got the head after all. He never had been much of a shot. The three eyes remained locked on his, the magnet so strong that as the beast fell to the ground the eyes pulled him out of the wheelchair and toward the fallen figure.

The beautiful woman crouched over the dark robes as the great brown eyes turned to her, the wound from the gun blast large and ugly on the broad forehead. Reverend Lovrun, out of the chair now, froze as he watched the two women look at one another and the big voice struggle to speak. Then, with a thunderclap, the crowd erupted in a spasm of pain and anguish.

The noise pulled the Reverend Arnold Lee Lovrun out of his stupor, and he ran, too late, down the row of wheelchairs and gurneys along his escape route. He had almost reached the edge of the field when a wheelchair rolled into his path, blocking his escape, his cowboy boots giving little traction to maneuver. He knocked over the chair, landing on top of its occupant as the sound of pandemonium swelled in his ears. Struggling to his feet, he received a glancing blow from a large black woman who appeared out of nowhere.

Then they were upon him, yanking out chunks of his hair, gouging at his eyes. With a sickening crack someone wrenched one shoulder from its socket, then the other, his screams lost in the deafening roar. He was dimly aware of his neck breaking, a snap that momentarily stopped the pain. He gasped for air, a last few choking gasps, then lost consciousness. His last memory before death was aural, the buzzing sound of the angry crowd, like bees from a disturbed hive.

Blood pounded in Mason's ears. Sweat poured from his forehead. His mind seemed to work in a different dimension, analyzing, questioning, struggling to comprehend. He had previously seen two purported messiahs die, one by his own hand, one by an apparent heart attack. Still, the shock lingered. He forced himself to take a deep breath. He sensed the crowd's agony, felt his own adrenaline. He stood.

The Bishop, his face pinched and grim, rose to his feet and shuffled past Mason toward the back of the stage. Out on the field, a large group huddled around the prostate figure lying in the grass. Young Assistants pulled hoods over their heads in a single motion. Someone commandeered a gurney, and with considerable effort the group hoisted Zhézush onto its narrow frame as a group of paramedics arrived from the other side of the field. A group of Young Assistants, alienlike in their hoods, helped clear a path toward the stage, wheeling and escorting the recently healed out of the way. Elisabeth clung to one side of the gurney, her formerly shimmering dress now blood-soaked and in tatters, the lovely face tear-stained and drawn.

Mason joined the Bishop at the bottom of the stage steps as the entourage passed. The wound was briefly visible: a black hole the size of a silver dollar in the middle of Zhézush's wide forehead. Dark blood saturated the white pillow under her head. Two paramedics worked swiftly and efficiently at resuscitation, one counting loudly and pumping furiously on her chest while the other gave mouth-to-mouth assistance, pausing every few seconds to turn his head to breathe.

Falling into line behind the gurney, Mason and the Bishop became a part of the exiting group as a brigade of hooded Young Assistants sealed off their flank against the surging, screaming crowd. Another black battalion plowed a course through the masses bunched underneath the stadium. A misting rain descended, cutting visibility. Wild and confused, the crowd made for the exits.

Outside the stadium, the rotating lights of an ambulance snaked through the milky precipitation. Young Assistants and police officers beat back the crowd, frantically attempting to clear a path. Thousands of frenzied hands reached to touch the fallen messiah, necessitating use of the officers' billy clubs to keep the body on the gurney.

With a final push the entourage reached the ambulance. Struggling paramedics loaded the stretcher. Police cut off others attempting to climb aboard. Trapped in the pack following the gurney, Mason caught a brief glimpse of a dripping, glimmering dress before the ambulance door slammed shut. Then the vehicle moved slowly away, its siren barely audible above the noise of the crowd spilling out of the stadium.

"Let's get out of here!" Mason yelled in the Bishop's ear, surprised to find him still at his side. Nodding, the Bishop jerked his head away from the stadium. Together, they plowed through the strengthening rain.

The force of the rain increased to needlelike intensity. Bursts of wind drove the moisture horizontal, flinging the stinging missiles into Mason's eyes and face. He stopped to wait for the Bishop, who trudged along behind, wet hair plastered to his forehead. With a final burst of energy they reached Mason's car, only to wait agonizing additional seconds as he fumbled to unlock the doors. They plunged in, exhausted, their wet smells filling the car. The rain pounded a drumbeat on the car's roof, but compared to outside it was as quiet as a tomb.

"She is dead."

Even in the darkness and wetness, Mason thought he could detect tears in the Bishop's eyes. "But how do you know? They may have been able to resuscitate her."

"I know." Long hands covered the dark face again.

"What should we do? We don't even know where they took her." Mason glanced at his watch. 12:45 A.M.

The Bishop did not speak for a few moments. "We must find Elisabeth," he said softly, his face still covered.

Mason sank back into his seat and wiped moisture from his face with the back of a hand. But where? He had no idea where the ambulance was headed. There were probably twenty or thirty hospitals in the Miami area. He could call the police department, but he was almost certain that would not produce useful information, at least initially.

Lightning flashed, followed by an immediate volley of thunder. The rain and darkness rendered the world outside opaque. They probably weren't going anywhere soon, given the weather and the chaos of the dispersing crowd. Mason grabbed the mobile phone, to touch base with New York, but found it dead, the batteries evidently left too long uncharged.

"Shit!" He gripped the wheel in frustration. He felt paralyzed, as if he'd witnessed a car crash but couldn't leave his own auto to help. He inched the vehicle forward, glancing at the Bishop's uncovered face.

"We should go to the hospital where the healings took place." The Bishop spoke tonelessly, almost without moving his lips. Mason nodded in the darkness; Dade Memorial wasn't far from the stadium, and maybe they could at least get someone to call other area hospitals for them. The thought occurred to him that Zhézush's body might by now be lying in a county morgue somewhere. He decided not to burden the Bishop with that consideration.

"Don't you think she might still be alive?" Mason asked as they sat at a standstill. Soaked humanity streamed by on both sides of the car, and thunder crackled in the distance. "I mean, with all of her healing powers, wouldn't everyone be better off if she simply healed herself and continued her mission?"

The Bishop gave an almost imperceptible shake of his head. "It was planned this way," he said sadly, lapsing again into silence.

"Planned by whom? God?"

The Bishop turned and looked at him directly for a long time without saying anything, as if Mason had uttered something disturbing or profound.

"Yes, I think so," he said finally, then turned his attention back to the window, and the rain and people beyond.

The traffic and weather turned the two-mile trip to the hospital into an hour-long ordeal. The Bishop remained completely uncommunicative, his chin cradled in a palm. By the time they finally reached Dade Memorial the rain had eased, though wind-whipped flags flying near the hospital entrance crackled and slapped loud enough to be heard inside the car. A phalanx of police cars and media vans jammed the hospital parking lot, validating the Bishop's intuition: the body had been brought here. Disembarking underneath a patient unloading overhang, the Bishop hurried into the building while Mason parked the car.

To Mason's surprise he found the lobby empty when he entered minutes later, save for a couple of police officers leaning against an information desk. "Was Zhézush brought here from the Orange Bowl?" he asked, acutely aware of how ridiculous the question must seem. "You know, the woman who's been on TV."

A beefy, red-haired sergeant eyed Mason impassively. "I'm sorry, sir, I'm not allowed to give out any information about that."

"What do you mean you're not allowed to give out any information?"

"Exactly what I said—"

The doors to the hospital entrance burst open and a group of soaked women rushed in, speaking rapidly in Spanish. A tall woman separated herself from the others and rushed forward to confront the police officers.

"Where is Zhézush?" she asked in breathless, accented English. "I know she was brought here!"

The policeman repeated his statement, advising the group someone from administration would arrive shortly to give an official statement. In the meantime, no one was permitted farther into the hospital.

Mason fished out his press card and handed it to the other officer. "I'm press," he said impatiently. "Where are all the other media?" He gestured toward the emergency room entrance.

"Sorry," the officer replied, firmly blocking the hallway. A squadron of security officers and policemen appeared behind him in the hallway and pushed past him, depositing several young men carrying television cameras and equipment into the lobby area. Mason counted four different affiliations. The entrance doors flapped open again to admit other wet bodies, including a few drenched Young Assistants. There was no sign of the Bishop or Elisabeth.

"Is she alive?" asked the tall Spanish-speaking woman in a squeaky voice.

"No," replied a tall man with a bushy beard holding one of the television cameras. "She was dead on arrival."

Silence blanketed the room, punctuated only by the movement of the electric doors as they admitted sodden followers into the room. Then the wailing began, a howling of primal pain wrapping snakelike around the lobby. The doors whooshed open again and again.

Cries of "Hallelujah!" and "Praise the Lord!" mixed with the anguish, signaling the arrival of protesters from the stadium. The wails metamorphosed into cries of anger, quickly escalating into a scuffle in front of the interior hallway entrance. Forced to move to maintain order, the police cleared the lobby in a rush of pushing, shouts, and whistles, forcing the growing multitude outside into renewed rain. As Mason was being ushered out the electric doors, he caught sight of the short hospital administrator from the previous day. With a shout and a wave, he managed to draw the man's attention.

"He can stay!" the administrator ordered. A plastic name badge identified him as John O'Rourke. The electric doors closed with a clap, and one of the officers pressed a switch on the door's side, sealing them momentarily from the throng outside.

O'Rourke's sweaty red face resembled an overripe tomato. "This is just unbelievable, isn't it? Just unbelievable." He produced a handkerchief and mopped his head.

"Where are Elisabeth and the Bishop?" Mason asked pointedly.

"Who?"

"The people who were with Zhézush when we were here before."

"Oh, yes. There is a room off the emergency room, a chapel of sorts reserved for grieving families. I will show you."

Mason followed O'Rourke back down the hospital's empty main corridor. "What is being done with the body?"

"I understand they want to send it back to Brazil, without a service or anything." He mopped his face again.

They stopped before a closed door marked "Chapel." Inside, Elisabeth and the Bishop sat in stuffed chairs to either side of a hooded Young Assistant, an especially stout and fierce-looking young woman whose eyes, squat nose, and puffed lips protruded from under the hood. The Bishop introduced her as Erlete, and she nodded almost imperceptibly in recognition. The hood unnerved him—it made the young woman look even more like a troll or alien. Her eyes stared at him, as if reading his thoughts.

Elisabeth rose to embrace him, her arms tight around his shoulders. Her face was moist on his neck, and he reveled in the closeness to her. Pulling away, she held him by the arms, her once-shimmering dress tattered and caked with dried blood. Tears flowed from the emerald eyes. "I have lost all that means anything," she said quietly. A new stream of tears made their way down the high cheekbones. She looked vulnerable, exposed, and beautiful.

"What happened? One minute you were there on the platform next to us, and the next thing I know, you were down on the field and Zhézush was dying."

Elisabeth pulled back, brushing tears from her face. "I had a sense something was about to happen," she said in the same quiet voice. "The Bishop says he was overcome by the same feeling. I tried to get there in time to do something, but I was too late." She paused, apparently on the verge of sobbing. "She and I . . . have been together for so long."

"Was Zhézush alive after the shooting? Did she say anything?"

Elisabeth shook her head. "I heard nothing, but there was much noise. It was chaos. We were lucky to get her out of there as quickly as we did."

Mason nodded. His reporter's instincts surged, in conflict with feelings of empathy. "The hospital administrator tells me there will not be a memorial service in the United States, that the body will be flown to Brazil."

The Bishop nodded slowly. "Yes, we feel that is best. It is what she would have wanted."

"Do you expect her to rise from the dead?" Mason cleared his throat and glanced at the Young Assistant, but the hood shielded her face from view.

The others looked at him in bewilderment. "Of course," said Elisabeth, recovering her composure. "That is why we want to have the body removed immediately to Brazil. We feel it is more appropriate she rise there. There is some concern about the logistics, however. If she is to arise on the third day, we must not have bureaucratic delays in the body leaving the U.S."

Mason walked over and switched on a TV in the corner of the room. A reporter's image filled the screen, apparently live from outside the hospital, breathlessly transmitting the confirmation of Zhézush's death. The picture flashed back to an anchor, then to footage from the service. Silently, the scene replayed itself, like a nightmare revisited: Zhézush among the wheelchairs, the man with the blonde wig, the gunshot.

The Bishop exhaled loudly as the news anchor reappeared on the screen, announcing that the unknown assailant had also been killed. The remainder of the room remained silent. Mason snapped off the set at the sign of the station's regular programming.

"Does anyone know who this guy was?" Mason needed to get on the phone to New York.

"I have not heard anything," Elisabeth said softly. "Probably someone associated with the religious fundamentalists against Zhézush." She turned and looked at Mason and the Bishop, starlike tears still staining her cheeks. "It really does not matter that much now, does it?"

The live transmission of Zhézush's Miami service had spawned a participatory chanting, swaying, and crying in the tiny church deep in the São Paulo *favela*, a wondrous noise that reverberated off the building's leaky roof and gave life to the remote ceremony. The sound of the gunshot, like the crack of a whip, dissipated the clamor into a deathly silence. Aide was the first to rise to her feet, unfurling her long, thin arms with an anguished, retching wail. With sickening realization, the others joined in.

Perola had told herself it was just a trick, a ploy to boost TV ratings, a pseudo-attack; the sight of the assailant's blood as the enraged crowd tore him limb from limb convinced her otherwise. The wails in the old church climbed an octave. It seemed hours to Perola before the bedlam eased to a murmur.

A bearded man burst into the small sanctuary, followed by two other men. "Have you heard? Did you see what happened? Is she really dead?"

Someone turned up the TV volume so that distorted sound blared over everything, returning the room to chaos. Remembering the phone in her purse, Perola stepped quietly outside and punched in Mason's mobile number but received no answer. An ominous rumbling could be heard across the *favela*, something she could not identify, too close to be an airplane, too constant for thunder. She stood for some time, trying to pinpoint it. A woman's sob broke above it, and suddenly she knew.

The noise was the hum of people, thousands upon thousands of people, talking, muttering, sobbing, shouting, reacting. The collective despair of a slum, a city, a nation. Without knowing why, Perola began to cry, the tears warm against her face. She stumbled back into the church.

Inside, the TV still blared, but the din around it had eased, the group now huddled around the screen. Pushing her way to the front, Perola saw the picture flash to a scene in front of what looked like a hospital. Aide and Vicente succeeded in further quieting the others so that the announcer's voice could be understood. The image of a woman reporter gave way to one of a nervous little man standing in front of a group of people. It appeared to be raining, and Perola recognized several Young Assistants in the crowd, their hoods pulled above their heads.

Her blood went cold. She barely heard the man announce in English that the woman named Zhézush da Bahia had been pronounced dead on arrival at the hospital.

14

And Pilate marvelled if he were already dead: and calling
unto him the centurion, he asked him whether he
had been any while dead. And when he knew *it* of
the centurion, he gave the body to Joseph.

Mark 15:44-45

He dreamed the dream again, for the first time in days. Things were different. This time he attempted to speak to one of the nurses, the ones who usually ignored him as he passed. He saw the nurse's beautiful face as never before, the round brown eyes, her dark skin in contrast with the white uniform. Grabbing her arm as she passed, he stopped her abruptly. Ever so slowly, her mouth formed a silent, questioning oval he associated with aliens on old science fiction shows, the ones who communicated with weird music without actually speaking. She led him by the arm to the building, stepping in front to open the green door. This time, he moved with trepidation into the cool, dark interior. The nurse released his arm and moved away, her white form disappearing into the blackness. He tried to follow but couldn't, afraid of falling in the shadows, of dropping through the building's floor. Paralyzed, he stood in the darkness. Gloom closed in around him, squeezing his pumping heart. He felt fear, fear of the unknown, fear of darkness, fear so great he wanted to wake, never to return to this building.

In the black distance a white shape appeared. His heart leapt; the nurse must be returning. She could lead him out of this place. The figure moved closer, hovering just out of reach. There was something familiar about its movement; he knew this figure. It was not the nurse. A beam of warmth radiated toward him. He wanted to run to it, to free his immobilized legs and throw himself into its wonderful familiarity, to stay in its grasp forever. Yet something kept him away, an external force that would not let him move. He felt pressure in the lower part of his body, pressure that would not go away, pressure so strong he could never reach the white figure, pressure that bared his weakness. Then he was awake, the pain in his abdomen the mundane urgency of a full bladder.

He stared at the blank ceiling. What was happening to him? He offered a silent prayer, a brief pleading for understanding. He remembered his earliest prayers, adolescent efforts offering good behavior in return for instant gratification. Had things really changed since then? It was all still egocentric, all *his* needs.

Wearily, he pulled himself to a sitting position. He flexed his triceps as he sat on the edge of the bed. Zhézush was dead. What did it mean? Other "messiahs" had died—this was what perpetuated the myth. A few "sightings" gave birth to another cult.

Still, he had seen the miracles himself: the little girl's legs straightened, the kids healed in the hospital, the magical voice that needed no amplification. Fakery? Perola's hesitation rang back to him from the first service in São Paulo when he had asked whether she believed Zhézush to be who she claimed to be. The healings were offered up as what—proof of God's power, or Zhézush's legitimacy? If Zhézush truly only wanted her message heard, why did she claim to be Christ returned? Wasn't there still some tiny element of faith involved?

He closed his eyes again, opening them behind the lids to a kaleidoscope of dots. He couldn't let himself believe that she was the *one*. What symbol would follow this death that could match the cross? Would schoolchildren be selling icons a hundred years hence of a fat lady with a bullet hole in her head? This death was plain, ordinary, and brutal, that befitting a child of the streets and pretender to the throne. No one would drink and eat in remembrance of this.

What if, instead of just a fraud, she was in fact the Evil One? Was he destined to find proof only of darkness? His stomach knotted in remembrance of the purple skin and bleeding wrists. It would be so easy to turn the world on its side, to bind the Church up in it. That was why Rome had recruited him, of all people, with all of his flaws. That was what they were really concerned about—a true Christ would eventually reveal himself and the world would be fine, so their thinking went, but the Evil One would be the destroyer. Particularly if he arrived in the guise of the returned messiah.

With a gasp he blew air pressure against his ears, trying to focus his mind. He needed to do his job, to verify details of the death with the police department, to track down information on the assailant, to find out what the Young Assistants and the rest of the entourage planned to do, to follow the movement of the body. He was concerned that he hadn't heard from Perola, despite leaving several messages. They needed the Brazilian reaction for the story.

He surveyed himself in the mirror, his thoughts on Elisabeth. Even in the pain and turmoil of the shooting's aftermath she had glowed with beauty. He had seen the looks the cops had given her as they swept by in the hospital hallway outside the little chapel, the glances even the nurses gave her. The thought of another liaison with her made his mouth go dry. Yet, his infatuation with her had dulled. Thoughts of her no longer clouded his every waking thought as they had several days ago. Security and serenity seemed more attractive now than exotica and passion.

The phone rang loudly, inducing a momentary panic. What was he afraid of? "Hello?"

It was Jay Summit, a young reporter from the national desk who had arrived in Miami the previous day and helped Mason craft a serviceable story on the assassination.

"I'm headed down to the police station to see what they've got this morning," Summit announced. "There's a press conference of sorts scheduled at ten. You wanna go?"

"Yeah. First I'll try and find Elisabeth and the Bishop. I'd also like to go see the body."

"So would I."

"Actually, I was hoping I might get you to track down what you can about the guy who shot her."

"You got it. The TV news is reporting he was a preacher from some little town near here. I'll see what I can find and give you a call on your mobile later."

"Anything else on the news this morning? I'm just rolling out of bed."

"Not really. The coroner's office said she died almost instantly. Apparently they've only got bits and pieces left of the guy who did it."

"I'll call Rhodes and the others. Give me a call." Mason hung up and dialed Rhodes, explaining their strategy.

"Keep a close eye on that fucking body," Rhodes instructed in a voice so loud Mason had to hold the phone away from his ear. "Of course, you're right. Somebody's gonna claim she rose from the dead, and we oughta be on top of it the whole goddamn time. Sleep by the fucker if you have to."

Dade Memorial's morgue provided an oasis of cold in a stifling basement where fluorescent fixtures provided the only light. Elisabeth had agreed, after a brief press conference held by the police department on the investigation into Zhézush's death, to request the police to allow Mason to view the body. Now, security guards flanked either side of metal double doors under an ordinary-looking sign proclaiming the room's function beyond. Another guard accompanied Mason, Elisabeth, the Bishop, and their police escort into the chilly interior.

Even the cold did not completely mask a formaldehyde smell. Two large feet protruded from beneath a blanket on a gurney in the center of the room, the dull puncture-wound scars on each providing immediate identification. The feet were enormous, bigger than he remembered, with great misshapen toes that seemed as big as the fingers on a baseball glove. He looked crossways at the others, each staring at the great feet as if examining one of the world's great wonders.

He shivered in the cold. The security guard strode to the front of the stretcher and pulled back the sheet, exposing Zhézush's large head. The eyes stared vacantly upward; a third opening in the middle of the forehead gave the eerie impression of an additional eye. The row of scars across the forehead was faint, yet visible. The group moved closer to the body, and Mason touched the rigid face. It was cold, colder than the room, so cold he feared his finger might stick to the clammy skin. The unfocused three-eyed stare held him in its grip, seeming to beckon him to do something, to warm the cold flesh with his own, to breathe life into the still body.

His breath came in short gasps. The messiah? The one? He wanted to believe it. He could feel his head dipping toward the corpse when another, warmer hand gripped his. Elisabeth whispered softly in his ear. "Let us leave this place." Her tone was firm and her voice steady. "There is nothing you or I or anyone else can do."

Mason grimaced. She was right; he pulled away from the gurney. He had intended to check the corpse's pulse, just to make sure, but the temperature of the body told him everything he needed to know. Nothing alive could be that cold. His head swam in the silence, in the certainty she was dead. The group stood silently for some time, long enough for Mason's feet to grow uncomfortably numb from the room's temperature. At last the Bishop bowed slightly to the attendant, who pulled the sheet up as the party made for the door.

The warmth of the hospital basement embraced them as they exited the morgue. "When does the body leave?" Mason asked.

Elisabeth and the Bishop exchanged glances. "We have arranged for a special Brazilian military plane to transport the body," Elisabeth replied. "This is extremely confidential. The Brazilian government is very concerned with how the body is handled."

Mason rested his hands on his knees. "No autopsy, I presume?"

The others nodded. "The authorities have been very helpful," Elisabeth said quietly. Unspoken was the question of any possible resurrection.

"Any chance of my catching a ride back on the plane? I assume that's where you will be."

"No. I am sorry," Elisabeth responded. "By request of the government, only Joaquim and I will accompany the body."

"Are you sure that's what you want to do? Every media outlet on the globe is going to want to know exactly what happens to that body and how it is handled. Wouldn't it make more sense to have an independent observer along, to attest to the fact nothing unusual has happened? Any claimed resurrection becomes that much more credible."

Elisabeth smiled. "An independent observer such as yourself?" She looked at the Bishop, who gave a slight shrug of his shoulders. "Your idea has merit," she said slowly, "but I do not think you qualify as independent. Many people are beginning to think you are one of us. Perhaps you are. We need someone truly independent. Perhaps that man from the *Global Press*—what is his name?" She looked to the Bishop again.

"Reynolds is his name," Mason muttered. He hoped she was only teasing him. Lose this inside track to Reynolds? Nausea crept through his abdomen.

"Yes, Reynolds. A pleasant man." She started down the hall, glancing over her shoulder at the Bishop as he began to follow. "Ask him to join us, will you?"

The Bishop looked at Mason almost apologetically. "Perhaps Mr. Mason has an associate who could also accompany us," he suggested to Elisabeth's back.

"Yes, I do. He would be most happy to participate." Mason hurried to catch up.

Elisabeth paused briefly at the top of a flight of stairs. "Fine," she said disinterestedly. "Tell him to be at the front door of the hotel at four o'clock."

They left through a side hospital entrance, activating another media swarm as if by electronic switch. As Mason hesitated, Elisabeth and the Bishop scampered into the police car that had brought them to the hospital. With a slamming of doors and a screech of tires the car pulled off, the Bishop's long face visible against the glass in the front passenger seat. Mason was left standing in the midst of the groaning, cursing reporters, some of whom briskly packed and piled into cars to give chase. Others stayed behind to question him.

"Hey, Mike, what gives?"

"You still on the story, or should we be covering you now?"

"Did you see the body?"

Ignoring them, Mason moved to reenter the hospital. The barbs became more pointed:

"Yeah, those guys with the *Herald* don't think they have to talk to us mere mortals."

"Hope you don't ever need a job, buddy!"

He passed a bank of pay phones in the hospital lobby, wishing for an old-fashioned phone booth with a door he could pull behind him and shut out the world. He succeeded in calling a cab, then punched in Summit's mobile number. Luckily, Summit had his passport with him and could get back from La Belle in time for the flight. The young reporter claimed to have unearthed some interesting information but would need more time for additional work. The connection was intermittent, and they agreed to try and connect again on Summit's ride back to Miami.

Several reporters lingered within eavesdropping distance of the pay phones. The jerks. They really were like vultures. Fortunately, there was no sign of Reynolds; with any luck the Bishop would be unable to locate him. Mason considered attempting to reach Perola or Rhodes, but decided to wait. With a sigh he pushed past the reporters and went in search of the taxi, renewed abuse echoing in his ears.

15

Command therefore that the sepulchre be made secure until the third day, lest his disciples come by night, and steal him away, and say unto the people, He is risen from the dead: so the last error shall be worse than the first.

Matthew 27:64

Perola met him in the swirling madness of the São Paulo airport. She seemed thinner, and tired. She hugged him tightly as they embraced.

"I am glad to see you, Michael. It is very troubling here."

"So I see." He was glad to see her, more glad than he wanted to admit. She seemed solid, grounded in reality. Dependable.

In contrast to his last visit to the airport, uniformed soldiers equipped with automatic weapons seemed everywhere, intermingling with the ubiquitous crowds. A huge, menacing throng waited behind the security checkpoint area, and Mason and Perola halted in front of it, unsure of what to do. Mason had given Summit Perola's mobile number, but she had heard nothing from him.

"Demonstrations and confrontations with government troops have increased," she said. "Although condemned by the government, an unofficial national holiday and day of mourning have been declared by Zhézush's supporters, drawing widespread support in São Paulo. Most stores have closed. Government offices have eked by on small staffs as employees called in sick. The streets have been full of people protesting the government's policies. Rumors have swept the city that Zhézush was assassinated by a Brazilian hitman sent by the government."

"Are you okay?"

"Yes, I am all right. It's just that . . . I do not know . . . something strange has happened to me. Several days ago I met this group of followers of Zhézush—I told you about that. A day or so later one of them appeared in my house, uninvited, and convinced me to stay with the group for a while. I was with them when Zhézush's death was broadcast. Over and over, the scene played on the television. The heartache and the anguish of the group were so real. I myself have felt so sad and distraught I have found it difficult to do my job. I feel perhaps I have been brainwashed or something." Her voice fell to a whisper. "Maybe it is a cult." She sounded scared.

Mason knew what she meant; he felt much the same way. Under ordinary circumstances, her death would have startled him, perhaps saddened him a little. Instead, he felt a profound sense of loss.

Miraculously, Summit materialized out of the crowd and made his way through the security checkpoint. After introductions to Perola, the three adjourned to a hard plastic table and chairs at a nearby fast food kiosk.

"Pretty uneventful trip," Summit stated wryly, rubbing the stubble on his jaw. He was young, younger than Mason had originally thought, maybe twenty-seven or twenty-eight. "You saw us board the plane and the casket get loaded in. Reynolds, bless his heart, insisted on checking the body before it was loaded, which pissed everybody off. You saw that, right? They had to get some special person to unseal the thing. Anyway, Elisabeth and the Bishop pretty much kept to themselves on the way down, talking Portuguese and stuff. Reynolds and I just kind of shot the breeze and read most of the way."

"Did the military people have much to say, or talk with Elisabeth and the Bishop much?" Mason asked.

"Nah. I'm not sure they spoke English. They didn't say anything to me. They certainly looked at Elisabeth and that tight dress a lot, but I didn't notice much conversation. We landed at a military base about an hour ago, and Reynolds and I watched as the body was unloaded. Reynolds asked that they open the casket again, just to make sure, but they refused. He got really agitated at that point, and they brought a car around for us.

I thought maybe we were gonna follow them to wherever they were going, but instead the guy zooms off and brings us back here. I thought Reynolds was gonna have a stroke, he was so pissed. Anyway, here I am, and my flight back leaves in twenty minutes."

"So you don't really know what happened to the body?"

"Nope."

"Were there other journalists at the base?" asked Perola. "That must have been the air force base just north of the city."

"Not that I saw."

"What happened to Reynolds?"

"He grabbed a cab as soon as we got here and went back into the city. Where, I don't know. Listen, I probably need to move down to the gate if I'm gonna catch this. I'll call tomorrow afternoon."

They bid Summit farewell, and Perola punched up Henrique's number on the mobile phone. "I will find her," she said, half to herself, then unleashed a torrent of mostly incomprehensible Portuguese. Apparently, Henrique did not know the body's location. Slipping the phone back into her handbag, Perola looked up at Mason, the circles under her eyes more pronounced than he remembered.

"He will call me back. I can also probably find out through the Zhézushians. Let me try something else." She retrieved the phone and punched in more digits, waited several seconds, then snapped the mechanism shut again.

The phone emitted a shrill beep as she returned it to the handbag. Mason recognized Henrique's voice as it filtered through the earpiece. Perola listened intently, a smile forming on her lips. *"Bem, bem. Obrigado."* She snapped the phone shut and stood.

"They have her at an office near the *Penitenciária*, the prison in north São Paulo. Henrique says there is a very strict armed guard. He doubts they will let journalists anywhere near it. We shall see, okay?"

They climbed into Perola's Fiat and began the trip into the city, the night breeze pleasantly cool after Miami's heat.

"So," she began conversationally, "is it true what has happened? Was she who she claimed to be?" She turned to face him in the darkness.

He fumbled for a response. "I don't know. I saw some things I have never seen before, things only something supernatural can explain, even taking into account extraordinary occurrences. You have seen her. You know. She had some . . . some power, like at the stadium, where she held the crowd in the palm of her hand."

"I do not know what to think anymore, Michael." She sounded tired and worried. "My country is on the verge of constitutional crisis, people are in the streets, and this woman seems to be a catalyst, you know? I too have seen her, seen the evidence of her powers. It is like I told you before; if she is not the Christ, she is remarkable in her own right. But you have seen much more than I. You have spoken to her, spent time with her. Would you have given all to follow her?"

He paused, taken aback by the question. "I don't know. I don't think so. She seemed remarkable, all right, but . . ."

They drove in silence for a time. A sense of déjà vu washed over Mason, a sensation of making his first trip into the city, that he had dreamed everything else, that Zhézush had never existed except in a tabloid's pages. He glanced at Perola, catching sight of a gold cross just visible in the opening of her shirt. He found himself thinking more about the cross, less about her chest. The warmth and motion of the car lulled him toward sleep.

He was dreaming, dreaming *the* dream again, and he knew he was dreaming, and he wanted to yell to Perola to break the dream, but he couldn't. The images flew by at an accelerated pace, the white-clad nurse strolling rapidly in front of him, the door to the green building yielding easily to his push. He rushed headlong into the darkness of the building, looking for the light he had seen before. Instead, the car's rapid deceleration and a man's voice awakened him.

They were at a military checkpoint of sorts. A uniformed man with several days' growth of dark beard leaned into the car, examined Mason carefully, and motioned to Perola to proceed. Mason wiped spittle off his face, and ran his hand through hair wet with sweat. He was shaking.

Perola laughed softly. "You must have been dreaming, Michael. Your hands and feet were moving and you were snoring at the same time."

Mason grinned weakly. "Yeah." He ran his hands through his hair again and rubbed his face vigorously. "I keep having this same dream, over and over. Anyway, what was all that about?"

"There are more military checks, given the city's state of unrest. They are looking for weapons and for those known to be subversive to the government. So far, at least, I do not fit into the latter category." She shifted gears and the old Fiat groaned. "I too am having strange dreams. What is it you dream of?"

"It's really not that much of a dream. The place is so real, so familiar, but I don't think I've actually ever been there. Nothing really happens. I just open this door. Sometimes there's a figure of light that beckons me." He tried to hide the tremble in his voice.

"Dreams are important. They tell us of the things that inhabit the corners of the mind."

Sweat poured from his forehead. "Listen, I want to tell you something." He had to tell someone. His voice sounded strange and garbled.

"Okay."

"I am . . . I was . . . a priest." He choked out the words. "It's not that I am not also a legitimate journalist—I am—but I have been similarly engaged by the Vatican to investigate these phenomena."

"Wow. You were a priest? You left the Church?"

"I determined early on I was not cut out for the priesthood. The vows, the celibacy." He winced at the word. Even after all these years.

"I resigned my position, became a journalist. Sort of by coincidence, I fell into investigating religious phenomena. The hierarchy at the *Herald* agreed never to mention my background. Neither I nor they wanted my objectivity questioned.

"I was approached several years later by a Church official I had once been very close to. He had read some of my articles and asked if I would be willing to work more closely with the Church to provide them hard information on the various subjects I encountered. I agreed. It tied in with what I was doing anyway, and I guess I had a reservoir of guilt from my resignation. So, for the past five years, in addition to the newspaper reports I have written, I have filed separate reports with Rome. I have been told only three people in the Vatican know of this arrangement: my contact, the Pope, and one other official. As you may know, the Church has a very arduous, methodical process when investigating so-called miracles. It generally takes years. I guess I provide a quicker take on the situation, so they can act swiftly if the need arises."

"And why would they need to act swiftly?"

"Well, things can move rather rapidly with these self-proclaimed messiahs. The Church is particularly interested in situations where clergy, particularly high-ranking clergy, leave the Church. Maybe that's one reason why they have me doing this—I don't know. In this case, they really seem as interested in the Bishop as in Zhézush. There is some evidence . . . God, I shouldn't tell you this . . . some evidence that there is an organized group of 'fallen' clergy, if you will."

A siren's wail broke out somewhere in the distance, then ceased just as suddenly. "I know this sounds crazy. You asked me once if I have seen glimpses of evil—I believe I have. One of my stories was about a French monastery where all sorts of weird things were happening—deaths in the surrounding area, weird sounds, bizarre meteorological phenomena. When I entered the place with another journalist, it was the creepiest thing I'd ever seen in my life. The place was empty, not a soul to be found anywhere, except one monk who had apparently gouged out his eyes with his own hands. All of the Bibles, and there were many, as you can imagine, were splattered with blood. There was a drawing on one wall of a multiheaded beast I can't erase from my memory. I informed Rome immediately, and within a fortnight the place burned to the ground. I'm not positive they were responsible, but . . ."

"Did you tell this to the Bishop?"

"No. Only you and I and the three people at the Vatican are aware of this."

"How do you communicate with these people, your contacts in Rome?"

"Various ways. You would think diplomatic pouch or something, but actually mostly by e-mail. I e-mailed an analysis of this situation the same night I filed the story." To the appropriately named Monsignor Deceptor.

"And does the *Herald* have any idea about this?"

Mason shook his head. "I am still a legitimate journalist. That job comes first. Nothing with the Church impacts on my objectivity as a reporter."

"And why do you do this? I guess I've asked you that before. Is it for the glory of God?"

Mason's stomach churned. "I wish it were that simple," he said softly. "I need confirmation: the one glimpse that will be the true explanation. The face of God, so to speak. I . . . I have to find it. I know I should see it in everything around me—a baby's laugh, a lover's smile, a flower in bloom. For some reason, that's not enough. Even what looks to be evidence of evil spurs me on. Maybe it's my own salvation, maybe it's penance. I have to know."

"Has it occurred to you that you may never find what you seek?"

"Yes. Or that I might find what I don't want to admit."

A news announcer's voice pierced the radio's low chatter. Perola turned up the volume. Something about a disturbance downtown, followed by a discussion of the arrival of Zhézush's body.

"What was that?" he asked when it was over.

Perola sighed. "There was another series of protests against the government today. They have been going on almost every day for weeks now, since before Zhézush left for the United States. It makes me angry, in a way. If this government is overthrown, people will say, 'Oh, it is just South America. The backwards continent. Only to be expected.' " She shook her head forcefully, swinging her long hair. "They also said Zhézush's body has been returned to Brazil but is being held by the government at an undisclosed location, pending burial. The service is to be open to the public."

"So, let's see, it's after midnight now, right? Zhézush was killed the day before yesterday, which makes this the third day. So if there's going to be a resurrection on the third day, it would have to be today, which is what, Sunday? That seems to fit nicely. I'm not sure when the burial is scheduled, but it sounds like she may not be buried before she's supposed to rise."

"Hmm. True." Perola pulled into a brick-lined plaza outside the *Penitenciária.* Guards sprang to attention, marionette-like, at yet another checkpoint. Perola rolled down her window.

"We are journalists." She flashed an identification card. "We have come to see the body."

The guard responded in a blur of Portuguese. Evidently, he was refusing to allow them entrance or to confirm the body's location.

Perola turned to Mason in exasperation. "I am not sure what to do from here."

"Ask them if either Elisabeth or the Bishop is inside."

Another flash of Portuguese. The man hesitated, then announced that he had no knowledge of such.

Mason and Perola looked at one another. In halting Portuguese, Mason asked to leave a message for Elisabeth or the Bishop. Without waiting for a reply, he hurriedly scribbled something on a torn notepad sheet and handed it to the guard, who looked it over dubiously before thrusting it down a trouser pocket. Perola reversed the car and parked on the street nearby, within sight of the checkpoint. They could see the guard talking with another man, who disappeared with what looked to be the note in hand.

"This is probably a long shot, but we'll see," Mason said in a low voice. "From the way he acted, it certainly looks as if at least Elisabeth and the Bishop are here. In the meantime, I wonder if you should try to contact the Zhézushians again. Wouldn't it be natural for them to be clamoring to view the body, or for Elisabeth to be in contact with them?"

"I would think so." Perola pulled out the phone again and punched in some numbers. Connecting this time, she engaged in a lengthy conversation. The guard shuffled out, peered at them, went back to his post. Mason's mind roamed in a fog of fatigue, replaying the dream again. He did not attempt to follow Perola's half of the telephone conversation.

She snapped the phone shut after several minutes. "The Zhézushians do not completely trust me," she said slowly. "Some of the leadership think I am bent on betrayal, given my occupation and my husband's position. There was a battle on this conversation between Aide, the woman who appeared in my house, and Vicente, whom I take to be the leader of the São Paulo Zhézushians, on whether I can be trusted with information. They are also concerned about speaking over the phone, particularly over mobile phones, which can be monitored by the government.

"In any case, Aide convinced Vicente to tell me what they know, which is not much more than we do. They do not know for sure the body is being held here, although they think it likely. Vicente said they have a number of people stationed near here. My guess is somewhere over there." She pointed to a dark area across the street from the guard post, where shapes moved in the shadows.

"Vicente says the authorities have been very close-mouthed about the location of the body for fear people will converge in great numbers and things will get out of control. After a rumor earlier this evening that the body was in the main square, more than fifty thousand people descended on the square. Vicente says no one has spoken to Elisabeth or the Bishop since the death. This is of some concern. They believe Elisabeth and the Bishop may have been taken prisoner. Vicente and Elisabeth had an understanding before she left for the United States about a procedure for establishing contact if an emergency arose."

Mason nodded, staring at the gold cross visible again in the opening of her shirt.

"Aide says she is of mixed emotions right now," Perola continued. "On the one hand, she is devastated about Zhézush. She had anticipated the death, but surely not in a way such as this. On the other hand, she is ecstatic about the response it has produced from people who want to join their cause. She was surprised I was able to get through on the telephone because the lines are always busy. As soon as the burial time and location are announced, they will organize a massive turnout for the event. Vicente estimates over two million people will attend and much of the rest of the country will watch on television."

"When do all the Young Assistants and everyone else arrive? I didn't see them on my flight."

Perola shrugged. "I do not know. I am not sure how they got to the U.S. in the first place. You told me there were hundreds, no?"

A uniformed soldier approached and leaned in Perola's window, cutting short Mason's response. "I have a message from your friends," he said softly in Portuguese, holding the white sheet of paper. "They will see you now. Pull your auto into the circle and park, then come with me."

They followed his instructions and exited the car into the cool night breeze. Bright fluorescent spotlight beams illuminated the circular drive. Mason glanced at his watch: two-thirty. A guard led them through huge metal gates connecting razor wire–topped walls, past armed soldiers who yielded at their escort's signal. With a monstrous clang the big gates shut behind them. Mason mentally kicked himself as he realized neither he nor Perola had left word with anyone of their intended destination.

They passed through yet another metal gate and more barbed wire, into a recreation area with basketball hoops, an oval track, and soccer field. Brilliant light bathed the area in a strange glow, and the smell of some flower Mason couldn't place permeated the air. More soldiers sprang to attention, flinging open doors to a building at one side of the recreation area.

They entered an empty corridor, their footsteps echoing loudly on brightly polished floors. The guard quickened his pace, forcing them to struggle to keep up. After turning several corners, they stopped before a door bearing the nameplate of General Raul Camargo. Their escort motioned for them to enter.

A tall, strikingly handsome man with a slight, dark mustache stood to greet them. Rows of medals and ribbons adorned his crisp khaki-colored uniform. He had the whitest, most perfect teeth Mason had ever seen, though they seemed too large for his mouth, as if transplanted from another, larger man. Mason found himself staring at them, inadvertently ignoring the outstretched hand.

"Welcome to Brazil," he said to Mason in perfect English. He kissed Perola's hand, and she murmured something softly in Portuguese in return.

They stepped farther into the room. Elisabeth sat regally in an armchair to one side of a polished mahogany desk, turning and smiling briefly at Mason, glancing with interest at Perola. The man Mason assumed was General Camargo motioned for them to be seated in chairs on the opposite side of the room. Three young officers leaned against a desk near the cavernous room's door. The Bishop was nowhere to be seen.

"I am Raul Camargo," the man said brightly to Mason, as if introducing himself at a job interview. He looked roughly forty, a few strands of gray hair visible at his temples, his movements those of an athletic man. He appeared as fresh as if he had just awakened, the crease in his pants perfect, his shirt and hair seamless and impeccable. Mason rubbed his eyes, feeling the effects of a long flight and little sleep. His head felt heavy on his shoulders. He squinted in the bright light.

"And I believe I know this young lady." General Camargo gestured to Perola with another wide smile. "Her husband and I used to be racquet-ball partners, although we haven't played in quite some time. He used to beat me more than I liked." He laughed, a throaty, masculine laugh that dissolved into another tooth-filled smile.

"Ms. Obrando has told me quite a bit about you, Mr. Mason, and I had heard of you before, even so. We probably would have become acquainted, but this acceleration of that meeting is welcome." Mason glanced at Elisabeth, surprised to hear her last name. Almost everyone referred to her only as Elisabeth.

"We were just discussing the plans for the memorial service and burial," General Camargo continued, seating himself again. "As you can imagine, given the effect this woman has on our citizenry, we must take precautions. We are concerned that once the location of the body is announced, hundreds of thousands of people will descend on that place. Thus, we are not divulging the present location of the body to anyone, including you. Our present plans call for the funeral mass to be held tomorrow afternoon in the *Estadio do Pacaembu.* Although this is earlier than the customary date, we believe that the circumstances justify it. To delay could bring additional problems. We will not have the ordinary funeral cortege. The situation is simply too unpredictable. As for the body, I think Ms. Obrando agrees with me that burial is not a viable option." He threw up his hands in resignation. "We feel there would be attempts to liberate the body from the grave, or constant demands to exhume it to confirm its existence. Cremation makes much more sense." He smiled again, as if prepared to serve as undertaker himself.

Mason glanced at Elisabeth, who stared without blinking at General Camargo. "Do you think that's what she intended?" he asked awkwardly.

"Yes," Elisabeth replied without looking at him. "She and I discussed it. Her return will be nonetheless triumphant from ashes and dust as it would be from a decomposing body. Brazil's place in the sunshine awaits. In the meantime, her citizens deserve order and protection from anarchy. I believe the General's steps are prudent."

Mason frowned, his head pounding from lack of sleep. "Where is the

Bishop?"

She turned and looked at him coldly. "He was not feeling well."

"General Camargo," Perola interrupted.

"Please, call me Raul," he responded in Portuguese. Another flash of teeth.

"Raul, when will the arrangements be final for the funeral? How will people be notified?"

"We are moving in that direction. We hesitate to spread the word until things are absolutely final. In that light, I ask that you not publish or otherwise notify anyone of this until we have made our decision. I am sure you understand."

"When will the cremation occur?"

"We were just discussing those details when you walked in. We do not want this to be a situation like the cortege of the Ayatollah, where the crowd pulled his body from the casket. We are considering having the cremation occur before the ceremony. That way, if zealots do overrun the proceedings, which we do not expect, the only result will be the scattering of the ashes at the stadium rather than somewhere else."

"Where would the ashes be scattered otherwise?" Perola asked.

Elisabeth spoke up. "It was Zhézush's wish that her ashes be disseminated in the ocean."

Mason cleared his throat. "Will it be possible for us to witness the cremation? It would certainly help in terms of anyone later claiming the wrong body was cremated."

General Camargo looked to Elisabeth, then glanced at the other officers across the room. "Let me think about that. Ordinarily, no. But these are not ordinary times, eh?"

He stood, indicating that the meeting was over. "Oh, and I must ask that you remain in our complex until the final decisions are made. It will be only an hour or two. I cannot take a chance on this information being leaked."

Light glinted again off the brilliant teeth. Mason's head swam.

"You will be very comfortable, I assure you," General Camargo continued, bowing magnanimously. "Thank you for your cooperation."

16

And it was Mary Magdalene, and Joanna, and Mary *the mother* of James, and other *women that were* with them, which told these things unto the apostles. And their words seemed to them as idle tales, and they believed them not.

Luke 24:10-11

The government car shimmied to a halt before a nondescript building on a downtown São Paulo side street. Mason climbed out of one door as Perola exited another. In front of them, General Camargo and Elisabeth disembarked from a similar car to the springing salute of hefty uniformed men. Grimfaced soldiers ushered them into the building's cramped lobby, overflowing with perhaps a dozen other people, where the air hung warm and pungent. Old, dirty carpet and peeling paint on the lobby's walls indicated the facility did not often host dignitaries. An odor with a burnt tinge, similar to the smell of a wood sander, permeated the area.

Mason looked around the small lobby, trying to match those present with the list Perola had relayed to him. Archbishop deLonious was readily apparent, his cape visible even in the dim light. General Camargo and a squat uniformed officer sporting a large bristly mustache stood off to one side. Elisabeth stood in front of the group, talking to a thin, gray-haired woman.

"That is Aide, of the Zhézushians," Perola whispered, following Mason's line of sight.

Mason nodded as he scanned the rest of the group. The short, balding man directly in front of him must be Guilherme Oliveira, the mayor of

São Paulo, and the distinguished-looking man in the dark business suit next to him would be Stefan Miklos, president of one of Brazil's largest banks. A large, round man with a giant ill-fitting toupee paced nervously back and forth in the back of the room, beads of sweat visible below the lines of his hairpiece.

"That's Manuel Texeira," whispered Perola, "the leader of the opposition party."

Texeira snorted loudly, wiped the back of his hand across his nose and gave a curt greeting to Mayor Oliveira. Perola identified the remainder of those present, including an extremely tall woman who towered over everyone, as members of the Brazilian media. "You notice there are no TV cameras, although several of these people are television people," she whispered again. "Apparently, General Camargo forbade broadcasting this."

"What do you know about Camargo?"

"He and Henrique are acquaintances from long ago. His star has risen rapidly in the Brazilian military, to the point he is now the commanding officer of the Brazilian army. This is unusual for someone his age. He is a bachelor, somewhat of a celebrity, often seen in the society pages with beautiful women. Recently, he played a small part on a Brazilian soap opera show that practically everyone in the country watches. He is—how do you say it?—media-genic. Why he is in charge of this particular situation, I do not know."

"How did Aide get invited?" Mason asked, watching the thin figure bend in animation as she spoke with Elisabeth.

"I do not know for sure. My guess is Elisabeth must have wanted her to be here and Camargo went along with it."

"Gentlemen and ladies." Camargo stood in front of the assembled group, teeth flashing. "You have been asked here today to witness and verify the cremation of a woman named Zhézush da Bahia." He signaled to an aide standing on the side of the room, who pushed open double doors behind Camargo to reveal a wooden casket on a wheeled cart. With effort, the aide and another man who appeared from behind the doors pushed the cart into the center of the room. With a theatrical flourish, Camargo pulled open the top of the coffin and invited the startled onlookers to peer inside.

Shuffling forward, the group peered timidly over the casket's edge. Zhézush's great body lay stuffed into the narrow box. Her shoulders were hunched to fit within the casket's frame as if wedged into a too-tight suit. Her arms lay propped across her midsection. She was dressed not in her ordinary dark robes but in a white cotton smock of sorts, the sleeves of which extended to her elbows, the bottom of which obscured her feet. Her hands were turned palms-down, the dull scars of the stigmata visible on her wrists. The great brown eyes lay hidden under dark lids, the third dark eye opened directly to the brain.

Several turned away in revulsion, but Mason lingered over the coffin. He had the overwhelming urge to reach down and touch the body, to turn over one of the great hands and rub the scars on the wrists, to feel the wound in the forehead, to verify again the coldness of the skin. He reached into the coffin almost subconsciously, only to be caught short by General Camargo's sharp rebuke. He pulled his hand back without touching anything.

The General introduced the small, balding man in the white lab coat who had helped push the cart into the room. "This is Marcos Villadares. He is in charge of the crematorium. He will explain the process."

Villadares launched into a high-pitched, lengthy discourse on how the body would be placed into a gas-fired furnace where the temperature would reach over 100 degrees Celsius. After only seconds in such heat, the body would be reduced to ashes. After allowing time for the furnace to cool, the ashes would be retrieved.

"There is only room for two or three people to observe the placement of the body in the furnace," General Camargo interjected. "I would suggest myself and two others. How about you, Mr. Mason, and the archbishop?"

At Camargo's direction, Mason and Archbishop deLonious followed Villadares through the double doors down a wide, poorly lit hallway, the coffin-laden cart rumbling behind them. The burnt smell intensified until they reached an opening at the end of the hallway housing what looked like four giant washing machines.

With a sickening screech, Villadares pulled open a door and rolled out a metal slab. Several grunting aides hoisted the coffin onto the slab's edge, and as one released a latch at the foot of the coffin, the others lifted Zhézush's head in an attempt to slide the body onto the slab. The wedged-in body didn't budge, forcing Villadares to reach into the coffin and pull on the large feet. For a second the body and coffin hung precariously over the slab and the four men struggling around it, then the body came free, almost knocking the slight Villadares over as the aides pulled the casket away from it. Dropping the casket, the aides reacted in time to grab the body as it began to topple off one side of the slab.

At General Camargo's request, the archbishop mumbled a prayer and made the sign of the cross over the body. Mason's eyes remained transfixed on the broad face turned toward him, eyes now half-opened, the grotesque orifice created by the bullet partially closed as the head rested on its side. At a signal from Villadares, the aides pushed the metal slab into the oven and slammed the door behind it, turning a metal lock.

Villadares moved to a set of controls on the side of the doors and turned a few knobs. Seconds later, firing gas jets whooshed as the incinerator rumbled to life. Mason stared at the door. The room warmed perceptibly, quickly becoming stifling. Mason wiped his brow with a shirtsleeve.

Villadares stepped forward again, his face alive with excitement and importance. "That is it," he exclaimed in his high-pitched voice. "It will take approximately twenty minutes for the ashes to cool. We may return to the other room now."

"I would prefer to stay and see the ashes," said Mason.

General Camargo had started to leave, but stopped. He turned and looked at Villadares, then shrugged his shoulders.

"What is to be done with them?" Mason asked.

"They will be safeguarded until their disposal in accordance with her wishes," Camargo responded. "A presentation will be made at the funeral service this afternoon."

Mason squeezed lemon into the tall glass, careful not to spray the white tablecloth or his luncheon host. An invitation to lunch with Gilbert Monterio Alves, the *Miami Tribune*'s longtime Brazilian bureau chief, had awaited him the night before when he returned to his hotel room. Even though Mason was beyond busy, plotting coverage of potential resurrection sites, putting a story together, and attempting to interview Zhézushians, he had decided to accept. Rhodes had been bugging him to meet with the local papers.

Monterio was a small, round man with a bald head, goatee, and an engaging laugh. He had seen the stories in the *Herald*, he told Mason, and understood Mason would continue his stay in Brazil for some period of time. They talked amiably of newspapers and foreign correspondents. Monterio had been around a long time and knew some of the *Herald* brass in New York. Although a native Brazilian, he had served in the U.S. for a number of years, including a stint as his paper's New York correspondent.

"I find the relations between races in your country fascinating," Mason said between bites of crêpe. "For instance, there don't appear to be any blacks in this restaurant."

Monterio looked around. "Certainly not by design or law," he replied. "Sometimes these things happen, not on the level of the United States. Do you find it odd that Zhézush is black?"

"Maybe not odd, but significant."

"I think so too." Monterio clasped his hands in front of him. "As you know, Mr. Mason, the story of Zhézush has, for better or worse, focused the attention of the world on our country. I and many other Brazilians are concerned our government currently balances on a narrow precipice. The *povão,* the masses, if you will, are agitated. The slightest provocation could send us over the edge, breaking the back of our constitution and sending us back into the military rule we fought for years to overcome. This in and of itself should be an international crisis, with the attention of the world riveted on the possible failure of one of the world's largest democracies; for some reason it is not. The rest of the world tends to ignore South America, Mr. Mason—perhaps at its peril. The situation with Zhézush could provide the spark that leads to conflagration."

He chewed lustily on a large dinner roll, then continued. "I think it was fortunate her death occurred in the U.S. If it had happened here, there would have been implication, warranted or not, of governmental complicity. I believe chaos would have descended. As it is, the government has handled things fairly adroitly. I was somewhat surprised they went ahead with the cremation before the funeral service, although in retrospect it was probably a sound decision. I was surprised the crowds contained themselves at the service."

"So was I. It was serene and sad, and crowded. And relatively uneventful. Were you there?"

"No," laughed Monterio. "I value my safety. I saw all I needed to on television. Of course, the paper had a number of reporters present." He shifted forward in his chair. "Tell me, Mr. Mason. What do you think will happen? You have followed this closely, perhaps more closely than any other journalist. You have experience with other such situations. You may have known her better than anyone in Brazil. Was she who she claimed to be?"

Mason coughed. "Will I be quoted on this?"

"Most assuredly not."

Mason weighed his response carefully. He did not know this man, this competitor, did not know the customs in the country. Whatever he said could come back to bite him. "I don't know, Mr. Monterio," he said truthfully. "I saw some things I have rarely encountered, even things that I have never seen before in my life. Maybe I was fooled. I will say there was something special about Zhézush. Whether she was Christ returned, daughter of God, from another world, I don't know."

"Do you expect her to rise from the grave?" Monterio's eyes narrowed.

"I expect something. As you indicated, I have experience in such matters. Whether there will be anything that can be verified is another question."

"How long will you be staying in São Paulo, Mr. Mason?"

"I'm not sure, probably a couple of more days."

"Would you care to join my wife and me this evening for the football match? We have an extra ticket, and it should be an excellent game."

Mason paused. Rhodes' growling visage passed through his mind. "I'd love to. Of course, if something happens, I might have to decline at the last minute."

Monterio smiled, light shimmering off his bald head. "I understand."

The message light blinked methodically, like a warning. Mason picked up the hotel room phone and dialed the operator, who linked him to a voice message. Jay Summit's voice filled his ear.

"Just wanted to report in after the service in La Belle. As you might expect, there were more media present than mourners. Mrs. Lovrun was again inaccessible. The police report was nothing of significance; the murder weapon was an old Smith & Wesson forty-five registered to the good reverend. One interesting thing—I was combing through the trash and found an overnight delivery box, evidently received several days prior to the murder. I wouldn't expect this guy to have received a lot of overnight deliveries. Anyway, there was no sender listed on the outside of the package, but underneath this box in the trash was an envelope with the address of the National Conference of Christians . . ."

Summit's message was cut off, and Mason pressed the necessary buttons to bring up the following message. Summit's voice returned. "Anyway, what I was saying, there's this envelope from the National Conference of Christians. I trust you're familiar with them—a big fundamentalist group, maybe the largest in the U.S., powerful politically. Inside the envelope is what looks to be a handwritten message from the Reverend Joe Farriday, the president of the NCC, to this Arnold Lee Lovrun. The envelope got wet and a lot of the writing is smeared, but the gist of the message seems to be an oblique directive for Lovrun to take action to stop the blasphemy of Zhézush. I'm gonna have the letter analyzed to try to reconstruct the smeared parts. If that's what it says, it's pretty wild stuff. Call me when you can. You've got my mobile number."

The hotel room's air conditioner slipped to a deeper gear as Mason replaced the receiver, and he shuddered in the sudden coolness. A directive that Zhézush be wiped out? His mind played through the possibilities—it would certainly be one helluva story. How did it affect the truth? He started to dial Summit, then decided to wait. He wanted to talk to Rhodes and the others about this development. They needed to get a quote from this Reverend Farriday.

Mason settled into his seat in what turned out to be the magazine *O Mundo Esportivo*'s box at Morumbi Stadium, the same arena where he had first witnessed Zhézush's service a little over a week before. The setting sun left the sky a peculiar golden color, radiating off the faces of the crowd opposite him even as the stadium lights beamed down on the field. A few pockets of empty seats glimmered like a receding hairline in the stadium's corners, growing smaller as the crowd continued to stream into the stadium. A slight, cool breeze slowly replaced the warmth of the day, rendering the temperature close to perfection.

He was seated next to Monterio's attractive young wife, Maria, and the crossing and uncrossing of her long brown legs competed with the sporting event for his attention. At least fifteen years younger than Monterio, she had a pug nose and impish smile and spoke fluent English with little trace of an accent. She carried on a lengthy conversation throughout the game with anyone who would participate, to the annoyance of several around her more intent on following the action on the field.

He had agreed with Perola to bring his portable phone to the stadium so he would be reachable in the event anything happened. São Paulo itself had been quiet during the day, as if the entire city lay waiting for something to happen. Rumors of Zhézush's appearance had swept the city. First there was the word on a radio station she had been sighted in Rio near the statue of Christ the Redeemer on Corcovado mountain. A local TV station announced a rumored sighting in Ibirapuera Park. Mason had rushed over, only to find a hundred or so people gathered together for a *candomblé* ritual of some sort and no sign of Zhézush. Perola had spoken with Aide, who informed her various groups of Zhézushians and others would be gathered in prayer vigils at points around the city in anticipation of the return: at the Catholic *Basilica Nossa Senhora de Assunçao* downtown, at the *Consolação* cemetery, and at the *Praça da Sé.* Aide had invited Perola to join them at the cathedral that evening. Elisabeth and the Bishop had remained incommunicado. Perola noted that, to her knowledge, the Bishop had not been seen since the arrival of Zhézush's body in Brazil.

The stadium crowd, roaring and focused, gave no indication anything special was in the air. The game between the SPFC and Corinthians football clubs, also being viewed by a television audience of probably ten million, according to Monterio, finished in a flurry of goals. The home team pulled out the victory with a beautiful save on a corner kick, and the game ended to ringing cheers and a victory lap around the field by several players. As in the U.S., battalions of uniformed police took up stations on the field as the game neared its conclusion, and more than once the stadium announcer warned spectators to stay off the field after the game. Mason had thanked Monterio for the ticket and was speaking with Maria when a stir in the crowd drew his attention back to the field.

A group of perhaps fifty people, hooded and dressed completely in black, had assembled at one lip of the stadium. Momentarily unprepared, the officers on the field formed into waves to repel the assault. Those nearest the encroaching group fell back as the intruders approached, giving way until the remaining officers could encircle the interlopers. Circling and encircled, the two groups moved slowly toward the middle of the field. The officers' unheeded shouts to desist carried to the stands. Those left in the stadium quieted at the prospect of further entertainment.

Suddenly, the black-dressed group began to scream in unison, a piercing, wailing sound silencing all other noise. Black hoods snapped back in a single group motion, revealing smooth shaved heads. The surrounding officers recoiled in bewilderment. Into the circle's center stepped a familiar figure, black hair flying. Heads ducked toward shoulder radios, beckoning reinforcement.

"People of Brazil!" Elisabeth's voice trumpeted through the stadium without benefit of any visible amplification. "Behold your savior!" With the flip of a wrist, she pulled the black cloak off of another figure now in the middle of the circle. Hands went to guns. The public address system coughed to life. "Ladies and gentlemen, please stay off . . ."

Released from the black cape, the large figure raised its arms skyward. Turning slowly in a tight circle, oblivious to the police officers and others slowly edging away, the figure clenched and unclenched its fists, large hands unfurling like flowers, then closing again. The bright stadium lights permitted no mistake in identity. Red television lights blinked in excitement. The crowd remained silent, as if turned to stone.

Zhézush stood at the center of the field.

Mason stood petrified, his mouth half-open. He had half-expected this, not here, but . . . His heart raced with something. Gratitude? Exaltation? The story would not end. It was more than just the assassination of a gifted faith healer; he had witnessed the cremation with his own eyes. Zhézush lived! He felt his knees tremble. Dimly, he was aware of Monterio's wife asking what was going on.

Could it be? How could it be? A final master illusion? His heart thumped so that he thought it might spin out of control. His mouth was dry, his face wet with tears. He mumbled something, something he later could not recall, something like a prayer of thankfulness. He would remember later he had never in his lifetime felt such exhilaration.

Almost immediately, doubt set in. The resurrection? At a soccer match? In one sense it was easier to fool a stadium from afar than one person at close range. The inexplicable could always eventually be explained, given enough time.

Those remaining in the half-empty stadium reeled in shock, unable to fully comprehend the magnitude of what played out before them. Elisabeth joined hands with Zhézush in the center of the circles, bolstering the big arms raised skyward in triumph. The crowd's silence suddenly broke in a great responsive thunderclap, flowing forever into a chaos of exhiliration, weeping, hugging, clapping, kissing, and shouting. Those in the parking lots turned in bewilderment at the sound, then rushed back inside. Staccato *samba* drumbeats punctuated the roar, emanating unseen from somewhere near the center of the field, as if combusted by the crowd's emotion. Mason surged toward the field, drawn as if by a magnet.

Somehow, Elisabeth's voice sliced through the clamor. "Let us tell the world!"

The crowd's roar reached a level of pandemonium.

"Zhézush has returned!" The stadium's concrete girders shook as if from an earthquake.

"Let us tell the government!"

"Governor! Governor! Governor!"

Again, Elisabeth's voice pierced the wall of sound. *"O Parlamento! O Parlamento!"*

The surging crowd took up the chant. The officers on the field gave way helplessly as the black-clad group moved toward the stadium's north end. The lower reaches of the stands poured over onto the field, creating a serpentine throng that trailed Zhézush's group in a giant, liquid parade. The human stream fluctuated, swelling and contracting in respiration as its current flowed out of the stadium toward downtown. The beat continued, spawning dancing human swirls on the throng's fringes; those crammed in the middle swayed to the sound in giant ripples. It seemed that all of São Paulo had dissolved into one gigantic, pulsating celebration.

Mason's feet led him inexorably to the field. He could not remember later how he got there, or whether he ever actually considered doing anything else. He was light-headed and giddy. Goose bumps pimpled his arms. Who could believe it? The thrill of participation, of being one with everyone, of overwhelming exhilaration. The beat flowed through them, connecting them. He found himself wanting to tell someone, anyone. Remembering the phone at his waist, he punched in Perola's number. The metallic recording of her voice mail failed to diminish the moment.

"She's alive!" he croaked into the phone. "She just appeared at the end of the soccer match in the middle of the field! There's a monster crowd heading for downtown São Paulo. I'll meet you there!"

He snapped the phone shut, suddenly realizing he had completely abandoned his host Monterio in the excitement. Catching sight of the bald newspaperman and his wife several rows farther up the stadium steps, he stepped out of the flow to wait for them.

"Do we walk or do we ride?" Mason shouted above the tumult.

"I think riding is foolish," Monterio rasped in his ear. "It will take as long or longer than walking. Have you had your exercise today?" He motioned with his hands, and they melted into the crowd's rushing waters.

The *samba* beat spurred Maria's brown legs into frenzied action. She glided seamlessly into the center of the crowd, her legs and feet a blur of motion, her upper torso a picture of effortless calm, a relaxed smile on her face. Monterio followed behind her, moving slowly to the now fading beat. Mason felt his own body move almost unconsciously in rhythm, subsumed again by the crowd, his mind floating in a manic haze, conscious of little more than movement and the all-consuming beat. It was as if a drug had rendered him incapable of assimilating anything other than the sensual.

He was not sure how long they had been moving. He remembered seeing automobiles caught in the flash flood of people, their occupants either happily abandoning their vehicles to the onslaught or fearfully burrowing down to ride out the tide. At some point, the beat became louder and the crowd began to bunch in front of him. A wisp of the acrid odor of tear gas clicked his mind into gear. They had reached the *Viaduto do Chá,* the viaduct in the heart of São Paulo. With a snap the beat ceased and the crowd grew still.

Elisabeth's voice boomed out of the darkness. "Today your savior has returned!"

Igniting again in sound, the crowd sent waves echoing across the plaza. Traffic halted on the freeways below them.

"Your government cannot deny this! The time has come for change!"

Another tumultuous roar. From somewhere behind the sound came the click of metal on metal and the rumble of engines. Almost immediately, a fog of tear gas descended on the plaza, its swirls reaching like tentacles to engulf the crowd. The gas obscured the streetlights and the light thrown off by nearby buildings, rendering the plaza opaque. Like a horse with a blanket over its head, the crowd moved wildly in all directions, trapped by the choking gas. Screams pierced the fog. Pulling his shirt over his face, Mason made for the direction of hazy lights to one side of the plaza, having lost all connection with Monterio and his wife. More screams, something that sounded like cannon fire, the sound of something big falling. Large dark shapes hurtling across his path. By the time he reached the end of the plaza, the fog had begun to lift, and he chanced a look back on the horror behind him. A number of people had apparently been forced by the blinded crowd against the fence protecting the plaza from the freeway below. As he watched, the fence buckled under the pressure. Dozens of screaming people disappeared over the side.

He wiped his face with trembling hands, the burn of the tear gas still in his throat and nostrils. Zhézush and Elisabeth were nowhere to be seen.

The whoosh of a projectile. Troops, marching. Should he try to make it to Perola's office? He had been there earlier in the day; it wasn't far. The noise and commotion clouded his thinking. The office seemed to make the most sense, as he could make it there on foot; traffic looked to be snarled downtown for the foreseeable future. Sirens blared in the distance. He edged away from the crowd, peering back over his shoulder in an attempt to catch a glimpse of the broad dark figure who had precipitated this tumult.

He made his way away from the plaza, dodging police reinforcements that rushed past in a metallic static of radio transmissions. With a flickering shudder, the streetlights and lights in nearby buildings went dark, leaving the entire downtown area in the pitch blackness of a moonless night. Heart thumping, he hurried on, trying to navigate the blackness of an unfamiliar city. A raspy voice called out from the darkness as he regained the center of the street, where the light of the few stars provided minimal illumination. Sirens continued to wail in the distance, and every now and then an automobile appeared, its lights puncturing the black to reveal scurrying humanity.

It took nearly half an hour to find the office. By the time he stumbled down the familiar narrow street, electricity had returned to the area. He found Perola on the phone in her office, hair matted, face smudged, her feet propped up on the worn wooden desk.

She grinned at Mason and waved him into a chair as she hung up. "Well," she said breathlessly. "So we see. You were right. She has returned, or so it seems. You saw her?"

Mason nodded, opening a small refrigerator and pulling out a soft drink. He felt groggy, as if he had come down from a chemical high. "Yeah. I half expected this, but it's still a shock." He took a big swallow out of the can. "The crowd from the stadium marched into a tear gas attack at the *Viaduto do Chá*. Were you there? A bunch of people got shoved through the fence onto the freeway. Then the lights went out."

"I know. I have just spoken to New York. The cable news networks have already aired footage of the march and the conflict at the plaza. New York is looking for a story for tomorrow."

Mason nodded. "Were you at the plaza?"

"Eventually, yes. I went to the cathedral when I returned to town, to meet Aide and the others. We had been there only a few minutes when someone ran in with the word Zhézush had appeared at the stadium and that a crowd was marching toward downtown. We all went to the plaza. It was several minutes before we could hear the drums. Within fifteen or twenty minutes we saw the beginnings of the march from the stadium. Our group was swelling rapidly. As the marchers arrived, so did army tanks and personnel carriers. They pushed us off the plaza and tried to prevent Zhézush and the stadium group from entering. She was at the front of the group, with Elisabeth. Aide and the others with me were swooning in ecstasy. Anyway, Zhézush and Elisabeth and several others left the remainder of the group and approached the line of troops. The drums were beating, the crowd chanting—it was like this force or something."

"That was about the time I arrived," Mason interjected.

"So you may have seen the rest, then. All of a sudden the drumbeats stopped and it got really quiet. Elisabeth's voice rang out over it all, proclaiming the savior returned. The crowd went crazy, troops panicked, tear gas dropped, and all was chaos."

"Did you see what happened to Zhézush and Elisabeth?"

"No. I was trying to avoid being trampled. Did you?"

"It was like a fog descended on the plaza. I couldn't see anything until later. I think we have enough to put a decent story together, huh? Why don't I take a stab at the first cut and you work the phones. Let's get the official government reaction, if we can. Let's talk to the hospitals. Let's try to locate the Zhézushians."

"So, is it real?"

"I don't know." His mind scampered over the question it had engaged but sought to avoid. "I really don't know. I doubt it, but the exhilaration is hard to describe. It's like the hospital healings. *Something* happened. Something large enough to spur thousands of people into near hysteria." He stopped, not wanting to put into words his own excitement. He would e-mail Rome later, after this emotion had subsided.

"One of your glimpses, perhaps?"

"Perhaps."

Electricity had returned to the *favela*, at least those parts served by electricity, by the time Perola made her way slowly past the now-closed guard post through streets choked with people and vehicles. The area hummed with activity, the air alive with an excitement usually reserved for the apex of Carnival. The anonymity of the chaos made the *favela* feel less dangerous; drunken *favelados* swaying in and out among the creeping traffic seemed more interested in revelry than violence.

It took almost an hour to reach the area near the shacks where she had sat with Aide, Vicente, and the other Zhézushians. Perola found the shanties dark and deserted as she approached on foot after parking in what she hoped was a safe area several blocks away. To her surprise, the unmistakable profiles of a pair of uniformed soldiers were visible outside the doorway of the green shack, the light from glowing cigarettes framing their dark faces. She stood for a few minutes in the shadows then slipped away in the darkness, back to her car and the relative safety of the crowds.

She dialed her message machine from the car phone, conscious of the danger the sight of a mobile phone might provoke among the *favela*'s young hoodlums. Nothing. She reached Mason a few minutes later.

"Anything happening downtown?"

"Not that I can tell. I've signed off on the story, and I'm getting ready to head down there now. Any sign of the Zs?"

"None. In fact, a couple of uniforms are stationed outside of the shack. They were the only ones I saw in the entire *favela.* I thought I'd swing by the cathedral and see if there's any sign, and keep checking my messages. I have to believe they will try to reach me."

Mason yawned. "I'll see you in a bit, then. There hasn't been anything new on the TV news. Definitely nothing new on the international networks."

"I will try to follow up with my government contacts," Perola promised. "Do you still think I should go to Bahia?" Their original plan had been for Perola to investigate Zhézush's origins.

"Let's see where we are by early morning. If nothing else dramatic has happened, why don't you plan on going? We've got to spend some effort checking that out."

17

And as they thus spake, Jesus himself stood in the midst of them, and saith unto them, Peace *be* unto you. But they were terrified and affrighted, and supposed that they had seen a spirit.

Luke 24:36-37

The flight to Salvador, the capital of the state of Bahia, was long and cramped. Detouring around bad weather, the plane landed three hours later than anticipated, affording Perola the opportunity to read and reread the Brazilian morning papers. The major papers featured large, front-page color photographs of the risen Zhézush at the football stadium, arms clasped above her head, and reported with great fanfare the details of her reappearance and march to the plaza. Little was said, however, of her current whereabouts or future plans. Perola felt some relief. No one had gotten much more than they had.

Judging by the morning TV news, little had changed overnight. She focused on the papers, noting with interest that one article described Zhézush as "melting into the night" during the fracas at the *Viaduto do Chá*. Another suggested that she might have been taken prisoner by the government. Perola reflected on the latter possibility as she settled into the back seat of a surprisingly new taxi for the ride to the Rialto Hotel. Why would government troops have been present at the Zhézushians' shack in São Paulo, if not to guard against a reappearance? The government—city, state and national—had to view Zhézush as the ultimate catalyst for sedition. If Zhézush and Elisabeth had managed to slip away during the tumult, the search would be intense. If not, God only knew what their fate might be. Henrique had been able to shed little light on the matter, bitterly informing her the São Paulo police had been relegated to providing protective buffers for the federal soldiers. State and federal bureaucrats now controlled all policy regarding the confrontations.

Perola squirmed in her seat in the slow-moving taxi, aggravated even to be in Salvador. She hadn't protested much when Mason had suggested it, but things seemed to be falling into a familiar pattern—the white, male "boss" took the good assignment in São Paulo where the action was; the female, black "employee" got stuck with grunt work in the hinterlands. She liked Michael Mason, but he barely spoke Portuguese and had been in the country a total of one week. What contacts did he have in São Paulo? She lay back, trying to force herself to be calm. Little was to be gained by picking a fight or holding a grudge.

Her thoughts jumped back to Mason: his revelation of his relationship with the Church, his constant searching for God. She had no doubt of God's existence, any more than she doubted Corcovado Mountain still rose above Rio. God was; the dilemma was determining what He wanted and why. In her experience, if you waited patiently enough, it was usually made apparent. All of the angst and intrigue of the search seemed to her unnecessary.

The taxi's jolt brought her back to the present. She would find what there was to find about Zhézush. Maybe something key, maybe not. She would do her job.

Quaint and colonial, Salvador and Bahia represented the root of black Brazilian life. Perola had not visited the city in years, and was surprised to find the streets relatively clean, the people smiling and friendly, with no sign of the youth gangs and desperate poverty plaguing São Paulo and Rio. Compared to São Paulo's perpetual smog, the air seemed pristine. A light breeze flipped flags on multicolored downtown buildings framed by wrought-iron balconies. Her hotel, an older, smaller edifice with a small neon sign proclaiming it the "Rialto," snuggled next to two larger buildings on the side of a cobblestone street that wound like a brook through the city's heart.

After checking in, she set about scouring the room for a telephone book or city directory. Finding none, she ventured downstairs to the desk and procured a dog-eared, outdated phone book and an even older city directory. Ancient fans creaked overhead as she sat in the quiet lobby scanning the two books, nearly oblivious of the few guests and hotel staff who came and went. She identified two orphanages from the old city directory and jotted down the address of the public library.

By two in the afternoon she was back in another *fusca,* winding through narrow streets alive with color and sound. At almost every corner, a musician of some sort picked a string instrument, rapped on a drum, or in one instance, blew melodiously on an ancient trumpet. Jackhammers and electric saws from new construction thudded and whined, car horns blared, motors coughed. The bells of a bicycle jingled as it passed. What seemed like hundreds of radio boom boxes competed for their place in the spectrum of sound.

The odor of different foods carried on the wind as if drawn by the music out of the old walls and streets. Skin color was noticeably darker here, the ratio of blacks to whites inverted from São Paulo's. Even the whites seemed darker, their bright clothing offset against smooth, brown skin. Evidence of mysticism and religion was everywhere, from the occasional street corner altar to the spires and crosses dotting the skyline. Even the taxi driver contributed his part—a string of crosses adorned his neck below a bushy white beard, and the taxi's dashboard served as a shrine of sorts for at least a dozen religious artifacts. His constant humming added a base to the kaleidoscope of sound.

A modern shopping center squatted in the area where the directory had shown the first orphanage should lie; a vacant building occupied the second orphanage's putative location.

"Tell me," she said to the humming taxi driver. "Have you ever heard of Zhézush da Bahia?"

"Aye," said the man as he wheeled the car around. "She is on TV, no? The one who heals?" He turned and flashed crooked teeth at her.

"Yes. I understand she is from Salvador."

"Aye, that is right."

"Do you know anyone here who knew her? Anyone with any connection to the orphanage?"

The man shook his head from side to side. "Maybe the police? I know other reporters have inquired about her."

Perola dropped back into the seat and directed the driver to the newspaper's offices, where she spent the remainder of the afternoon poring over old papers from the period in which Zhézush might have been a resident of the city. She found several references to one of the orphanages, São Luis, but little else.

Hungry and exhausted, she caught another taxi back to the hotel. A phone check of her message system yielded nothing new, and neither Mason nor Henrique was in. The international television news network had nothing additional on the story. Dining alone in the spacious old dining room, she contemplated her next day's agenda—more newspaper research, a visit to the Salvador social services office. Her resentment at being in Salvador boiled up again. This had been a complete waste of time. She would not call Mason again this evening; if he wanted her, he knew where to find her.

The only waitress in the dining room, a young woman of maybe nineteen, stood attentively several feet away from Perola and the other diners, an elderly couple and a young woman and her small child. The others soon finished and left, leaving Perola and the waitress the sole occupants of the room.

"How are you today?" asked Perola, hoping conversation would diminish her malaise.

"Okay. And you?"

Perola nodded, her mouth still full of fried fish.

"What brings you to Salvador?"

Perola explained that she was a reporter doing some research. "Have you heard of Zhézush da Bahia?"

"Yes, of course," the girl said brightly. "She is on the television every night."

"I have been trying, without much success, to find out some things about her childhood. She is from Salvador, you know. She was an orphan. The most likely place she stayed has been torn down."

"Oh, I see," the girl said pleasantly. "My great aunt was the assistant director of an orphanage a long time ago."

"Which one?"

"I think it was called São Luis, or something like that."

"That may be the one!" Adrenaline crept into Perola's system. "Does she know of Zhézush?"

"I have never asked her, but maybe. She is quite old. If you would like, I could arrange for you to speak with her. Maybe tomorrow?"

"Yes, yes. That would be wonderful. Any chance of doing it tonight?"

The girl looked thoughtful. "I could call and see. She goes to bed early." She disappeared into an alcove off the dining room.

Perola finished her dinner. Maybe this trip would not be a total bust.

The girl returned several minutes later. "I get off work in an hour. Why don't I ring your room then, and we can go visit her. She is very old and forgetful, so do not expect much. But sometimes she can remember things that happened long ago more clearly than those that happened yesterday."

True to her word, Lina called some forty-five minutes later and invited Perola to meet her downstairs.

"Let us see," she said when Perola arrived. "I have a bicycle, but it really is not too far to walk. Shall we? I'll bring the bike. It will take maybe twenty minutes."

The walk was pleasant in the cool evening. The sounds and smells from earlier in the day had diminished into a muted rustling of music and traffic. The odors of alcohol and spicy food filled the air. Lina moved down the curving streets and alleys at a pace that hardly gave time for appreciating the surroundings. Chattering almost the entire way, she explained that she was studying to be a nurse but worked thirty hours a week at the hotel restaurant to pay for her schooling and help support her family. She had a boyfriend named Braulio, whom she would like to marry one day, but only after she had received her degree and he had become more established in his job. By the time she slowed at a small cobblestone plaza where the aroma of cooked meat hung like a cloud, Perola had worked up a sweat.

Lina darted down a small side street and halted before a three-story apartment building. She used a key to enter a ground-level apartment, pulling the bike in after her. Piles of furniture, books, and other belongings were everywhere.

"Auggh," Lina muttered. "Please excuse the mess. My family, they never throw anything away. We might need it someday, they say! Meanwhile, we cannot walk for the clutter." She shifted some boxes to reveal three small stuffed chairs, then uncovered a battered coffee table by moving another pile of papers and books. "Please, have a seat." She motioned to one of the chairs.

A frail, dark, white-haired woman emerged from the piles of furniture and boxes, hobbling forward slowly with the aid of a wooden cane.

"This is my Aunt Elsa," said Lina.

The older woman smiled in greeting, spreading her hands against a faded calico dress.

"Would you like some coffee?" Lina asked. Perola nodded, and Lina made her way to the kitchen.

Dona Elsa's memory proved beneficial, but erratic. She remembered Zhézush and Elisabeth well. She couldn't recall what years they had lived at São Luis, although twenty-odd years ago sounded about right. She couldn't really remember anything of the circumstances surrounding their tenure at the facility. She certainly would not have suspected that Zhézush would be healing people and claiming to be Christ returned.

Dona Elsa did have several specific recollections that proved interesting. "I remember it being very unusual for a girl to be named Zhézush," she said in a creaky voice. "When she first arrived, we thought for several days she was a boy. Finally, she blurted out to us—I guess she must have been four or five years old at the time—that she was a girl. We felt bad because of our mistake, particularly since she was not an attractive little girl, you know, overweight and such. But she adapted well. She was there . . . oh, maybe five years or so?"

The coffee arrived. Elsa took a sip. "The other one you asked about—Elisabeth. I remember most how smart she was. In those days, there was no testing as there is now, but that child could have been a genius. We were all amazed at what she could do, with numbers, with spelling—anything."

"When did they leave?" asked Perola. "And did they leave together?"

Dona Elsa couldn't recall anything about their departure or where they might have gone.

After chatting for a few minutes more, Perola thanked Dona Elsa and

Lina and stood. "Do you have any records or anything from this period, or know where any might be?"

Dona Elsa shook her head, tilting her coffee cup back. "After the school was demolished . . . I do not know what happened to anything. I had retired by then."

Perola left her card and returned to the hotel, declining Lina's offer of an escort. After a bath and a brief conversation with Henrique, she fell into a shallow, restless sleep in which she dreamed of an orphanage being slowly destroyed by fire.

The next morning she arose early, groggy after a poor night's sleep, and spent the day moving among the library, the newspaper office, and various government offices in a mostly futile attempt to gather useful information. She found nothing further at the newspaper and little new information at the library. Salvador birth records for the period she estimated to be relevant yielded no record of the births of either Zhézush or Elisabeth. The state child welfare office did maintain some old records regarding São Luis, but the information proved bureaucratic in nature: reports of regulatory visits and safety code violations, censuses for several years, and one listing of children for an indeterminate year, which did not reference Zhézush or Elisabeth. Perola limped back to the hotel about four to report to Mason.

"Anything happening there?" she asked.

"Not really. Some minor protests at the university. Nothing like several days ago. No sightings of Zhézush or Elisabeth or any of the others. I'm starting to think the government has absconded with them. Why don't you catch the evening flight back tonight? I have a feeling something may happen tomorrow."

The phone rang as Perola was packing her bags. The halting voice on the other end of the line sounded familiar, but it took several seconds before she recognized Lina.

"Dona Elsa has had a stroke. I am at the hospital. The doctors do not expect her to live." Her voice broke into a series of sobs.

"Oh, dear. I am very sorry."

Lina regained her voice. "I just wanted to tell you that she told me something to tell you. She was babbling incoherent stuff, and suddenly she made sense for a few minutes and asked to speak to you. I explained you were not here. She said Zhézush had a sister who also stayed at the orphanage. She called her Zelinda. That was all; everything was nonsense after that."

"I see," Perola murmured sympathetically. "Thank you very much for calling. Is there anything I can do for you?"

"No, no. I probably should go now. I see the doctor coming out of her room. I just wanted to let you know . . ." her voice trailed off.

Joaquin Sebastião Silva's nose touched the cell's metal bar. For a moment the smell of moist iron overcame the overwhelming fecal stench. The cell's five other occupants lounged in postures of boredom, apathy, or suppressed aggression. Designed for one or maybe two, the cell constrained six bodies like a cage. Sleep was possible only in shifts.

He wondered that he was still alive—or maybe he wasn't. Death would come soon in this place, regardless, from illness or violence or madness. She must still need him for something, though for what he wasn't sure. He wondered at her rejection, attributable without doubt to his own weakness. She had seen it, known it all along. Yet in a strange way, amidst the depths of self-flagellation, the thought crept by that his weakness had saved him. He dwelled on the thought, turned it over, examined it. He felt somehow renewed, refreshed. Cleansed?

He laughed aloud, startling the other inmates. He turned to them—José, the Butcher, Brolio, Renaldo, the Quiet One. "Your sins are forgiven," he said to them. "Christ died for you."

The Butcher spat at him; the others ignored him.

"Get this fucker out of here before I kill him with my own hands," shouted Brolio to an invisible guard. "If you want him to live, put him in solitary. We need no priest."

"Jesus loves you. Zhézush."

Closeted in the familiar confines of the Hilton bar, Perola sipped a Coke as Mason downed more coffee. She had arrived back in São Paulo earlier in the afternoon, after another morning of relatively unproductive research in Salvador. Searches at the newspaper and the birth registry had yielded no record of a Zelinda, Zhézush's purported sister. A message from Lina had awaited her at the Hotel Rialto. Dona Elsa had died during the night.

São Paulo had remained quiet during her absence, with no further sign of Zhézush or Elisabeth. Several of the morning papers reported disturbances in Rio's *favelas*, with one report that over ten thousand protesters had battled police with rocks and crude weapons. It was unclear whether the protests were related to Zhézush or were purely anti-government.

Henrique was to join them later, having confirmed in an earlier conversation that the São Paulo police were bracing for an assault similar to Rio's. Large numbers of government troops remained in the city, as much a fixture now in the downtown area as the young executives in ties and suits racing among the city's skyscrapers.

"I've been completely stalled on any meeting with anyone of importance in city, state, or national government," said Mason. "The mayor's office promised they would call me back; they haven't. I couldn't get past the operator at the governor's office."

Perola pursed her lips. "I will see what I can do. No announced press conferences or anything?"

Mason shook his head. "Do you think there's any possibility that the government could be in danger?"

"The national government?"

"Yeah. Some of the international news outlets are speculating that the instability makes things ripe for a military move."

"What makes you think Brazil's government is any more likely to falter than that of the U.S.?"

"Well, for one thing, it's not just me—Monterio at the *Miami Tribune* mentioned it yesterday. Plus, there's recent history. Brazil has had a military government within the past thirty years."

"That was before the Constitution. The world gives us no credit. To you, we are practically incapable of governing ourselves or doing anything more constructive than making money for you. The slightest tremor and Brazil might collapse."

"Okay. The government's not going to collapse. I'll take your word for it." He looked surprised at her vehemence. "It's just that I expect the editors to ask about it when they see some of the international coverage. Anyway, there's something else you ought to know." He described Jay Summit's findings.

"Joseph Farriday," she mused, composure regained. "That name sounds familiar."

"He and his group are very well known in the U.S." Mason glanced around the bar, then poured more coffee. "What's our next move? This place is suddenly swarming with foreign media. I saw Maria Espinosa of Global News in the lobby this morning. They're probably about ready to start doing live anchors from Brazil."

"I do not know. The Zhézushians seem to have vanished as completely as Zhézush, Elisabeth, and the Bishop. Their phones have been disconnected, government troops occupy their dwellings, no one has contacted me. It is as if they have disappeared from the face of the earth. All of the thousands of *ajudantes*, where are they now?"

The phone in Perola's purse rang. She fished it out and flipped it open. Henrique's voice echoed through the receiver.

"Word is on the street that Zhézush is to appear in Rio tomorrow at noon. The Rio police say the radio stations there have been getting call after call about it. It may just be rumor, but they say that she is to appear on the beach at Ipanema near the Hotel Vilarejo."

Perola relayed the information to Mason, then called her friend Iraci in Rio. Iraci worked for the *Noticias* newspaper and had also heard the rumors.

"I understand the police are going crazy, worrying about the crowds and the tourists," Iraci whispered. "I would not be surprised to see the army barricading the beach in the morning." Iraci too was worried about the government's stability. "There was a large protest here last night, people waving little Brazilian flags and copies of the Constitution. Military intervention is what everyone expects to happen, and expectations usually become reality."

"But the Constitution . . ."

"Do you think that the big corporations are going to sit idly by, constitution or no constitution?"

“I think we need to be in Rio,” Mason said as she hung up. “Why don’t I go over tonight and you meet me in the morning? That way, if something happens here, you would be in position to respond.”

Perola nodded her silent agreement.

If São Paulo was on edge, Rio had started to totter. There seemed to be as many troops as people in the city, soldiers clustering on street corners, in alleyways, in front of government buildings. The city’s residents congregated in the streets and across the *calçadas,* the black-and-white mosaic tile pedestrian thoroughfares, impossibly clogging traffic. Drumbeats competed with boom boxes, car horns, shrieking children, and police bullhorns. On one street corner a classical wind quartet played patiently, as incongruous as if dropped in from another world. But for the massive military presence, the atmosphere would seem almost like that of Carnival. The green-clad soldiers turned the mood from celebratory to anxious, and the shouts of the people outside Mason’s hotel window rang with anger rather than joy.

The Vilarejo stood at the end of São Conrado beach, not far from Ipanema, its view down upon the famed white sands, with their volleyball nets and usually thousands of brown sunbathers in stringy swimwear. Today, however, the beach sat empty, its sands marked only by an occasional lost toy or the flutter of a piece of trash. From his room facing east, Mason gazed down the vacant beach, back toward the city. Empty kiosks littered Avenida Niemeyer, running the length of the beach. A fleet of military vehicles covered the boulevard like a convoy of ants, extending almost to the horizon. Soldiers scurried furiously around the vehicles, forming a wall to deny beach access to the thousands of people behind them.

Mason took the elevator to the first floor, into a sea of commotion. Military personnel stalked the broad hotel lobby, having apparently commandeered large portions of the facility’s common areas, leaving flustered tour operators to explain the situation to frightened tourists. Families attempted to divert small children intent on the beach to the crowded pool area or back to their rooms. Outmanned hotel security personnel gamely tried to create some sort of order. Ubiquitous street peddlers, taking advantage of the chaos, hawked metal license plates stamped "Rio" until forced away by hotel employees. A large American woman with an enormous straw hat wailed above the tumult, demanding to be taken into town on her last day in the city.

Mason forced his way through the throng to the hotel's front doors, only to be blocked from proceeding farther by a wall of soldiers, guns in hand. Other military personnel with bullhorns were visible farther down the beach, pacing back and forth in front of the surging crowd. Snatches of metallic words echoed across the empty beach: "Stay calm! Return to your homes! Nothing is going to happen today! It is for your own safety!"

The amplified urgings, if anything, spurred the crowd. It seemed a darker group than those who had marched from the São Paulo stadium. Several held aloft banners and placards, exhorting the returned messiah to "Save Us!" and "Free the People!" Mouths moved silently, their words unheard in the commotion.

A drumbeat sprang from out of the mayhem, the sound of a multitude of invisible drummers, igniting the onlookers to rhythmic life as if at the flick of an electric switch. Fear showed on the soldiers' faces, fear of being outnumbered, of being no longer in control. Fear that could instill panic—and violence.

Regaining the security of his room, Mason threw open the sliding glass door fronting a small balcony that faced the eastern beach. A pleasant breeze blew in from the ocean, carrying the sound of the *samba* beat and the noise of the crowd like a raft on the sea.

He noticed a ripple in the crowd several hundred yards away from the hotel. Soon, the entire crowd's attention became focused on the beach volleyball complex situated perhaps a quarter mile farther along the beach, its bleachers and advertisements sparkling in the late-morning sun. Five figures emerged atop a metal building that served as part of the complex, three unknown to him, the other two familiar even at such distance: a round, squat figure in a dark tunic and a shapely figure in a white dress. Acidity lurched through Mason's stomach.

"My people!" The voice thundered across the beach, over the heads of the military, through the thousands, maybe hundreds of thousands, gathered along the beachfront. All conversation ceased, leaving only the lapping waves and the cries of gulls and terns. All heads turned to face the figures on the roof.

Zhézush lifted her arms above her head. "God is love," rang the voice. "I am love. I am yours."

The crowd convulsed in excitement, then surged in a gigantic tidal wave over and through the military blockade to encircle the volleyball complex. The troops scattered like birds, some taking cover in the safety of the vehicles, others joining the current of the crowd.

"It is not necessary that you believe in me, but that you believe in yourself, that you believe in your world and those beside you." Again, the familiar ethereal quiet. For some reason the words sounded to Mason more metallic than usual; perhaps even Zhézush had to succumb to using amplification to project over the waves. Goose bumps formed on his arms and back. He pulled a pair of binoculars to his eyes and focused in on the rooftop. The other figures surrounded Zhézush, shielding her from . . . from what? Another gunshot? He stared, perplexed. Still, there was no mistaking that figure or that voice.

"*You* must stop injustice! *You* must save your children! *You* must save your world! If your government will not do it . . ." A long pause permitted the crowd to growl in response. ". . . you must do it for them."

Frantic now, the crowd roared its approval. The drums recommenced their cadence, somehow audible through the other noise.

"Do you see injustice?"

The response shook the Vilarejo's foundation.

"Do you want to change your world?"

Sound waves crashed forth, as if the crowd intended by its own voice to lift the figures heavenward.

"How do you change things?"

"Love . . . Peace . . . Justice! Love . . . Peace . . . Justice! Love . . . Peace . . . Justice!"

The drumbeat accelerated, people swirled, sound lifted off the beach like a fog. The figures atop the volleyball complex disappeared. It was like the climactic moment in a huge sporting event, Mason decided, frozen in time as spectator response reached the apex. Jerking and twitching to the beat, the crowd reached in all directions, completely consuming any remaining green military uniforms and vehicles. Mason turned from the window to the television, where a camera broadcasting from the opposite end of the beach relayed equal chaos. The noise from the crowd completely drowned out the TV's sound. Only a differing vibration from the ringing phone alerted him to pick it up.

"Michael!" He could barely recognize Perola's voice above the din.

"Where are you?" he shouted.

"Not far from the hotel," she gasped. "I think I can make the front. Yes, ahhh." A blast of static followed, then her voice grew clearer. "It is very dangerous out here. Someone could be trampled in this crowd. I am inside now. What room are you in?"

Fifteen minutes later she flopped down on one of the room's double beds. "It is very wild, yes? Did you see and hear her?"

Mason nodded and closed the sliding glass door. "I heard her loud and clear. Where were you? Did you have a good view?"

Perola shrugged her shoulders. "I was maybe fifty yards away. Her back was to me."

"Where did they go when it was over?" Mason asked.

"I do not know. It was as if they vanished. One minute they were there, and then . . ."

A blast from the television caught their attention. "A curfew has been imposed for this evening at seven o'clock," proclaimed a red-faced announcer. "Repeat, the City of Rio de Janeiro has imposed a curfew from seven o'clock tonight until six tomorrow morning. All citizens are to be off the streets by seven!" The announcer shuffled some papers nervously, glancing furtively at the camera.

Mason returned his attention to the beach, still alive with humanity. "What next, eh?" He pulled a soft drink out of the mini-refrigerator.

"I do not think that Rio has had a curfew for at least twenty years, maybe longer." Perola bit her lip in concern.

"I think we need to commandeer some help." Mason jerked his thumb in the direction of the TV. "The report before you came in said huge crowds are on the streets in São Paulo, as well. We probably need to have people here, and in São Paulo, and someone in Brasilia."

Perola stared out the window at the crowd. "You are probably right. If the government were to capitulate, where would it be? Brasilia? If Zhézush is to show herself again, where?" She paused again. "How quickly can you get someone else to come in?"

Mason grabbed his mobile phone and punched in New York, flipping the TV channels at the same time to see if the international news networks were carrying any coverage of the events at São Conrado beach. Minutes later he had Rhodes and other *Herald* managing editors on the line. He filled them in on the events at the beach and attempted to assess the current situation.

"The rumors are that the military could be moving in to take over the government within a week. These returns of Zhézush seem to serve as catalysts for disturbances and protests against the government. There are so many people, it just simply overwhelms whatever military is brought to bear. Wait, here it comes on INN." Footage of the beach filled the TV screen. "Are you guys tuned in there?"

They watched the coverage in silence for several minutes. "Anyway," Mason broke back in, "we probably need some more bodies here. I'd like somebody in Rio and somebody in Brasilia. Perola and I will return to São Paulo, one or the other of us prepared to venture out as necessary."

There followed considerable debate as to the merits of who, when, and why, but eventually the editors agreed to send back Roberto Smith, the bureau chief who had joined the call mid-way through, and to move Eva Montaigne over from Buenos Aires. Smith would proceed to Rio, Eva to Brasilia by the following morning. Mason spent a few more minutes coordinating with Smith, then signed off.

"My guess is things are going to shift back to São Paulo," Perola said, opening the refrigerator and pulling out another soft drink. "I am glad we will be there."

She had almost completed her sentence with the word "together," he thought with satisfaction. The sight of her slender body stretched out on the hotel room bed sent his pulse into gyrations. The room felt suddenly warm.

"Does it seem odd to you that the Bishop has completely disappeared? That the *ajudantes* are nowhere to be found?" Perola sat up, pulling her knees under her chin. "I want to work the streets and see what I can find.

When do you want to head back?"

Mason walked to the window to survey the dispersing crowd. "Soon. How did you end up getting over here?"

Perola smiled. "The Fiat is still running. I parked several miles away. I hope she is still there." She looked out at the beach, where patches of white sand showed again among the bodies.

"Are you planning on driving back?" He felt foolish, as if asking for a date.

"Well, I'm not planning on leaving my car in Rio." She smiled again, the face-lightening smile. "But I think we should give it several hours before we attempt to go anywhere. Is it story time?"

Mason pointed to his laptop, poised at a desk a few feet away. "After you."

18

For I have heard the slander of many: fear *was* on every side: while they took counsel together against me, they devised to take away my life. But I trusted in thee, O LORD: I said, Thou *art* my God.

Psalm 31:13-14

The sun had fallen behind Rio de Janeiro's green hills by the time Mason and Perola made their departure from the city. Traffic on the expressway from Rio to São Paulo, busy at any hour, moved at a sclerotic crawl. Accidents and stalled vehicles dictated a pace of barely two miles per hour; Mason was certain he could have bicycled the route more quickly. By the time they reached the Cruzeiro exit, the pace had begun to quicken, affording an adjustment to their estimated post-midnight time of arrival. Warnings of military roadblocks and inspections peppered forth from the radio, but so far they had seen nothing. Perhaps the officers were too busy dealing with traffic issues.

Miraculously, little violence had been reported in Rio following Zhézush's appearance. By the time Mason and Perola departed, the beach had taken on a normal afternoon flow of brown flesh and crying vendors. The radio reported no disturbances downtown or elsewhere in the city. The crowds had melted away as quickly as they had generated, the *samba* beats burrowing into the ordinary noises of the city.

The international news networks had expanded their coverage of the story, with a skepticism and a paternalistic "oh, what have we here?" tone that had made Perola slam down her notebook in disgust. United States news networks had also shown keen interest, and it was rumored that at least one of the prime-time anchors was on her way to Brazil for a series of broadcasts. International coverage was rife with speculation that the Brazilian government was near collapse, as evidenced by an article in the *Washington Banner* predicting Brazil would fall under military rule within thirty days.

So far, other than the incident at the *Viaduto do Chá,* no clashes with government troops had been reported in São Paulo or any other city. Neither the federal government in Brasilia nor the governments of the states of Rio de Janeiro or São Paulo had made any public statement on Zhézush, a tactic Mason and Perola agreed was probably a correct play of the government's hand. The military had minimized confrontation while maintaining order, and the troop commanders in Rio had shown good judgment by shrewdly melting away when Zhézush's appearance convulsed the masses. No death squads or troops had overrun the *favelas,* no one anybody knew of had been detained without warrant, there had been no house arrests and, until today, no curfews. The military had seemed content to let groups gather, even demonstrate, provided that they did not resort to violence or looting.

"I wonder where this is all heading," Mason mused as they barreled along the crowded freeway. "You know, Zhézush and everything. Will she eventually 'ascend' and depart? Or will there be some finality, some cataclysmic something, civil war or what have you, that will take her from public sight?"

"I do not know," Perola said slowly. "You would know the pattern better than I. Did not Christ reappear only to the believers, at first? Did he ever reappear to the masses? I cannot remember."

"His return crystallized the belief of the true believers, who in turn spread the word. Here, it is almost as if the reappearance is designed to convince the world. A very public, media-type thing."

"I have thought a lot about what you told me the other night, about yourself."

Heat crept up his neck, and he turned to face her.

"It is interesting. You search so hard for God. He is like a lover you do not trust, one you must continually check on to prove his fidelity. Perhaps you should step back and let Him, or Her, find you."

He swallowed hard. Trust, faith, fidelity.

"Tell me more about why you entered the priesthood," she said.

"I was young. I convinced myself the Church was my path. I realized after some time that it wasn't."

"Anything specific?" She was probing, a good reporter.

"Yeah." He sighed. "A young woman seduced me. It wasn't so much that I sinned, but I felt I couldn't go back. I languished for a time in a sort of purgatory between the Church and the secular world and eventually just drifted away."

"And you have never married?"

"No."

"Come close?"

"Not really. I guess that's another quest. I'm always looking but never finding exactly what I want."

"And what is it exactly that you want?"

He looked at her, at the friendly, open face, the partly open shirt. Why did sex always seem to get in the way of love?

"Look!" Perola jammed a finger in the direction of a road sign, then swerved the car onto an exit ramp, rattling Mason against the dashboard.

"What?" He was relieved to discover that the car was not crashing or otherwise destructing.

"That sign. Look what it says." The Portuguese came so rapidly he lost translation.

"Whoa. Slow down! What are you saying?"

"The sign said Zelinda," she said more calmly. "That was the name the old woman in Bahia gave me, the woman who had been at the orphanage where Zhézush lived. Zhézush's sister's name. I had forgotten that this was also the name of a town. Maybe the woman meant the town, or some other connection, yes? Maybe. I think it is worth a visit—it is not that far. What do you think?"

"Let's just make it quick, okay?"

Several dingy-looking bars, a post office, and a small bank flanked Zelinda's dirty town square. The few trees were windswept and dismal, offering little in the way of shade or color. Down the road, the neon of more modern establishments glinted in the dusk of early evening. The only moving creature in the downtown area, an older woman of apparent Indian descent, scowled at them as their car passed. As they watched, she squatted and urinated in the middle of the square.

"Seen enough?" Mason asked.

"I guess. Oh, well." She pulled the car in a tight U-turn to return the way they had come.

"My God!"

"What?"

"Go straight here." He had glimpsed something that couldn't be, something that sent tremors throughout his body. As the car grew closer, the tremors became convulsive shakes. His breath came in great gasps. For an incredible moment he felt that he had died and his soul had become suspended above the car, such that he could see and hear everything perfectly, but from a vantage point outside his body.

"Are . . . are you okay? What is it?" Perola navigated the car around a curved embankment, past metal fences and into the terraced, antiseptic-looking grounds of a medical facility.

"The São Paulo State Mental Hospital," she read slowly. "That is it. That is what I remember about this place. There is this big mental hospital here." She turned to Mason. "Are you okay? You look sick."

Mason sucked in air in an elongated gasp. He too remembered this place, but from his dreams, from the dream, the dream that had recurred so often it felt a permanent part of his psyche. Everything was positioned as it should be, the white-clad nurses crisscrossing the lawn, the building with the green shutters, the curving driveway, the green door.

"Michael, are you okay?" Perola's voice broke through the haze.

"Yes, yes," he muttered. "It's just that . . . that this is . . ." He took in another breath, his hands shaking, his stomach twisted and sore. "I have been here before. I have dreamed of this place."

Perola crossed herself involuntarily, something Mason had never seen her do. "You mean the one you dream again and again?"

Mason nodded. He exhaled loudly, his gaze riveted on the scene in front of him.

"What should we do? Do you want to go in?" Perola pulled the car off the road and silenced the engine.

"I don't know." Mason felt as if he were back in the dream. Things were moving slowly, languidly, the white figures crossing the lawn in rhythm with his breathing. The desire to go inside was there, the same as in the dream, the desire to walk across the expanse of green lawn and open the large front door. "Yes, I do want to go inside," he said hypnotically, his voice coming back to him in a long echo. Sideburns of sweat rolled down his face.

Perola started the car again. The driveway curved ahead of them toward an old iron gate, where a sentry spoke with the occupants of another auto.

"Wait!" Mason blurted suddenly. "Turn around."

Perola stopped the car in confusion. "What is it?"

"If we saunter up to the gate and ask to go in, we'll be tossed out on our ears. We don't know anyone here. Let's go back into town and formulate a plan. Plus, look over there." He pointed to an area beyond the sentry's post, where a contingent of soldiers lounged in the last rays of the day's sun. "Doesn't that strike you as strange, that the military would be hanging around a mental hospital in the middle of nowhere?"

Perola murmured her agreement.

"I don't think it's just a coincidence. There has to be something significant here."

They retreated to a restaurant on one side of the dusty downtown plaza, purchased coffee, and huddled over a crooked wooden table in a dark corner. Mason ran his hands through his hair, then rested them on the table. He was still trembling.

"It's six-thirty," Mason said finally. "If we're going to do something today, we'd better do it. I don't believe we stand a chance of getting in there at night." They sat silently for a few minutes. "I think I've got an idea. A crazy idea. Have you ever considered becoming a nurse?"

Twenty minutes later the old Fiat sputtered to a stop in front of the sentry's station, Perola in the driver's seat, Mason in the back. He lolled his head from side to side in what he hoped was an accurate portrayal of someone mentally ill, keeping his arms behind his back, as if manacled.

The sight of the hospital through the sentry's gate sent his central nervous system into overdrive, his stomach into heaving spasms. Vomit spewed profusely on the car's back seat. He came up for air in time to hear Perola address the guard.

"I am escorting Mr. Salles back to the hospital," she said efficiently.

The guard gave Mason a curious look, recoiled in disgust at the regurgitation, then scanned a list. "Salles, you say? I see no Salles."

"I called just a short time ago. You can check with Dona Moreira inside if you wish." They had obtained the name of the hospital's administrator earlier.

"Nah." He took another look at Mason and the vomit. "Okay." He ushered the car on through.

"Michael, you are sick! I should have known this. We should abandon this effort."

"No. I'm sorry about this. I'll clean it up."

The car crunched down a gravel driveway toward a parking lot on the side of the building. Perola located some rags in the trunk, and in a whirlwind of effort they cleaned the car as best they could.

Leaving Mason in the car, Perola marched up a short walkway and entered the building through the large front door. Mason stretched around in the car to glimpse the building's front, his stomach still quivering. His entire body shuddered in a feverish rush as he watched the door he had dreamed of so many times slowly open.

Perola disappeared for a few long seconds, then emerged pushing a wheelchair, which she negotiated down a metal ramp and wheeled to the car. A white-jacketed orderly appeared in the doorway and started to follow, but she dismissed him with a few crisp words. Unlocking the Fiat's back door, she pulled Mason out into the wheelchair. He lolled his head around, then quieted as she nosed the wheelchair back up the metal ramp until he sat only inches away from the door, the great, magnificent door of his dreams, now gilded gray in the twilight. Silently, Perola pushed it open.

The door yielded slowly, the entrance dark and inviting as always. Perola returned to the wheelchair to push him inside, leaving the opening yawning in front of him. For a moment he was suspended in the dream again, his legs unable to move, the pain back in his abdomen, his entire being consumed only by the desire to enter. Spittle rolled from his mouth.

A white-jacketed attendant brought him back to reality, her squat features and severe haircut stimulating a chill of recognition. "May I help you?" She addressed herself to Perola in a tone that suggested help was obviously needed.

"Yes, I am returning Mr. Salles," said Perola impatiently. "Is your supervisor in?"

"I am the supervisor," the squat woman replied. "I know no Mr. Salles."

"Well, there must be some mistake," Perola said in surprise. "I have just driven from Rio. Mr. Salles' physician was to have called earlier. Perhaps you have some message from the hospital in Rio?"

"Nothing I am aware of, but perhaps it came in only recently. If you would like to accompany me to my office, perhaps we can clear this up." This was the opening they were looking for. Mason lagged behind as Perola followed the supervisor down a short hallway. As they disappeared into an office, he whisked the wheelchair toward an open, recreational-type area. Four people occupied the room: a young white woman of about eighteen lying curled in a fetal position on a couch, an enormously fat black man leaning heavily on a fragile-looking broom, and two elderly black women sitting in front of a mute television screen, murmuring unintelligibly to one another.

The fat man looked up as Mason wheeled over to them. "I have seen you before, no?"

"Have you people ever heard of Zhézush da Bahia?" Mason asked breathlessly in the best Portuguese he could muster. Time was of the essence; Perola would be able to hold off the administration for only a few minutes.

The fat man looked at him blankly. The two older women resumed their chattering, the sound clacking like knitting needles in the cavernous room. Mason groaned inwardly, still numb from having actually entered the building. This had been a stupid idea. What had they hoped to accomplish? Conversations with the patients? They would probably end up in jail in the middle of nowhere. He should have come here alone, if at all, and not subjected Perola to this risk.

"I have heard of her." The silky voice emanated from the sofa. "Who has not? Maybe some of those around here." She gestured dismissively at the others in the room without looking up.

"I am told she had a sister," said Mason, glancing furtively back over his shoulder toward the administration office.

The girl wrinkled her face in what appeared to be a smile, still facing a wall opposite Mason. "Yeah." Silence ensued, broken only by the old ladies' muttering.

"Did you know this sister? Zelinda? Was that her name?"

"Yeah, I knew her. She was a patient here." The girl turned slowly to face Mason, revealing large sunken eyes in a skeletal face. Nausea and adrenaline burned again in Mason's throat. "Her name is not Zelinda." Again, silence.

"What happened to her?" Again, a look toward the administration office. Time was running out.

The girl shifted again, face back to the wall. Another excruciating silence. "She was taken away a week ago," she said finally.

"Carolina!" Mason jumped at the sound. A white-suited female orderly had crept unseen into the room behind him. "What are you talking about?"

The girl sprang from the couch, her sunken eyes wide and terrified.

"Who is this?" The orderly looked quizzically at Mason. "I have never seen you before. What are you talking with Carolina about?"

Mason shrugged his shoulders, providing Carolina an opportunity to dart from the room. The orderly gave chase, barking into a radio pulled from her back pocket. Heart pounding, Mason turned his wheelchair in the direction of the administration office. Another orderly rushed past to join in Carolina's pursuit. The old ladies in front of the TV continued cackling. The fat man looked on impassively. The door to the administrative office remained closed.

"Her name is Magdalena," came a whispered voice from behind him. He turned to see the fat man bearing down on him.

"Thank you," Mason whispered back. "How do you know she is Zhézush's sister? Did she tell you? Why was she here?"

The man grinned, a big, toothless grin exposing blackened gums. "No, she did not tell us. She is mute; she does not speak. We see it on the TV." He pointed in the direction of the other room. "We see that the woman performing the miracles is identical to our Magdalena. We know that they are sisters. Twins. Identical."

"But why . . ." Mason's whisper died out as the administration door opened to the sound of Perola's angry voice.

"Okay. I will return him to Rio!"

The fat man scurried back in the direction of the main room as the administrator stepped out of her office. Dona Moreira's gaze moved from Mason to the rotund form retreating down the hall. "What is going on here?" she hissed.

"We are leaving," shouted Perola, moving quickly to grab the back of Mason's wheelchair and propel him toward the door.

Dona Moreira darted into her office, and Perola shifted to a trot. As they reached the front door, an image painted above the door caught Mason's eye. A beast with seven heads—the same he had seen in the French monastery. His heart pounded wildly. He fought the urge to leap from the wheelchair.

"Quickly," Perola muttered as she attempted to negotiate the wheelchair ramp outside the front door. "Did you discover anything?"

Mason could hear shouts from the building's interior. "Yeah."

They reached the car, its interior still sour with vomit. Perola gunned the motor to life. Several white-suited attendants spilled from the building's front door, beckoning them to return. With a spray of gravel, Perola drove the old Fiat back to the front gate, disrupting a flock of ducks that had ventured into the car's path.

The sentry at the front gate loomed before them, evidently alerted, positioned in the middle of the roadway. With wide flaps of an arm he signaled for Perola to stop. To the sentry's left, the military personnel visible earlier scrambled to action.

Perola gunned the motor. The high-pitched revving further galvanized the soldiers, now twenty-five yards away, grasping weapons. The sentry hesitated for a moment, began to draw his pistol, thought better of it, and dove out of the way as the Fiat whined past in a curtain of dust and gravel. Ducking in the back seat, Mason heard the sound of automatic weapons being discharged. Perola yelled in excitement as the old car careened out of the hospital entranceway and toward the town square.

"Keep going!" Mason shouted, twisting in the seat in search of pursuit. "Holy shit. I'll bet every cop in southern Brazil will be looking for this car within minutes. Let's get back on the freeway. Maybe we can lose ourselves in the traffic."

"What did you discover?" Perola asked over the racket of the wound-out engine.

"You won't believe it. I can't believe it. I can't fucking believe it! Zhézush has a sister, all right. A twin sister. Who was housed at this Zelinda Hospital until a week ago."

"No!"

"So say a couple of the patients. Of course, they're crazy, right? I'm beginning to wonder about our own sanity, pulling this stunt. How did we think we'd get away with that?"

"I pondered the same question as I spoke with Dona Moreira." They reached the on-ramp to the freeway and darted back into the thick of the heavy traffic. "She was not easily fooled. I think she sensed something was up almost immediately. But we did it! Did you see the look on the face of that guard when I almost ran him over?" She rolled her head back and laughed.

Ordinarily he would have shared in her excitement. Instead, he felt spent and exhausted, as if the survivor of a violent illness. Disappointment closed in like a black curtain. "The whole damn thing's been a sham," he mumbled to himself after a few minutes. "From A to Z, manipulation, trickery, and deceit." He tilted his head back against the car seat and watched the headlights zoom by in the opposite lanes. "They planned this—someone did—secreting the mute sister—"

"She is mute?"

"Yeah. I mean, it's too bizarre, isn't it? It must be her—this Magdalena—we've been seeing as the resurrected Zhézush."

"No way. How could she sound exactly the same?"

"I don't know. I think they bring her out and somehow replay Zhézush's words. I thought it sounded different. In Rio no one was allowed close to the area where Zhézush stood, and she stayed in the shadows where the cameras could not get a full view. Maybe they have her lip-syncing, or something."

"There is another answer," Perola countered. "An equally bleak one. What if they killed this twin sister, so the original Zhézush could be said to return?"

Mason blanched. "I saw her shot," he stammered. "I touched the body in the morgue."

"But whose body? Couldn't they have swapped bodies between the stadium and the morgue?"

His stomach turned in on itself. "There is something else," he said huskily, when he could continue. "I saw a sign at the hospital. A depiction I have seen once before. Of evil." The words hung in the air like oil on water.

"So maybe your glimpse is not of God," Perola said quietly. "If this is true, we have the investigative story of all stories."

"I guess so." She was right. This was a reporter's dream—if they could produce any evidence, which they probably couldn't. Instead, he felt only despair, and a kind of desperate loneliness. He had caught himself almost believing this time, only to be dashed against the hard rocks of reality. Slumping in the car seat, he thought back to Zhézush, her words to him, the miracles he believed he had seen. And what of the dream? Somehow, he had been led to this—it couldn't be mere coincidence. The thought sent renewed shivers down his back. Then again, maybe there was no sister, maybe he had only fallen for the ravings of institutionalized nuts. Realistically, how much could he rely on anything said by any patient at a mental hospital? Still, what were the soldiers doing there? His mind swirled in a nauseous maelstrom.

"What are you thinking, Michael?"

"That I've been used. That I'm as far from the truth as I've ever been."

"If you have been used, so have millions of others. The beauty of it all is that perhaps now we have some knowledge to expose this for what it is and make things right. Have you considered that perhaps your dream led you to the truth? Instead of being angry, perhaps you should be grateful. Now, we know."

She was right, again. He looked over at her in the reflection of the oncoming headlights. At least maybe there would be some closure to the whole bizarre mess; at least the dream might be banished forever from his subconscious, the search temporarily closed. Still, his mind hung on a highwire. He would report to Rome—what?

"Do you feel any disappointment?" he asked. "Somehow I got the impression . . . I don't know, almost from the first time we spoke about her, that you thought she might be the one. That she might in fact be who she claimed to be. Don't you feel . . . regret that this is not so?"

She did not answer immediately. "I cannot anticipate the path of God," she said, finally. "Nor do I try. I said from the first that if Zhézush was not the Christ returned, she was truly a special being. I still believe that. I said a few moments ago that maybe now we know the truth. Well, we may know part of the truth, or we may be letting ourselves be fooled again. I doubt we will ever know everything. Our job, or at least my job as a reporter, is to report what I do know."

He smiled to himself in the darkness. These were words he should have said. Flexing the muscles in his shoulders, he sat up in his seat. The instinct for self-preservation had begun to feed energy back into his veins. "You know, we are likely the most hunted couple in Brazil. Dona Moreira has certainly been on the phone. The soldiers from the hospital will be pursuing. We need to abandon this car if we want to avoid being taken into custody." Left unsaid was what might happen if they were taken into custody.

"Yes. We need to stay alive." She pulled out the phone and punched in some numbers, holding the wheel with a knee. "Henrique, my father is sick," she said slowly and distinctly. "I will meet you in twenty minutes." She clicked off the phone.

"We have a signal," she explained somewhat sheepishly. "I have never used it before. Henrique will be concerned. We are to meet at a restaurant I know is safe."

"If we can get there." The traffic had worsened as they neared São Paulo, even with the benefit of ten lanes moving in either direction. Without warning, a siren blared behind them. Swirling blue lights engulfed the car. As they watched in panicked silence, a police car blew by in the median some four lanes over. Mason released his breath in a long gasp.

"We must get off the freeway. They will block this road."

Perola fought her way across multiple lanes to exit at the next interchange.

"Is there a subway line near here?" Mason ran his fingers through his hair again.

"I think so. Yes, there should be one at Vila Matilde."

"Can we make it to wherever we're going on the subway?"

"Yes."

Perola found a parking spot on the street near the subway entrance. They abandoned the Fiat, descending concrete steps into the station's spotless interior. Mason glanced behind for signs of pursuit. Nothing. Only a few people milled around the damp station: scattered businessmen reading newspapers, a pregnant mother scolding a young child, a fat policeman leaning on a rail conversing with an idle maintenance worker. Mason glanced at his watch, back to the station's street entrance, over to the policeman, then back to Perola.

"They must have planned it for a long time," he said in a low voice. "Whichever way they did it. To fool the world."

"Or at least fool us," Perola responded. "Is it the government?"

"Maybe. Certainly Elisabeth." The memory of her brown skin sent his head spinning. "Why would the government do this, though? I mean, if anything, this has contributed to the civil unrest. Maybe it's the military."

A rumble and screeching of brakes preceded the train's arrival. With a shudder the doors wrenched open. Perola and Mason entered, casting last looks back at the station entrance and the fat policeman still engrossed in conversation. As the doors flapped closed again, Mason caught sight of a figure hurrying down the station's entrance steps. A squat figure, dressed in black, with close-cropped black hair. A hood of some kind on the back of a black jacket. His heart skipped a beat. The train groaned in acceleration, clacking into a smooth whine as it gained speed.

"Did you see that?" Mason whispered to Perola, jerking his head back toward the lights of the station.

"What?"

"A Young Assistant. *Ajudante.* Whatever. She ran down the steps just as the train pulled out."

"Are you sure?"

"Absolutely."

"Do you think she was looking for us?"

"It seems odd she just appears out of nowhere."

"Did she see us?"

"I don't think so." Mason shivered and grasped his arms in the cool of the air-conditioning. "They give me the creeps, like they're everywhere and nowhere." He scanned a metro map on the car's wall. "I don't like the feeling of being hunted. I'd feel better if we were somewhere safe and out of sight."

"Like the U.S. Embassy?"

"Yeah, or the Church." He ran his hands again through his hair. "I hope it doesn't come to either. Maybe we're overreacting."

"Maybe. We can see what Henrique thinks. Maybe we should shave our heads or something, disguise ourselves." She laughed, a short, quirky laugh that quickly dissolved.

They changed trains at the central *Estação da Sé,* mixing with the crowds boarding the southbound line toward Liberdade and Vila Mariana. Groups of military personnel paced nervously in tight bands but generally let the crowd come and go. Mason and Perola edged, heads down, toward the center of the stream of commuters. As they waited on the next platform for the southbound train, Mason raised his head to chance a look around. Coming toward them along the platform marched a group of five black-clad, short-haired women, arms almost linked. Even from a distance he could see their eyes darting to and fro as they searched among the crowds.

"Oh, no." Perola saw them also.

"We gotta move. Come on!" Mason pulled her toward a stairwell away from the approaching women. They scrambled up the crowded stairs, almost knocking over a stooped old woman, and emerged into the cool breeze of early evening. A giant poster of Zhézush stood before them, flapping against the wall of a building across the street. It showed her eyes lifted skyward, mouth open as if seeking assistance.

"Wow. Where do you suppose that came from? The Zhézushians?"

Perola stood rooted for a moment. "I suppose. It is so . . . fast." She recovered herself quickly. "This way." She pulled Mason toward a sidewalk on Avenida 23 de Maio, stopped, and hailed a taxi with a practiced wave. They clambered in and she gave the driver the address. With a grunt and a flick of the steering wheel he roared away from the curb. Upscale São Paulo played out before them in a flash of hills, trees, neon, and people.

Perola pulled out her phone and punched in some numbers. "A message from Aide. She wants to meet." Mason could hear the rattle of the recorded message through the earpiece. "A message from my friend in Rio. Apparently a public transportation strike begins there tomorrow. There is talk it may spread to São Paulo." She snapped the phone shut and stared out the window. "Do you think I should return Aide's call?"

"Probably. Let's make sure it's from a safe phone. I wouldn't divulge anything about Zelinda. Let's see what she has to say."

The taxi driver pulled onto a side street and stopped in front of a small restaurant advertising itself as the Mona Lisa. Mason paid the driver, who pulled into a quick U-turn. Inside, they found Henrique conversing with a tall man with a bushy mustache who looked to be the proprietor. Still clad in his uniform, Henrique rose to meet them, concern showing on his face.

"What happened?" he asked anxiously as he embraced Perola.

"We will fill you in," she responded quietly. "Shall we sit down?"

Over a bottle of wine Perola told Henrique of their discoveries in Zelinda and the apparent pursuit by the *ajudantes* and the military. "I am frightened, Henrique, truly frightened," she finished, wrapping her fingers around the stem of the wine glass. "These people know who I am, where I live, who you are, what you do, everything. I do not believe the three of us are safe."

"What would you have me do?" asked Henrique, arms outstretched. "I cannot just walk off my job. I must stay, even if it becomes civil war." He smiled, the big, white-toothed shark smile. "Danger is part of my job."

Mason pressed his lips together. "As it is ours, at times. We need to get the word out. I need to contact New York. Do we have enough to go on?" He looked at Perola. "We still need *proof*."

She nodded her agreement, then turned to Henrique. "We have talked about seeking refuge at the embassy or the Church, if things get too dangerous."

"I do not seek to minimize what you have told me," Henrique said carefully. "At this point, anything is possible. My advice is to lie low for several days, see what happens. São Paulo is a massive city; it is the perfect place to hide. If they are after you as you suspect, they will expect you to head for the embassy or the Church. You must go elsewhere. In the meantime, I will keep my ear to the ground, as you say, and let you know what I hear. If they are coming after me, I will know soon enough. I think I am quick enough to dodge them."

"Where should we go?" asked Perola. "Obviously, the apartment is out. I would think a hotel room is not appropriate."

"What about your friend Margarida, up in Liberdade? She is close to downtown. You could probably walk from here, even. She would be glad to do it, yes?"

"Yes, yes, that would be good."

Their food came, great heaping portions of steaming pasta and vegetables. Mason ate ravenously, as if freed from a long sickness.

"Use the phone at Margarida's, not your cell phone," said Henrique between mouthfuls. "Be careful. Do not call the house to check your messages. And whatever you do, do not call me at the station. If you need to get in touch with me, leave a message on my other machine. I will check it frequently."

"I received a message from Aide, from the Zhézushians," Perola said in a halting voice. "Should I return it?"

"Yes, but again, be careful." Henrique's voice was calm and firm. "That could easily be a trap. When was the last time you spoke to her?"

"Several days ago."

"I would call her from a pay phone. If she wants to meet, stall her. We would need to think of a proper place. That may be difficult. Antonio!" He summoned the maitre d' over and obtained a mobile phone. "Do you know Margarida's number?" he asked Perola.

Margarida was happy to house them for several days, at first assuming Perola had left Henrique. Only a fierce denial and partial explanation of the situation convinced her otherwise.

"We will walk to her house and find a pay phone on the way to call Aide," Perola announced, strength returning to her voice. She grasped

Henrique's hand as they stood to leave. "Please. Take no chances. If they are coming, get out."

"Be careful." The shark's smile flashed again, and as they stepped outside the restaurant he kissed Perola lightly on the cheek. Then with a wave he was gone into the night, the patrol car's lights disappearing down the narrow alley.

Returning to the lights and bluster of Avenida 23 de Maio, they waded into the river of northbound pedestrian traffic and its cloak of anonymity. The great ant hill that was São Paulo churned with activity—cars, noise, smog, bicycles, people, litter. Horns barked, vendors squawked. Military personnel gathered in the traffic arteries. Perola kept her hands thrust in her pockets, her head down, her peripheral vision alert for black-jacketed *ajudantes.* After several blocks, she spotted a bank of pay phones and nudged Mason toward them. He remained in a nearby shadow as she inserted her phone card to make the call.

A man's voice she did not recognize answered the phone on the second ring. A few seconds later, Aide's husky whisper filled the receiver.

"How do I know that it is you? Give me some sign. Tell me something that only you would know."

Stumped momentarily, Perola allowed the phone line to evaporate into silence. "The day you entered my apartment, I was wearing a yellow robe."

Further silence. "So you were," came the whisper finally. "So it is you. The rumor on the street is that you are dead." Perola gulped, acid churning in the pit of her stomach. "It is not safe that we talk on the phone," Aide continued. "We must meet."

"That may be difficult," Perola responded. "What did you have in mind?"

"The place where we first met. Do you remember it?"

"Yes. I have been there recently. It is not safe."

"I know. But I will leave a message there under a blue flowerpot four doors down. It will specify the place. Pick it up by six A.M." With a click the line disconnected.

Perola hung up the phone and ventured back onto the sidewalk, where Mason rejoined her. "Let's get out of here," he whispered. They fell back into the pedestrian flow.

"Well, what did she say?"

Perola glanced around nervously. "Wait until we get to Margarida's, okay?" she whispered. Another trip into the *favela* to pick up a note? The prospect seemed particularly uninviting.

Another fifteen minutes of maneuvering through streams of pedestrians and automobiles. Exhaustion crept in behind her eyes. Despite the full dinner, her stomach rippled and rumbled. By the time they reached their destination, her thoughts centered only on sleep.

Margarida was a gray-haired, sprightly woman of about fifty, a former co-worker at the *Noticias* newspaper. She ushered them into her elegantly furnished apartment, where soft classical music played in the background and a hyperactive dachshund ran in circles.

"I want to know everything," Margarida exclaimed in Portuguese when they were seated, clasping her hands in front of her. "You were so mysterious on the phone. Are you sure you and Henrique are okay? With this handsome man along with you, no?"

"No, no," Perola replied, shaking her head definitively. She introduced Mason. "I guess I should start at the beginning." She told Margarida the entire story, including a description of the events in Zelinda. The monologue went on for twenty minutes, long enough for a serving of pungent coffee and large sweet rolls. She finished with a description of her conversation with Aide.

"She wants me to go pick up this message in Bras," Perola explained. "The same place where just days ago I saw soldiers. I am concerned about this. But the conversation seemed genuine. She did not want at first to believe it was me."

Margarida reclined in her chair, as if knocked backward by the force of the story. "This is truly . . . unbelievable."

Mason's gaze shifted to Perola. Even through the haze of fatigue, she could tell what he was thinking: had they divulged the story of all stories to a competing journalist? She shook her head definitively. Margarida was beyond trust.

"What is to become of our country?" Margarida asked Perola plaintively. "This craziness—the military is everywhere, this Zhézush, and now you tell me it is all a fraud!" She swung her legs underneath her and reached into a leather pouch for a cigarette. "It saddens me, for I fear that we are poised before an abyss into which we are destined to fall." A plume of smoke wafted its way toward the ceiling. "I have an idea, though, about your rendezvous. I have a neighbor, a teenage boy who sometimes does errands for me. Kind of a tough guy. I think he could be hired to pick this up for you. You want me to call him?"

Mason and Perola looked at one another and shrugged simultaneously. "I hate to bring someone else into this," Perola said, her chin resting in her hand, "but I dread the thought of going there myself."

"Nonsense," said Margarida, reaching for the phone. "This kid is in Bras all the time. It is nothing for him. He will be much safer than you. I will insist he be careful." She barked a few commands into the mouthpiece, then pasted the bright smile back onto her face. "Not to be too mysterious, but perhaps you two should not be here when he arrives; you know, so he does not know of you. If you will describe the location carefully to me, I will relay it to him."

Perola drew a map, then withdrew with Mason into a small den cluttered with knickknacks. A few minutes later a rap came at the door, and they heard Margarida's muffled instructions. A soft voice. More instructions from Margarida. Then the squeaky hinges and the gentle catch and pull of a deadbolt.

Mason reached Rhodes at home.

"Where the hell have you been? I've been trying to get you all day. You don't fucking call anymore?"

Mason relayed the situation, and Rhodes calmed. "Of course it was all bullshit. Didn't I tell you from the first moment? But good work. I'm gonna tie in Lanny, okay?" Lanny Briscoe was an assistant managing editor. "Hold on a minute."

Lanny's Midwestern twang filled the line a few minutes later, and Rhodes brought him up to speed. "Can you get a story out tonight?"

asked Rhodes plaintively.

Mason signed. "I'll see what I can do. I'm exhausted."

"Get me something tomorrow. Shit, if something happens to you, what have we got?"

"Not a damn thing!" Mason snarled, conscious of his rising voice in Margarida's serene apartment. "I'll call tomorrow." He slammed down the phone. Let Rhodes and the others come down and risk their lives on the front line and see how they liked it. He groaned and rubbed his temples, then returned to the living room. The conversation had given him a headache.

Margarida and Perola sat in front of a small television set jammed in one corner of the room. Footage of the strike-related traffic jams in Rio played across the screen, the blaring of car horns audible behind the announcer's voice.

"The strike is expected to hit São Paulo tomorrow," Margarida said ruefully, turning to him. "I remember the last time. The entire city shut down." She sighed, crossing her legs.

Perola lounged on a sofa, her eyes heavy with sleep. "I think I am too old for this," she said softly. "I was shot at today! Then chased by these . . . these people." Shivering, she pulled a blanket around herself. "Now strikes and more turmoil." She closed her eyes.

"Do you want to lie down?" Margarida asked Mason.

"Ah, no. Thanks. I think I'll stay up and watch TV for a little while." Margarida disappeared back into the kitchen area. Mason looked over at Perola, fast asleep now, shook himself, and pulled out the laptop. Perola hadn't flinched at carrying out the nurse charade, crazy and risky as it had been, nor had she complained about the danger they had been thrust into or its inconveniences. Her probing questions had made him reexamine things about himself he hadn't thought about in years. The more he was around her, the more he realized how truly remarkable she was.

Margarida returned a few minutes later with some warm bread and more coffee, which he gratefully accepted. She returned silently to the back of the apartment, leaving him alone with Perola and the television. He began to pound out the makings of a story, only to reconfirm what little they had: the words of a dying Bahian woman, a confirmation from patients at a mental hospital. With the flick of a button and the use of Margarida's phone line, he sent a copy of the draft to Rome, including a brief description of the drawing of the beast at the mental hospital. No matter what Rhodes wanted, there wasn't enough here to justify their conclusions. They needed something definitive, like a picture of Magdalena and Zhézush together, copies of records showing residence at Zelinda, or best of all, evidence of lip-syncing fraud at another Zhézushian appearance. Chewing his lip, he pondered how they might pull off such a thing. If they knew in advance where she was to appear, maybe a high-powered telescope with a camera or . . . ?

A rap at the apartment door jolted Mason to his feet. Pulling a groggy Perola with him toward the kitchen, he glanced at his watch: one-fifteen. Margarida passed them on the way to the door. He heard the chain unlatch, the rapid prattle of a youthful voice, followed by Margarida's smoother tone. She reappeared in the kitchen a few moments later holding a folded blue envelope, which she gave to Perola.

"Well?" Mason asked impatiently as Perola scanned the paper underneath a broad lamp.

"She wants to meet in front of the *Igreja de Santo Antonio* at six in the morning." She glanced at her watch.

"Where is that?" Mason scanned the scrawled message.

"Not far from here. Did the boy have any problems?" She squinted at Margarida from underneath the lamp.

"No. He said there is much activity in the area, many military. He says he is quiet as a mouse and dark as a shadow. It is good you did not go yourself."

The phone rang shrilly, startling them all. Margarida answered it on the third ring. Relief quickly showed in her face.

"It's Henrique!" she whispered to Perola, cupping the phone.

Perola cradled the phone as if it were an infant, muttering only monosyllables at first, then unleashing a torrent of words and tears. She relayed the contents of the message received by the neighbor boy. Should she go to meet Aide? The receiver buzzed in response. After a few moments, she said goodbye and replaced the receiver, then relayed the conversation.

Henrique had been calling from a pay phone near the apartment. He knew the *Igreja de Santo Antonio* well—a wide plaza affording maximum visibility and little opportunity to hide. He would swing by the place now, again about an hour before the scheduled rendezvous. If everything looked good, he would call Margarida's a half hour or so before six and let the phone ring three times only. If for some reason they did not hear from him or the phone rang only twice, that would be the signal to stay put. In the meantime, she was to get some rest.

They sat looking at one another, wide-eyed with fear and fatigue, until Mason suggested that they follow Henrique's advice and try to sleep. He lay down on a sofa in a spare bedroom. Margarida returned to her room. Perola busied herself in the bathroom, where the sound of the running water failed to mask her sobs.

19

For the time *is come* that judgment must begin at the house of God: and if *it* first *begin* at us, what shall the end *be* of them that obey not the gospel of God?

I Peter 4:17

The ringing phone again. One ring and Mason sprang out of half-sleep. "Don't pick it up," he hissed in the direction of Margarida's bedroom door. Two rings and he was on his feet. The luminescent clock on the table in the room where he had dozed off glowed 5:25. Three rings, then silence. The coast was clear.

Margarida emerged from her room, a robe partially draped around her shoulders. "Shall I make you coffee?"

"No, there isn't time."

"Ready?" Perola appeared in the hallway, her voice husky from lack of sleep. She shrugged on her jacket. "You must not come, Michael. They will be looking for the two of us. It would be better if I go alone."

"No way. I'll follow from a distance, if you want, but I'm coming."

"Michael, why endanger yourself? You do not know the city. If something happens to me, at least you can continue."

He shook his head. "Let's go."

He followed her out of the warmth of the apartment into the cool of a foggy early morning. They zigzagged a course paralleling Avenida 23 de Maio, strangely quiet now that the crowds from the evening before had dissipated. Only the grind of truck engines and the clank of early morning deliveries broke the calm. Here and there a voice cut through the mist.

Scattered car lights pierced the fog, their beams miniature searchlights bouncing up and down. Mason and Perola stayed in the shadows, edging around a homeless woman asleep on a step, skirting past a pot-bellied man walking a poodle on a leash. No sign of the military, which Mason knew must be ensconced in the main thoroughfares or manning transportation links in anticipation of the strike.

"Come on!" Perola whispered, navigating somehow in the darkness.

He fought back an urge to hold her hand, to pull her back toward him. Instead, they pressed on, moisture melting on their faces, turning their hair matted and wet. A gray streetlight. Another turn in the fog.

Something skittered by Mason's leg, eyes glowing green for an instant then gone. A kid raced by on a bicycle; how could he see in this stuff? Perola stopped for a second, hesitated, then pressed ahead again. Mason glanced at his watch: 5:50. They were almost at a run, his breathing heavy. He felt sweat mixing with the moisture on his forehead. They rounded a corner, and a plaza appeared in front of them, the outlines of a church visible beyond it until an impenetrable wave of fog obscured the view.

"You should probably stay here," Perola whispered, turning in a circle as she scanned the shadows. The fog shifted, exposing the church again, then redraping it in curtains of gray. "I thought I saw a figure in front of the church," she breathed to Mason, her white teeth visible even in the darkness. "Wish me luck." She vanished, swallowed whole by the fog. He caught sight of her once more as she moved toward the church, the breeze latching onto her damp hair so that she seemed to float like a ghost. Mason shivered and looked skyward, where the first glint of pink showed through the fog.

Perola advanced toward the church's entrance as the breeze grew stronger. Fear clawed her stomach and rasped in her breath. The clip-clop of her footsteps on the concrete plaza echoed like thunder. The figure she thought she had seen earlier stood straighter as she grew nearer, and by thirty yards away she recognized Aide's thin shape. Looking to her right, then left, Perola searched for others, friend or foe. Aide's gaze locked with hers at ten yards.

"You are alone," came the low rumble of Aide's voice. It was more of a statement than a question.

"Yes, and you?"

"More than you can imagine." Aide smiled wanly. "Come. Sit. We have much to discuss and little time. Things are dangerous." She motioned to a small bench in the shadows of the cathedral's door.

"You have seen Zhézush?" asked Aide softly.

"Only from a distance."

"And?"

Perola peered at her through the mist. "And, what?"

"Is it she? The messiah resurrected?"

"I am unsure. She certainly looks the same, but . . . I cannot tell. I think something is different." Perola swallowed uncomfortably. "I have tried to get in touch with you. I went to the house where we first met. All I found were soldiers. No sign of the Zhézushians. No calls. No word."

Aide laughed softly, the sound tinged with bitterness. "I do not believe this woman is our resurrected messiah," she said quietly. "I too have seen her only from a distance, but I have seen the military only too closely. They have been everywhere, questioning our people, taking them away. We have been hunted like stray dogs. I escaped only by hiding in a basement for several days. We have had no contact from Zhézush or Elisabeth. Zero." She spat onto the stone flagstaffs, anguish evident in her thin face. The morning light had begun to brighten the fog, rendering it even more opaque.

"What about the posters of Zhézush? I saw several last night."

"I do not know who has produced them. No one in our group."

Perola hesitated, then relayed the events at Zelinda. When she had finished, Aide sat silently, then fished a long cigarette out of a tattered pocket. A butane lighter flashed and then extinguished. She puffed on the cigarette for several minutes without saying anything, the smoke merging with the fog.

"I do not know what to believe anymore," she said sadly. "I only know I will follow Zhézush wherever she leads. I must go now." She stood and stretched, sending the ember flying into the darkness. "Where will you be?"

"I do not know. We may attempt to leave the country if things get out of control. And you?"

Aide stared out into the fog. "Everywhere I can," she said slowly. She turned back to face Perola. "A small group is meeting later this morning, about nine. Come and bring your friend, but take care. Go to the Y, ask for Emmanuel. Tell him you have vegetables. He will lead you to us. Also, here are several numbers." She handled Perola a crinkled slip of paper. "Can you memorize these quickly?"

Perola peered at the numbers and nodded.

"Call only from a pay phone that takes coins," Aide whispered. She kissed Perola lightly on the cheek, her lips as cool as the morning air. "You and I are in much danger. We know the truth, and they know this. We are liabilities that must be crushed." She paused to wipe moisture from her long nose. "Take much care," she said again, softly, then disappeared into the fog.

Perola looked around for signs of a trap. Betrayed by a kiss? She started back in the direction in which she had left Mason, then broke into a run, her footsteps clattering again on the concrete plaza.

Mason was not where she had left him. Her breath came in great heaves. Something clutched her arm, and she screamed in spite of herself, a piercing wail that knifed through the mist. Knees buckling under her, she turned to face her attacker.

"Sorry! I didn't mean to frighten you." Mason's familiar voice was a mere whisper. "I didn't want to take the chance of yelling your name across the plaza." They peered into the gloom for signs of anyone who might have been alerted by the noise. Only the distant sounds of the city interrupted the quiet, and nothing moved save the shifting fog curtains. The sky had lightened considerably, but the mist and fog remained thick.

"Let's get out of here, okay?" Mason whispered. "I thought I heard something earlier. I don't want to wait around to find out what it is. Are you okay?"

Composure somewhat regained, Perola straightened. "Yes. Follow me." Squaring her shoulders, she started back toward Margarida's.

They had taken only a few steps when a large, dark figure emerged from the fog directly in their path. This time, Perola emitted only a small yelp, backpedaling immediately.

"Perola!" Henrique's voice was calm and smooth as always, and she melted toward it with a surge of emotion. "Come, we must go," he said urgently. "It is no longer safe here."

The three of them hurried down an alleyway made briefly visible through a break in the fog. They did not see a dark figure that followed at length behind them, its face obscured by a black hood drawn up against the cool mist.

Back in the safety of Margarida's apartment, they sipped strong, wonderful coffee and plotted what to do next.

"Have you seen these?" asked Henrique, producing a leaflet from his pocket. Neat, symmetrical type proclaimed a rally in support of the transportation strikers to be held at 5:00 P.M. at the *Viaduto do Chá.* A sentence near the bottom of the page galvanized their attention: "Our resurrected savior Jesus Christ is expected to participate in a show of support for the strikers."

Perola looked at Mason. "I will be surprised if the government permits this. Things are too tense, the potential for violence too great." She reached to turn on the TV. "Should we meet with the Zhézushians?"

Henrique sighed and stirred his coffee. "It is dangerous everywhere. You are most certainly wanted. Yet, the number of police and military stationed in Bras is limited. We are protecting the assets, not the slums." He grinned wryly.

"I say we have to do it," Mason cut in. "I'm not ready to give up and head for the border just yet. We would be smart to plot an escape route, but in the meantime I say we do our jobs." The morning TV news was delayed in coming on, apparently preempted by an unusually lengthy weather report. The forecast was for overcast skies and rain later in the evening.

"In terms of leaving the country," Henrique continued, "I believe smuggling you into an embassy will be anticipated, and therefore difficult. There are, of course, hundreds of churches in which to seek refuge, but are you really safe there? It seems to me the better way would be to try to run the Argentine or Paraguayan border. There are back roads that are not well monitored. I have the four-wheel-drive vehicle. If we could get out of the city, I think that would be the best bet."

Official-sounding music blared on the TV, and the image shifted abruptly from the beleaguered weatherman to that of a man in a blue suit seated behind a large table, flanked by flags.

"Governor Melo of São Paulo," Perola whispered for Mason's benefit.

"The government of the State of São Paulo, working with the mayor's office and . . ." Mason could not understand the next few words ". . . have agreed to impose a curfew for the City of São Paulo, effective at four o'clock this afternoon. Anyone found outside after such hour, except on emergency business, will be subject to detention and interrogation."

"How can they do this?" hissed Perola. "The legislature has not acted. What power has Melo to do this?" The image shifted back to normal programming, a morning children's show. Perola flipped the channel, searching for more news.

"I am not sure, but it looks like he has done it," Henrique said. "It may be all the more important that you meet with Aide." The others nodded in agreement. "Unfortunately, I do not think I can accompany you. I must return to work."

"Have you slept?" asked Perola, concern in her voice.

"I have slept enough." The shark's grin flashed as he pulled on his coat. Perola followed him to the door. "You know how to reach me," he said softly, almost inaudibly. He kissed her lightly, then more fiercely. Mason turned away.

The door slammed. Henrique was gone. Perola stood alone in the vestibule, her arms wrapped around herself.

The Y was even more crowded than when Perola had interviewed Moraes only days before. Trash still blew among the few straggly trees and overturned appliances, but the crunch of humanity had stilled, as if a wandering herd of range animals had stopped to graze. A threatening ceiling of low-lying clouds magnified the crowd's noise. Perola had to shout to make herself heard. "Who do you suppose we ask about this Emmanuel?"

Mason shrugged his shoulders. They had made it to Bras without incident, having hitched a ride in the back of Margarida's mammoth Buick for most of the way before covering the final distance on foot. The effects of the public transportation strike were already being felt, as travel by automobile had ground almost completely to a halt. Signs of military or other authority diminished as they edged further into the *favela.*

"How about this guy?" Mason pointed in the direction of an enormously fat man seated on an upside-down crate.

"Excuse me, sir, do you know Emmanuel?" Perola asked politely. "We have vegetables for him."

The man eyed her impassively from watery, red-rimmed eyes. He jerked his elephantine neck in the direction of a group of women standing nearby. "You mean that Emmanuel." It was more of a statement than a question.

Out of the middle of the pack of women bounded a lighter-skinned young boy, eyes spaced far apart, his forehead chromosomally oversized. Perola recognized him immediately.

"I have come to lead you," he said in an odd, chirpy voice. "Please follow."

The boy led them through a rabbit's warren of nooks and holes, eventually ending up on the far side of the Y. He scurried down the road, muttering happily to himself, his arms in such constant, comical motion it looked as if he was trying to lift his stout body into flight. After a time he darted into a dirty alleyway, dodging beneath flapping laundry and over a makeshift plywood bridge spanning a trickle of foul-smelling liquid. They emerged into a small plaza fronting an ancient-looking building identified by faded lettering at its top as some sort of school. Emmanuel pulled open the partially unhinged door and ushered them inside.

The building's interior resembled a big barn, with wooden rafters stretching to a dimly lit ceiling and a narrow balcony of sorts running the length of one wall. Down below was an area which had apparently been used as a bar. The floor was a polished linoleum, the only thing in the establishment that appeared relatively new. The place smelled of dust, beer, and urine.

"This is a *quadra,*" Perola whispered, "the building housing a *samba* school. They train here for the Carnival. Long ago, when the Catholic officials expressed displeasure with the dancing and music blacks wanted to include as part of their religious services, separate organizations developed, the forerunners to these schools. Today, every community, particularly every black community, has a *samba* school."

Emmanuel ran toward a group of people gathered on one side of the building and plopped into their midst. Perola recognized the familiar faces of the Zhézushians: Vicente, his head wrapped in a large gauze bandage; Velda, her jaws working vigorously on an overmatched piece of chewing gum; and Aide, wrapped tightly in a blanket as if somehow chilled in the stuffy room. Others materialized on the balcony, apparently serving as lookouts. A large, muscular man closed the door behind them and pushed a big wooden deadbolt against it.

Aide stood to greet them. "Welcome," she said in a low voice. She gestured for them to find a seat on the floor with the others.

"I have disclosed to those present the information you provided me," she said to Perola. "It fits with the remainder of our puzzling knowledge. Why would our Lord appear to so many, but not to her faithful? We believe this lookalike person or sister or whatever lives and is being used and manipulated for evil purposes, but we have no proof. We must decide what we can do to assure ourselves, although some are already convinced." She resumed her seat, wrapping the blanket back around herself.

Vicente stood, his bandage flapping like a flag. "We must expose this deception. We have all seen the fliers—Zhézush is scheduled to appear at the rally at the *Viaduto do Chá* this afternoon. I believe we should find a way to display this fraud to the world. This will be our chance!" He swung his arms for emphasis, threatening to upset the turbanlike gauze on his head.

"What would you have us do?" asked Aide.

"Will it not be dangerous?" chimed in someone else.

"Of course it will be dangerous," Vicente sneered. "But in terms of service to our Lord, what more could one be asked? Exposure of this deception spreads our message of truth. Nothing must stop that."

"So, what is your plan?" Aide seemed impatient.

"I do not have it firmly formulated," Vicente admitted. "But it would seem that somehow we must put this imposter in the position of actually having to speak to us, to allow us to confront her. We must deny her the ability to utilize prerecorded messages and the like."

"But how?"

"We should infiltrate the secured area and assassinate the infidel!" This from an elderly man clad in a faded golden robe.

The room erupted in shouts of disapproval.

"Zhézush is love, not violence!" gasped Aide. Others nodded vigorously in agreement.

"We do not even know for certain it is not her," exclaimed a dark woman, her hair piled on top of her head. "Maybe she has her reasons for not appearing to us, perhaps to test our faith."

Muttering and shuffling disagreement filled the room.

"What has happened to the *ajudantes*?" asked Perola above the noise. The room plunged into silence.

Aide eventually answered, discomfort evident on her thin face. "We do not know. The *ajudantes* have always been a separate group. They were recruited by Elisabeth personally, and while they have attended our meetings and worked closely with us, their loyalty appears to be with Elisabeth. It is amazing because it seems they have multiplied into a vast number. During the period after our savior was killed, we mourned together and planned for the return. You were with us, you saw their presence at the cathedral when we awaited Zhézush's reappearance. We all went to the *Viaduto do Chá* together and rejoiced upon the wondrous news. But in the days that followed, when we received no contact, some of us expressed doubts. When these were shared with some of the *ajudantes*, we were looked upon almost as heretics. Perhaps they have been misled, as have so many others."

"And Elisabeth?"

Another long silence. "She is either the right hand of God, or she represents evil in its absolute form," Aide finally answered. "None of us has spoken to her since the cremation. Some believe she has a political agenda." She gestured around the room.

Mason shuddered. The sickening realization he had fought to exclude entered his stomach. Had his lust driven him past truth, to despair? He struggled to clear his mind. "I have an idea," he said, glancing from Perola to Vicente. "But first, do we expect that a rally and an appearance by Zhézush will actually take place, given the curfew imposed this morning?"

The room's clear consensus was that the rally would proceed despite the curfew. "The police and military, powerful as they are, cannot stop crowds of this size," affirmed a thin man emphatically.

"If people could see that this woman is not actually uttering the words they hear, that would go a long way to proving to ourselves and to the world this is not the returned messiah. There are two things we need—one is a telescopic camera, the other a diversion. The majority of those actually in the crowd, including ourselves, will not be close enough to detect the fraud. However, a camera could tell."

"But how can this diversion be achieved?" asked Vicente. "What you suggest requires a closeness that will be impossible with the security detail."

"I don't think it needs to be extremely close," Mason said. "Only enough to cause the imposter and the others to fall off stride. It may not even be necessary. If this woman is really just lip-syncing to the recorded words of Zhézush, how close could she be? Maybe she's a savant or something, but she's been in a mental institution, for God's sake. And I am still not sure this isn't the original Zhézush. But a diversion would at least partially resolve this issue for us. And if we could capture a charade on film, well . . ."

"But how would the diversion work?" Aide asked.

"My thought was that something like a smoke bomb would do it, if strategically placed. Harmless, but disrupting."

"And where would we get that?"

Mason looked at Perola. "Can Henrique help us?"

"Possibly. If I can get in touch with him." She looked coldly at Mason. "I do not like to drag him into this."

"What about the camera?" asked Vicente, more animated now.

"I think perhaps I can help there too," Perola said softly. "It is odd, no, that the newspaper reporters want it captured on film to prove a point?" She laughed softly. "I can take care of the camera."

"If we can capture this on film, will it not also be seen on TV?" asked Aide.

"Possibly," Mason admitted. "If so, so much the better—that way millions see it immediately. I have a feeling, though, that it will take more sophistication than that, that they will have the imposter behind some sort of reflecting glass or something so that the ordinary viewer will not be able to catch this right off."

"I think your plan is worth a try," said Aide. "We have little to lose. If you can procure the smoke device, we should be able to take care of planting it in the crowd. Maybe then we can assure ourselves, huh?" She smiled at Mason, a thin, unenthusiastic effort, then turned to Perola. "You know how to contact us. You remember the numbers? Take good care. Go in peace."

20

For false Christs and false prophets shall rise, and
shall shew signs and wonders, to seduce, if
it were possible, even the elect.
Mark 13:22

The Zhézushians had been right. The rally would be held despite the curfew. A mob had overrun the *Viaduto do Chá* shortly before five, melting over and around the government's anticipatory defenses. Wisely retreating in the face of the onslaught, the troops had held their fire, forcing the crowd flow into preconceived directions like water through a sieve. From his perch in a window of a nearby apartment building, Mason detected no recognizable media coverage. He spotted several handheld video cameras in the surging crowd, but so did the security forces. As he watched, one cameraman was escorted away; uniformed officers pursued another beyond Mason's vision.

Of course, other media sources could have had the same foresight to rent an apartment with a clear view of the plaza. Stretching back in his chair, Mason surveyed the scene below. The cameraman Perola had engaged aimed his video camera at the back of a flatbed truck parked at one end of the plaza. Large Plexiglas plates were draped across the truck bed like oriental screens. Bulletproof glass? Nothing behind them yet, but perhaps that was the point. He was willing to bet their purpose was more for obfuscation than protection. At the cameraman's suggestion, he peered through the viewfinder to get an idea of the picture available if and when Zhézush/Magdalena appeared. As near as he could tell, the Plexiglas did obscure the view, but probably not fatally.

Mason fidgeted and looked at his watch. The flare Henrique had obtained was to be set off within one minute of when Zhézush began speaking. Perola had insisted on being on the ground, to better enable her to report on the rally as a whole. He would stay with the camera.

If their ruse worked, what would they do? He hadn't spent much time pondering that question. Probably try to smuggle the tape to New York, let the guys there analyze and string the proof together. On the other hand, maybe the only proof uncovered would be that Zhézush had in fact returned, or never left. He pondered the possibilities, trying to gauge what his reaction would be. He felt detached from it all, up in a window, safely above the fray. He would rather be on the ground with Perola.

The transportation strike had essentially ground the city to a halt. No buses ran, no subway trains moved, even a number of taxi drivers had stayed home. The resulting gridlock had begun early, and by mid-morning a number of drivers had simply given up and walked away from automobiles rendered useless. Others had simply opted not to venture into work at all, but instead used bicycles, motorbikes, or feet to move downtown. The city appeared to be awash in enough military personnel to invade a neighboring country, but the soldiers mingled peacefully with the hordes, futilely encouraging traffic to move enough to reposition military vehicles.

By about 3:00 P.M., handheld and truck-mounted loudspeakers had begun broadcasting the government's curfew edict, directing that the streets be cleared. Surprisingly, even the traffic seemed to comply, for within an hour the streets were nearly clear and the military patrols more pronounced. Tanks became visible along the southern end of the plaza and along the freeways below. Then, as if from a bottle unplugged, the flow of humanity surged to the viaduct. From his perch in the apartment window overlooking the *Viaduto do Chá,* Mason estimated the rippling and teeming crowd at over fifty thousand and growing. They looked like insects set to devour a field.

Five o'clock came and passed. The crowd grew restless; the military hunched into its positions. Finally, at about twenty minutes past, a familiar dark figure mounted the truck bed, followed by two others. Mason trained his binoculars on the trio, partially visible through the Plexiglas screens. Zhézush, Elisabeth, and another woman he did not recognize.

"How much can you see?" he asked the cameraman. The view through the binoculars did not show a particularly clear image of the subjects' faces.

"Okay. Want to look?"

Mason peered through the viewfinder. The camera lens was stronger than the binoculars, the image clearer. "I think this'll do it." His voice caught in a watery gasp.

The crowd's chant surged through the partially opened window. A drumbeat began somewhere in its midst, triggering a concomitant swaying and a rhythmic stomping of feet. After several moments, the large figure raised her hands in the air, and the noise ceased as abruptly as water turned off from a spigot.

The melodic voice rolled across the plaza. "My people!" Mason refocused the binoculars on the figure's face. The lips were moving, but the image was not near clear enough to track against the words echoing through the hushed masses.

"May I take a look again?" he whispered to the camerman.

"God is love! I am love! I am yours!" Seen through the viewfinder, the lips moved much more clearly, tracking the words perfectly. A sinking feeling settled into the pit of his stomach. Had they jumped to preposterous conclusions? He glanced at his watch—only a few seconds to go until the planned detonation of the smoke bomb.

He sat back from the camera, his hands trembling. What would the smoke do? Would people panic? Would others be hurt? They hadn't really considered these things in the zeal to know and expose. A violent spasm shook through him. He wanted to call the whole thing off, to let things play out as they would, to report the news, not manipulate . . .

A slight whooshing sound carried across the plaza, followed by a small plume of smoke emitted from the center of the crowd. Seconds later, a flare burst brightly overhead, surprisingly visible against the late-afternoon haze. Necks craned momentarily skyward, while Zhézush's words continued to pour out across the plaza. Mason grabbed the binoculars.

The lips had ceased moving. The sound of Zhézush's words also ceased, but not fast enough.

"We were right!" Mason shouted. "You got it all?"

The camerman nodded. "I think so."

The sound of Zhézush's renewed words lulled the buzzing crowd back into silence. Mason picked up the binoculars. Magdalena/Zhézush's lips had resumed moving to the sound—a fairly adroit recovery—probably enough so no one would notice, except someone looking for it.

"Let us thank God for all that we have . . ." The magical voice rolled on. Mason focused the binoculars on Elisabeth, seated behind the larger figure. Even through the Plexiglas it was obvious her face was contorted in anger. She seemed to be staring at him, even at the great distance, and suddenly her countenance broke into a knowing smile. Hastily, he put down the binoculars. Surely she could not recognize him. He pulled back into the room.

A chill swept through his body. Suddenly he felt visible and vulnerable in the apartment window. Perhaps he should join the safety of the crowd—after all, they had the video. The portable phone next to him jangled sharply. He could not bring himself to look in Elisabeth's direction.

"Are you going to answer?" asked the camerman.

"Yeah. Hello?"

Perola's whispered voice penetrated his ear. "Well? What did you see?"

"We got it. They recovered quickly, but there was no question."

"Great!"

"What should we do now?"

"I guess just watch the rest of the rally and see what happens." He could hear others in the crowd shushing Perola to be quiet. "I must go. We will meet as we decided before. Ciao."

He turned to the camerman. "Could I go ahead and collect the videocassette? We could record the rest of the rally on a separate tape."

"Sure." The cameraman popped out the tape and handed it to him.

A banging somewhere in the apartment building caught his attention. Muffled mens' voices, then more banging. It sounded as if someone was knocking on apartment doors. His heart leapt into his throat. The military? Elisabeth's henchmen? "I'm gonna peek out and see what's going on."

Mason crept to the apartment's auxiliary door to the hallway. Easing it open a crack, he peered down the hall. A pair of soldiers, rifles slung across their backs, were knocking on a door at the far end of the corridor. Behind them stood a squat figure in a hooded black jacket. Mason shut the door, his mind churning. The group must be making the rounds of apartments facing the plaza. They would be at his door in a manner of minutes. He could play possum and not answer, but would they force their way in? He could use the cameraman as a front and hide somewhere in the apartment, but would they search it? Or he could try to escape down the hallway. With the nervousness of a hunted animal he returned to the window.

"Listen, there are soldiers in the hall. I think they're searching these apartments. We need to clear out."

The cameraman grinned. "No problem! I can go in two seconds."

"Okay." Mason stuffed the videocassette into his jacket and edged back to the door. With a nod to the cameraman he slipped out of the room and ran for the red exit sign on the side of the building opposite from where he had seen the soldiers.

He had almost reached the stairwell when a woman's voice called from behind. "Excuse me . . ." the voice began in Portuguese, but he did not turn.

Ducking into the stairwell, he careened down two flights of stairs, the cameraman on his heels. The apartment had been on the eighth floor. Would it be smarter to get off on another floor and take the elevator the rest of the way down? He hesitated, then burst into the sixth floor hallway. No one in sight. The cameraman's breathing behind him. Footfalls on the stairs above them before the stairwell door slid silently shut.

A few great bounds to the elevator door. They would be sitting ducks for anyone who glanced down the hallway. Mason prayed to the elevator gods for swiftness. With a deafening clang and jerk the car rumbled to a stop, its doors easing open with infuriating slowness. Mason pulled them wider apart, then dove inside, the cameraman literally on top of him. Standing, Mason jammed the button to close the doors. Was that footsteps in the hallway outside? *Close,* dammit!

With a shudder the door closed and the elevator resumed its downward journey. Mason's mind kicked into gear again. Would the lobby be covered with *ajudantes* or other officials? He jammed at the button for the basement, and the old elevator creaked past the ground floor uninterrupted. Another lurch, another painstaking drag of the elevator doors. No one in the hall, a darker hall this time. The smell of urine and garbage. Something like cabbage, rotten cabbage. Mason ran toward a red exit sign. It ended at a metal door, bolted from the inside, crammed with huge buckets of stinking garbage. He shoved past, wrenching open the door.

Daylight. Heat, smoke, and noise. Sirens, one on top of another. They were in an alleyway, blocked with more mammoth garbage cans, but devoid of people. Only two directions. Mason chose left, running as if warding off tacklers or shrapnel, the cameraman behind him step for step. The tape jostled in Mason's jacket as he moved, bumping up against the cell phone. Should he try to call Perola?

The alley emerged into a side street, which Mason guessed led back to the *Viaduto do Chá*. A steady flow of people streamed away from the noise, and the acrid odor of tear gas hit him in the face. The military must have dispersed the rally. He ducked into a door stoop and pulled out the phone, the cameraman rushing past with a semi-salute and then gone. He had punched in only a few digits when an explosion rocked the building's foundation. Shattered storefront glass flew in all directions, mowing down people like a scythe. Suddenly he could see nothing but glass, smoke, blood, and writhing bodies. A woman ran past, an enormous jagged edge of glass impossibly embedded in the side of her head. She made it half a dozen strides before collapsing in the middle of the street, her head flopping like a dead chicken's. He felt moisture on his arm, noticed a flow of crimson running from his shoulder down the length of his arm. His mind suddenly cleared, and he examined the wound, determined it was minor, then resumed punching the digits of Perola's mobile number.

No answer. A squadron of riot troops, shields in hand, appeared at the end of the street nearest the *Viaduto do Chá,* pushing people before it like a street sweeper. Mason edged into the flow in front of their path. The unfamiliar street spilled into another, broader avenue, equally clogged with those in flight. He stepped over the prostrate body of a woman, evidently trampled by the stampeding hordes.

Behind him the sound of heavy machinery cranked up, sending a shudder through the packed street and initiating a flurry of renewed effort at escape. Stepping over another trampled victim, an elderly man with his glasses crumpled beside him, Mason noticed what looked to be a gilt-edged Bible caught in the dead man's grasp. He started to stop, opening his mouth to protest, but the wave of those behind him pulled him forward, like a twig in a stream.

The flow of people thinned after several blocks, enough to allow him to duck into a doorway and catch his breath. He tried Perola's number again; still no answer. Ruling out returning to the office or the hotel, he decided to make for Margarida's apartment. At least there he would be able to use the phone to reach New York and e-mail Rome, and maybe Margarida had heard something from Perola. The thought of her threw clouds of concern across his mind. Had she been injured in the melee or taken into custody? Surely, even if she had been forced to temporarily turn off her phone, she would attempt to contact him when she reached safety.

He threaded his way back in the direction of Margarida's flat, the videocassette clutched against his chest. He found himself on Rua Direita, past the Municipal Theater, everyone hurrying, black and white, head down, as if trying to catch a phantom bus. The farther from the *Viaduto do Chá*, the more deserted the streets, evidence the curfew was in effect. By the time he neared Margarida's he imagined himself the only thing moving. Behind drawn shades, human shapes shifted, huddled in fear, their faces peeping into the street from time to time to eye the curfew's transgressor. Undoubtedly some were notifying the authorities of the violation; sirens and police could only be moments away. He began to run, heedless of the clatter of his shoes on asphalt streets, until he came to the block where Margarida's apartment lay nestled snugly along a row of identical, nondescript units. Chest heaving, he knocked on the door in what he hoped was not a panicky banging. No answer. He began to hyperventilate.

"Come on, be here!" he muttered, half to himself, raising his fist for another rap on the door.

The door opened an inch or so, revealing Margarida's beady dark eyes.

Then a few inches wider, enough for him to squeeze through.

"I was not expecting you," Margarida whispered. "Is everything okay? Where is Perola?"

"I don't know," Mason gasped. "We were separated at the rally. In the chaos afterwards, I haven't been able to find her. I tried to call her mobile phone, but there's no answer. I thought she might have tried to contact you." He pulled the videocassette from his jacket and placed it on a coffee table.

Margarida shook her head. "I have not heard from her. What chaos occurred?"

Mason narrowed his eyes. "Was there nothing on TV?"

Another shake of the head. "No. I have had the news on all afternoon. Only discussions regarding negotiations between the government and the labor unions on the strike." She reached for a coffee cup.

"There was a major commotion at the rally. I didn't see the whole thing, but I got the impression that government troops moved on the people and they panicked. All I know is I came out of a building where I had been watching the rally to find explosions, flying glass and people being trampled to death."

He paused and gulped down some proffered orange juice. "They must have a news blackout going." Another gulp. "No coverage." He shook his head and peered through the shutters, half expecting to find pursuers outside. Instead, the last of the sun's rays shone on an empty street.

The phone rang, its shrill pitch catching Mason in the pit of the stomach. Margarida hurried to answer it.

"Yes. Oh, yes, it is you!" She cupped her hand over the receiver and whispered conspiratorially. "It is Perola!"

Mason felt his pulse begin to return to something approaching normal.

A frown crossed Margarida's face. "Yes, yes. Where are you?" A blinding burst of Portuguese Mason could not understand, then goodbye, and she was hanging up.

"Well?" asked Mason impatiently. "She is okay?"

Margarida stared at her coffee cup. "She is on her way here," she said finally over the cup's rim. "Apparently Henrique was seriously injured in the melee this afternoon. Another officer told her this, but no one seems to know where he is being treated or what his condition is. She lost her mobile phone in the chaos; that is why you have not been able to contact her."

Mason glanced at the videocassette on the table. Margarida followed his line of vision. "I told her you had the cassette," she said quietly. She took another sip of coffee. "She is upset, particularly about the difficulty in obtaining information about Henrique. I have told her I will assist her as I can. I will call the most likely hospitals to see if someone is listed under his name."

She picked up a phone book the size of a giant cake, and after a few minutes began punching numbers into the phone.

The basement of the old church reeked of mold and mildew. Mason crouched with the fifty or so others, some seated in lawn chairs, the remainder on the damp floor. It was midnight, or thereabouts, following the massacre/riot at the *Viaduto do Chá*. The straggly group of Zhézushians met covertly, in violation of the curfew. Vicente was there, as were Aide, Velda, and Emmanuel, the retarded boy. Mason recognized others who had been present the previous day.

Perola sat on the floor next to Mason, arms gripped tightly around her legs. No information had been obtained by calling area hospitals, and Perola had been reluctant to contact friends in the police force for fear of exposing them or herself. Her face looked worn and fatigued. Dark patches had formed under her eyes.

The incident at the *Viaduto do Chá* had in fact been something near a massacre. According to Perola, during the resumption of Zhézush's talk, after the flare disruption, an officer with a megaphone had mounted the stage and again interrupted the dialogue, urging the crowd to disperse and comply with the curfew. At the first sign of hostility from the onlookers, tanks positioned on one side of the plaza had rumbled to life, launching the assault by a massive riot squad, which thrust the throng into a stampede. The explosions Mason had encountered occurred moments later. Perola assumed they were artillery shells or mortars fired by the military. She estimated the casualties at over a thousand, many of them trampled in the waves of fleeing people. The television news had been completely silent on the matter, a number of stations off the air. Only on the radio could any description of the carnage be heard, and then only in snatches, as if the stations that remained operative sought to continue to transmit by reporting the event only minimally in clandestine bursts. One excited announcer described a street so littered with trampled bodies it looked like a giant steamroller had passed through, flattening everything in its path. Another announcer passed along a blood bank's urgent appeal for donors.

Mason had filed his story and his report to the Vatican from Margarida's hours earlier. He had also spoken to Rhodes and other editors earlier in the evening about what to do with the videocassette. Whereas the story could be transmitted electronically, the cassette tape, at least under the present circumstances, could not. Ordinarily, Mason would have downloaded the tape at a broadcast facility for immediate transmittal to New York, but this had been deemed too hazardous. Given the state of the country, broadcast facilities would be under intense scrutiny. After discussing various options, consensus had been reached to have the tape duplicated. The task was risky, given the curfew and the probability the military knew the tape existed, but Perola felt strongly that they could safely obtain the copy. The plan assumed the airport was still operating, which as near as those in New York could tell was still the case. The international news had been reporting the military's intervention in certain areas of Brazil, but so far there were no reports of a takeover of the government itself.

The decision had eventually been made to have Margarida's runner, accompanied by another Zhézushian, take the tape for duplication, drop a copy back at Margarida's, and take the other copy to the airport for delivery to a courier arriving on an overnight flight; the courier would have the tape back at the *Herald* by late the following afternoon. Perola had reached Aide by phone and learned of the meeting to be held, surprisingly enough, in the basement of an evangelical church not far from Margarida's apartment. By the time they were ready to leave, the neighbor boy had returned with the duplicated tape. Perola had been right—in a city the size of São Paulo, the task had been relatively easy, even with the curfew.

Mason had listened from an alcove as Margarida gave the unseen boy explicit, rehearsed instructions on the copy's delivery to the airport. A grumble and snort signified his apparent understanding. She returned with the other copy and handed it to Mason, who punched it into Margarida's video machine. Zhézush's broad form filled the screen, relatively clear behind the Plexiglas. They watched in silence as the tape played out. Perola turned to Mason, who nodded. There was no mistaking the slip, or the recovery.

They left the apartment shortly before midnight. By the time they found the dour little chapel, the others were already there, gathered in whispering clumps in the moldy basement lit only by rows of candles along its walls. Mason sat down next to Perola on the floor as Aide stood to address the group.

"I would like to offer a prayer," she said solemnly. Heads bowed in anticipation. "Oh, great God," she continued, "lead us in your way. We are lost. Treachery and deceit are all around us. Light our path, so we might follow you. In the name of our savior, Zhézush." Hands crossed chests in the sign of the cross.

Aide lifted her head once more, and Vicente stood to join her. "We are aware of several things after today," she continued in the same solemn tone. "We have proof the woman appearing before the crowds is not Zhézush, but a lookalike who mimics her words. We have captured this proof on film. Many of us saw it with our own eyes. We knew but did not want to believe it. Now we believe.

"We are also aware that what is left of the government is completely dominated by a ruthless military whose goal is to preserve order and their own power. Their indifference to the people is evidenced by the slaughter at the *Viaduto do Chá* today. Thousands of helpless, unarmed people were killed or wounded. Our Vicente was taken prisoner but managed to escape in the confusion, for which we are eternally grateful. But we are in danger, and I am afraid this violence is only the beginning."

"If this woman is not our savior, when will Zhézush return?" asked someone from the back of the room. A muttering assent echoed softly through the gathering.

"We do not know," Aide replied. "But it is not our place to know. God will act as He sees fit. Our job is to spread the true word of Zhézush, and so we must expose this fraud. We must also stand up for the rights of our brothers and sisters, as we have been taught."

"Our friends Michael and Perola," Aide said, pointing in their direction, "have captured this deception on film. As reporters, they are committed to exposing this truth to the world. As we speak, a messenger is taking their videotape to the airport, where it will be flown to New York, put into newspapers, and shown on television around the world. This is the first step. The next step is to spread our message, first among the *favelas* as always, then among the greater masses. I fear there will be much destruction in the days ahead. We must be ready to offer an alternative of love and peace."

"It is probable we will never be able to meet like this again," Vicente said, his eyes shifting nervously. "We have taken a great chance by violating the curfew to be here tonight. Strategy for the dissemination of the word has been formulated; it is now time to implement that plan. I believe you are all fully informed of your role. Are there any questions?"

An older man in the front struggled to speak. His face had been damaged such that portions of the black skin gave way to strips of tan. "How do we communicate with each other?"

"Any way we can," Aide said. "We will be hunted, we know, even as now we may be sought. Our task is to link up as we can, to spread our chain across this city and this country. There will be much confusion. Our members may be thrown in jail, but we have legions of friends. The truth must guide us."

The sound of a siren filtered through to the church's bottom, fading, then growing louder. Another joined it, then another. Vicente and another man moved swiftly to extinguish the candles, plunging the room into dank darkness. Competing mechanical wails grew closer, then ceased abruptly. The church basement was as quiet as a tomb, its occupants scarcely breathing. Seconds passed into minutes. Shouting erupted outside at an uncertain distance.

The door to the stairwell burst open, revealing a slim figure outlined against the light from above. "It is okay," came urgently whispered Portuguese. "The sirens are at a disturbance several blocks away."

Grunts and sighs of nervous relief greeted the announcement.

Seconds later a match flared and a candle sprang to light.

"We must disperse," said Aide softly. The others murmured in agreement. "God go with you."

21

If I say, Surely the darkness shall cover me; even the night shall be light about me. Yea, the darkness hideth not from thee; but the night shineth as the day: the darkness and the light *are* both alike *to thee.*

Psalm 139:11-12

Silently, one or two at a time, the group dissipated, funneling through the church's several doors into the dark streets beyond. Another power failure or shut-off had plunged the area into inky blackness, providing cover for the departure.

As Mason waited in line with Perola for their turn to exit, a voice whispered in his ear. "I need to speak with you." It was Aide. Mason motioned to Perola, and they stepped aside, into an alcove housing an old upright piano.

"I have some information." Aide's narrow face was hidden in the shadows. "Bishop Silva is being held at Carandiru prison. I do not know why, or under what circumstances, but I am certain he is there. No one else among us is aware of this. I ask that you tell no one. Also," she said quietly and moved forward so that the gleam in her eyes was visible, "I have information with regard to your husband."

Perola drew in her breath sharply.

"He is safe at the home of a friend in Ipiranga. He was rescued, if you will, from the military hospital in Cambuci this morning."

Perola's knees started to buckle, and Mason braced her fall. "He is . . . okay?"

"Yes."

"Who else knows of this?"

"Obviously, those at the hospital know he is gone. With respect to his location, only the informant and myself."

"Where is this place?

"I will take you there, but I want to ask a favor of him and of you. We must get inside the prison to speak with the Bishop. Henrique must help us arrange this."

"But I do not know that he can do this."

"It is of vital importance to the truth. I fear that Bishop Silva will not be alive much longer."

"Why have I not heard from Henrique?" Tears filled Perola's eyes.

"He has only recently regained consciousness," Aide responded. "He is fine, my dear. You will see. Come."

She motioned them out the door and into the moonless night. Vicente bowed as they passed him, whispering his thanks, his eyes averted. A hulking young man Aide called Felipe joined them and led the way down the darkened street to a beat-up Ford parked at a curb.

"Is it safe to drive with the curfew?"Mason asked.

"In a city this size, they have no hope of strictly enforcing any curfew," snorted Aide. "The key for us is to avoid the places where it is most likely to be enforced."

The four piled into the old car, which rumbled to life and rolled away from the curb, gathering speed like a freighter. Pavement flashed by beneath rusted floorboards. The radio scratched and coughed, as if trying to stay alive. Intermittently, a news announcer's voice came through. Something about a bombing somewhere. Looting.

"What happened to Henrique?" Perola wanted to know.

"There were explosions at the rally. He was nearby, and part of a building fell on him. He was knocked unconscious. One of our people, a paramedic, rescued him. Later, this same paramedic assisted in spiriting him out of the military hospital where he was recovering. We were concerned the military might discover that he was there and start asking difficult questions. We moved him to the safe house. He is much recovered and receiving good medical care."

"What happened to Vicente?" asked Mason.

Perola coughed. “He was, as you know, responsible for the smoke bomb. I was standing only a few feet away from him when an officer pushed through the crowd, caught him by the arm and dragged him away. They never saw me, and Vicente never had the opportunity to discharge the flare. So, I did it.”

“What?” Aide and Mason stared at her.

“Henrique had given me two. I had the other one in my pocket.”

“Why didn’t you tell me?” Mason wanted to know.

Perola shrugged her shoulders. “I guess my mind is on Henrique. What happened to Vicente after he was captured?”

“Apparently, the officer chained him to a police car while the riot raged around him,” Aide responded slowly. “He says something must have happened to the officer, for he never returned to the car. After several hours, Vicente was able to pick the lock and escape.” She sat silent for a moment. “Undoubtedly, he was targeted because he is a known member of our group. We are most fortunate at his return, for an interrogation could have proved devastating.” A frown creased her face.

Another auto whizzed past, its lights dancing as it took on the road’s large potholes. With a groan the old Ford slowed, and Felipe wheeled it into a side street, then killed the motor. They coasted to a stop next to what appeared to be a five- or six-story apartment building. Aide climbed out, motioning for the others to follow. Deftly producing a key, she unlocked the main door and led them into a dimly lit vestibule, then across cracked parquet floors to a small elevator. With a creak and a jerk the lift opened, its harsh yellow ceiling light throwing uncomfortable illumination outside. Somewhere deep in the building a dog barked. The door shut, cables groaned, and the lift shuddered upward.

The doors opened again on the fourth floor, and Aide led them down a darkened hallway. Seconds later her key clicked loudly in a door lock, and they were inside. Perola pushed anxiously to the front. The dwelling was dark and quiet and smelled of rubbing alcohol. A tiny woman materialized and ushered them to the back of the apartment. The woman and Perola entered a bedroom as the others followed behind.

Henrique’s broad form lay propped up on a bed, his eyes large and glistening in the dim light.

Perola rushed to him. "You are okay."

"Yes," he whispered back. "I am much improved."

Aide motioned to Mason and the others, and they adjourned to a small living room. With the flick of her wrist, a small lamp crackled on. Mason glanced at his watch: 2:20 A.M. He could hear Perola and Henrique conversing in the other room. Tentacles of jealousy wrapped around him. He sat and rubbed his face with his hands.

"Assuming someone is able to get into the prison to speak with the Bishop, what do you propose to do afterward?"

Aide smiled again, a lopsided smile that seemed to lengthen her already long face. "We spread the word, my child. We know the truth." She pulled a small radio off a nearby shelf and worked the dial, listening intently at each sound, as if searching for a shortwave transmission.

Using Perola and the tiny woman as crutches, Henrique limped into the room and settled heavily into a lounge chair. The lamp's light highlighted deep circles under his eyes. Otherwise, he looked the same.

"It is good to see you, Michael," he said languidly.

"Tell us what happened," Mason responded.

Henrique shrugged and repositioned himself in the chair. Perola moved to sit cross-legged on the floor next to him.

"There is not much to tell beyond what you probably already know," he said slowly. "I was maintaining my position at the *Viaduto do Chá* during the rally. I was some distance from the stage, at the outer fringes of the crowd, so it was difficult to tell what was happening. A flare was shot off somewhere in the crowd, and then some government official took over the stage and attempted to shut down the rally. The crowd protested, the tanks moved, people began flying everywhere. Suddenly, there was an explosion. Everything near me was flattened. Someone—I do not know if it was another officer—picked me up and moved me out of the flow of the stampede. I awoke to the aftermath, to dead bodies on the streets. I was placed in an ambulance and transported to the military hospital. The doctor said I had sustained a concussion and gave me medicine that made me sleep.

"When I awoke, I experienced some discomforting things. Some military people came to see me. They had a lot of questions, mostly questions about you, Michael, and about Perola. I pleaded fatigue, amnesia, headaches; I stalled. There was no phone in the room I could use to call. I knew they would be back. An orderly entered my room shortly thereafter and told me he had instructions to transfer me. I was afraid and began to fight him, then he told me he was sent by Aide. Then I knew, and I cooperated. We arrived here a few hours ago."

He turned to Perola and squeezed her arm. "Perola believes I should consider returning to the hospital, but that is suicidal. Dona Martina is providing me good care here. I will be fine, but I will be a hunted man. I cannot return to my job. It is probably best I leave the country, that Perola, Michael, and I attempt to get out while we can. We could probably hide in São Paulo for some period of time, but what is the point? To live in hiding squeezes the juice out of life. Maybe at some point things will change and we can return." Dona Martina brought him a glass, from which he drank thirstily.

"Perola has informed me of Aide's request regarding Carandiru prison. This will be extremely difficult. I have a slim idea, one not likely to work. My father was friends with a man I think is still the prison's chaplain. I can contact him and see if he would be willing to help us. The risks are huge, as he would most likely be risking his life to do so. I feel uncomfortable even asking him to do this, but I will. I have not spoken to him in many years, do not know for sure he is still alive. I will call him when it becomes light. Let me ask this: is it necessary that one of us speak to the Bishop, or could this man act as a transmitter?"

"We need contact with someone from our group," Aide said firmly.

"I'll go." Mason stood and faced the others.

Aide nodded. "You have spent more time with him than any of the rest of us. In fact, we do not really know him at all."

"But, Michael, you barely speak the language. The entire military contingent in São Paulo is looking for you." Perola glanced from Henrique to Mason and back.

"No more so than they are looking for all of us."

A rap came at the apartment's door. Aide made her way silently to the door. A man's muffled voice sounded. Seconds later, the door swung open and Vicente entered. Even more disheveled than usual, his small dark eyes glittered as they took in the room. The others sagged in silent relief.

"I could go," Perola offered.

"No." Mason turned to Henrique. "What kind of plan do you have to leave the country?"

"An unformed one." His teeth flashed. "Probably the best bet would be to drive to the Argentinean or Paraguayan border and cross there."

"Let us rest now," said Aide. "We have much to do tomorrow. There are blankets and pillows in a closet here. We can sleep for several hours, then prepare tomorrow morning."

"Wait, turn that up!" Perola moved toward the small radio and adjusted the volume. The announcer's garbled voice grew louder.

". . . the communique by General Camargo indicates few changes are expected during this interim period of governance . . ."

"The military has taken over!" Perola exclaimed.

". . . only several hours ago. The spokesman for the military government describes the transfer of power as orderly and peaceful. The court system and government will continue to operate as before, and most institutions will continue to function, although the national legislature will recess for several months. As for São Paulo, the curfew is expected to continue for several days, although it could be lifted as early as tomorrow."

"A sad day for Brazil." Aide walked over to a small television set and flipped it on, but found nothing on the announcement. "People proclaim Brazil's newfound prosperity, but at what price? Those who have benefitted want to preserve it at all costs—the lower inflation, the consumer goods, the trips to Disney World—even at the cost of democracy itself. Others of us, we have received nothing."

She shook her head, turning to Mason. "You Americans," she spat, her eyes flashing, "with your capitalism and your trickle-down. At the bottom, there is not much trickle, no? And to you, maybe this is not a big thing. It is, after all, South America."

Mason ducked his head.

"To the U.S., we are still the little one," Aide continued, "to be dealt with as an inferior. But know this: you are witnessing a world-changing event, no less than if the government of Japan or, God forbid, the United States had broken." Aide's thin face had turned a mottled charcoal. *"O fim do mundo.* You may have just seen the beginning of the end of the world."

Mason started to scoff, but the sound caught in his throat. His thoughts flew to Elisabeth, then to Zhézush. The magical voice seemed to pound inside his brain.

No one said anything. A chair scraped loudly.

Perola broke the silence. "We cannot go back downtown, can we?"

Mason shrugged his shoulders. "Not if we don't want to be taken into custody."

"If General Camargo and his cronies are now running the country, where are Elisabeth and the fake Zhézush?" asked Perola.

"More importantly, where is the real Zhézush?" asked Mason.

The others stared silently at him, as if he had committed a grievous blasphemy.

Lazy morning light filtered into the room, playing across bodies sprawled on the floor in various stages of slumber. Perola picked her away across the floor, careful not to disturb the sleeping. She stopped as she caught sight of Mason's prone figure. Several days' growth of beard made his face darker; the course of his sleep had caused his shirt to roll up, exposing his lean stomach. Perola stared at him in the half-light.

The thought of leaving the country and almost everything she had ever known was overwhelming. She wished it to all be a dream, and when she closed her eyes and leaned against the tiny kitchen's cracked counter, it was not that hard to imagine it so. The country would return to normal, she and Henrique would return to their jobs, Mason would return to wherever he came from. Stability and moderate prosperity would return. For a brief moment she was dreaming, and the figure of Zhézush appeared to her, mouthing words she could not understand. Then it was gone, and she was awake, the morning light cold and cruel.

There was no sense denying reality, she told herself. They were in danger. They might survive for months, maybe years, on the run in São Paulo, but to what end? Henrique was right—there was little more they could accomplish under these circumstances. To leave without saying goodbye, though, would be hard. Her sister lived in Rio; Henrique's brother lived in São Paulo. She supposed they could call them once they left the country. But what would they do then? Where would they go? Fear stabbed at her. She imagined a future filled with menial work and loneliness.

The coffee maker coughed and wheezed. She stood over it like an expectant mother, drinking in the sweet aroma. Henrique was awake in the other room, but no one else stirred among the sleeping. Her thoughts drifted back to Mason, and then to Zhézush and the circumstances that led them to this predicament. Was the hand of God really at work here? Was it possible the forces of evil, locked in a dance with a putative equal, had gained an advantage?

She thought back to *candomblé* services she had attended as a child, to *Exu,* the icon of the devil that peered from a million tiny statuettes. In *candomblé, Exu* was the messenger between the deities and mankind, someone to whom offerings were given at the start of every service, an entity recognized and respected. Crossing herself, she placed her hands near the coffee maker to ward off a chill. *Exu* seemed to be everywhere these days—in her mind, in the chaos engulfing her life and her country, in her husband's injured body.

"Hey." Mason's voice made her jump. She hadn't seen him rise from the floor.

"Hey," she replied, her shoulders slumping. She wanted to grab his arm for support, but didn't.

"Sorry. I didn't mean to scare you."

"It is okay. I . . . I know how you feel sometimes when you say you think you are going crazy." She smiled, sort of. "Do you believe in the Devil, Michael?"

"I think so. I've seen things I attribute to evil. Is there one governing force? I'm less certain. What do you think?"

"I believe there are forces of evil, perhaps as powerful as the forces of good. They are locked in a struggle for each soul, each country, each world. Many believe good will always triumph. I am not so sure."

Mason eyed the freshly made coffee. "What is the point of evil? If there is a Satan, what is he trying to accomplish and why?"

She shuffled her feet, and stared out across the sleeping room. "The same could be said for God." She poured Mason a cup of coffee, then one for Henrique and another for herself. How could she explain the fact that *Exu* hovered all around her? Mason would not understand.

"There is something I have been meaning to mention to you," she said as she picked up the mugs. "I think I have it in my satchel. I will be right back." She returned moments later carrying a copy of a faded picture of Elisabeth and a dark-haired man, apparently pulled from a newspaper or magazine article. Mason's eyes narrowed as he examined it.

"The Reverend Joe Farriday? They know each other?"

Perola shrugged. "I thought his name sounded familiar when you mentioned it. I had a friend check the computer files at *Noticias.* This Reverend Farriday visited Brazil last year, apparently as part of some kind of worldwide evangelical convention. Judging from the date, his stay in Brazil was not long before the onset of Zhézush's rise to popularity. I don't know how he met Elisabeth, or what the connection is, but the picture is interesting, yes?"

"I'll say." Mason turned it over in his hands, as if expecting to find more on the back. "There's almost a trail from Elisabeth to Reverend Farriday to the murderer, isn't there? At least a connection." He handed the paper back to Perola. "Let's get this to New York." He smiled. "Good work."

She dipped her head modestly. Ordinarily she would have been defensive. Of course she did good work—what did he expect? But his compliment rang true, and she felt flustered instead, draining her coffee with nervous little drinks.

"Henrique has made contact with the prison chaplain," she whispered.

Mason's eyebrows arched in surprise. "Already?"

"Yes. He decided to go ahead and call."

"And?"

She cleared her throat softly, the sound like a cloth against wet wood. "He will help us."

"When do we make our move?"

"Come with me. Henrique is awake. He can explain everything."

They found Henrique sitting up in a small double bed, looking more rested than a few hours earlier. "The chaplain—his name is Nicolau Pareja—suggests we make our attempt this afternoon. He has a regular visit with certain prisoners today. One is Bishop Silva. He is permitted to enter their cells, with a guard remaining stationed nearby. He has suggested that you arrive at the east gate at approximately two P.M., wearing the vestments of a church official. Keep your head covered and mention only his name. You will be searched at least once. If you are asked anything, say only that you are in training with the chaplain. He will do his best to be waiting for you."

"You know, Michael," Henrique continued, his voice dropping into an even softer whisper, "this is exceedingly dangerous. There is no shame in saying no. There are any number of things that could go wrong. If you are recognized or detained within the prison, I fear no amount of diplomacy or intervention could save you."

Aide crept quietly into the room and stood at the foot of the bed near Mason.

"It is exceedingly dangerous, no matter what I do," Mason said. "I will go."

"Let us keep this matter to ourselves," Aide suggested quietly. "There is no sense involving anyone else in the details, even among our group." She directed her head toward the opposite room, where Felipe and Vicente still slept. "That way, if someone is caught, there is less chance of betrayal."

"What do you want me to ask of the Bishop?" Mason rotated his neck.

"We seek answers," Aide replied. "Are we correct in our view of the fraudulent nature of this return? Did he know of this sister of Zhézush? Why is he being detained when Elisabeth is not? Why were we never contacted after the supposed return?" Her eyes shone with tears. "These and other questions."

A knock came at the door, and Felipe entered the room. "There is an announcement on the television," he said, rubbing his eyes. "You may want to watch."

They trooped into the other room, where a somber announcer's voice reverberated. ". . . in accordance with the provisions of the Brazilian constitution, the armed forces have temporarily taken control of the government. All constitutional rights will remain in place. President Domingues has offered his resignation, effective this morning. The transfer of power is temporary and has proceeded smoothly, without violence. . . ."

"What is he saying?" hissed Perola, angrily stamping a foot. "The president? They have trashed the constitution! There is no provision for this!" The announcement ended and gave way to regular programming. She switched the channel to the International News Network.

"Economic growth at the expense of repression," Perola spat. "The modern Brazilian miracle. Our economic boom emphasizes luxurious consumer goods, which furthers the misery of the poor. Our per capita income rises, yet we have an infant mortality rate double that of other countries with our income."

Mason made his way to the phone. Perola assumed he was calling New York and soon could hear his part of the conversation over the drone of the TV set. Apparently Rhodes was not yet in the office.

"What are you talking about?" The tone in Mason's voice caused the others in the room to turn. He cupped his hand over the phone's end. "The courier never made it to the airport," he said, haltingly.

A dagger of fear struck Perola. She looked to Henrique, who had entered the room and stood leaning against a doorway. "Margarida?" Each of them mouthed the word. Perola reached for her mobile phone and punched in the number. There was no answer, and the usual merry click of the answering machine failed to materialize.

"I am concerned," said Henrique. He looked to Aide. "Perhaps I can have Felipe run me over to check on her?"

"No!" Perola blurted. "If something has happened to her, they will be watching her place, no?"

"She is right," Aide admonished Henrique. "It would be foolish. Perhaps there is another way." She rousted Vicente, still dozing on the floor, and the two spoke in low tones.

"Vicente will have someone go by her apartment," Aide announced. "Someone reliable." Vicente ran his hands through misshapen hair and a scraggly growth of beard. His eyes darted wildly around the room. With a grunt he raised himself to his feet and asked for the phone.

"Who accompanied the runner?" asked Mason.

Aide motioned to Vicente, now huddled like a bear over the phone, sniffing and snorting. "One of his people. Isaias, I think. He is checking on this as well."

Perola could catch only a few words of Vicente's conversation. "Madness . . . of course, let me know . . ." He replaced the phone with a loud "harrumph" and made for the coffeepot. "We will know something within the hour," he said to no one in particular.

"The runner?" asked Mason.

"I do not know yet. We are checking."

It was Aide's turn to grab for the apartment's phone, so Perola went to work on her mobile unit. Contacts at *Noticias* and the *International Press* confirmed the television announcement. The official communique had been broadcast at 1:00 A.M., then rebroadcast several times during the night. There had been no violence or protests that anyone was aware of—yet. Large military contingents were in place at strategic locations around the country, particularly at government facilities in Rio and São Paulo.

Someone flopped the morning papers in front of her, and she skimmed them. Big headlines, not as hysterical as she had imagined. Speculation regarding the detention of Zhézush by the military, denied by a spokesman for the council. Projections of the impact of the takeover on the Brazilian economy for the remainder of the year. Surprisingly angry op-ed pieces denouncing the failure of democracy. A brief article caught her eye.

"Michael!"

He looked up from the television.

"The mental hospital. It has burned to the ground!"

The others turned to look. Color drained from Mason's face. Perola started to say something, but stopped at the look on his face. Just like the monastery he had mentioned to her. Rome?

The phone in the kitchen rang. Felipe picked it up, then summoned Vicente. As Perola watched, he listened silently for a few moments, bushy black hair obscuring his face, then muttered an almost incoherent "Oh, my God!"

Aide scuttled over from across the room. Perola put the papers away. Henrique limped into the room.

"What is it?" Perola asked. Fear pounded again in her chest.

"Margarida's apartment has been ransacked," he said tonelessly. "Torn to pieces. There is no sign of her. Paulo and Isaias have vanished."

Henrique's gaze locked on Perola's. Fear fluttered between them like a magnetic charge. She had never known him to be afraid. It terrified her.

"I fear the worst," he said disconsolately, motioning her back into the bedroom. "I hope we did not bring ill upon her." His gaze broke from Perola's.

She nodded, wiping her face with a sleeve, stifling a trembling indrawn breath. "Can they be far away?" she asked when she could regain her voice.

Henrique looked out the small window into the morning sun. "Probably not. They must have followed us to her place, or traced the delivery boy back to her. How they got him, I do not know." His eyes returned to Perola's. "We must keep moving," he said softly, "like criminals on the run. Nowhere are we safe until we are out of the country."

He beckoned her to him and held her against his chest. She could feel the throbbing of his heart against hers. They stayed locked together for a long time, until Mason's knock at the door signaled it was time to go.

Late morning heat seared through skin and clothing, drawing steam from the wet pavement and fogging Mason's cheap sunglasses. He sank into the car's crushed velour back seat, grateful for the blasting air conditioner. A different car, another American behemoth. Felipe took the driver's seat, and the car took off carrying its single passenger. Mason felt abandoned and alone, and fought the urge to tell Felipe to turn the car around. He found a dark robe and clerical collar on the seat beside him. His disguise? He slipped them on, embarrassed to meet Felipe's eyes in the rearview mirror.

He had rehearsed the plan with Henrique enough to ingrain it in his memory: the car would drop him at the prison's main gate; he would proceed from there to the reception area. Hopefully, Father Pareja would be waiting. If he was not, or Mason was refused admittance, the plan called for Felipe to circle back by the gate twice for a possible pick-up. If things went well, Mason would leave with Father Pareja, who would give him a ride to the *Vila Alpina* cemetery, where he would rendezvous with Perola and Henrique. Slowly, Mason slipped the videocassette and his mobile phone under the seat.

Felipe slowed the car and turned into a side street. Mason sat up straighter in the back seat, senses heightened. They couldn't be at the prison yet, of that he was certain. Was this an ambush? Could Felipe be trusted?

"Por quí estamos parando?"

Felipe pulled the car to the curb adjacent to a boarded-up building where grass two feet high sprouted between cracks in the sidewalk. Like a bullet, a small figure rocketed from a crevice between two buildings and wrenched open the car door nearest Mason. Before he could react, the figure was in the car, slamming the door shut, and Felipe was accelerating away from the curb. Emmanuel, the Down's child, sat motionless on the seat next to Mason, his eyes unblinkingly locked in place.

"What's going on?" Mason gasped to Felipe in English. Felipe's eyes flitted to the mirror, then back to the road.

Emmanuel's face twisted into a vacant smile. "Do not be afraid," came a voice, not a child's voice, from the child's lips.

Sweat froze on Mason's forehead. Light moved in great swabs of gray and black around him, and he struggled for air. The voice had been hers, Zhézush's, as surely as he had ever heard it. He rubbed his ears. A part of his mind contemplated the possibility he was hallucinating—maybe a drug slipped into his drink? Schizophrenia?

"You are surprised, no? Like many others, you expected my return in the same body, the same form. Do not be deceived. Take nothing for granted, and investigate everything. And maintain your faith in my message. Love."

Mason's mind floated somewhere outside his body, as if through death he viewed the scene from a distance, dispassionately listening in on a different world. All sense of the moving car, of Felipe, of the rendezvous with Father Pareja—vanished. He was bound up in the voice, in the pleasure of the sound of what could only be a creator. Nothing else mattered.

"There is a difficult road ahead. Remember only that I will be with you. The struggle between good and evil is not a simple one. You will be tempted. The strength of the opposition is formidable; do not underestimate it. They will exploit your weakness."

Mason's mouth formed unspoken words. The child cocked his head knowingly.

"Beware of treachery from those closest to you. Eventually, you must rely only upon yourself. You have the tools to succeed. Use them."

"You are . . . ?"

The child's lips puckered into a bemused grin. "Yes."

"Then the resurrected Zhézush is a fake?"

"You know this to be true."

"Please." Mason reached out a hand to touch the child's arm. It felt warm and human and normal. "Help me to understand. Am I dreaming? Am I insane?"

"I have spoken to you through your dreams, but this is not one. Listen carefully, for time is short. It is vital that you spread the word, the true word, as you know it. Expose the deception."

"But how?" Mason clutched the arm again, afraid the child would vanish into nothingness.

The quizzical smile returned. "You know my message: Love. Peace. Justice."

"But, I do not underst—"

The car slowed and turned sharply. Mason glimpsed gates and barbed wire.

"You must go now," said the smiling child/Zhézush. "Have faith."

22

And the Lord said, Simon, Simon, behold, Satan hath desired *to have* you, that he may sift *you* as wheat: But I have prayed for thee, that thy faith fail not and when thou art converted, strengthen thy brethren.

Luke 22:31-32

Mason stumbled through the sticky heat. The sweet smell of cut grass sprang up at him, lodging barely noticed somewhere in his brain. His knees trembled, jellylike, such that he considered grabbing a post for support. He felt himself enter a portico, heard himself respond mechanically in Portuguese to a guard's questions:

"I am to meet Father Pareja. Yes. Father Vasilinda."

Mechanically, he handed over identification Aide had produced, then stepped into a cubicle to strip for a young, hatchet-faced man. Off came the robe, his underwear. The young man looked on disinterestedly, declining to pursue the search further. Mason shrugged the robe back on, tightening the belt around his waist, fastening the sandals back to his feet. Back to the portico for a plastic-shielded ID badge. All the while calm now, almost oblivious to it all. His mind on her, it, whatever. Madness. Fear of insanity, but not of this.

He moved with a prisoner's measured tread, the hatchet-faced man leading the way. For some reason it was peaceful to be behind bars, to be locked away from the world, like a priest in an abbey. A door opened to the inside. Heat. Tattered paint on the wall. A locked gate with iron bars. Keys jangling. The creaking of metal hinges. A broad brown man in clerical robes beyond the gate. Mason's mind beginning to click again.

"How are you?" asked the brown man warmly, pulling him into a giant hug and kissing him on both cheeks. Mason returned the gesture.

"We have much to do," said Father Pareja, turning to leave the hatchet-faced man behind. Another guard, a burly *mulatto* with breasts like a woman's, followed along behind them. "It is so good of you to assist today! God's plan surely shines for us."

Mason grunted affirmatively. Sweat rolled down the sides of his face, the heat unrelieved by sporadic overhead fans. God's plan. What was it? His body felt numb, his skin rubbery.

Father Pareja bustled down the corridor into the cell block, where sullen-faced men stood packed in cell-cages.

"Hey, Pop, you got some new help today, eh?"

"What is this young buck, eh papa? You dipping your tool?" Muttered laughter. The scraping of feet on a concrete floor.

Father Pareja ignored the taunts, waving jovially to a number of inmates and voicing greetings to others. "Thursday, Emilio. No, Thursday. I will see you! Do not despair. Octavio! Hello there!" He moved past the last cell into a narrow corridor where the smell of fecal matter hung heavy. Shouting erupted further down the hallway. Another metal door loomed in front of them, another guard moved to admit them. They were in a quieter, somewhat cooler area now. Concrete block walls muffled a scream into nothingness. Father Pareja stopped before a metal door, beckoning the large-chested guard following them to open it.

"Oh, João, I apologize. I did not introduce you. This is Father Vasilinda." He gestured in Mason's direction. "He will be assisting me today and again in the future." The older man beamed, as if he had relayed the greatest possible news.

The cell door swung open to reveal a dark space illuminated only by strands of daylight shining through high overhead bars. The concrete walls had been dulled at their bottoms, perhaps by human contact, returning to a whitewashed color only at about eight feet or so. A tiny sink stood forlornly in one corner, and a metal cot occupied most of the rest of the space. No evidence of a toilet, only the small hole in the floor near the sink. A bony, tattooed man clad in blue prison garb sat on the cot, rocking slowly back and forth. He looked up at Mason and opened his mouth, revealing a single gold tooth in the scarred crevasse formed by his lips.

They stepped into the cell and stood awkwardly at the foot of the cot. Even the floor did not offer sufficient room to sit. The door clanged shut behind them. João waited outside, the sound of his breathing audible through the barred door.

"This is Senhor Souza. Senhor Souza, meet Father Vasilinda."

The gold tooth glinted in acknowledgment.

"How are you, my friend? Have you had a good week?"

The thin man nodded affirmatively and continued to rock. "Why do you bring a friend?" he asked finally, his tongue twisting around the single tooth as if seeking lost support. "Are you leaving us?"

"Of course not!" Father Pareja's voice boomed off the concrete walls like a cannon. "I am going nowhere, but in my elderly state, I can always use the help. Are you . . ." His words broke into Portuguese Mason did not understand. ". . . and do you have anything to confess?"

Senhor Souza shook his head vigorously.

"Would you like us to pray for you? Come, Father, let us pray for Senhor Souza." Mason sank to his knees with the round old man.

The ritual was completed for others: Senhor Villasantos, Senhor Navarre, Senhor Calvacado. Mason fell into the rote pattern, his mind disengaging from his body again to view the process from afar. The child. Zhézush. His search for true signs of God. The disappointments of the past ten, twenty years. The relief. The ecstasy.

Father Pareja ended a session with Senhor Neves, a short, completely bald man who sobbed during the entire encounter, and proceeded to a room in front of which a guard sat tilted back in a wooden chair, drawing on a cigarette.

"Good afternoon, Senhor Barria!"

The guard grunted in response, his eyes on Mason.

"This is Father Pareja's assistant," João jumped in, helpfully. "He will be joining him for the future. We hope we are not losing Father Pareja!"

"Of course not."

Senhor Barria produced a ring of keys and swung open the door to the cell behind him. The cell's interior looked the same as all the others, the same cramped space, the same overwhelming stench of decay and excrement, the same crushed bit of humanity slumped on the floor in a corner.

The Bishop's gaze remained on the floor as they entered. He looked older, thought Mason, and frightfully thin, perhaps twenty pounds less than only weeks before. Dots of hair sprinkled his unshaven face, as if ants had attacked and overrun him. Dark veins stood out in shrunken arms.

"Good afternoon, Father Silva!"

"Good afternoon, Father."

"I have an assistant with me today, Father Vasilinda."

The Bishop did not look up. Mason cleared his throat softly. "Good afternoon," he said quietly. A glance showed the guard Barria hovering at the door.

The Bishop's gaze was on him now, bloodshot eyes seeking confirmation. The slumped figure moved away from the corner toward them.

"It is my pleasure," the Bishop whispered hoarsely, grasping Mason's hand in a shriveled claw. "Indeed."

"How are you, my friend? Have you had a good week?" The ritual continued.

"Ah, has it been a week?" The Bishop's dour features attempted a smile.

"Do you have anything to confess?"

A pause. "Yes, father." The whisper's harshness cut like a saw. The Bishop kneeled painfully, and they followed. "I . . . I have sinned greatly." He coughed, as if the effort were too much for him, the bones of his bowed neck strained and visible above the prison uniform. "I have taken part in a deceit against God's name."

Another pause. Shouldn't Father Pareja say something comforting? Mason wondered if Barria still had his face pressed against the cell door.

"I was . . . I am a priest. A bishop. You know this. I reached a point in my life where I believed myself to be happy, but somehow I needed more. Into my life swept this beautiful creature. I was tempted, but I resisted this temptation. Then she came to me one night. She was so strong! I weakened, and I fell into her grip. It was wonderful and terrible—I was consumed with guilt and passion. She took me, made me hers. I was powerless. I tried to break away. I went away for some weeks, praying, begging to be released from her. And when I returned, she . . . she . . ." His voice caught and disintegrated.

"She told me she was pregnant," he whispered finally. "She demanded that I leave the church to follow this . . . this faith healer she supported, this woman who claimed to be Christ returned!" He lifted his head, tears running unheeded down the emaciated channels of his face. "I told her she was crazy, that this was blasphemy of the worst sort, that I had devoted my entire life to Christ, that this would be the ultimate betrayal. It would ruin my life, I told her. But . . . the child! She gave me no other option. She threatened to expose me, showed me pictures she had taken of us. I almost took my life, wanted to take my life. When it came down to it," his voice broke into a sob, "I was too weak to pull the trigger."

"And the child?" Mason whispered, after a time.

"There was no child," the Bishop managed through clenched teeth. "I do not believe she was ever pregnant. She used me, and I allowed her to do so, and at some point I was almost grateful for it." The whisper dissolved again into wracking sobs.

"Bless you, my son." Father Pareja said softly, making the sign of the cross over him.

The Bishop flung a sleeve across his face. The rasping voice continued. "I left the Church. A thousand times, I asked God to kill me, to prevent me from perpetrating this fraud. But Elisabeth, she . . . she is so powerful, so persuasive. At this point Zhézush was not well known—she had only been in São Paulo a few weeks. When the story of my defection hit the papers, interest began to pick up. Within weeks she was attracting large crowds. There was a group of us—myself, Elisabeth, Cunha—who plotted strategy to enhance her visibility, as if she were a household product. We orchestrated the healings, recruiting subjects we thought could be 'turned around,' as we put it. Elisabeth recruited the network of *ajudantes* to assist us. It became an extremely well organized effort. I found myself believing as we got further into it. Maybe it was rationalization—it must have been—maybe it was the only tonic my mind would accept. That, and her power. Anyway, we decided ultimately that for true worldwide exposure, Zhézush needed to go to the United States, where international media coverage is so much greater. So, we went. The coverage was all we could hope for and more. Then the murder took place. We flew back with the body. I was incarcerated almost immediately, separated from Elisabeth. I know almost nothing beyond this point, only what I have heard thirdhand and through snatches of news reports—that Zhézush has returned, that the country is in chaos, that the military has intervened.

"What of Zhézush?" asked Mason.

The Bishop did not answer immediately, his head still bowed toward the concrete floor. "When I first met her, I considered her a puppet, a vehicle for Elisabeth. As time went on, I witnessed the effect of her voice in her services. I began to believe she had some powers of her own, perhaps of a mystical nature. After seeing the healings, my vision began to change further. For you see, after a time, we could not screen in advance every person to be healed. There were just too many. Word of her powers had become too widespread for us to maintain complete control. Yet the healings continued. I saw deformed legs become straight, impossible afflictions healed." He glanced up at Mason. "I told myself, surely the hand of God is in this. Perhaps she is the one, after all. I argued with myself. I accused myself of attempting to justify my own abomination, of blasphemy of the worst kind. I pondered whether this was the work of Satan, of healing powers utilized to deceive and benefit an overall evil scheme. Yet I continued to see the healings, day after day. And I came to ask, how could this wonderful thing be evil?"

A banging of the cell door's metal bars startled them. "Hey, how long is this?" Barria's face thrust through the opening.

"We are in confession!" Father Pareja hissed angrily. "Do not interrupt again!"

The face disappeared.

"What of her death?"

Again, no immediate reply. A drop of moisture rolled off the Bishop's face onto the concrete below. Sweat? A tear?

"Her death . . ." he began finally, then lapsed into silence. "Her death was planned." The room seemed to shrink around them. Mason glanced again to the door. No sign of anyone.

"One night in São Paulo, before we left for the United States, I overheard Elisabeth and Cunha talking. They were discussing her . . . her res . . ." He stopped again, his face behind his hands. "Her resurrection. I knew then she would be killed. Oh, God . . ." The sobs returned, his body heaving spasmodically. They waited for the paroxysm to ease. Mason shifted his weight, easing the pressure on his knees.

"But I did nothing. I was the weakest of the weak. I was not sure how, or when, this would occur. Then Zhézush began saying certain things, as if she knew she was about to die. I could not sleep from the strain. The day of her death—you were there, Michael—I had a foreboding. I remember Elisabeth going out onto the field after Zhézush began her healings, something she rarely did. I felt death, as strong as granite. I knew she was gone before I heard the shot."

"What is Elisabeth?" Mason asked softly.

The Bishop shifted his weight back onto his haunches. The deep-set eyes stared unblinkingly. "She is the other one," he said slowly. "Evil."

Even in the heat of the cramped cell, Mason shivered slightly. "Did you ever know a Reverend Joseph Farriday?" he asked, his voice faltering.

The Bishop frowned. "He is American?"

Mason nodded affirmatively. "Zhézush's killer received a package from him just before the murder. I discovered a picture of Farriday and Elisabeth together in São Paulo last year."

The Bishop rocked back and forth on his knees. "Yes, I remember him. Perhaps Elisabeth used him to help set up the murder? I would not doubt it."

"What about Cunha?"

"Yes?"

"Tell me about him."

"Oh, he was an evil man, not particularly smart. He joined forces because he had nothing better to do, because it afforded him the opportunity to regain the limelight."

"What about his death?"

The Bishop shrugged bony shoulders. "That remains a mystery. My guess is Elisabeth did it somehow, but I have no proof. It may have been completely natural. Did the autopsy ever find anything?"

"They're still waiting for some of the test results." Mason lowered his voice further. "Do you fear for your life here?"

The Bishop shrugged thin shoulders. "I am almost dead. Why she has allowed me to live this long, I do not know. I can only imagine I am a safety valve, to be used in the unlikely event I am needed."

"Did you know Zhézush had a sister? A twin?"

The Bishop's shoulders sagged further, his body melting into the floor. A long silence ensued. "Yes," he whispered bitterly. "I knew this part of the plan, as well. She was to be kept in seclusion, to be brought forth to complete the deception. . . . Has this happened? I doubted that it could work, but I should not have underestimated. . . . How do you know this?"

Mason glanced nervously again at the cell door. "It's a long story, but it has happened. To all appearances, it has worked. At first I thought perhaps the sister had been killed in Miami, that Zhézush was part of the plan." He looked sidelong at Father Pareja, who sat silent, his mouth open, fishlike.

"What convinced you that she was not?"

Chills swept up his spinal column, like a force trying to find its way out of his body. "I also was . . . a priest. In addition to my duties as a reporter, I report to the Vatican on phenomena such as this. We captured the deception on tape. More than that, the real Zhézush has appeared to me. Not the sister. Not in the form of the body we knew, but as a child. But the voice. The *voice! It was her!* I am sure of it! I . . . I . . ."

Tears flowed, blocking his vision. A swipe with a forearm restored eyesight. The Bishop rocked further back, almost to a reclining position, his eyes shut tight as if to trying to dam a flow of emotion. Father Pareja's leathery face pinched itself tight. No one said anything. The tiny cell seemed on the verge of explosion.

"Uhhh . . . ahh!" The Bishop broke the silence. His head rolled back exultantly, fists clenched in front of him. The sound brought Barria to the door; the others did not turn to look. The Bishop rose and grasped Mason around the neck, pulling him close. "You would not lie to me! Not now. I . . . I have dreamed of this, prayed for this! You have no doubts? What did she say?" His voice returned to the rasping whisper.

"That there is evil all around," replied Mason, his voice catching. "To have faith. To spread the true word, the word of the deception." He paused. Tears reached his mouth. The cell seemed to expand, then retreat upon itself. "I've searched most of my life for this."

"Hey, hey! What is going on?" Barria's nose poked through the cell door's bars.

"We are almost finished," Father Pareja said respectfully, bowing in the guard's direction. "Please allow us another moment."

Barria looked on balefully, remaining at the door.

The Bishop returned to his knees, his head bowed once again. "I can receive no greater gift," he said, almost to himself. "I can go now, in peace."

The opening of the cell door flushed a small breath of cooler air into the cramped cell. A tall, unsmiling man entered, a nervous Barria on his heels. "I told them to hurry it up," whined the guard.

Father Pareja stood, bowing in deference to the tall man. A military-like nameplate on the man's chest flashed briefly in the spindles of light, its lettering indecipherable. A scar ran down one cheek, rendering his face a scowl. His chest and shoulders bulged with evidence of regular exercise. He eyed Mason with a questioning look.

"This is Father Vasilinda, who will be assisting me in the future," said Father Pareja. "Father Vasilinda, here is Mr. Villacruz, assistant warden.

"Who approved this?" growled Villacruz. "This prisoner is to have no visitation."

"Except clergy," Father Pareja bristled. "No one is denied our visit."

"Who approved your assistant?"

"It has been in the works for some time. You know this." He smiled, in an attempt to soften the words. "I will not be around forever, you know."

Mason's eyes caught the Bishop's nervous hands. They seemed to be forming and reforming into some sort of sign. . . . The Bishop was signaling him, he realized, in sign. "Dream." Mason recognized that word. He strained to make out the letters that followed: "V-I-C-E-N-" Vicente! He nodded vigorously that he understood, shielding his eyes with his hand so he could continue staring at the Bishop's partially hidden hands.

"Let us go to my office. I would like to review this man's credentials." Villacruz commanded everyone's attention. Mason's eyes strayed briefly back to the Bishop's hands.

"T-R-A-I-T—" It was enough. The message had been received. Was the

Bishop's dream equally prescient? Perola and Henrique and the others could be in grave danger, maybe already captured. His heart thumped at the thought.

Father Pareja turned to the Bishop and embraced him, whispering into his ear. The Bishop nodded, then turned to Mason. For a long moment they stared into one another's eyes, then closed into an embrace.

"God's grace be with you," whispered the Bishop. "Thank you."

Then they were off, back through the corridor, through the gauntlet of cells and taunts and smells. Several guards hovered in one cell, trying to block with their bodies the screams emanating from inside. Hands banged on metal bars. The concrete floor magnified the sound, blurring it all into something concretelike itself, punctuated only by the screams. Then they too stopped, and only solid noise remained.

They emerged from the cell block and entered an adjacent building. A blast of air conditioning chilled the sweat on Mason's back. Villacruz ushered them into a cramped, sparse office smelling strongly of dead cigarettes. A window air conditioner hummed and strained.

"You have been here before?" he asked Mason.

"No." Pause. "Today is my first day."

"You are a foreigner?" Villacruz's interest seemed piqued.

"Yes, he has been assigned several months ago to Mato Grosso parish, which serves this prison," Father Pareja jumped in.

"Quiet!" Villacruz held up his hand. "I am speaking to Father . . ." He studied the papers in front of him. "Vasilinda. So, where are you from, Father?"

"I am originally from the United States." Mason tried to hide his anxiety. This was leading down a dangerous path.

A buzzing sound interrupted them. Villacruz pulled out a pager, placed the device at his ear, then stood abruptly. "Stay here," he ordered, then strode past them out of the room. Footsteps sounded in the hall. Voices melded together, their pitches rising in excitement. From somewhere beyond the building a siren sounded. More footsteps. A loudspeaker blaring unintelligible words. The faint smell of smoke.

Mason turned to Father Pareja. "Let's get out of here!" he whispered urgently.

Father Pareja nodded in agreement. "I do not know what is going on, but we should go to the gate."

They stood and left the room. The building was now strangely quiet and seemingly vacant, and they crept unhindered to the exterior door. Outside, the quiet gave way to bedlam. A small column of smoke rose from the cell block like a dull gray flower. Fire engines streamed through the prison gate, horns blaring, yellow-jacketed firefighters poised for action. A honking alarm suddenly kicked on, engulfing the area in further noise. Blue-suited prisoners streamed out of the cell block into a barb-wire-enclosed recreation area.

"The Bishop." Mason searched Father Pareja's face. "Can you lead me back to him?"

The older man shook his head. "It is suicide, my friend. Remember what you have been told."

Another trio of fire trucks rushed past. Behind them came a coughing sound, then a gush of water as the first tanker truck kicked into gear. A truckload of military personnel careened into the courtyard, hurriedly disembarking behind the fire trucks.

Mason and the elderly priest moved toward the gate. Wind whipped against the priestly robes. Father Pareja gasped for breath, and Mason slowed down. They reached the exterior sentry station just as the guards waved through another series of fire trucks.

"Where are you going? No one can leave!" The surprised guard turned to the figures behind him.

"It is only I, Miguel," responded Father Pareja.

"Oh. But I have my orders."

"Please. Father Vasilinda must return for an emergency matter."

Miguel's answer was lost in the roar of another truckload of military personnel.

"Go!" shouted Father Pareja in Mason's ear and pushed him toward the doorway to the outside.

Stumbling, Mason made his way through, glancing back to ascertain whether Father Pareja was following. The elderly priest was arguing with the guard. The crack of an explosion broke Mason's line of vision, shaking the ground and flinging him sideways and onto his back. Struggling to his feet, he turned to see the entire prison complex slowly consumed in smoke. Yellow flames shot from the roof of the cell block. Father Pareja's white robes slowly disappeared from sight.

"My God," he muttered, mesmerized. What had caused the thing to ignite? He thought of the Bishop, alone in the cramped cell.

A bleating car horn finally caught Mason's attention. Felipe gestured wildly from a corner a hundred yards away. Half running, half staggering, he made his way across a mowed field. Another explosion shook the ground. He expected to feel a bullet from the sentry tower any second—how could he not look like an escaping prisoner? The smell of smoke blanketed the area—plastic, noxious smoke. Above him an electrical transformer popped in protest.

He fell into the car. Felipe swung hard in a tight circle, then sped away against oncoming traffic. Mason reached underneath the seat to retrieve the videotape he had left earlier. He held it warily in his hands, half expecting it to disappear.

"It is like a jail break, eh?"

Mason did not respond, slumped into the seat. He felt emotionally and physically spent, kept alive only by the fear pumping through him, a wounded animal having temporarily eluded its pursuer. A furtive glance behind them produced no evidence that anyone was following.

Vicente, traitor. He had never intended to set the smoke bomb, had faked his capture. He hadn't been informed about the visit to the prison, but maybe by now he had figured it out.

"I must get word to Perola," he shouted to Felipe above the car's engine clamor and the blasting hot air from open windows.

"We are going to meet her," Felipe responded.

"No, you don't understand . . ." Mason suddenly remembered the mobile phone he had stashed in the car earlier. Pulling it from the floorboard, he punched in her mobile number. No answer.

"Where were they? Do you know the number?" Mason was literally shouting in Felipe's ear now. The driver pulled his head away.

"I do not know the number."

Mason eyed him suspiciously. "Who exactly is meeting us?"

"Well, Perola and Henrique, and I guess Aide. I do not know who else."

Felipe seemed frightened, heightening Mason's angst.

"What happened to Emmanuel?"

"Who?"

"Emmanuel. You know, the kid. He was in the car earlier."

"Y . . . yes. I know Emmanuel, but he was not in the car earlier. I have been told that he is dead—trampled at the service riots. I have not seen him in some time. Are you feeling okay, Mr. Michael?"

Mason did not answer. Evil all around. Do not be deceived. Christ, he had been deceived so many times he didn't know what was real and what wasn't anymore. Wasn't that the test for mental illness? He punched in Rhodes' number on the mobile phone.

"Yeah?" The familiar arrogance was almost comforting.

"Aaron, Mike Mason." Static drifted over the line, then cleared.

"Hey! What the hell's happening? I can't fucking keep track of you."

"I know, I know. Listen, it's probably not safe to talk on this phone, but I wanted to get to you. I saw the Bishop. He confirmed everything." Mason covered his mouth in an effort to keep Felipe from listening. "I'm going to try to leave the country and bring my copy of the tape out with me."

The car slowed, interrupting him. Mason cupped his hand over the phone's receiver. "What's the deal? Checkpoint?"

"No, I thought so, but it is only someone's flat tire. We are almost to the cemetery."

Mason returned to the phone. "Listen, I've got to go. I'll keep you posted."

"Okay. Listen, Mikey, where ya tryin' to come out, huh? Maybe we can get ya some help."

"I'm not sure. The others were working that out. Paraguay or Argentina, I think. I'll let you know."

"Take care, kid."

The concrete hills of *Vila Alpina* stretched before them in the afternoon sun. The day seemed clearer than usual, the sun resilient instead of oppressive. Rows of mausoleums and headstones stretched into infinity, like the soldiers of a thousand armies standing watch over the central circle near the entrance. A blue American car idled alongside one edge of the circular roadway. Mason turned in his seat, searching for signs of cars following or nearby. Nothing. His anxiety began to ease. Felipe swung the car slowly through the cemetery's entranceway and into the circle. Perola's profile grew visible inside the blue car. Pulling out his phone, Mason punched in her mobile number once more.

"Yes?" Perola's startled voice came over the line. "Who is it?"

"It's me. Who else is with you?"

"Henrique, Vicente, and Aide. Is that you in the green car?"

"Yes." Mason ordered Felipe to stop the car across the circle from the blue car, maybe ten yards away.

"What are you doing?"

"I tried to reach you earlier. I have some disquieting news. First, I have seen Zhézush, the real Zhézush. She appeared to me in the form of Emmanuel, the Down's syndrome child."

"Michael, I—"

"Stop! Don't say anything. Just listen, okay?"

Perola murmured her assent. He could hear the other voices in the car, questioning.

"I saw the Bishop. He affirmed almost everything. He also told me that he thinks Vicente is a spy for Elisabeth."

"What?" More voices around her, louder this time.

"I think you should run for it. Does he have a—?"

A figure exited the passenger's side of the car, flinging the door shut behind him. Scraggly hair flopped wildly as he scrambled, crablike, away from the car. Other doors opened. A shout echoed across the circle.

"Perola, get out!" Mason screamed into the receiver.

It played out in slow motion. Vicente turned, twenty yards from the car, and aimed what looked like a video remote control device. Perola and Henrique were exiting opposite sides of the back seat. The blast of the explosion seemed caught in time, the orange ignition preceding by a split second shock waves that reared Mason's car up like a bucking horse, knocking him against the car door and out onto the hot pavement. Dizziness engulfed him. He lingered for seconds near unconsciousness. The acrid odor of the explosive brought him back. Eyes burning, he scrambled to his feet.

Dead silence met him. Where the blue car had once sat flames and pieces of twisted black metal rested in a shallow crater, as if the car had been swallowed by the earth, then parts of its smoldering chassis spit back. A tire freed of its harness spun crazily, silently, toward him, jumped a curb and veered off to his left. Flames lapped from an object in front of the crater. A body.

He stumbled toward it, tears from the smoke and realization hampering his vision. He stopped to wipe the moisture from his eyes and glanced around for Felipe, finally noticing the prostrate form wedged between his car's front and back seats. Still no noise, like a silent movie.

In the distance, the faintest sound of sirens. He hesitated, snapping his head back and forth between his car, the burning metal, the body. The green Ford looked none the worse for wear. Hesitation again. Then, into the driver's seat. A shove sent Felipe's body into the back seat. Dead or alive? Friend or foe? There was no time.

Turn of the key. Cough, then catch. A spin into reverse. His eyes searched the blast scene for signs of movement. None. No one could have survived, he knew. Still, one last look, around the other end of the circle.

There! Movement behind a crumbled mausoleum front. A man, his shaggy hair singed on two sides. Raising his arm. A gun.

The dull crash of bullet into glass and metal, as if a thousand miles away. The car, still running. Somehow, into reverse again. Another thud. The car shimmying, like a buffalo speared in its side. Then off, in blue smoke.

Where? The unfamiliar streets rolled by. Unconsciously, almost, Mason pushed the accelerator harder. Numbness overtook him. He was a shell, moving on synapses he barely controlled. A police car, lights flashing, sped the other way. Mason's hands shook on the steering wheel, presaging spastic quivers of his entire body. His breath caught in a great choking gasp. He was sobbing.

Had the inflamed body been Perola's? His mind recoiled. Should he have searched for her? Could he go back now? The absurdity failed to extinguish any of the pain. He drove on, blindly.

Street signs whirled past: Orlando Calisto, Melida Costa. A traffic light at Herwel. An interior sense of direction told him he was headed east, but it could be wrong. Passengers in other cars, glancing in his direction. Was the curfew still on? He couldn't remember. His mind struggled to right itself. What was the date? Who was president? He glanced at his watch for reassurance. 3:40 P.M.

A slowdown in traffic ahead. Cars ground to a stop, brake lights blinking angrily. A woman with a large hat—was it a woman?—sauntered by on the sidewalk. Faint whistles from some of the cars. Something was wrong with his hearing. A large billboard advertised Kaiser beer. The people in it looked happy, relaxed, as if they could look down on it all and see it only as a silly game. Cars inched forward. A woman and her mother in the car next to his, smiling. Distant music buzzed like an insect.

Blue lights flashed ahead. A glimpse of uniform. He realized it must be a checkpoint, that he would undoubtedly be discovered. Halfheartedly, he pulled blankets from the car's floorboard over Felipe's form in the backseat—maybe it resembled a pile of jumbled laundry. The cars inched forward. His gaze played over frame houses and side streets. He could abandon the car and run, if he had the energy.

Perola. His mind tripped over itself in anguish. He was responsible; he had brought her into this entire mess. The one woman who meant more than anything—had he loved her? She was someone else's wife, yet he had felt closer to her than if they had actually . . . What could he have done? His heart felt like it had stopped beating.

He twisted in the seat, regaining some senses. The videocassette—was it still here? His fingers wrapped gratefully around the hard plastic. Blue smoke to catch up with the line. A flip of the cassette into the crowded glove box, then out again. Hastily, under the seat. His hand found the mobile phone; shaking fingers punched in numbers. Nothing. He cast it aside.

Now second in line. Maybe a half dozen uniformed officers, state police. Dark green uniforms darker with sweat. He slumped in his seat.

"May I see your license?" The voice seemed far away, as though a window separated them.

Mechanically, he pulled his wallet from a pocket.

"You are an American?"

A weary nod. The large, shiny black face bent closer. Oddly shaped teeth dominated a large mouth.

"You are a reporter, Mr. Mason?" In English, now.

He looked up. "Yes." His own voice sounded odd. Thick, drugged, distant.

"Many are searching for you." The face very close to his now. "Can you follow instructions?"

Hesitance. "Yes."

"Take this road until you reach a sign for Sapopemba. Approximately four kilometers. Turn left at the sign. Go two blocks, park on the left. The establishment is called *Túmulus.* They are expecting you. Stop for no one." With an official abruptness the officer was away, waving impatiently for Mason to move ahead.

He sat dumbfounded through another impatient series of waves. More car horns behind him. Into drive and lurching forward, leaving blue smoke. Open highway in front of him. Four kilometers. His mind spinning again. Friend or foe? He had imagined himself detained, searched, captured. Instead, he was free.

His spirits lifted minutely, the will to live cutting through the fog of numbness and grief. He forced himself to count the kilometers off. One. Traffic was lighter, faster. Two. Three. A big dog bounded alongside on the sidewalk, racing or chasing. Four, and there was the sign. Metal groaned as the big car turned.

Two dirty blocks. Nothing moving, mostly warehouses and dust. A peeling soft drink sign garnished a yellow window. The sign for *Túmulus*—wasn't that Portuguese for tombs?—was small and faded. Fear built again in his stomach. He stopped the car and got out, afraid to leave Felipe's body or the cassette. Several minutes went by as he loitered helplessly, looking at the small dark window next to the *Túmulus* door, the only *Túmulus* window. Finally, he grabbed the cassette, tucked it under his jacket, and made his way across the street.

Closer proximity to the filmy window did not improve the view. The establishment appeared to be closed, if not abandoned. No movement inside, no light, except for strands filtering in from the same window. A dusty table and chairs. He edged back from the building, looking for another entrance. Perhaps a warehouse in the back? He glanced nervously at the car, then circled the building. Large metal garage doors at the back showed more recent signs of use, with the pattern of truck tires visible in the dirt alleyway.

He banged on the garage door. No response. Returning to the street, he knocked on the door with the little window. Nothing. His hand gripped the knob, and it turned easily. Slowly, irresolutely, he entered. The smell of cut wood and sawdust greeted him. Stepping forward, his shoes made clacking noises on the concrete floor. He cleared his throat. The sound seemed like a vacuum inside his head.

"Hello!" he called, unsure of his voice's volume.

Nothing. Then, a shuffling from the back of the building. A door opened and shut. Another person entered the room, the dim light obscuring his face. The easy swagger of a young man.

"Who is it?" a voice called softly in Portuguese.

"Michael Mason." The words sounded silly. What was he doing here?

"Ah." The figure moved into view. Maybe twenty years old, black, but with hair dyed blond. His face scarred or tattooed. Eyes that jumped.

"Follow me." The youth turned, sending a plume of dust into the air, and moved quietly toward the rear of the building. Mason followed, shoes flapping against the floor. They worked their way among scattered tables and filing cabinets into a large warehouse, apparently the area beyond the garage doors at the back of the building. Fluorescent lights illuminated several large work stations, surrounded by saws and piles of lumber. The smell of sawdust and wood and glue intensified. To one side of the warehouse, stacked row upon row, thirty feet to the ceiling, lay the finished product: hundreds of wooden caskets. A battered half-ton truck, its back yawning open, apparently being loaded. A greasy forklift in front of the truck, its arms uplifted with a load of three caskets. Mason shuddered and sought the safety of a wall to lean against. An image of a bullet in the back of his head flashed through his mind.

"This is your ride to São Angelo," said the young man, with a nod of his blond head toward the truck. Another man appeared from the front of the truck, short, mustached, a gold chain hanging from his neck.

"Thanks." Questions surfaced, unasked. Who were these people? What were their names? Why were they doing this? What was in São Angelo?

The short man beckoned Mason toward the back of the truck, then hopped onto its bed in a spry half-jump. Mason moved forward uncertainly. What was he supposed to do—ride in the back with the caskets? The short man jumped up on the pile in the truck and wrenched open the lid of a casket near the top.

"No. No." Mason was on the truck bed now. "You want me to—no."

"You have little choice, my friend," said the blond from behind him, now also on the truck bed. "You will be fine. It is not far. There is plenty of air—see?" The short man pointed to holes around the casket's lip. "We have provided padding for your comfort. Here is a water bottle and a sandwich. Do you need to use the restroom?"

23

As it is written in the prophets, Behold, I send my messenger before thy face, which shall prepare thy way before thee. The voice of one crying in the wilderness, Prepare ye the way of the Lord, make his paths straight.

Mark 1:2-3

Perola's eyes fluttered open, then closed again. Some whir she could not identify droned beside her, contributing to her pain. She coughed and sputtered, besieged by pain that plagued all consciousness. The sweet blackness of unconsciousness closed around her until she fell gratefully into it, only to be pulled out again by a choke-inducing substance at her nose.

She opened her eyes to let in the pain. She was in a hospital. A white-suited nurse stood over her, passing the vile substance back under her nostrils again. Another cough. Every nerve in her body felt inflamed and uprooted. She fought back the scream that welled deep inside her. No one could endure this pain. Comforting darkness closed around her again.

"Listen to me!" Another face near hers. She recognized the flawless features, as if from a previous life. Elisabeth.

"Where is he?" The eyes burrowed in. Perola struggled to remember. What had happened? Mason had gone to the prison, and they were to meet him—was he still there?

"Another dose, nurse." Elisabeth pulled away, then returned to her position inches from Perola's face. "You see, my dear, you can hide nothing from me. Nor can you die without my consent. So you will hang, in this painful limbo, until I get what I want."

Perola's mind floated untethered. She felt the prick of a needle somewhere in the forest of pain. Almost immediately, numbness entered her body, working its way among the jumble of nerve endings. The blackness around her receded.

"Where is Michael Mason?" whispered Elisabeth conspiratorially, now a best friend.

"He went to the prison to meet the Bishop," Perola heard herself say, her voice flat, a million miles away.

"And from there?"

"He was to meet us, at the cemetery."

"Where was he to go from there?"

"We were leaving the country. Argentina, I think. Henrique had it worked out."

"Where?"

"I do not know."

"You are sure?"

A pause. "Yes."

Elisabeth leaned back from Perola's chest. The pain intensified again. Perola could see bandages on her arms, charred flesh where her fingers used to be. The pain built to another crescendo. She gasped for breath.

"Monitor her closely," Elisabeth commanded the nurse. "If she says anything at all, I want to know. I will return shortly."

Perola closed her eyes, trying to divert her attention from the pain. Helplessly, she opened them again. A figure leaned over her. The nurse, this time. Something familiar about her. Was she hallucinating? A single chipped tooth. Vile breath. The nurse lovingly raised a syringe. Another prick of pain, barely noticeable. Then, the sweet blackness closing in around her.

"Goodbye, dear," said Velda. "We will meet again soon."

He awoke, screaming, from a half-dream of being buried alive. The truck rocked from side to side, its cargo bumping and shifting. The heat was not as unbearable as he had anticipated, but the lack of air circulation left him with an overpowering feeling of suffocation. Twisting in the box, he slammed his nose against the air holes, like a dog straining at a fence. The darkness of his tomb made the air seem thicker, crushing his chest in a malevolent vise. Hell could not possibly be worse than this long, slow death.

At some point the truck had stopped. He had heard voices, the sound of the rear door opening, prodding among the boxes. He had wanted to shout, to be rescued, to be freed from his prison, but the pressure on his lungs and head had been so great he had only managed a feeble, unnoticed yelp. With the slamming of doors the truck had pulled away again, abandoning him to the torture of the shrinking box.

His mind reeled through periods of lucidity, dream, and hallucination. During the lucid periods he attempted to sort out pieces and events, struggling to make sense of the child/Zhézush, his/her message, the Bishop's revelations, the ambush at the cemetery. It appeared Elisabeth and her group were now completely aligned with the government, or at least with the military, against whatever vestiges of the old Zhézushians remained. He supposed those who had helped him escape, the officer at the checkpoint, the employees of the casket company, were somehow tied in with Aide and the old Zhézushians, those whose natural inclination was to distrust the military and the government. Still, why were they helping him? How did they even know who he was? How was he to know them? He felt the hard edge of the videocassette beside him in the darkness. Was this the prize everyone was after—to protect or to destroy?

Consciousness gave way to vivid dreams, in which a great horned figure chased him down a hole, then heaped debris on top of him. He felt the heat of the beast's breath, saw the sharpness of the horns, sensed oxygen slipping away. The debris kicked up a dust, choking him in a vicious tourniquet of filth. Just as the dust closed in and the last gasp of air vanished, a slender hand reached through to pull him out. A human hand, pink and tender and fleshy, its nails white and gleaming. He reached for the hand in a surge of gratitude, only to realize that it was connected to an alien arm, a red, hairy thing, an appendage of the beast. Drawing back in horror, he watched as the hand changed into a cruel claw, which grasped and cut him. Then the claw withdrew, plugging the last gap in the debris, blocking all light and air.

His screams woke him. Visions appeared on the plywood inches from his face, first of Zhézush, her round body jiggling like gelatin, then of the child Emmanuel. He closed his eyes, blinking them open again, but the image remained. It changed like a kaleidoscope, now of the Bishop, his face in his hands, now of Perola, her eyes large and afraid, struggling to escape the blue car. He pounded on the walls of the casket, desperate to break the field, determined to wake himself, but knowing he was awake. The vision slipped to one of Elisabeth, silky hair shapely and perfect, her mouth luscious and inviting. He struggled against the casket, as if bound in a straightjacket, banging his head on the plywood. Blood found its way down his forehead, plaguing his eyes, salty against his lips. The image of Elisabeth remained, his mind playing down her body, first on her neck, then her shoulders, down to her exposed breasts. Flinging himself again against the confines of his prison, he rocked the casket, sucking precious oxygen. With a great creaking the lid of the box opened. Light and eyes peered inside. He screamed again and passed into unconsciousness.

He awoke on a couch, in an un-air-conditioned apartment, an overhead fan bathing his face with warm air. Stretching, he felt no boundaries; the claustrophobic confinement of the casket was gone, a horrendous nightmare over. His muscles relaxed, his breathing in rhythm with the circular movements of the fan. He must have dreamed the entire episode. Surely it had been a hallucination of sorts, brought on by conflict and fear.

He sat up, wincing at the soreness. His hands played across his face, finding a tender scab on his forehead. He was clad only in the same foul-smelling T-shirt and underwear he had been wearing for days. Where was he? Where were his clothes? Light pierced a hole in a metal shade across a window. The sound of utensils against a sink came from somewhere below him. The room smelled of dog, though he saw no sign of any animal.

His feet found the floor. He remembered. It had not been a dream. He had been transported in a wooden box out of São Paulo, supposedly to somewhere on the coast. Treading softly to the window, he pulled open the blind. The clutter of a crowded dirt alleyway stretched before him, quiet in the afternoon sun. Dwellings of cardboard, concrete block, and a hodgepodge of other materials faced him across the narrow passageway. Flaglike clothing fluttered on clotheslines. All manner of rusty metal antennas elbowed and stretched their way to the sky. It could be São Paulo, or Caracas, or Athens, or anywhere.

The sound of a scrape against one wall sent him back to the center of the room. Padding in bare feet to the only door, he listened to movement behind it. From behind the peeling panels came the sound of breathing. Then a snicker. The high-pitched giggle of a child. He tried the doorknob. Locked.

"Hello! Who is there?" He realized he had spoken in English, and tried again in Portuguese.

More giggles. The sound of an animal's nails clattering on the wooden floor. A soft bark, then a child's voice, shushing the animal.

He sat back on his haunches, examining the room in more detail. It was small, maybe ten by twelve, matching twin beds pressed against two walls. A dirty oval rug anchored the room's center. Against the other wall, a simple chest of drawers lay partially opened, clothes spewed from its top. Yellowed posters decorated two of the walls, advertising—he squinted to see in the half-light—some sort of beverage. A scantily-clad young woman. A race car.

Steps clumping up stairs. Another voice, whispering. The child's voice, in response, plaintively explaining in Portuguese, "But I did not open!"

A key scraped. The door opened an inch. He moved silently backward, staring at the widening crack, which abruptly slammed shut, then opened again. This time, wide enough to reveal the faces of two boys, maybe seven and ten. Below them a dog of uncertain origin, poking its head around the door.

Mason pulled a blanket around himself.

The older boy stuck his head into the room. His skin was light brown, offset by wide white eyes. An almost-shaved head like a chocolate egg. The dog ventured farther in, followed by the smaller boy.

"What is your name?" asked Mason softly.

The boys hesitated, looking at one another for assurance. "Roberto," said the older one, finally. "He is Julio." He gestured at his brother. "We wanted to see the man who stays in our room."

Mason smiled. "Are your parents home?"

Both boys shook their heads vigorously. "The father will be back soon," offered Julio eagerly.

"I see. Where do you live?"

"In Gloria," Roberto responded.

"Is that a city?"

"It is like a city," said Roberto importantly. "It is a part of Rio de Janeiro."

"Ah, I see." He had been taken all the way to Rio. No wonder he was so sore. He had been in the box a lot longer than an hour or two.

"What is your dog's name?"

"Savage," replied Julio shyly.

Footsteps sounded somewhere downstairs, and the boys scurried to shut the door. A loud voice in the stairwell, calling, then angry. Thumps on the stairs. Then, a respectful knock, the click of a key, the turning of the knob again.

A slight, bewhiskered man in clerical garb entered, bowing to Mason. "My apologies, your worship. I hope my boys did not trouble you. They are most curious." The whiskers formed a yellow goatee around his mouth.

"Not at all. They were fine."

"I am Father Molina, priest of the Gloria parish.You have been sent to me by a friend. I have agreed to help you leave the country. This is something I have some experience with. I have helped others in difficult circumstances." He stepped over to Mason, extending a leathery hand.

More voices downstairs. This time, the warm timbre of a woman. Several women. "Our sanctuary is downstairs." Father Molina smiled benignly.

Lighter clumps on the stairs. Mason retreated to the bed, pulling the bedclothes around his dirty body. Two youthful nuns in dark habits entered the room, one stout and smiling, the other lithe and serious.

"This is Sister Heloisa," Father Molina pointed to the thinner one, "and Sister Esmeralda. They assist me with my duties and with the school here." The two nuns bowed and backed out of the room. "You are a very famous person," Father Molina said brightly.

"I am?"

"Yes. Your picture is all over the news. There is a large reward for information regarding your whereabouts—twenty million *reais.*" He pursed his lips. "Roberto, Julio. Downstairs with you, okay? Do not bother Mr. Mason any more."

The boys scampered away. Savage remained behind with Father Molina.

"I praise God for your presence," said Father Molina, moving closer and grasping Mason's hand again. Savage rustled forward and began licking the other hand.

"You take a major risk by hiding me," said Mason. "It is I who praise God for you."

Father Molina shrugged. "We will provide you safe passage, and all will be well."

"What exactly is the plan for that?"

"Tomorrow night, a freighter leaves for Miami. I have papers for you to be aboard that boat as a cook. Your name will be Benito Banderas. The docks are only two blocks from here. It will be dark; we can get you there unseen."

"Once I am on the boat?"

"It is up to you. We could try to get in touch with someone in the U.S., to intercept the ship."

Mason sat back on the narrow bed. "Explain something to me, Father. Why are you willing to risk your life to do this? What is going on? What group are you a part of?"

The yellowed goatee parted to reveal teeth capped in silver. "I am part of the Church, my friend. A Monsignor Deceptor asked me to help you. From Rome."

24

. . . and, lo, I am with you alway, *even* unto the
end of the world.

Matthew 28:20

The tiny shower produced a spitting spray of lukewarm water, which Mason nonetheless reveled in. He tried to imagine the water cleansing his aching psyche, washing away the hurt of Perola's death. Rome was somehow aware of his predicament—at least there was that. He wondered if the Bishop was still alive, concluded that he probably wasn't. Even if by some miracle he had survived the fire at the prison, he almost certainly was of no further use to Elisabeth and the others.

They were all dead or probably dead now: Cunha, Perola, Henrique, Aide, the Bishop . . . Zhézush. Only he and Elisabeth remained alive. Elisabeth and a thousand *ajudantes*, all looking for him. With a start he remembered the videocassette, hurriedly wrapped a towel around his midsection, and returned to the boys' room. He found his clean pants, hanging on a chair, his watch and wallet, but no sign of the tape. The floor squeaked behind him and he whirled quickly in surprise, momentarily dropping the towel.

"I am sorry," whispered the thin nun Heloisa, a tray of food in her hands. "I thought you were still in the bath." Her gaze searched briefly over his body, then returned to the floor.

"It's okay." Mason secured the towel around himself and moved forward to accept the tray. "Thank you very much."

Her eyes lifted off the floor to meet his for a charged second, then lowered again. "I go now," she said, backing out of the room. "We will be in the room across the hall. Please call if you need anything." Savage poked his head in, then retreated.

Mason devoured the food, scarcely slowing to take notice of its content. He could not remember the last time he had eaten. The sight of his pants returned him to the harsh realization that thousands were actively seeking his capture, that millions would gladly turn him in and collect on the more-than-substantial reward. Was this the best the Church could do? His spirits sank again. He tried a few push-ups, hoping to reboost his circulation and energy, but quickly gave up in despair. What was the point?

He wondered what Rhodes was doing. Probably rushing in someone else to finish the story. His phone—what had happened to it? He searched briefly through the room.

A polite knock at the door interrupted him. Father Molina peered through the open doorway.

"Hi."

"Hello. I just wanted to make sure you have everything you need. We go to bed early on nights we do not have services."

"Thanks. Listen, when you unloaded me, was there a videocassette inside with me? Or a portable phone?"

"Oh, yes, yes. At least, as far as the videotape. Is it not in here?"

Mason shook his head.

"I will have to ask Heloisa and Esmeralda. They may have put it somewhere for safekeeping. I do not know anything about a phone." He moved excitedly out of the room, calling Heloisa's name. A few moments later he returned holding a dirty white cassette.

"You don't have a player, do you? A videotape player?" Mason indicated the cassette.

"Ah, no."

"That's okay. How about a radio? I'm not ready to go to bed just yet."

"But of course. Roberto!" He clapped his hands together, and the older boy quickly appeared. "Where is your radio?"

The boy attacked a pile of debris on one side of the room, eventually emerging with a battered boom box. He plugged it into a wall outlet, and a stream of flat, tinny-sounding music sputtered forth. "See?" The boy held it up to Mason, excited that the visitor would want something of his. Father Molina edged out of the room.

"Thank you so much," said Mason. "I will take good care of it tonight."

The boy hopped on the bed and propped himself up on his elbows, evidently anxious to stay. Behind the door came the wails of his younger brother, denied equal opportunity.

"You are a fugitive, no?"

"Well, yes, I suppose so."

"How does it feel?"

"Not too good right now. It's hard to relax."

"Have you been shot at?"

"Yes."

Roberto's eyes grew large. "Were you hurt?"

"No. Maybe you had better go back to your brother now."

The boy obediently slid off the bed. "Do not worry," he said earnestly. "We will not let you be discovered."

"Thank you." Mason fiddled with the boom box, clicking through several music stations before settling on a newscaster's serious tone.

". . . and the interim coalition government indicated no businesses are expected to be nationalized or otherwise subjected . . . to government control . . ."

He struggled to keep up with the rapid Portuguese, made more difficult without benefit of seeing the speaker. ". . . Nations around the world have acknowledged the legitimacy of the interim government, as ambassadors from Japan, Russia, India . . . today paid their respects to General Raul Camargo and Elisabeth Obrando, the leaders of the coalition . . ." Elisabeth, a leader of the governing coalition? His mind reeled. From liberal activist to right-wing collaborator, all to the benefit of her own power.

". . . the Brazilian stock market, which had suspended activity on Tuesday, resumed operations today, down twenty-four. . . . General Camargo announced that the inflation index for the current month showed minimal movement, which he attributed to the strength of the Brazilian economy, even through the governmental transition. When asked, the General predicted . . . the general assembly would reconvene in approximately two weeks. The curfew, still in effect for São Paulo, Rio, and most of the country, is expected to be lifted within the next few days. The spate of suicides since the change in government appears to have eased, as none have been reported during the past twenty-four hours . . .

"In other news, the manhunt continues for the fugitive American newspaperman accused of the murder of one of his co-workers and her husband. Forty-three-year-old Michael Mason was last seen heading south from São Paulo in a green American Ford. He is considered extremely dangerous. A thirty million *reais* reward has been established by the government for information leading to his arrest. He is described as white, approximately six feet two inches tall, with dark wavy hair . . ."

Mason pulled his legs up underneath himself, squeezing into a ball, as if the action would render him less noticeable. Elisabeth was co-leader of one of the world's largest countries. He was a fugitive with a huge ransom on his head. It seemed unreal, as if he had dreamed it, and for a few seconds he comforted himself with the thought that he had simply slipped out of reality. Recovering, he shifted his gaze around the room, fighting the impulse to run. He was completely at the mercy of these people he had never met before, strangers on whom his life now depended. His mind played over the plan Father Molina had laid out. How could the nicotine-stained clergyman be so certain this would work? At least some of the operation evidently depended on forged papers of some kind; nothing about the man brooked any confidence as to the likely efficacy of such instruments.

Shivering, he pulled the blanket around himself. How could he hope to get away with it? His thoughts careened back to Perola. Grief overwhelmed him. The bastards blaming him for the deaths of Perola and Henrique, probably getting away with it. The image of Perola's white teeth and laughing eyes flashed by, bringing new sorrow, flowing into a complication of feelings for this colleague and friend and . . . and what? The sense of loss was huge, too huge. There had been something more than friendship, he was sure of it, and he had realized it only too late. What else could he have done? He should have known the rendezvous would be a trap, should have recognized his true feelings. It was all mixed up together. Why had he allowed Felipe to proceed?

His eyes caught on an object poking out from under a blanket near the end of the bed. With a swipe he picked up the hard plastic shell of the videocassette and ran his fingers down its spine. Was it relief he felt, or additional anxiety? Could the contents of this flimsy contraption really be that important? He thought back to his conversation with the child/Zhézush, trying to remember exactly what he had said. He had warned him of treachery, and temptation.

Scrolling the radio dial, he floated in a half-daze. For some reason he felt like a prisoner awaiting execution, time suddenly stalled and slow. One way or another, he told himself, it would be over within the next twenty-four hours. Another news broadcast detailing his description and the manhunt shook him out of his reverie, and he dropped down onto his knees beside the bed, offering a silent, simple prayer for salvation. No bartering. No conditions. Just a plea for help. Her words came back to him, floating, gossamer-like: "Remember only that I am with you . . ."

He must have dozed off, for when he awoke the room had darkened to grim shadows. Blood pumping, he searched for the noise that had stirred him. It came again, a scrape at the door, then the click of a key turning in the lock. Bounding off the bed into a defensive crouch, his dulled mind tried to formulate some sort of strategy. Light streamed around the door's corners, like water gushing over a dam, framing the intruder in its beam, showing the unmistakable shape of a woman.

Heloisa closed the door quietly but firmly behind her. She paused at the door, still clad in her habit, eyes searching but evidently not yet adjusted to the gloom. He could see her quite clearly, and his breath caught as she flicked off her robes to expose transparent underclothes affording a view of her youthful body. Her lips parted in a smile as she caught sight of him. Moving forward, she reached behind her neck to release the catch of the flimsy clothing so that it dropped like rain on a slick surface. She stopped a few feet away from him, the coif the only bit of clothing that remained, her body gleaming like precious stone. He remained crouched, looking up at her, his throat constricting in a swallow so loud it sounded like speech. Slowly, silently, she pressed herself closer to him, and then he was on his feet, backpedaling, whispering something to her, pleading. She pursued, one hand clutching his neck, the other on his crotch.

"Heloisa, no! I don't think this is good!"

She pressed relentlessly onward, her mouth hot on his. He was helpless against it—the ultimate sacrilege, the ultimate excitement, the familiar falling spiral. He raised an arm in futile protest. The movement dislodged the coif, revealing close-cropped hair. Something hard glittered and fell to the floor, skittering under the bed. He stared stupidly at it, then at her. She was sobbing now, her eyes red even in the darkness. "They will exploit your weakness." The words came back to him.

"What?"

She pulled away suddenly, her eyes sparkling, then turned, exiting, her round buttocks dipping and flattening as she stooped to retrieve her discarded garments. She reached swiftly under the bed, then continued toward the door. He followed after her in a helpless half-trot, catching her hand as she prepared to pull open the door. What had she retrieved?

The hot eyes shone on his, her jaw locked in place. "Why not submit," she said softly. He hesitated, then grasped her hand and pulled it open, revealing a small knife. "For safety," she whispered between red-eyed sobs, then opened the door and left the room.

He leaned against the door, his hands upon his head, his groin locked in place. Depletion washed about him in an overwhelming wave. Had she meant to kill him? The close-cropped hair—an *ajudante*? His stomach catapulted.

Should he try to leave? His eyes spun to the room's only window. He crept to it—locked or nailed shut. Back to the door, his full weight against it. Was Heloisa regrouping with the other one? Would a thousand *ajudantes* be upon him?

He returned to the bed, nauseous and dizzy, tucking his trembling hands under his arms to calm their movement. From across the room the radio announced yet again his description and the details of the reward. He held his head in his hands, lapping the warm, wet, salty tears that ran down his face and into his mouth.

After some time he arose. He tumbled off the bed and cocked his ear at the door—silence. Easing open the room's door, he made silently for the bathroom across the hall. He grabbed some scissors and went to work, whacking his thick hair back into an uneven stubble, leaving the several days' growth of beard alone. The effect was not exactly flattering, but different. For good measure he trimmed his eyebrows back to almost nothing. Perhaps he looked less like the image splattered across every TV screen in Brazil. Back in his room, he heard a door slam below, footsteps on the stairs. His stomach tightened anew.

A soft knocking at his door paralyzed him, and with wordless trepidation he watched the knob slowly turn. Roberto's small head peeked around the door's edge.

"Mr. Mason? Is that you?"

"Yes, it's me." Mason's shoulders collapsed in relief. The first grim glimpse of dawn crept through the window.

"I must talk to you. It is extremely important." Savage, the dog, bounded into the room.

"What is it?"

"You are in danger."

"Yes, I know."

"No, you do not understand. I watched Heloisa enter your room. She left the house just now. She is to betray you, I think, for the reward. I knew she would do this. There is no time. You must escape now!"

Spasms hit Mason's stomach with such force he feared he might lose control of his bowels. "But—"

"Hurry! I have a plan." Roberto pushed Mason ahead of him. "Go!"

Mason snatched the videocassette off the table as he tumbled out of the room. Down the stairs and into the dim light outside. Pausing, paralyzed again. Roberto pushing him from behind. Stares from some on the street. Trying to blend in. Roberto in front of him, churning on short legs. The dog following along. Christ, he might as well give up now.

His eyes adjusted to the street. Roberto veered down an alleyway, then another, then into a dark crevice between two buildings. They rested against a pile of rotting mattresses, breathing hard.

"What is your idea?" asked Mason.

"We must get to the airport," Roberto responded. "I have friends."

"Maybe you should circle back around and see if Heloisa has really come back with the authorities or anyone else. Is it possible that you were mistaken?"

"No! She would suspect me if she saw me. Believe me, she is evil."

Mason covered his face with his hands again. Was he insane? He had placed his entire security in the hands of a ten-year-old boy. Father Molina's plan had seemed risky, but at least it was something. This was suicidal. Why throw his fate to the winds in a blind faith that he would somehow be protected? He should go back to the house and alert Father Molina.

The crisp, rhythmic sound of boots on pavement filled the alley. Mason edged more deeply into the crevice. A quartet of green-jacketed soldiers marched by, eyes ahead, guns slung loosely over shoulders. The smell of burning cigarettes lingered behind them, long after their muted conversation and ordered steps echoed down the passageway into nothingness.

"Come!" Roberto shot out into the alley.

Mason followed as the boy veered in the direction from which the soldiers had approached. They ducked down a steep hill, through a foul-smelling, trash-filled ravine, underneath a railroad trestle, emerging onto a more affluent street of trim, white-washed houses.

Mason struggled to keep up, wiping sweat from his newly shorn scalp as the humidity closed in around him. The boy darted down another side street, then another, into a congested area of multi-laned automobile traffic. Corcovado Mountain loomed suddenly above them, majestic above a layer of haze. Mason stopped to catch his breath and take in the statue at its top: Christ the Redeemer, arms outstretched, welcoming all, but not them.

"Come on!" Roberto's high-pitched voice beckoned him from across the road. He pulled his gaze away, waited for a car to pass. Something in the car caught his eye, diverting his attention. The front-seat passenger wore a black shirt, with a . . . hood. Short, severe hair. The car passed, breaking the connection, but he saw the figure turning. Brake lights flamed. He scrambled across the road, joining Roberto down a muddy embankment.

"I think I was spotted!" His breath came in great, shuddering gasps.

"Come!"

Off again, down a narrow pathway, through refuse-strewn streets. Lungs searing. Following. Sweat penetrating his eyes, stinging and blinding him. Groping his way around an overflowing dumpster pillaged by pigs and dogs. Shrugging against his face with first one shoulder, then the other, trying vainly to clear his vision.

"Wait!" Roberto and the dog were fifty yards ahead of him now, barely visible.

Car tires crunched on the street behind him. The Young Assistant? He whirled, running blindly half-backwards, stumbled and fell. The car bore down upon him. With a panicked thrust of his shoulders he tried to propel himself out of the way.

A monstrous bumper. The sizzle of the tires burned past his ears. Somersaulting backward over a shoulder, then a crack and a jolt of pain as it popped out of socket.

"*Louco!*" a youthful voice rang out. The car careened away.

Crazy. Synapses in his brain moved in agreement, before descending into a cacophony of pain.

He had never known such pain. Despite his anguish and Roberto's assistance, the shoulder refused to re-seat. He choked back a scream, relegating himself to a few quivering whimpers. They were inside a nearby house, owned by a relative of Roberto. Mason's good shoulder was braced against a concrete block wall. At his direction, Roberto worked the other.

"All right, try again. No . . . auggrr!" Just as he felt he would pass out from the agony, a slight pop and a deadening of nerves signaled the shoulder's realignment. Gingerly, he moved his arm in a low semicircle. Not full range of motion, but better. He slumped against the wall, drained. "Is there anything to drink?"

"I will get some juice." Roberto disappeared into a small kitchen, returning with a bottle of soda. "Will this be okay?"

Mason nodded, grasping for the drink like a dying man.

"We can rest here for a little while," Roberto said. "My uncle will not be home for some time."

"What would he do if he knew that I was here?"

The boy grinned. "Turn you in for the reward. He is not so religious, like Father Molina."

"How much farther is it to the airport?"

"Several hours, on foot. Not too far."

"Yeah. Listen, kid, what exactly do you have in mind, huh? I can't just show up at the airport, buy a ticket, and get on a plane. They'll want to see a passport, and then I'll be screwed."

"I have friends who work there. Other friends who steal there. We will smuggle you onboard."

"Right. I've got a better idea. Is there a phone here?"

"Yes, of course."

"Take me to it." Roberto led him down a short hallway.

"But, who will you call?"

"Someone who can help me. Someone in the U.S."

"Do you not think that they will trace the call?"

"How?"

"I have seen it in the movies. You will use a credit card, right? They know the number. The minute that number shows up—boom, they are onto you!"

Mason shook his head and picked up the phone. The kid's imagination was out of control. For all he knew, the thing with Heloisa had been completely fabricated. He could be resting comfortably in the room above the church, waiting for nightfall and his trip to the docks. Instead, here he was with this kid and a dog, running around in broad daylight so that every *ajudante*, soldier, and ransom hunter in the country could pinpoint his location. He dialed Rhodes' number in New York, then waited for the beep.

Instead, an operator came on the line. "May I help you?"

"Yes, I am trying to place a credit card call."

"Card number?" He rattled off the *Herald* number. A series of beeps and whirs followed.

"I am sorry, sir. That card number is not valid. Do you have another?"

"How could that number not be valid?" He realized he had slipped into English. "May I place a collect call instead?"

"One moment, sir." Another delay. Jeez, maybe the kid was right. There was something screwy about this.

"Did you think you could escape me?" The voice floated to him across the wire, cramping his stomach with the force of a sledgehammer. "Why fight me? It is much easier if we are together."

Elisabeth. How? The voice sounded so supple, so inviting. Why was he fighting it? They would catch him anyway. The thought of her embrace warmed him.

"I am with you always, as before. Remember this."

Chills swept up his spine and across his scalp, blotting out the warmth. He jammed at the phone's disengagement button, missing it several times before he could bring the line to silence.

He stared at the phone as if it were alive. His gaze rose to meet Roberto's. "They will be here soon. You were right. They tapped the card somehow."

Like a rabbit Roberto shot out of the house through a side door, into yet another alleyway. Tires squealed on the pavement above them. Farther away, sirens blared.

Clotheslines, animals, people, pavement. The smell of bread baking. Teens dancing before a motley assembly. An old man, angry over his upended card table. Across a minefield of broken bottles. Other boys about Roberto's age, with torn clothing and dirty faces, acknowledging their flight as a normal occurrence. Skirting the edge of a holding pond, exposed momentarily to the world, then disappearing again into another cluster of buildings. He glanced behind once—no pursuit. Sweat pouring into his eyes again, burning. His lungs as if a flame had been placed underneath them. How much farther could he go?

Roberto ducked into a large building. Mason followed inside, into a gymnasium of sorts. Wooden steps led to a second-story balcony. The floor appeared polished, gleaming in the gloom.

"Thank God. I've got to rest for a second." Mason plopped onto the floor. "Why don't we take a taxi?"

"The taxi drivers are all looking for you. They want the reward. They are looking for someone of your description who wants to go to the airport."

Mason's breath still came in gasps. "How far to the airport?"

"A ways. But we could wait here for a while. It is probably safer than on the streets." He turned to the dog. "Home, now!" Savage's jumping tail stilled, and with a sad look he edged out the open door.

Mason leaned against a cool wooden wall. His shoulder throbbed with pain. "Why help me, Roberto? You could turn me in yourself. Make millions for yourself. I mean, I'll probably be caught anyway. It may as well be you who makes the money."

The boy frowned and shook his head. "It is what Father Molina would wish for me to do," he said calmly. "He took me in when no one else would have me, taught me that the truth is much richer than wealth could ever be. I believe you are of God. That is all that matters."

A door to the building creaked open, admitting a shaft of light and a large black woman, her hair piled on top of her head. She did not catch sight of them immediately, but Roberto was already on his feet, edging back into the shadows.

The woman screamed as if she had sighted a cockroach.

Escape, their flight picking up speed, through the loose boards from which they had entered, out into the damp, hot sunshine. Down a stream bed, into a crowded, bustling street. Trying to blend in with the crowd, head down. Rounding a curve, confronting a giant billboard, his own face peering down from it. His breath knocked out of his body, leaving him croaking.

"Jesus!" His body locked in place, staring up at his image.

"Come!" hissed Roberto.

The trance was broken, his feet moving again, respiration intact. His gaze still on the billboard, with its reward offer twenty feet high. A police car passed slowly, going the opposite way. Roberto ducked into a storefront.

"We must obtain some disguise," he whispered in Mason's ear. "Even with your haircut, you will be recognized. Your picture is everywhere! Do you have any money?"

Mason fished out several bills. They appeared to be in a shop that sold religious artifacts. Strange-looking images abounded: a fierce bronzed figurine labeled both "*Iansã*" and "St. Barbara," another of an equally ferocious St. George. More, along another wall—images of *Yemanjá*, goddess of the sea, bearing a striking likeness to the Virgin. An entire wall with statuettes of the crucifixion, some large, some small, some bathed in bright red blood, others bronzed or gleaming alabaster. Christ's face in many different shapes, from the long tresses and pink skin of an Anglo to the curly hair and thick lips of an African, his countenance ranging from serene to tormented to unconscious. In the largest sculpture, almost four feet tall, the scars in the side and forehead were displayed in agonizing detail, so real Mason felt compelled to run his fingers along the side of the rib cage, across the gaping red wound. To his shock it felt warm, and when he pulled his fingers away, a red residue remained on them. He felt his knees begin to buckle below him.

What was happening? His thoughts raced back to Zhézush's death. Should there be artifacts of a wide black woman, blood oozing from her head? It didn't seem so unrealistic now. For a moment he thought he could see a row of them, off behind some tourist trinkets. Had her death really been any less majestic than Christ's? Gunned down by a zealot. Betrayed. The *one*.

"Here." Roberto thrust a cap and some sunglasses into his hands. "This might help."

Mason continued staring at the image.

"Are you okay?"

"Yes, yes." His eyes lifted to meet the boy's. He managed a half-smile. "I guess I'm ready." The residue on his hands made stains on the cap's bill.

"It is a beautiful thing, no?" Roberto gestured in the direction of the statuettes. "Maybe you can come back and get one sometime."

"Yeah, maybe."

They made for the street again. Above and around the door, another wall full of images, this time of a man in a white suit and hat, carrying a walking stick. The figures peered from all different angles and positions, some with the hat in his hand, others with the stick raised in warning or defense, all with eyes that seemed to pierce and invade. The faces alternately laughed and threatened, as if cajoling viewers to stay in the store. Something about their eyes struck Mason, and he halted in front of them.

"What are those?"

Roberto had to reenter the store to answer him. "*Exu*," he said solemnly. "The Devil. The messenger between the gods and mankind."

Mason swallowed. The daggerlike eyes pricked his skin, as if they could enter his bloodstream. His thoughts ran to Elisabeth, to Zhézush, to the intertwining of good with evil. Dark with light. Could there be one without the other? His eyes swept above the statuettes to a painting on the wall. A multiheaded beast. The beast. A chill swept up his back.

"Let's go," he croaked, but Roberto was already out the door again.

Mason donned the hat and sunglasses and caught up with Roberto half a block down the street. Other pedestrians had thinned, leaving them alone and vulnerable.

"Do you believe in the Devil, Roberto? In *Exu*?" It was ludicrous to expect any meaningful response to such a question of a ten-year-old, but he had no one else to ask.

"*Exu* is *candomblé*. But, yes, I believe. My father says the Devil's cleverest ploy is to persuade you he does not exist. I see his signs all around. Do you not?"

"I suppose so." More signs than he wanted to admit. He wondered if he would be tortured when captured. Too bad neither the *Herald* nor the Vatican issued poison pills like the ones spies carried in the old secret agent movies. Not that he really had any secret but the truth. His fingers traced the outline of the videocassette he carried underneath his arm, and his mind played through again the possibilities for copying it, forwarding it separately, or leaving it behind. Maybe he should write everything down, in true journalistic fashion, so that it stood a small chance of being discovered later by some enterprising reporter, long after his demise. Of course, that's what he should have done when he had the time back in the room at Father Molina's. He chafed at his idiocy. He had been so caught up in his own emotional turmoil, in Perola's death, the ride in the coffin, in Heloisa, that he hadn't done his job.

The street had become more industrial, with fewer trees. The only people visible were engaged in loading, unloading, or driving trucks and delivery vans. A huge semi-trailer blocked the sidewalk, forcing them to skirt around it into the street. Rounding the other side, they encountered a group of soldiers lounging in the sun. There was no place to run or hide.

"Papers!" The sound rang out from a lead soldier, who approached laconically, his arm resting on a submachine gun. The other hand reached toward them expectantly. Mason looked to Roberto, who was fiddling with something in his pocket.

"Aieee!" A tremendous cloud of smoke appeared simultaneously with the yell, blanketing the soldiers in a blue ball.

"Whh . . ."

Roberto's insistent hand met Mason's, guiding him away, down a narrow crevice between the buildings. The sound of automatic weapon fire exploded behind them, followed by shouts and bellowing.

"Jesus Christ, what did you do?" gasped Mason. "Are you crazy? They'll kill us!"

"Yes. We must hurry."

They ducked down another alley in the honeycomb of buildings and trucks. Roberto hesitated before one truck, then scooted up a ramp and into the trailer behind it. Reluctantly, Mason followed him into the darkness.

"Over here." Roberto beckoned him over behind a row of boxes. Together, they wedged down into a corner. The sweet smell of cardboard mixed with the odor of their own perspiration.

"This truck will be moving soon. It will take us to the airport."

"How do you know?"

"I have done it before, many times."

"There will be blockades. They will search everything."

"That is why you must be very quiet, like the mouse." Mason could see Roberto's teeth in the darkness, could feel his breath against his face.

"I just spent hours on one of these, riding in a fucking coffin." Mason's voice was rising. "I can't do it again!"

"Relax. The guys who run this line, they are my friends. We will be okay."

The trailer shuddered with the weight of someone on its ramp. A low whistle reverberated against the metal walls. Then more weight on the ramp. The sound of boxes being stacked, toward the end of the trailer, the movement forcing slight drafts of air. Perspiration ran off Mason's nose, splashing onto the cardboard box in front of him. His wet arm rubbed against Roberto's, water on water. He shifted the position of the videocassette. The movement caused the box stacking to suddenly stop. For an eternity they sat silent and breathless until the weight reappeared on the ramp and the thud of cardboard on cardboard recommenced. The clang and clatter of the ramp rolling into storage position, a few indistinguishable words, then the slam of the trailer door. The meager light vanished. Seconds later, the truck's engine rumbled to life behind them.

25

And he said unto them, These *are* the words which
I spake unto you, while I was yet with you, that
all things must be fulfilled, which were written
in the law of Moses, and i*n* the prophets,
and *in* the psalms, concerning me.

Luke 24:44

So what do we do when we get to where we're going?" Mason shouted over the diesel's drone. "We'll certainly be found when they open the back of the trailer."

"Remember, these are my friends. They are used to us stowing away in here. They knew when they heard the noise earlier we were here, but they did nothing."

Mason cleared his throat. The sad truth was, he had to trust this kid. What other choice did he have?

Roberto scrambled out from behind the boxes that shielded them, climbing to the top of other boxes on the trailer's side.

"Come. There is more air up here." He pointed to vents which ran the length of the trailer's top. Mason clambered up to join him. The trailer rocked as the truck negotiated a turn, shifting the boxes precipitously.

"So how do you have all of these friends in warehouses and the like?"

White teeth flashed again in the darkness. "Father Molina took me in a year ago. Before that, I am a child of the streets. I barely knew my mother. I never knew my father at all. I do not know what happened to them. I existed by stealing—that was how I ate. I would take bananas off a vendor's cart and run. Sometimes I served as a lookout or courier for the drug sellers. That is how they know me on the trucks. There are many,

many like me in Rio. Then the death squads came, men who would come at night and shoot street boys like me as we slept. I wandered one day into Father Molina's church. He took a liking to me, took me in, along with Julio. He is not my real brother—well, I guess he is now. Father Molina gave me clothes, he fed me, he put me into school. He has been very kind to me. By helping you, I repay him for his kindness."

The truck slowed to a stop. Voices outside. "This may be a checkpoint," whispered Roberto. "Back to our hiding place."

With a series of clangs the metal trailer door slid open, admitting light and air into the sweltering box. Mason and Roberto burrowed into the pile of cardboard containers. Ever so slowly, Roberto pulled cartons over their heads, so that they lay buried. The trailer shifted slightly to accommodate the weight of someone on the bumper.

"What have you got here?" The voice was startlingly clear and close.

"A shipment of medical supplies. Here are the papers." The other voice was farther away, outside of the trailer.

Through a crease in the boxes, Mason could see a man in a red baseball cap, poking his face through an opening. The man ran his hand across boxes in the area near the top of the trailer where they had just been sitting, a puzzled look on his face.

"Hey! How come something is wet up here?" Mason's heart sank. Their sweat was to give them away.

"We just loaded the truck, yes?" came the muffled reply. "It is hotter than December. You see that I am still dripping, no?"

The red baseball cap chuckled. "I know you are right, my friend. This time, okay. But next time, I get the dogs to check it, right? Some kids attacked soldiers a few blocks from here. They are cracking down on this shit. Things are different now."

The trailer door rolled again, bringing down the curtain of darkness. The conversation continued outside, now unintelligible. The brief breath of air from the opened door vanished as if a hose had been pulled. Slowly, quietly, Roberto pulled the boxes from above their heads. The grumbling rumble of the diesel engine kicking to life allowed them to move with more abandon, until soon they were sitting back near the vents at the top of the trailer.

"So far, so good," Mason mouthed in Roberto's ear. "We've been lucky."

"Yes, most lucky." The truck picked up speed, increasing the trickle of air near the vents. They rode in silence for some time. Outside, horns honked and tires sizzled on the roadway. Through the vents came glimpses of green grass. Mason wanted to ask again for an explanation of Roberto's plan, but held himself back. Finally he could contain himself no longer. "So, will your friends meet us at the airport?"

"I do not know. Possibly."

Mason halted the next question in his throat. If he was to survive, he told himself, he had to have faith in this kid. There was absolutely no way he could escape on his own. The chances with Roberto and his friends probably weren't much better, but they were at least on the chart. Leaning back against the trailer's swaying side, he adjusted his still-throbbing shoulder and closed his eyes, listening to the whirring of the trailer tires and the chugging truck engine. He squeezed off a prayer, not so much a request as an attempt to establish contact. What faith did he have in anything? After all that had happened, how certain was he of God, or fate, or prayer? Maybe the whole thing had been a wild hallucination, a delusion of black-jacketed pursuers and his own importance.

And then he was sleeping, plunging back into a dream, *the* dream. It welcomed him like an old friend, the images clear and precise, as he had always known them. He stalked the green lawn with confidence now, nodding to the nurses who passed in front of him, free of the urgency he had previously felt. The trip to the door was faster, smoother. When he grasped the door's handle, he was certain of what lay inside. The interior remained as gloomy as always, but he plunged ahead, entering the area with the couches and the television. He paused, momentarily confused, suddenly unsure of what he was looking for or why. Then a figure entered, dim at first, but growing brighter. Thin, waiflike, childish. He recognized the girl from the hospital in Miami. She moved forward, her face changing, until she was older, the girl he had seen at the mental hospital, the one who from the couch had told him of her knowledge of Zhézush. Brighter still, the figure metamorphosed again, slipping slowly into Perola's visage. Brilliant white lips moved in silent words he strained to understand. His heart ached in happiness and longing for her, and he reached out, but she was changing. The shimmering skin around her face lengthened and stretched until it was that of an old woman, almost transparent, dulled lips still moving incomprehensibly. Wrenching his body toward her, he tried to catch the words spilling forth before she vanished into nothingness. Just as she disappeared before him, the whispered words reached his ears: "Love. Peace. Justice." Then she was gone, and he was alone in the darkness.

Something sent him tumbling out of the dream, propelling him against the cardboard cartons in front of him. The truck had stopped. A shrill beeping signaled its shift into reverse. Roberto beckoned him away from the trailer door.

"Come!"

They crouched near the door at the top of the trailer. Away from the vents, the heat boiled down mercilessly. He was conscious of his sweat dripping like a faucet onto the cardboard below him, and of a growing, tremendous thirst. As he pondered the possibility of unconsciousness, voices rumbled outside, and the trailer door clicked in the process of being unlocked. Roberto grasped his arm.

"Follow what I do," came the whisper.

With a shuddering roar the door rolled open, admitting blinding light and a rush of cool air. Roberto was down from the boxes, onto the trailer's bumper almost before the door was completely up. Scrambling and half-falling, Mason followed.

"Hey!"

They were past the startled workers, three of them, before anyone could react or resist. Roberto darted down a giant loading dock, dodging other trailers and workers. A forklift careened by, its driver shouting obscenities. No one else in the huge, busy place seemed to pay any attention. They were out of the loading area and into a row of houses across the street within seconds. Turning, Mason saw no one in pursuit.

"So far, so good," he panted as he caught up with Roberto. The boy had squatted by a water spigot on the side of a house, his face in the stream. Mason followed suit when Roberto came up for air. The force of the warm water made it difficult to drink, but the spray tasted wonderful.

They stayed for some time, trading turns at the faucet, rejoicing in the breeze and the bright sunshine. Still, no one seemed to be following.

Eventually several boys about Roberto's age wandered over and stood nearby. The oldest, a skinny, rough-looking kid with abrasions on his face, said something to Roberto in a coarse dialect Mason could not understand.

Roberto smiled in return. "I have a project I would like your help with."

The boy did not return the smile. Another kid sidled up on a rusty bicycle. Mason eyed escape routes, uncomfortable with the tone of the situation.

Roberto seemed nonplussed. He reached into a pocket and to Mason's shock pulled out a big wad of bills. "I want your help to smuggle him on a plane."

The other boy's eyes lit up, and he snatched at the money. Roberto held it away from his grasp. "Do we agree, brother?"

The skinny boy considered for a moment, glancing around at his compadres, then nodded. A plane zoomed close overhead, blanketing them briefly with its shadow. The boy looked at Mason. "Who is he?"

Mason wanted to shout. Was Roberto crazy? Every billboard and TV screen had pictures of the "criminal and traitor." How could they not recognize him? These scruffy hoodlums would turn him in for the reward in a heartbeat.

"He is my friend."

Another long look from the skinny kid. "Okay," he said finally, showing two missing front teeth. "*Último*."

Roberto handed him the bills, which he counted for a second, then jerked his head for the others to follow.

They scrambled single file down a series of alleyways, then across a large field. The airport came into sight, its flat expanse of runways and taxiways isolated like a dry lake amidst the development around it. Landing lights blinked blue and yellow in the sunlight. A cluster of planes gathered around the terminals, like fat geese at a feeding trough. Tall fences with barbwire across their top protected the landing area. In front lay a major thoroughfare jammed with stalled, honking cars—what looked to be the main highway to the airport. The source of the bottleneck: a security checkpoint at the airport's entrance. Slow-moving, uniformed guards inspected trunks and checked identification in each vehicle.

The older boy, whom the others called Mingo, conversed rapidly with Roberto. The others boys stared at Mason, who looked uncomfortably away. After a few minutes, Roberto came back to speak with him.

"He wants to wait until dark. Only a short time."

"Roberto, don't these guys recognize me? Why don't they just turn me in for the reward?"

Roberto smiled. "Probably they recognize you. But you do not understand. They do not trust the government. They assume the reward is a hoax, that no one will ever give them millions of *reais*. Cash in hand, however, is another thing."

"Where did you get that cash?"

Roberto did not answer, flipping a sideways smile and sidling away. Mingo backtracked, leading them along a filthy streambed to a multicolored row of shanties. He entered one, instructing the others to wait outside. The area was alive in the twilight. A band of chickens squawked underfoot, a nearby infant cried shrilly, and an old man with a shaved head sang softly on a makeshift porch. The smell of cooked food mixed with stale beer and a sour odor Mason could not identify. Lights blinked on, illuminating a ghostly strand of electric lines and television antennas running upward like spiders' webs.

Mingo emerged with plates of steaming food, rice and some kind of vegetable, which the others gratefully devoured. Surprisingly cold bottles of beer were also provided, and Mason and the youngsters downed them quickly and easily. By the time they were finished, it was completely dark. They departed minutes later, back to the main roadway across from the airport. The line of cars remained at a standstill, the checkpoint bathed in the flashing blue lights of a nearby police car.

Mingo was running now, dodging in and out of cars across the roadway, into a clump of bushes on the other side of the road. Mason followed behind the others, glimpsing rubbery faces of automobile occupants fearing robbery. They gathered on the other side of the roadway, pressed between the bushes and the fence, only three of them now: Mingo, Roberto, and Mason. Deftly, Mingo pulled open a cut in the fence and squeezed inside, motioning the others to do the same. They were in, visible and vulnerable on the well-lit expanse of the grassy area adjacent to the tarmac. In front of them, the lights of a jetliner moved in their direction, then turned, the blast of its engines obliterating all other sound.

Mingo signaled, and they followed in a mad dash across the flat expanse, some two hundred yards to the edge of the terminal. It took only a minute or so, but it seemed like hours. Miraculously, no cry was raised or alarm sounded. They reached the corner of the terminal and ducked into a recess beneath a vacant loading bridge.

"They will have seen us from the tower," Mingo said rapidly in his odd dialect. "We have only minutes."

A thin, bearded man emerged from the shadows beyond the loading gate and moved toward them, lugging a plastic carton. A plastic identification badge flapped in the breeze. Mingo stepped out to meet him, still shielded by the loading bridge, and they conversed for several seconds between jet blasts. The man abruptly turned and walked away, leaving the carton. Mingo lugged it over to the others. Another boy, tall and gangly, emerged from the shadows.

"Who is that?" Mason asked Roberto, motioning to the new youth.

"Another friend. He will be with us when we are caught, so that they will think all of the trespassers have been captured."

"Okay." Mingo gestured for the others to huddle around him. "The handlers will be returning shortly." He looked at Mason and motioned to the plastic carton. "Get in."

"What?" He did not understand.

"You must climb inside the animal carrier," whispered Roberto. "That is how you will be smuggled onboard."

"But, I can't fit in there!" Mason lapsed into English again. He moved as if to run.

"You can. Have faith—there is little time!"

He kneeled to look at the contraption, which stood maybe three feet high. He hadn't realized what it was. Part of its air openings were taped shut. Its door couldn't be more than a foot and a half wide.

"How am I supposed to . . ."

"Squat and back into it. We will help you." Mingo glanced back over his shoulder.

Feeling foolish, Mason squatted in front of the carton, trying to roll himself into a ball. Ducking his head, he tried to put one foot backwards into the carrier, succeeding only in toppling it over.

"Hurry!" hissed someone in the group.

He tried again. Someone held the carrier in place. Easing backwards, one foot in, then two, but his torso still outside. He appeared to be stuck, his rib cage too big to fit through the tiny opening.

"Police!" He tried to move forward, to pull out of the thing. Instead, hands met his face and chest, pushing him backward. With a bang the carrier tipped over onto its back, the impact jolting him inside. Hands firmly shut its door, the latch inches from his face.

"Goodbye, Michael," whispered a voice from outside. "God's grace to you."

The light echoes of youthful feet in flight. Then nothing but the wail of the jets.

He was cramped, doubled over, his face against his knees, his back stretched as if on a rack. His side ached from where he had been forced into the box. His shoulder still throbbed. Feeling with his fingers, he felt the videocassette on the carton's floor. At least it had made it. He could not last long like this, he knew.

The sound of footsteps, then a grunt as the carrier was lifted. It had wheels on its bottom, apparently, for after a dizzying turn he was placed in an upright position and rolled. A bump in the pavement tilted the carrier precariously to one side, then toppled it, jamming his body and injured shoulder against the carton's side in a shower of pain. With a curse the man outside righted the carton and resumed pulling it, slower this time. Spots flashed before Mason's eyes, and nausea crept up his belly.

After some time the rolling stopped. He felt someone twisting the handle attached to the carton's top, perhaps applying a tag. Then, grunts, as someone, maybe two people, lifted the carton onto a conveyor belt of some kind. An itch developed on his back, magnifying in maddening intensity since he had no way to scratch it. Shifting his weight, he attempted to relieve the strain on his knees and the balls of his feet. He would be crippled from this contortion, he decided, if he lived.

The conveyor belt went up an incline, then made a turn. The smell of jet exhaust washed through, heightening his nausea. Then more grunting as someone lifted the carton and shoved it into a darkened space. Voices, nearby and far. A puppy barked somewhere close, undoubtedly similarly imprisoned. More discourse, something about a divorce. Disparaging words about a new boyfriend. The clang and scraping of other luggage, muffling the conversation, fading farther away.

Finally, the great crunch of metal doors swinging shut, as if on a tomb. Darkness. Silence, except for the puppy's whimpers.

Lt. Luiz Marco Santos rubbed his hands across his oily, scarred face. He had been on duty for over thirty hours straight, managing airport security during the period of high alert. The coffee in the cup he held in his hand tasted like sludge. He was tired, and he wanted a bath and a cigar. Rising slowly from his seat, he stared at the three juveniles sitting in front of him in the windowless white room. All this hype about "Public Enemy Number One," all the reported sightings, and he gets this: three scruffy kids breaking onto airport property, claiming they wanted to stow away to the United States. More likely, they wanted to pick the pockets of the wealthy people coming off the planes or changing their money. The tower had spotted them immediately. He sighed. Some in his position would simply shoot these three and be done with it. Who would ever know that they were gone? But he would not do that. His instructions were to call anything in to headquarters, which he had done. Now, he would wait.

His assistant, Georges Nguini, an intense, capable man, barged into the room. "Headquarters wants to come interview these three."

Lt. Marco Santos shrugged in surprise.

"Apparently, Elisabeth Obrando herself wants to come talk to them," Nguini continued.

Lt. Marco Santos pursed his lips. It could be his imagination, but it seemed the color was draining from the face of one of the kids.

He had lost all track of time, absorbed in pain, from the ache in his bent neck to his throbbing shoulder to the burning in his knees and back. It had to have been at least two hours, he told himself, but he couldn't be sure. The puppy had progressed from whimpering to mournful howling, back to whimpering again. Once, the plane had shuddered, as if the loading bridge was being disengaged, but nothing else had followed. For all he could tell, the plane remained on the ground.

Tensing his muscles, he tried to keep the circulation going in his left leg, which felt asleep or dead. He shifted backward in an attempt to reach a sitting position, but succeeded only in rocking the carton. His back hurt, but the worst pain was mental: at least twice, claustrophobia closed around him. He shook the carton violently, begging aloud to be freed, heedless of the danger or the circumstances. He was beginning to hallucinate, he knew, and he tried without success to focus his mind on something—anything. Choking, he prayed for unconsciousness, uncertain of whether his lips formed words. The dark comfort of sleep seemed the only thing that would enable him to retain sanity. He was going mad.

Lt. Marco Santos had never seen such beauty, anywhere. Not in the movies, not on television, not in any magazine. He could look at nothing else, think of nothing else, conscious of his open-mouthed stare but unable to do anything about it. She was dressed simply, in a white dress, not the sort of thing you would think a political leader of her stature would wear. Nor did he really understand why she was here. There was a small entourage with her: a woman with short hair in a hooded dark jacket, a military man of high rank, an enlisted soldier. But all eyes were on her. It was as if nothing else in the room existed.

Elisabeth turned to the enlisted man. "Are any of these the one?"

The man pointed to the smallest of the three boys, the darkest-skinned one who sat on the end. "I think it was him."

"You said you found a smoke bomb on one of the boys," she said to Lt.

Marco Santos. "Which?"

Lt. Marco Santos' heart jumped as she addressed him. He pointed, wordlessly and importantly, to the same boy.

"Take the others away," Elisabeth ordered. Nguini moved to comply.

"Now, my friend," she said softly to the remaining boy. "When you tossed a smoke grenade at this soldier today, there was a man with you. Where is he now?"

"I did not . . . aieeeahhh!" The boy screamed as Elisabeth slammed her foot onto his ankle.

"There is little time. Look into my eyes." The boy tried to divert his gaze, but locked back onto Elisabeth's. She held his gaze for several long seconds, then pulled away.

"Halt all planes," she ordered Lt. Marco Santos. "Immediately."

The vibrations from the jet engines rattled the luggage compartment, sending the puppy howling again. Otherwise, the drone produced a kind of serene calm. Unless he was hallucinating, they were airborne; he had felt the liftoff and the gravitational pull as the plane nosed upward. In a moment of lucidity, he realized he had no idea where the plane was going, or what he would do when it got there. Then the pain took over, plunging him back into an abyss of despair and hallucination. His back felt as if someone had knifed it at several different points, his feet as if they had been cut off. Protecting the videocassette with one hand, he released his bladder, sending a trickle of warm liquid down his leg and onto the carton's floor. A broad band of sparkles and dots danced before him, and consciousness slipped away.

Francisco Lopez Reyes, pilot of Argentinas Aero Flight 107, asked for the message to be repeated.

"Repeat. We have information you may have a bomb onboard. Rio is requesting that you return immediately."

"I am closer to Buenos Aires," Lopez protested. "It would be safer to land in B. A."

"Agreed."

"So, permission to land in B. A.?"

There was a silence. He could hear conversation among the air-traffic controllers. "Granted. Runway one nine. Clear to land."

Lt. Marco Santos pulled out his service revolver and released the safety. The boy stood in front of him, knees together, hands behind his back. Bile bubbled up in the back of the lieutenant's throat. He did not relish this directive.

"Love" said the boy.

Lt. Marco Santos stared. "What?"

The boy stared back.

"I'm sorry, kid. It's my job. An order."

"Peace."

The kid's voice seemed deeper now. The gun wavered in the outstretched hand.

"Justice."

Lt. Marco Santos felt faint. The room seemed to have blurred around him, the colors mixing and reforming. Was it a heart attack? And then the kid was by him, down the hall in another flash, manacled hands swinging behind him. Lt. Marco Santos struggled to the room's door, looked left, then right. The kid was gone.

Lt. Col. Gilberto Mannas rolled his F-15 fighter slightly, aligning the target. His blood pumped furiously, all senses on go. Things had been tense since the collapse of the government, and he and his cohorts had been half-expecting to be called to manage some crisis. When the call had come to intercept an enemy target, he had been in the air on a live ammunition training exercise. Thank God, he had been the closest to the enemy aircraft. Now was his chance to shine, the chance he had waited an entire career for.

Checking his gauges, he lined up the target on his screen. Several miles away now, well within range. He knew that the target was well outside

Brazilian airspace, that he was certainly outside the protection zone. He radioed for confirmation. Did they still want a hit?

"Affirmative," came the automatic reply.

His speed was such that he saw the target now, only a mile or so away. Easy pickings. Maybe three thousand feet up, descending. Practically over the city of Buenos Aires.

He searched for intercepts on his screen, becoming more uncomfortable. The red and white logo of Argentinas Aero became visible below him.

He hesitated. A passenger jet?

"Confirm. Target is a passenger jet?"

"Affirmative," came the frantic reply. "Hit!"

He hesitated again; his finger cradled the firing switch. Was it loaded with explosives? Terrorists? Somehow, he knew that it was not so. He imagined he could see women's and children's faces in the tiny windows.

What would happen if he did not fire? He had never disobeyed an order in his professional life. What of his wife and kids? Failure to act would undoubtedly mean hardship for them, maybe death. On the other hand, what of the families of those on the passenger jet?

He sat, paralyzed, his hands trembling. Tears ran into his eyes, blinding him. Was it courage or cowardice to disobey? Would he be plunging a knife into his loved ones by turning away?

"Hit! Hit!" The words echoed against his skull.

He could do nothing, and by doing nothing he had chosen a path. He was a failure, to his family and to his country, too weak even to take his own life. Mindlessly, he switched the radio frequency and veered toward the Argentinean coast. Out of the corner of one eye, he watched the passenger jet lumber on toward the Buenos Aires airport.

Slowly, painstakingly, the bomb squad moved through the luggage compartment. Protective gear wrapped around them like space suits, dogs in tow, they carefully removed the luggage, one piece at a time. The dogs seemed calm, interested only in one of their kind which yelped from a plastic carrier. One of the canines, Lady, whimpered before another large carrier. An officer eased up and put his eye to an air hole.

"Holy Jesus." He crossed himself hurriedly. "There is a body inside."

He awoke to searing whiteness—white walls, white ceiling, white sheets on his bed. But for the tube protruding from his nose and the pain in his back, he would have presumed that this was the start of the afterlife. A woman in white clothing bent over him, speaking to him, words he only partially understood. Spanish. A television droned somewhere nearby, also in Spanish.

A man moved upward into his vision. He recognized the stubble of hair on his head, the bearlike posture. Aaron Rhodes.

"Hey, Mikey! You made it! Nice haircut!"

He closed his eyes again, tried to focus his mind. What had happened? He had been with the boy, Roberto, they had sneaked onto the airfield . . . it all came back. He opened his eyes again, unsure if Rhodes' round face would still be there. It was.

"The bomb squad found you, Mikey. They had been told a bomb was on that flight. Instead, they found you, in a damn animal carrier! More dead than alive. Doctor said you were almost completely dehydrated. Hell, you've been out for over twenty-four hours. Long enough for me to get down here after they called the *Herald*." He moved closer, so that his face encompassed almost all of Mason's vision.

"You're a smart kid, you know that, Mikey? I hadn't heard from you in days—we were worried. Word filtered back from the other media outlets about the manhunt. We figured you would go to the embassy. We had it all set up to get you out from over there. Anyway, you made it. I'll bet you've got a helluva story."

"The tape?" He whispered the words through chapped lips.

"Ahh, bad news on the tape. There's nothing on it. I looked at it a few minutes ago."

"What?!" Mason strained against the tubes and restraints. The room swirled in a fog of colors. "How can that be?" he choked. "You're kidding me, right? You're fucking kidding me! I risked my life for that damn thing! That was our evidence, our proof!"

" 'Was' may be the operative word. There's nothing there, kid."

"No way. There must be some mistake."

"Kid, I'm tellin' ya. We can wheel a damn VCR in here if you wanna see for yourself. There's nothin' on the damn thing."

He slumped back against his bed, numb. His mind lost traction, uncomprehending.

"I'm sorry, kid. Listen, I don't wanna upset you. I know you've been through some shit. The doctor will be here in a few minutes. I had them post some guards by your door. *Herald*'s expense. You see, Brazil is demanding your extradition. The guards have already had to turn one intruder away, some weird-looking woman with a black hood."

Mason slumped back in the bed. The room descended to silence, except for the babble of the TV, now in English.

". . . and in Brazil, news that one of the country's leaders has died . . ."

"Turn that up!" he whispered to the nurse. She moved to comply.

". . . General Raul Camargo, one of the governing junta in Brazil, was found dead this morning at his home. He was forty-eight. General Camargo was one of the leaders who stepped forward to seize power when the government of Brazil collapsed last week. His death was apparently from natural causes. Police report no sign of a struggle or other abnormality, with the exception of unconfirmed reports regarding the odd blue color of the corpse. An autopsy is expected. The Brazilian ruling coalition has announced that Elisabeth Obrando, a civilian leader of the coalition with ties to the faith healer Zhézush, will assume power. For an analysis of these developments we go to . . ."

"Turn it back down."

"Wow. Whadda ya think, Mikey? When can we get a story together?"

Mason smiled. Warm darkness closed behind his shut lids, blotting out the confusing light. Truth floated in the sea of black, understanding surrounding him. He knew now what had happened, and almost why, what to do. Fear no longer plagued him.

"Soon," he heard himself say. "I want to spread the word. The truth, the joy, the warning. The *faith*. For it has started in Brazil . . ."

He left the sentence unfinished.